• Private Screening for a Captive Audience •

"Where's the show?" Billy yelled. Angered, he made a move to stand, but right away he found that he couldn't.

"Hey!" he cried, struggling to get up, but he was stuck in his seat; it felt like something huge and heavy had sat on his lap, pressing him there with its force.

All at once, he felt a jolt of pain—deep and cutting.

"Help me!"

The pain quickly gathered force, until it became unbearable, matching the wild, panicked beating of his heart. He tried to cry out again, but his tongue lay in his mouth like something huge and dead.

Billy stared at his right arm, which began to move in a series of strange, spasmodic jerks. Suddenly, he watched in horror as the flesh began to move. He watched as a jagged line formed along his arm—a deep and bloody scratch.

No! What's happening to me? No!

The lips of torn flesh now spewed out blood and sinew, exposing cords of red-slicked muscle. Released from the ruined arm, they dangled and twisted, glowing within the dim light of Odeon. . . .

SCREAM PLAY

DOUGLAS SOESBE

CHARTER/DIAMOND BOOKS, NEW YORK

For Ruth and Keith, my mother and father,
and for the Laurelhurst Theatre,
Portland, Oregon

SCREAM PLAY

A Charter/Diamond Book / published by arrangement with
the author

PRINTING HISTORY
Charter/Diamond edition / September 1990

ISBN: 1-55773-387-2

Charter/Diamond Books are published by The Berkley Publishing
Group, 200 Madison Avenue, New York, New York 10016.
The name "CHARTER/DIAMOND" and its logo are trademarks
belonging to Charter Communications, Inc.

PRINTED IN THE UNITED STATES OF AMERICA

10 9 8 7 6 5 4 3 2 1

• Prologue: August 1931 •

MAYBE IT WAS the way the wind blew, so sudden and strong out of Main Street, but the boy who loved movies knew that magic was in the air.

On the night the Odeon Theatre opened for the very first time, Jack MacGruder stood with the rest of the crowd, his bony legs pressed up against the barricade that kept them away from the festivities. Usually empty by eight o'clock, the street was filled with the things of celebration. Vendors sold balloons and souvenirs, while down the block a marching band formed, followed by a team of horses with cowgirl riders. The cowgirls held up pink silk banners, which fluttered in the new stir of wind: *Congratulations, Odeon*.

But now all was still.

The marching band stood frozen. The instruments were poised, but not yet played. Horses shuffled restlessly while everyone waited behind the barricades: Henry Wallenberg, mayor of the town that bore his name, was about to pull the switch.

Jack MacGruder was small for sixteen, so he had to stand on tiptoe to see. He kept his eyes fixed upon the marquee—fifty feet wide and made of copper and glass. In a second the glass tubes that swirled along its rim would come to life.

The crowd applauded when Mayor Wallenberg pulled the switch. The neon offered up only a weak little pulse at first, and Jack was disappointed. But the purple gas quickly grew brighter; it buzzed and hummed, then rushed through the tubes of glass like blood through transparent veins.

Gasping, Jack realized the tubes formed letters—great ornate loops of sculpted glass. He jumped when he heard another noise—a loud snap—followed by a new surge of purple light, which danced out a name:

O D E O N.

The light was unstoppable now: It splashed across Odeon's great facade—a cathedral window framed by four Corinthian columns, carved with birds and flowers. Above it, a vertical sign stabbed the purple sky. Gothic letters flashed the same proud message to all of Wallenberg: *ODEON*.

Now the street came to life again. A whistle blew and the marching band started up; the horses with the cowgirls pranced proudly behind. Fancy roadsters with fenders awash in klieg light pulled up before the theatre, unloading well-dressed guests.

The boy who loved movies watched wide-eyed, imagining it was one of the Hollywood premiers he had read about in his movie magazines. Jack MacGruder had never been so excited in all his life.

"Jack!"

The boy cowered and turned to the voice, which belonged to Mr. Peabody, the manager of Odeon. His fat stomach was cinched by a scarlet cummerbund.

"What are you doing out here, Jack!"

"Watching the celebration, sir."

"You know that the staff isn't allowed out here!"

Jack opened his mouth to speak, but Mr. Peabody cut him off. "If I catch you away from your post again, I'll fire you!"

"Yes, sir!" Jack cried, and with a quick, dutiful salute, he bounded his way into Main Street.

Stupid, stupid, he thought, angry at himself for getting caught. Mr. Peabody had warned the ushers they were to stay at their posts.

But as Jack elbowed his way through the crowd, he decided he didn't care.

It was Jack, after all, who had waited two long years for this. It was Jack who had stood day after day at the construction site, watching as a gaping hole in the ground yielded first a steel frame—Odeon's spine—later the theatre itself. He felt he had a right to see the theatre come to life, usher or not.

After entering the theatre by a side door, Jack ran up a flight of stairs toward his post in the balcony. In the mezzanine he stopped at a huge mirror, where he checked his uniform. Made of forest-green wool, it featured brass buttons that worked down a double breast, and the boy who loved movies loved it. Jack decided he was a soldier in some exotic foreign army.

Carefully, Jack adjusted the matching fez to an angle he found more flattering. The fez accented his long face, which, with its stern features, seemed mature beyond his years. Some told Jack that he didn't seem like a child at all, but more like a grown-up man who posed as one. Lonely boys who loved the movies were like that, most of Wallenberg supposed, and when he'd stood for two years watching the rise of Odeon, they hadn't thought a thing of it.

Jack turned and started up the second stairway, but he stopped when he heard a roar of voices, which filtered up from the enormous lobby below. Not able to resist a look, he moved down the stairway and up to the rail that overlooked the lobby.

The lobby glowed, and Jack realized he had never seen it fully lighted before. Three crystal chandeliers lit walls that were twenty-five feet high. The ceiling—a spectacular dome within a dome—was frescoed with cherubs that flew through a tangle of arabesques. Designs of sculptured plaster swirled to the floor, ending at the carpet—a rose-colored chenille. Guests poured in from the forecourt through a bank of tall bronze doors.

"Little boy!"

The hairs on the back of Jack's neck stood on end. He knew that voice, and it scared him, even more than Mr. Peabody's. He turned around slowly and faced Forbes Carlton.

"Hello, little boy," said Carlton, whose thin, wormlike lips managed an unfriendly smile. He clutched an ivory cigarette holder. At its tip a Camel burned furiously.

"Hello, sir," Jack said, silently cursing his luck. He would rather have run into Mr. Peabody than Forbes Carlton. *Any*body but Forbes Carlton.

Carlton was tall—incredibly tall, Jack thought—and too thin, it seemed, to be alive. As he walked to the rail, the fabric of his tuxedo buckled across emaciated shoulders. He blew out a ring of smoke, which turned a lazy circle above the crowded lobby.

He pointed to the frescoed dome. "We copied that from a ceiling in Italy, line for line. Mrs. Wallenberg demanded perfection. Mrs. Wallenberg *always* demands perfection."

Jack didn't like Forbes Carlton, even if he was the man who had designed and built Odeon. He remembered the day two years ago when Carlton arrived from San Francisco. He had brought with him a flurry of publicity that was unusual for the small town.

"Famous Architect to Build Movie Dream Palace in Wallenberg," the local headlines read.

Carlton eyed the boy's uniform. "So I see you got a job here."

"Yes, sir." He stood up as tall as he could. "This is the biggest night of my life, sir."

"You like the movies?"

"I *love* the movies."

"Why?"

"Dunno. Guess 'cause things are prettier in the movies. Things are more fun up there on the screen sometimes."

"Are you a lonely little boy?"

Jack shrugged, feeling very uncomfortable. He didn't like these questions. They seemed stupid and they embarrassed him. "Sometimes, I guess."

When Carlton turned again to the lobby, his black pompadour glistened in the clear white light of brand-new fixtures. "You're just a child," he said, "and children don't know. They don't know the hell of things."

"What, sir?"

Carlton aimed a skeletal finger into the lobby. "She's lovely, don't you think?"

Jack saw that he was pointing toward Mayor Wallenberg's young wife, Edith. Beautiful, she was dressed in a pale blue gown that featured shapely legs. A plunging back revealed the broad expanse of creamy white shoulders.

"Yes, sir," agreed Jack. In fact, he had always thought Edith Wallenberg looked like one of the movie stars he kept in the scrapbook under his bed.

Carlton spun to him. "A child doesn't know the hell of things!"

Jack startled. "What, sir? . . ."

"A child doesn't know the hell of loving someone you cannot have!" Carlton cried.

When Jack shrugged his confusion, Carlton glared at him. "You have nothing to say, little boy?"

The boy shook his head, feeling an excruciating shyness. It was the feeling he always had when straying too far into the world of adults and their strange preoccupations with love.

Why didn't they find their happiness at the movies? he wondered. Movies were important, not life.

Carlton turned away angrily. "Then go back to your post," he ordered. "Go back to your post and be a good little usher."

"Yes, sir!"

Jack was only too happy to escape the tall, cadaverous man, and he turned and ran up the stairway, taking as many steps at a time as he could, looking back only once.

Forbes Carlton was already gone.

When everyone was seated and the movie was about to begin, Jack paused at the edge of the balcony, where he looked down into the magnificent theatre.

A crimson curtain draped Odeon's screen. The wall of bloodred fabric stretched between matching pilasters. A flock of cherubs flew all the way up to Odeon's head—the mighty proscenium, which was carved with sunbursts and garlands. Birds soared proudly through frescoed clouds.

The lights were dimming fast now, and Jack knew that he had to leave. Mr. Peabody had made his orders clear: All ushers were to stand at attention outside the doors once the show began. But when Jack reached the exit, he couldn't bring himself to walk out.

I've waited too long for this!

He remembered all those nights he had lain awake dreaming of that magic moment when the curtains would part across Odeon's screen for the very first time.

The boy felt charged with new courage. After looking both ways for Mr. Peabody, he headed for an empty seat in the last row, where he slipped into the embrace of rich upholstery.

As the lights bled to almost nothing, he could barely read the cardboard souvenir program he had scooped from the floor.

8:00—DEDICATION

8:30—MOVIETONE NEWS

9:00—LAUREL & HARDY COMEDY

9:30—*CITY LIGHTS*, STARRING MR. CHARLIE CHAPLIN

Now the light was gone.

Whispers ceased in the total darkness.

He looked up at the portholes, where a column of arc light spilled forth. The excited boy followed its course to the curtains, which parted before him—a smooth and elegant bloodred shimmer.

But just as he started to applaud, Mr. Peabody grabbed his shoulder.

"Come with me!" he ordered.

All alone in the men's room, Jack stood forlornly in his underwear.

He stared at his uniform, which lay before him, draped across one of thirty washbasins that lined the great tiled wall. Now the smell of fresh wool made him sad. Mournfully, he touched one of the buttons he had polished with Brass-O the night before.

After wiping away what remained of his tears, he reached for his own clothes—a frayed cotton shirt and knickers. They looked so crummy to him now, and ordinary. Civilian clothes, Mr. Peabody had called them. Jack felt as though he had been dishonorably discharged.

Once he had dressed, Jack offered up a salute to the mirror. But it was a flimsy salute, he knew. It was a defeated wave of goodbye, not the gesture of proud respect he had offered up to Odeon from behind the barricade.

Imagining that he had been summoned before a firing squad that waited beyond the rest room door, Jack gathered up his uniform. He held it proudly against his chest for a final time, then turned heroically to leave.

But at the door he heard a noise. He spun around to it, facing the row of toilet stalls that lined the other side of the room.

The huge men's room, with its thousands of pieces of tile, was a system of hard echoes, and for that reason Jack wasn't certain if he had heard the sound at all. His own footsteps, after all, had sounded thunderous to him. He cocked his head to hear, but now all he heard was a faint drip in one of the basins.

When he turned to leave, he heard it again—muffled, like a woman crying.

Cautiously, he stepped to the stalls—fifteen of them, he counted, and larger than any he had ever seen. With their heavy mahogany doors carved with a single elegant *O*, they were more like small rooms.

"Is anybody here?" he shouted.

After his echo died away, a low moan answered him, drifting from the farthest stall.

Frightened, Jack walked up to it and tried the handle, but it was latched from the inside.

"Are you all right?" he cried.

After a second he looked down and saw the blood. It flowed from inside the stall.

Instinctively, Jack rushed at the door, slamming at it as hard as he could. He banged until his fists throbbed with pain, but the heavy door was stubborn; as with everything in Odeon, it was sturdy and built to last.

He looked at the floor, where the pool of blood had grown larger. The thick red liquid now touched the tips of his brand-new shoes.

Stepping back with a cry, the boy looked up at the top of the stall door, deciding he would climb over the top.

With a deep breath he leapt in the air, grabbing at the ridge along the top of the door with both hands. As he climbed, the soles of his shoes slipped noisily across the door's slick surface.

When he reached the top, he stared down into the stall.

"Mrs. Wallenberg!" he screamed.

Naked, she lay sprawled across the toilet. Her arms and legs, crazily akimbo, were slicked with blood. Beside her, the beautiful blue dress lay wadded up and soaked through with blood.

When he looked into her eyes, he begged for a sign of life, but the eyes that returned his gaze were glassy and unblinking.

And the boy who loved movies knew that she was dead.

Two hours later Jack stood alone in his secret place—a thick bower of trees and shrubs that overlooked all of Wallenberg, accessible only by a small trail hidden from Main Street. He had gone there after the sheriff released him. Now he watched as an ambulance carried Mrs. Wallenberg's body away.

"Little boy!"

Jack froze with terror, trying to pretend that he hadn't heard the voice behind him.

Not you! Not you! This is *my* place. No one else is supposed to be here!

But now he heard the twigs as they snapped beneath the intruder's weight, and he knew that Forbes Carlton was moving up close behind him. Terrified, Jack turned and faced the tall, skeletal man whose body was drenched in purple light.

"I followed you," Carlton said. "I followed your fear."

"Go away!"

But the tall man ignored him, continuing his slow approach through moonlight.

He carried something in his hand—pale fingers clutched it greedily. Jack squinted and saw that it was a carpetbag.

Forbes Carlton stood before Jack, offering up the carpetbag. "Now, little boy, you will know the hell of things."

"What?"

Carlton shook the carpetbag. "Look inside, little boy."

"Why?"

"Look inside and know the hell of things."

"No!"

Carlton grabbed him, his fingers wet and cold. "Look inside, damn you!"

Jack felt a rush of bile as it roared to his throat and he tried to swallow it back, afraid that he might throw up.

With a cry he pulled himself free and began to run.

Keep going, keep going! he thought, frantic, and he tried to imagine the distance that formed between himself and the corpse-like man with the awful carpetbag. Twigs smashed violently beneath his feet as he ran.

Yes, yes! Just a little ways!

But now he could hear the lumbering approach of Forbes Carlton, and he could tell that he was following close behind—closer and closer.

He felt something—bony and cold—as it grabbed at his neck. Carlton's hand!

The icy strangle of flesh tugged and tugged at him. He tried to keep running, but Carlton's hold grew stronger.

"No! No!" he screamed.

But now the boy's feet tangled up in the thick brush and he fell to the ground, where Carlton pinned him.

"Look inside!"

"Leave me alone!" he screamed, and he kicked and thrashed, trying to get free, but the tall man was surprisingly strong.

Finally, the boy's strength deserted him, and he lay helpless, gasping for breath. He looked at the carpetbag, which Carlton dangled before him, now only inches from his face. He saw that the bottom was soaking wet. Liquid fell away in large drops: thick red drops.

"No!" he screamed, realizing what it was. The bottom of the carpetbag was soaked with blood!

Carlton's eyes were crazy in the moonlight. "What do you love?" he cried.

The boy thrashed and screamed, refusing to answer, his voice lost in his paralyzed throat.

"I asked you what you loved, little boy!"

"Please . . ."

"You love Odeon, don't you?"

Jack nodded.

"How much?"

"A lot."

Carlton fingered the top of the carpetbag. "Then look inside, little boy. Look inside the carpetbag and know the hell of things!"

Jack tried to look away, but Carlton grabbed him from behind the neck, pressing his face to the gaping lips of the carpetbag.

"No!" Jack screamed, and he tried to keep his eyes closed, scrunching the lids together as tight as he could.

"Look inside, damn you!"

Jack felt the icy fingers along his face as Carlton tried to pry his eyes open.

"Yes, little boy! Look inside and know the hell of love!"

The boy who loved movies could no longer resist the force of Carlton's fingers, and he opened his eyes so that they flooded with purple moonlight.

Or was it the light from Odeon? he wondered, but as he lay on the ground and gasped for air, he realized he could no longer tell one from the other; the movie theatre seemed as large and bright as the huge summer moon that hung in the black sky above him.

Now that his eyes were open, the boy had to look.

He had to look inside the carpetbag.

And when he did, he screamed.

• One •

It was two o'clock in the afternoon in Los Angeles, and Karen Webster still had four vampires to see.

"Can you do a Lugosi accent?" she asked.

"The best."

"Let's hear it."

Karen watched as the old man shifted in his seat and prepared to perform. Skeptical, she glanced at his eight-by-ten headshot, which lay between them on her desk. As usual, it bore no resemblance to the man who had shuffled into her office moments before: It was Hollywood phony—an airbrushed, glossy lie. It could have been his son.

Now the old man squinted at the page of copy Karen had given him. He pursed his lips, then cleared his throat with a thunderous sound. After raising his frail arms dramatically, he began to read. He did not sound at all like Bela Lugosi.

With a polite nod Karen excused him and went on to vampire number two. He was better, but still not quite what she was looking for.

"A vampire in a soap ad?" he asked huffily.

"Yes," she answered, studying him in that strange, dispassionate way required for casting someone in a part. He was suddenly less a human being than a stick of furniture.

He was better physically, she thought, but she could tell already that his voice was too high. It would never produce the thick, unctuous basso of Lugosi.

"You see," Karen explained, "the vampire has to get blood-stains out of his cape. He walks into a laundromat and he throws the cape in a washer. Our client's soap gets out all of the stains."

"Is it night?"

"Of course," Karen answered. "Vampires only come out at night."

She thought about it for a second and laughed.

"Don't they?"

"Just checking," he said.

When neither he nor the vampire who followed proved acceptable, Karen began to worry.

Am I being too picky?

It was, after all, the first time she'd been responsible for casting a major part in a client's commercial all by herself. Karen realized that an anticipated promotion depended upon how she handled such increased responsibilities. Perhaps because it meant so much, she was trying too hard.

Wouldn't be the first time, she mused.

"I got him!"

Karen looked up at Tyler Briggs, who bounded into her office without knocking. Tall and gangly, the nineteen-year-old office boy rubbed his long hands together, imitating a mad scientist. "Vampire number four's here!" he said.

"Oh?"

"He's perfect!"

"I hope so," Karen said.

Tyler stepped forward. "I mean, this guy's General Delivery, Transylvania."

Karen laughed. "Thanks, Tyler."

Tyler's face, an explosion of acne, suddenly changed expression. The eyes grew wide behind the thick glasses and he looked at her adoringly.

Karen looked away, embarrassed. She knew that Tyler had a crush on her and she did her best to discourage it. "Tell him to come in," she said, busying herself with the papers on her desk. "I've got a four o'clock appointment across town."

Intrigued, Tyler moved up to her desk. "Where you going?"

"Tyler!"

"Sorry," he said with a shrug, then reached for the paperweight on her desk. It was a glass ball filled with water and bits of white plastic. He had given it to Karen for her birthday.

Tyler sighed, then shook it furiously, watching as a blizzard raged across the miniature plastic village locked inside. "Rosebud!" he whispered.

Karen grinned. "Yes, Tyler, you've told me. The sled."

"Orson Welles was only four years older than me when he made *Citizen Kane*."

Karen decided to indulge him. "What year was it released, Tyler?"

"Forty-one! RKO. Script by Welles and Herman J. Mankiewicz. Photography by Gregg Toland. Music by Bernard Herrmann . . ."

"That's amazing," she said, busying herself once more with paperwork.

Tyler ignored her hint and sat on the edge of her desk. "I'm dynamite at Trivial Pursuit . . . the pink square, I mean. People don't ask me to play anymore, though. They think I sit up nights memorizing the answers." His face broke into a wide grin that revealed his braces, and he poked a finger at his temple. "I got it all up here. All of it. Ask me something. Ask me something!"

"Tyler! The vampire. Remember?"

"Yeah, yeah," he said, getting up. "Vampires on parade!"

When he got to the door, he snapped his fingers like he'd just remembered something.

"The Nu-Art's showing a couple of old William Castle horror movies this weekend," he said. "Maybe you'd like to go, huh?"

"I don't think so, Tyler."

"C'mon, it'll be fun! They're showing *The Tingler*."

"The what?"

"*The Tingler*. It's this great old movie from fifty-nine, see. There was this director . . . name was William Castle, and all his movies had these really terrific gimmicks. In *The Tingler* he wired up all the seats so the projectionist could zap you when things got kinda scary and stuff. They're gonna show it that way at the Nu-Art. First time in years!"

"I don't think so."

"How come?"

"I go to the movies rarely enough, Tyler. I don't think I'll choose one that requires a smack of voltage in the behind."

"But it's art, Karen!"

"I don't like horror movies," Karen said.

Tyler looked as if he had just been slapped.

"Don't like horror movies!" he cried. "Why, that just isn't natural!"

When Tyler ushered in the next vampire—a distinguished-looking gentleman in his fifties—Karen was encouraged.

God, maybe Tyler's right. Maybe he *is* perfect.

After he was introduced, he bowed with a courtly flourish that Karen recognized as exactly right for Count Dracula.

"Here he is," Tyler announced, slipping into his Karloff impression. "Fresh from the grave and ready to go to work!"

Embarrassed, Karen moved to the vampire. "I'm sorry," she said, "we get a little informal around here sometimes."

"Please," he said. His accent was thick—perfect, as far as Karen was concerned. "Playfulness at work increases productivity. There was a study done."

Karen shot a look at Tyler and he scrambled out the door.

Once again, Karen studied the vampire. Indeed, he looked better and better. When she offered her hand, he took it and kissed it with a click of his heels.

If he can only read the script as well as he looks and acts, he's got the job.

Moving to her desk, Karen glanced at her watch. She saw that it was almost three and she realized she had exactly an hour to get through the interview, then drive from Century City to mid-Wilshire for her four o'clock appointment.

I can't be late. I can't! she thought, already nervous and preoccupied.

Karen knew that her appointment with Estelle Hopkins was the most important of her life.

"Here you go," she said, handing the vampire his script.

The courtly old gentleman read it first to himself, then aloud. When he finished, Karen applauded and leaned forward.

"Perfect," she said. "You are a perfect vampire."

Karen found it an odd place to look for a child.

She had expected the adoption agency to be lively and filled with the spirit of children. Instead, the room in which she now sat seemed cold and blank. It had no more character than the other offices in the huge building on Wilshire—the offices of insurance brokers, lawyers, and accountants.

Could this really be the place where I'll find a child?

Karen stared at the walls. Whereas she might have expected bright colors, even a sprightly design of wallpaper—little cowboys or angels? she considered with a smile—they were painted an impersonal beige. There was a single picture, a blue and gold abstract, which hung perfectly straight in a chrome frame.

The desk before her, which belonged to Estelle Hopkins—now

fifteen minutes late for their interview—was orderly, marked by
its unbroken row of supplies: a stapler, a ruler, a spotless green
blotter, a cup of pencils that were sharpened to perfect points.

Behind the desk, file cabinets loomed. They were all shut tight,
with tiny keys protruding from their locks.

Karen looked at them. She imagined that they contained the
names of children. Would one of them become hers? she wondered. An unwanted child, she thought—a boy or girl, it didn't
matter—waited somewhere for her.

At thirty-three years old Karen knew that she was ready. She
would take that child to the center of her life. She would hold it,
protect it, and love it in a way that she herself had never been
loved. She would give it everything she had.

Yes, it's time.

A door opened and Estelle Hopkins entered. She was an
attractive woman in her fifties, and Karen decided that the brisk,
officious moves suggested confidence. When she sat at the desk,
she apologized for being late, then opened Karen's file folder. She
examined it soberly while tapping one of the pencils with the
perfect points.

Karen felt self-conscious. The chair in which she sat was of an
unyielding design, and she could not find a comfortable position.
Each time Estelle turned a page in the file, Karen would shift, her
tall, slender body resisting the shape of the grey metal chair, and
she felt all her movements turn to graceless fidgets.

Miss Hopkins paused and looked up from the file. Her eyes,
intense behind tiny spectacles, studied her unabashedly, and
Karen knew that she was being judged.

Appearance. The first important thing is appearance.

Karen tried to convince herself that she had come to the
interview looking the part. She had worn clothes she thought made
her look officious, those she hoped would imply the responsibility
of parenthood: an emerald-green suit with cardigan jacket, a white
silk blouse with ruffled bib. After sweeping up her hair into a
graceful chignon, she had applied only minimal makeup.

Miss Hopkins spoke as she continued through the file. "Were
these self-explanatory?" she asked, referring to a batch of special
forms that Karen had filled out for the meeting.

Karen nodded, feeling suddenly anxious. It troubled her that the
forms she had filled out told so much about her life.

She had received the packet of forms several weeks ago, and
she remembered the night she sat up filling them out: the financial

report, the medical report, and finally, the most troublesome of all, a form that required her to write a brief autobiography.

My past won't be a secret anymore! she thought, shifting once again in the excruciatingly uncomfortable chair.

Karen bit her lip as she watched Miss Hopkins read the forms.

Miss Hopkins continued to speak as she read. "How did you happen to pick our agency, Miss Webster?"

"Actually," Karen said, smiling, "I found it in the telephone book. Funny, but I'd never thought of an adoption agency being in the yellow pages before, but . . . there it was . . ."

Karen stopped abruptly, worried that her remark had made her appear frivolous.

"There's a certain mythology built around adoption." Miss Hopkins smiled. "I suspect that nothing here is quite what you imagined."

"No. Quite frankly, it's not."

"This will only be the first of several interviews, Miss Webster. Subsequent to this, there will be two more meetings—both of them with other prospective parents. A social worker will then be assigned to you. There will be an in-depth interview, followed by a detailed examination of your home, usually done in a surprise, drop-in fashion. The social worker will also drop in to see you at work." Miss Hopkins smiled again. "In the end the social worker will know more about you than perhaps you do yourself."

She folded her fleshy arms and leaned forward. "Quite frankly, the social worker will be aggressively nosy. He or she will become . . . well, let's be honest, a pain in the neck. I hope this doesn't bother you, Miss Webster."

"Of course not."

"Good. You're in a minority here, Miss Webster . . . being a prospective parent who is *single*, I mean."

"Oh?" Karen had dreaded the subject. Even though she was confident, her status as a single parent worried her. A part of her wondered if it was fair—didn't a child *deserve* both parents?

"We have no objection to releasing a child to a single parent, Miss Webster . . . in fact, it's become somewhat common . . . but there *does* come with it a set of considerations peculiar to the case."

"Such as?"

Miss Hopkins picked up a pencil. As she spoke in a soft, measured tone, she rolled it slowly between thumb and forefinger.

"For instance," she began, "what we do *not* want is someone whose aloneness could affect the child in a negative way."

Karen stiffened. "What do you mean?"

When Miss Hopkins laid down the pencil, Karen noticed how soft her hands were, and there was no wedding ring. The perfectly pressed handkerchief that poked from her breastpocket suggested a life of fussy independence. It screamed to Karen that the woman was lonely.

Did Miss Hopkins long for a child too? she wondered.

"For instance," Miss Hopkins said, "if the child is expected to become the entire focus of the parent's life, then we fear the child would be . . . well, to put it delicately, Miss Webster, smothered by good intentions."

"I understand," Karen said.

"We expect a well-rounded atmosphere for the child."

"Of course."

Miss Hopkins picked up the file. "It says you've been at your current job for two years."

"Yes."

"The Hurst Webber & Pyle Advertising Agency in Century City, right?"

Karen nodded.

"And what exactly do you do there?"

"I'm assistant to one of the account directors. Lately, I've been getting more and more involved in the commercials themselves."

Miss Hopkins smiled, which Karen found encouraging.

"I'm up for a big promotion," Karen blurted. "In fact, I'm keynote speaker at a company/client banquet this weekend." Karen stopped, fearing that she sounded desperate.

Was it arrogant, she wondered, to bring up the promotion? She felt paralyzed by self-consciousness.

Now Miss Hopkins reached for the form that contained the autobiography she had written. Karen felt a deep and terrible dread as she tried to remember the precise order of the words she had typed there—the wash of ink that told her life so unflinchingly. She had written it as honestly as she could, and now she regretted it.

Why was life so much easier when you lied?

"Miss Hopkins," Karen said suddenly.

The woman looked up, adjusted her glasses. "Yes?"

"I wrote about myself very candidly."

"Good. We expect that."

Karen desperately judged the moment. Should she speak up now or let the woman read for herself?

She decided to blurt it out. "Miss Hopkins, I cannot bear children of my own because . . . at seventeen I damaged myself. I gave myself an abortion. It was a mistake, I know. A terrible, awful mistake . . . I have suffered for it . . . very much . . ."

"I see." Miss Hopkins paused for a moment. "And the father? A high school boyfriend?"

"I never knew who the father was."

Karen saw the baffled look in Miss Hopkins' eyes.

"I was raped, Miss Hopkins. I was raped by someone I did not see."

"My God . . ."

"You should also know that I've been in therapy, Miss Hopkins. That's in there too. For three years now. I had a . . . well, a small breakdown in the summer of 1980. I do feel that I'm fine now. I do."

Karen searched Miss Hopkins' eyes for a flicker of disapproval, but the woman's expression was not to be read. Karen glanced again at the looming file cabinets. The locks seemed stronger to her now. They would keep her from the child she had dreamed of.

"I appreciate your honesty, Miss Webster. It demonstrates that you are taking this all very seriously."

"I want a child," Karen said. "More than anything, I want a child."

"Yes," Miss Hopkins said, "I know."

And then she closed the folder.

A half hour later Karen worked her way home through traffic. The radio told her it was ninety-eight degrees and another blast of August heat could be expected tomorrow.

Stopped in a clog of traffic, Karen saw that the mountains were still on fire; great ropes of smoke twisted up from the brown, dead hills. Helicopters hovered like great black birds above the Hollywood sign. The radio went on to say that a family of four had been murdered in the San Fernando Valley. The oldest son—a boy of only fifteen—was the principal suspect.

Heat.

It always made things worse, she thought, and as she drove in fits and starts up Sunset Boulevard, Karen pondered the absurd:

Did the heat bake the brain cells? Did it somehow make it easier to go insane?

Karen tried to remember how hot it was the day she had the breakdown. But it *wasn't* hot, she remembered. No, she thought, it was a cool day, moody—one that had threatened rain.

Karen remembered how it started. She had gone into a supermarket, a simple errand for bread, some milk, some cheese.

Did it matter what?

While writing a check, she had felt it—a vague disorientation, followed by an uncontrollable urge to cry. All at once, she had felt her legs grow useless beneath her, and then she had fallen. She remembered the box boys—five in all—who had tried to subdue her there, while she screamed and cried and raged.

One box boy in particular had stood out, and Karen knew that she would always remember his face—something in his sensitive gaze had soothed her. Even through her pain, he had seemed strangely familiar and kind, and when he smiled at her, she had stopped struggling.

And then she had spoken the words—the mysterious words she had never understood: *Don't worry. A man cannot get pregnant. Don't worry.*

It was the last thing she had said before passing out on the supermarket floor.

Even now, Karen wondered if she would ever know what the words meant.

They remained at the center of her struggle like a strange and haunting riddle.

Karen stopped for another light. She felt a film of sweat gather along her face, and she reached into the glove compartment for a Kleenex. Dabbing at the few beads of sweat, she studied herself in the rearview mirror. She liked what she saw: an attractive, responsible woman with a promotion on the horizon. And she was reasonably certain that Estelle Hopkins had liked her too.

Yes, she thought, I *did* impress her. I did.

But how much else had Estelle Hopkins seen in her face? Karen worried.

Karen wondered now if she should have told the rest of the story, all that had led to the rape, the abortion, and the breakdown. She wondered now if she should have told about the boy with green eyes.

Should I? she wondered. Should I have told about the boy I loved? The boy I lost?

Even now, it amazed Karen what tender feelings he could still inspire in her. It had been so long. Karen was sixteen that idyllic summer of her life.

How absurd, she decided. Of course I shouldn't have talked about the boy with green eyes. Who would give a child to a woman who still felt pain over a love she lost when she was sixteen?

The light changed to green and Karen started up again, agitated by the boy's memory. It bothered her that the feelings, so ancient, still seemed so very much alive.

What bothered her even more was the intense anxiety she felt. Am I all right? she wondered.

The heat seemed all at once intolerable, and she felt dizzy, a gathering sense of despair. It all seemed so familiar, she thought, gripping the steering wheel as tightly as she could.

She had felt this way before, she realized. She had felt this way just before the breakdown.

Please, don't let it happen. Don't let it happen again. Not now.

When Karen walked up to her apartment at seven-thirty, she saw the man with the muscles.

He was sprawled across a chaise longue by the pool. His body, clad in a Speedo, was poised to soak up what remained of the day's sun—a dying, smoky light. Alan Fitschew was the manager's son, and Karen did not like him. He was supposed to do work about the complex, but Karen knew that he rarely did anything—except drink beer and offer himself daily to the sun.

The trick was to get inside her apartment without waking him, and she unlatched the gate quietly, then tiptoed across the courtyard. Moving past, she noticed the six-pack of beer and the ashtray that overflowed with butts. The faucet in her apartment would continue to drip while Alan, the aging surfer, lay in stupor.

The apartment complex was classic Southern California transient. Two stories of identical units, as impersonal as those of a Ramanda Inn, surrounded the pool area with its flimsy patio furniture and rusty hibachis. Karen lived on the second floor, where her windows were obscured by a mass of unkempt palm trees. They would sway in the night, groaning to the Santa Anas, and she often lay awake as the dried fronds scratched noisily along the slate roof.

Karen had lived in the Los Feliz Gardens for two years now. It was a temporary shelter, which, by way of procrastination, had grown much too permanent. With its coin-op laundry, vending machines, and tenants in constant turnover, the Los Feliz Gardens did not seem to her like anybody's home. Karen had already decided it would not be a good place to raise a child.

Karen moved gingerly up the steps to her unit, all the time keeping her gaze on Alan, who was still asleep. Just as she reached her door, a beer can fell from Alan's large, bronzed fist. It skittered along the cement and rolled into the pool, where it was buoyed by the stagnant ripples. Alan raised a sleepy head.

Unlocking the door, Karen smiled weakly at Alan, who loped across the courtyard beneath her. She knew he would start all of that foolish flexing, which was designed to advertise his muscles. Karen found his body absurdly overdeveloped: The muscles seemed gorged beyond their intention.

"I'll get to that faucet tomorrow!" he cried.

"Fine," she said, then she entered her apartment as fast as she could and closed the door.

Once inside, Karen knew immediately that something was wrong. She knew that someone had been in her apartment. It was a creepy feeling, like that sixth sense she'd heard about from people who'd been robbed. They knew they'd been robbed the minute they walked in, even before finding the evidence.

But when Karen looked about the front room, she saw that the VCR, portable television, and stereo were all where they should be.

Weren't those the things that burglars always took?—and she decided her instinct had been wrong.

But as she moved to lay her handbag across one of two wicker chairs that faced the front window, she found the first clue that someone *had* been in the apartment. The chair—usually at a precise angle to the window—had been moved.

Violently.

It had been pressed up against the window, so that a flap of drapery lay sloppily across the armrest. She was certain it hadn't been that way when she'd left for work, but after adjusting the chair to its proper position, Karen decided she must have bumped it without realizing it.

And yet, she had no recollection.

When Karen turned away from the chair, she noticed something else: A drinking glass lay broken on the floor, the shards in a pile beneath the coffee table.

Karen walked up and stared at the shattered pieces for a long time, her mind once again racing with possible explanations.

The night before, anticipating the interview with Miss Hopkins, Karen had been unusually preoccupied. She now tried to convince herself that she had simply been distracted enough to knock over the glass without realizing it.

Yet Karen, who prided herself on a devotion to order, knew that it was unlikely. Before going to bed, it was Karen's habit to tidy up the apartment, and she remembered having done so the night before.

Karen entered the kitchen, where she fetched a broom and dustpan. Moving through the familiar space, she could not shake the awful feeling: *Someone has been in my apartment!*

Karen looked about the small, functional kitchen, looking for further clues, but as far as she could tell, everything was as it should be. The refrigerator hummed out its cycle; the set of yellow canisters sat undisturbed along the tiled countertop. Three dishes she had used for breakfast sat in the sink, right where she had left them.

The faucet dripped.

Alan, she realized, and she felt a sense of relief. Of course, it was Alan Fitschew, she thought.

But why? Why would Alan enter, break a glass, and then not fix the faucet? Besides, she thought, Alan had just said he'd get to the faucet tomorrow, and there was no need for him to lie. Alan *never* did what he was supposed to do, and it was part of his arrogance to be proud of the fact. And why, even if he *had* broken the glass, wouldn't he have picked up the pieces to disguise his clumsiness?

Karen moved to the front room, where she quickly swept up the shards. Who? she thought, who? and she carried the pieces into the kitchen and dumped them into the wastebasket.

There's a logical explanation, she thought, replacing the broom and dustpan. There has to be.

Karen stood still in the center of her kitchen and studied where everything was. She thought of that old game in which someone removed something from a room and you had to be observant enough to guess what was missing.

The utensils, she realized.

There usually hung on the wall above the stove a set of three plastic kitchen utensils: a mixing spoon, a serving fork, a ladle. Now all three were gone.

Karen felt a rise of panic, then moved in a frantic search about the kitchen. She checked in the sink, looked along the counter and stove, then pawed through the cupboards and every drawer.

The missing utensils were not to be found.

An hour later Karen sat in a warm bath, where she sipped a generous bourbon and water. Yielding to the drink, she tried to relax.

But reluctant fingers now probed at the top of her groin. She found the spidery arrangement of scars, the irrefutable proof that she had long ago sabotaged her happiness.

From the depths of an old despair, there rose up in Karen now a morbid computation: How old would the child be today had it lived?

Seventeen years, she figured. Seventeen years, two months, forty-seven days.

She wondered what the child would look like by now. What interests would it have, what talents? What would make it laugh? Would it be doing well in school?

Karen pulled her hand from the scar, for she knew what would happen if she kept thinking that way. It would be so easy to obsess herself into a long, debilitating depression. Ever since the breakdown, Karen had learned not to let such thoughts intrude.

After all, she remembered, that fateful day at the supermarket had begun the same way. She had walked into the supermarket thinking about her unborn child, wondering, just as she did now, how old it would have been had it lived.

Karen's therapist would later insist that the box boy had been the target of Karen's projection: He was, after all, a young man who had smiled at her kindly, triggering some lost maternal need.

But why had she uttered those words: *Don't worry. A man cannot get pregnant. Don't worry.*

Karen heard a noise just outside the bathroom door.

"Who's there?" she cried.

It was a skittering sound, like something moving. Karen listened carefully, but all she could hear was the faucet dripping in the kitchen. Alone in the tub, she had that feeling again—the one she'd been having for several weeks.

Karen had the feeling that something else—something very much alive—was in her apartment.

Moments later Karen stood naked before the full-length mirror in her bedroom. Her hair fell in a damp splay along her back, and she worked at it furiously with a brush. When the stubborn tangles were removed, Karen slipped on a blue kimono, then turned to hang her clothes in the closet.

There she noticed her new dress, which she had bought for the company banquet at which she would make the keynote speech. A royal-blue silk with a subtly scalloped neck, it was the finest piece of clothing she had ever owned, and the touch of cool silk calmed her.

When she had put away her clothes, Karen gathered up the new leather pumps she had worn to the interview, then knelt to the closet floor, where she withdrew a shoe box. Lifting the lid, she noticed something.

Odd, she thought, but the tissue paper, which was empty that morning, now appeared to contain things: objects—three in all.

When Karen touched the tissue, she felt something hard inside, and she slowly unwrapped it, the paper crinkling noisily. Pulling back the final layer, she saw them: the plastic utensils from the kitchen.

Once again, she tried to explain the inexplicable.

After a light supper of salad and toast, Karen sat at the kitchen table, where she tried to concentrate on a stack of paperwork, but she was much too distracted.

Her gaze fell to a milk carton, where the eyes of a lost child stared at her balefully.

Why, Karen wondered, did the children in such pictures always look so sad? The photograph, after all, was taken *before* the child was missing, before it had slipped into abuse. It was as if the child had already sensed what terrible fate lay ahead.

Karen had checked all of the windows and both of the doors, but none appeared forced. Meanwhile, she could find nothing of value missing. Even a small wad of cash, which she'd carelessly left in view on the nightstand, had not been touched.

But someone was here, damn it!

Karen thought again of Alan Fitschew, and she pulled back the curtain to look toward the pool. At nine-fifteen it was still hot, and a few tenants played in the water, their cheerful cries echoing out of the muggy night. Karen saw that the chaise longue was empty.

But it couldn't have been Alan, Karen thought. He was obnoxious, to be sure, but he didn't seem the type for subtle pranks. The image of Alan Fitschew kneeling before her closet, his hard flanks bulging with muscle while he wrapped a mixing spoon in tissue paper, seemed ridiculous to her.

Karen released the curtain, then considered what she should do. She could call Mr. Fitschew and register a complaint, but she doubted that it would do any good. She had even considered calling the police.

But what in the world would I tell them? *Officer, someone took a plastic serving fork, wrapped it in tissue paper, then put it in my closet.* She pictured a policeman laughing as he made out his report.

Karen shuddered as she remembered the noise she had heard while in the tub. It was the noise she'd been hearing for two weeks now, and always at night, just after she had gone to bed. At first she'd thought it was the skittering of palm fronds across the roof, but she knew it wasn't. A soft padding, it was the sound of something moving—stealthily, and on all fours.

For several nights, suspecting it might be a rat, she had got up from the bed to search the rooms, but had found nothing. Just when she had decided to report it, the noise had stopped. Karen decided it must have been the pipes, or maybe the faulty water heater, and she'd forgotten all about it.

Until now.

An hour later Karen put out the trash. She did not want the broken pieces of glass, the plastic utensils, or the tissue paper inside her apartment. It was as if her fear had endowed them now with a spooky kind of power.

The air smelled of smoke, the pungent odor from fires that devoured nearby hills, and as Karen walked up the driveway toward the dumpster, she heard the dull thrum of helicopters.

What was it about Los Angeles, she wondered, that always made you think it was about to end?—fires, gas leaks, mudslides, earthquakes. Was it possible to feel safe here? she wondered, or was it precisely that—the danger—that lured so many? Did people come here to die? Had *she* come here to die those seventeen years ago, or was it only to escape what she had done—her terrible past in Wallenberg?

Karen lifted the lid to the dumpster. A full moon filtered through a tall eucalyptus, throwing jagged patterns of light across the week's garbage. Holding her breath against the smell of rot, she dropped her bundle into its center.

Something ran through the nearby bushes.

A dog?

A cat?

Karen heard movement, and she trained her attention on the muggy night, where sound traveled full and heavy. It was the press of tiny paws against dry earth.

Something brushed against her leg—a touch of damp fur. She cried out, kicking her foot, but whatever it was ran away. She heard it crash through a tangle of ivy.

It's not a rat, she thought. It's much too large for a rat.

Karen stared at her apartment house. It was only a few yards away, yet it could have been a million miles—fear expanded distance the way heat expanded air, and she could not find the courage to walk through night toward home.

She stood beside the dumpster, the backs of her naked calves pressed to its surface. She could feel where the cake of rust dug into her flesh, perhaps drew blood; she thought of spores as they passed the barrier of skin and raced into blood, the possibility of contamination, the threat of disease.

It was always like that when she panicked: One fear would trigger another, then another . . .

"You all right, lady?"

Karen swung to the voice, a child's voice, so gentle in this night of threats it arrived with the gentle clarity of a bell. She saw that it was one of the children who'd been playing in the pool.

"Hello," Karen said, smiling, pulling herself away from the dumpster.

The child, a little Spanish boy, stood soaking wet. His swimsuit was decorated with cartoons of huge, frolicking eels.

Karen knelt to him. "You'll catch cold, darling."

"Were you crying?" the little boy asked.

"No, sweetheart," Karen said, and she hugged him close. The odor of chlorine rose up off the boy's dark skin, and Karen could feel the swimsuit soak through to her own clothes, but she didn't care. "I'm fine," Karen said, "just fine."

And as Karen held this unknown child in the night, she convinced herself that she *was* all right. She convinced herself that she was not having another breakdown.

This is real, she thought.

Very real.

• TWO •

As USUAL, he was thinking about the movies.

If this were a movie, he grumbled to himself, I could stick out my thumb and get a cab in a second.

But it wasn't the movies, and Paul Chesney was weary. He'd been trying to get a cab for several minutes, but there were none to be had. Getting a cab in Los Angeles was almost impossible.

Not even Bette Davis could get a cab here, he decided, conjuring up a scene from some old movie in which she snapped her fingers and summoned a cab immediately, as if dispatched from heaven.

Frustrated, Paul turned and looked at his car. Now a hissing heap of a thing, it had overheated on his way to the hospital. Only moments before, he had pulled the car to the side of Hollywood Boulevard, where it now sat like some beached metal whale, a cloud of steam escaping from beneath the dented hood.

Looking at it, he felt like a loser. Car trouble *always* made him feel that way. He decided that when the universe had had quite enough of him, it would overheat his engine.

He looked at his watch, saw how late he was, then dropped his arms to his sides, exasperated.

Of all times. My son's in the hospital and I'm without a car. He thought of William Holden's line in *Sunset Boulevard*, the one that said being in L.A. without a car was like having your legs cut off.

You were right, Bill, he thought, taking a handkerchief from the pocket of his jeans. He used it to shield his hands as he lifted up the hood. It was a futile move, he knew, for what could he really do? Paul knew nothing about cars.

He stared at the grimy engine, with its confusing labyrinth of wires and metal surfaces. He smelled the water as it sizzled and evaporated off the hot parts. A new blast of vapor finally led him to the offending hose. A rupture ran the length of it, releasing steam that blew out in angry puffs, as if from monstrous rubber lips.

"Christ!" Paul yelled, slamming down the hood. He pictured his son lying in the hospital bed, waiting for him. And now he wouldn't be there because of a damned rubber hose.

When he turned around to the street, he saw a bus approaching, belching black smoke as it shuddered up Hollywood Boulevard.

But as it came within a block of him, Paul realized it wouldn't do him any good. Even if he understood the mysterious numbered codes that marked its destination, he still wouldn't know the transfers involved, and now, patting his pockets, he realized he had no change.

Your son could be dying, he realized, and the driver would want the fare to the penny.

He stared at the cars that passed by, and he began to wonder if he could hitch a ride. But the drivers, poised at their steering wheels with faces bathed in the sweat of the August heat, did not look in a charitable mood.

Could he get one of the cars to stop?

Paul Chesney was tall—six feet six in his bare feet, and he was husky; a shock of long blond hair dangled above a well-lined, masculine face. Friends told him he would have made a great, brawling Irish poet, if only he'd been able to handle the booze. Now it occurred to him he might use his size to advantage.

Anything, he thought, anything to get to his son.

Paul took a deep breath, then bolted into Hollywood Boulevard, where a chorus of honking horns greeted him.

When Paul threw up his husky arms, a car came to a screeching stop, and he thought of that scene from *Invasion of the Body Snatchers* in which Kevin McCarthy stood on the freeway and tried to stop the advance of the pod people.

"What're you doing, asshole?" a man yelled from the driver's seat.

Paul stood up full, then strode to the car. He knelt to the passenger window. "I need a ride."

"You gotta be kidding, jerk!"

Paul held up cash. "It's my boy. My boy's at the hospital. Cedars-Sinai. My car broke down. I'll pay you to take me there."

The man rolled his eyes derisively. "Oh, give me a break, buddy!"

"I swear to you!"

"Sick, huh?"

"Swear to God."

"You aren't shittin' me?"

"No!"

"Fifty bucks, huh?"

"It's yours!"

"Get in," the man said, but after they had driven a block, he added, "But I still think you're an asshole."

Paul ran the whole length of the hallway at Cedars-Sinai. Up ahead, he could see his ex-wife, Rita, who sat before the nurse's station, flipping through a copy of *Vogue*. By the time Paul reached her, he was out of breath.

"You look awful," Rita said.

"I love you too. How is he?"

"Not good."

"I want to see him."

"Can't."

Paul hated the way she said the word, like a spiteful child hoarding candy.

"Bullshit!"

The cords along Rita's slender neck constricted, always a signal that she was furious. Funny, he thought, but the things you remembered most about old lovers were the things they did when angry: necks constricted, hands opened and shut into tight red fists, voices slipped into foreign registers.

"The hell I can't," he said, and he turned to the nurse's station, slamming his fist on the desk. "Where's my boy?"

Rita touched him gently along his back. Her touch was acquiescent, reminding him of her talent for the art of avoiding scenes.

"You can see him in an hour," Rita conceded coldly, forcing a smile.

"Fine," he said, remembering her smile all too well—its empty gesture of reconciliation. How many fights over those ten years had ended in the stalemate contained within that cobralike smile? he wondered.

Paul gestured to the small couch. "I'll wait."

"Very well," she snapped, and Paul decided that her crisp

condescension matched her clothes: a neat grey suit with fashion-
ably oversized jacket, silk blouse, and pearl buttons. Her hair was
different, a trendy cut with spiky thatches inspired by punk.

"You look good," Paul said, and as he sat on the couch it
occurred to him he didn't know if he was lying or not.

"Thank you," she said.

Rita seemed genuinely touched, and when she looked away,
Paul caught a flash of something girlish and vulnerable—enough
to remind him of the woman he had married.

It hurt to look at the woman he had loved and see the enemy.
Almost everything about her had changed. Gone forever was the
spontaneous woman he had met in the midseventies—the sentient
girl who would have pitied the brittle, protected woman she had
now become.

Paul remembered all those nights they had made love in their
first apartment on Wilcox in Hollywood. Their bodies would
smash together beneath the weak, rosy flicker of votive candles
purchased at the liquor store. On the bedside table beside them sat
a joint, a roach clip, a half-empty bag of Oreos, devoured in the
laughter of shared private jokes. The room smelled of incense; the
tinny stereo played the Stones, Joni Mitchell, Leonard Cohen,
over and over, until the grooves had all but worn away, making
gibberish of lyrics they thought so profound.

What was it, Paul wondered, about that first apartment shared
with a lover? What was it that stayed on and haunted the both of
you, as though those ancient spaces still had something to tell you;
as though there were messages in the bad plumbing, secrets in the
floorboards?

In those days, Paul and Rita were linked by dreams: He was
going to be a director; she was going to make documentaries, but
none of it had happened. As with so many Hollywood fantasies,
it had lacked a final reel. Their relationship had locked down into
a kind of perpetual state of becoming.

Whenever Paul drove by that old apartment now, he would light
a cigarette and stare at the windows, wondering what other lives
went on behind them. He would summon up bits of their past like
favorite scenes from movies, and he would know that a part of
himself—frightened and sad—would never let go.

Paul looked up at Rita, who paced the hospital corridor.

"How bad was he this time?" he asked, reaching for his
cigarettes. He noticed the sign on the wall—a cartoon cigarette
trapped within a circle, a violent red slash through it.

Another coy reminder: If you don't clean up your act, you die.

"He's pretty bad," Rita said, pulling nervously at the straps of her tan leather purse. "I'm afraid he's getting worse."

Paul looked up at the clock. He saw that he had exactly fifty minutes until he could be with his son.

Scowling at the nurse, he lit a cigarette, as if to prove that after all these years he could still do something rebellious.

Paul entered Kenny's room as quietly as he could, Rita and the doctor following behind.

When he reached his son's bed, he saw that Kenny's eyes were closed in sleep. "Hey, pal," he whispered.

The boy—lanky, surprisingly tall for his age—now seemed more and more to Paul some fascinating new version of himself. Beneath the blankets, he could make out the outline of long legs, which were as yet out of proportion to the torso. It was an awkward relationship of limb to limb that promised a spurt of growth.

Just like your old man, Paul thought, smiling.

"He's grown," Paul said, and he touched the boy beneath the covers. The warmth of his son's body—so full of life that it could penetrate even the blankets—filled him with emotion.

"He *is* very tall for his age," the doctor said.

"Gary says he'll probably play basketball," Rita offered.

Paul yanked his hand away. The mention of his ex-wife's husband had made him feel an intruder, as though he had no right to touch this boy. He thought of the huge house in Coldwater Canyon, where Kenny lived and played within spaces Paul had never seen.

"He's taller than *I* was at this age," Paul said.

Paul remembered his own year of extraordinary growth—that summer he had done nothing but lie in bed and grow. Helpless within the furious complexity of his body's work, young Paul had lain there dreading scenarios born of the sci-fi/horror movies he loved.

Will I end up like Glenn Langan in *The Amazing Colossal Man*? Will I become so huge they'll have to put me in a circus tent?

Only the reverse scenario had frightened him more: What if I end up like Scott Carey in *The Incredible Shrinking Man*? How terrible to end up like the ill-fated Carey—reduced to but a puny inch in height, forced to retreat to the basement, where he would set up housekeeping in a matchbox and wage war with spiders.

Carey became so small that his wife no longer knew he existed. She had driven away from the house without hearing her husband's screams for help from the basement.

He reached out and stroked Kenny's hair. Even the color was the same, Paul thought—warm and sandy, a tarnished tawny gold, as Rita had called it. When he was Kenny's age, Paul would plaster down the stubborn thatches with Brylcreem.

What was that stuff the kids used now? he wondered, and it hurt him that he couldn't remember.

More and more, he was afraid he knew too little about his son—the telling details that a parent should know—for now they picked up the thread of their relationship like a chapter in some old Saturday afternoon serial.

Father and son, he mused, the cliff-hanger of Paul and Kenny. To be continued.

"What do you think of this man?" the judge had asked the boy, pointing at Paul, who sat nervously at the long table opposite.

"He's my dad!" Kenny had said impatiently, shrugging, as if to say, "What the hell do you think?" and the courtroom that awful day a year ago had erupted into laughter. The boy had taken down the judge, stabbed with a joke, and even the court reporter's fingers—until that moment a dizzy dance—had stopped and curled into question marks: Just how *did* you record the laser power of a child's innocence?

"You feel comfortable with your dad?"

"Sure."

"You feel he protects you?"

"Yeah," Kenny had said, offering up another little shrug beneath his new sport coat. He then turned to Paul and smiled so full and wide that even Rita—meticulously dressed to Paul's right—had seen their connection and hated it. She turned her frustration to the nervous fingering of a diamond necklace, another ostentatious gift from Gary.

When it had come Paul's turn to testify, he had only hoped to do as well as his son.

"I understand, Mr. Chesney, that you're now enrolled in a chapter of A.A.?"

"Yes, Your Honor."

"You have your own business, it says. A video store in Silverlake? Is that right?"

"Yes, Your Honor. Eight months now. So far, so good."

"And it says you've published a book? Film history?"

Paul had smiled at that one. He had received his first royalty statement only a month before the custody hearing. His book—an examination of the prolific career of Roger Corman, undisputed king of the Grade C horror flicks—had sold under five hundred copies.

"Horror and sci-fi, Your Honor. I'm afraid it didn't do too well. Not a whole lot of money in monsters."

The judge had laughed at that, and Paul, smiling at Kenny, knew that he and his son had forged some sort of a victory.

How humiliating it had been an hour later to watch him move down the courthouse hallway with Rita, who had predictably won custody. Paul would have his son on alternate weekends.

Paul turned to the doctor. "How long will he be here?"

"He might be able to leave in the morning."

A dread rose up inside of him. "Will we have our Sunday together?"

"We'd better talk," Rita said.

They sat opposite each other at a table in the hospital cafeteria, where Paul sipped coffee and listened to Rita describe the events that led their son to the hospital that day.

"He was fine all morning," she began, "but about lunchtime he got irritable. He wouldn't sit to anything. That's the way it always starts, you know."

"I *do* know," Paul said. "I was there once, remember?"

"Don't snap at me!"

"I'm sorry."

"I was in the front room. I heard him start that awful humming sound . . . you remember how it always began that way . . ."

"Yes!"

It irritated Paul that she thought he could ever forget. There wasn't a day in Paul's life that he didn't think back to that awful moment when they realized something wasn't quite right with their son.

It began with the voices.

From the throat of the boy they loved came a series of bizarre noises that later articulated into words.

But they weren't Kenny's words; they were the words of other people: characters. Soon it seemed that the boy was acting out stories born of some deep and private hallucination.

One night they found him in his room, where he was naked and shivering in a corner. When Paul tried to gather him up in his arms, the boy fought him off.

The boy then spoke in an old man's voice. He talked of his grandson, who was dying a horrible death from cancer, and Paul and Rita stood aghast, watching as their boy acted out the grandson's death. When he finished, Kenny tossed himself across the imaginary grave and wept so hard he got sick.

Just when they were certain the boy suffered from multiple-personality disorder, a different diagnosis came: The boy was schizo-affective, often a prelude to full-blown schizophrenia.

Even now, the term rattled Paul's insides. It stabbed him with a triple assault of sadness, guilt, and shame; how could anyone this innocent—the boy he loved so much—be expected to endure such pain?

Rita continued her description of what had happened that morning. "I approached him, Paul. He was wearing the yellow rain slicker. Do you remember? The one he wanted so much?"

Paul nodded, remembering Kenny's odd obsession with the yellow rain slicker. He had seen it one night when they all went to the Glendale Mall, and he had wanted it so much he soon became obsessed. Paul had finally bought it for him.

Rita went on. "He wore the yellow rain slicker this morning, and he was holding a paper sack. He was laughing. This awful laughter. He was using a voice that I hadn't heard before."

Rita pointed to his cigarettes. "Give me one of those, will you?"

Paul handed her a cigarette and lit it for her. Afterward, he touched her hand, realizing he had not touched Rita so gently in years. It angered him that the only thing that could make them close now was Kenny's illness; it was the only intimacy they had left. "Go on," he said.

"I went up to him, Paul, and I tried to get ahold of him, but he broke away. You know how strong he gets at times like that. He ran out of the room . . . screaming at the top of his voice. Only the voice had changed by now. It was a scream . . . a *woman's* scream, and he ran all the way to the bathroom, still carrying that paper sack. He got down on the floor, right there by the toilet, Paul, and he just sat there a long time. He finally started pounding at his groin . . . as hard as he could . . . I thought he would hurt himself . . ."

Paul could see tears forming in her deep blue eyes, and he hated himself for the sudden tenderness he felt. The boy's misery was making him love her again.

"Then what, Rita?"

Pulling a handkerchief from her purse, she dabbed at her eyes. "He just kept screaming like that . . . until he was exhausted. Like all the times before. And then he stopped. Just stopped, Paul, and he slumped there against the toilet. I went to him and held him. I carried him into the bedroom, undressed him, and saw the awful bruises. The bruises that he'd made from hitting himself like that. I felt his forehead and I realized he had a terrible fever. I called the doctor, then you."

"What about the paper sack?" Paul asked. "What was in the paper sack?"

Rita put out her cigarette. "I went back to the bathroom. The sack was still on the floor. I picked it up and looked inside."

"What was in it?"

"The things that were missing," she said.

"What things?"

"Lately, things have been missing, Paul. Little things around the house . . . insignificant things, mostly. I haven't thought much about them, really."

"What was in the sack?"

"Stuff from the kitchen. Some plastic utensils. A mixing spoon, a fork, a ladle."

• Three •

CARL IRVINE WATCHED them as they lined up for the Friday night movie. Keeping his eye on the long line of kids that spilled from the forecourt, he worried.

He kept his vigil from a rocking chair. It sat before the window of his room at the Wallenberg Hotel, which was just across Main Street from Odeon. The lights of the great marquee had snapped on a few minutes ago—at six-thirty exactly, according to Carl's watch, which he now checked again.

Carl wore a child's watch, and on its face was a big fat bear, its paws pointing out the time. A honeycomb had fallen to the bear's side, so that the bear was surrounded by bees that flew in a furious swarm to the 12. Carl had never quite figured out what the cartoon was supposed to mean, but he guessed it had to do with the way time went—it moved too fast, and it left you feeling angry.

But it was a child's watch, he thought, and what would a child know about the awful thing that time did to you?

Carl studied the watch, grimacing as he tried to calculate. Five hours and twenty-five minutes, he eventually figured, that was how long he had until it was time to show up for work at Odeon. That's when he'd have to walk in with his pails and his mops and his disinfectants.

"Perfume for stinking Odeon," he'd announce to all the old folks downstairs in the hotel lobby on his way to work.

Carl was grateful for the extra time he had tonight. It was all because old Jack MacGruder had booked a triple-bill Karate-Thon, and it took a long time to get through three pictures. He wasn't allowed inside the theatre until the last customer had left, for old Jack MacGruder didn't think it looked good to see the janitor hanging around.

It hurt Carl's feelings, but he realized that Jack MacGruder still had his rules. Wearing his tuxedo every night, Jack MacGruder still ran Odeon like it was something grand; he'd tear your ticket in half with a flourish, then smile and say, "Enjoy the show"—even if he knew damned well that the movie was rotten and stupid.

But Carl couldn't help feeling a little bit sorry for Jack MacGruder; after all, the old man had given his whole life to Odeon. Carl figured that Jack loved Odeon the way most men loved a woman: possessively, and filled with lots of ideas about forever. And Carl knew that Jack MacGruder couldn't accept what the old place had become. It was a crumbling, stinking relic, as far as Carl was concerned.

Carl looked at the chipped plastic letters affixed to the battered old marquee: KARATE-THON. ACTION. Beside them, the bilious orange and green logo for the California lottery—Jack's latest scheme to bring in customers. Carl noticed that the letters were hanging all loose and crooked. He thought of an old woman in an ancient gown, the frayed edges falling away from wrinkled shoulders.

Most of the people in line were kids—teenagers, mostly. They were the only ones who came to Odeon anymore. Most of Wallenberg stayed home now with their TV, video machines, and cable. Some even ventured the ten-mile drive up the 101 to Haleyville, where Carl heard they had this new multiplex with a whole lot of screens in one theatre.

But Carl never mentioned the multiplex to Jack MacGruder. If he did, the old man stiffened up and looked offended, like Carl had said something sacrilegious. Afterward, he'd lecture Carl on the good old days of movies, when theatres were palaces, not little holes in the wall. Jack MacGruder found the multiplex an abomination, so Carl just shut up about it.

Now Carl began the slow rise from his rocker. The process of getting out of it was long and painful for him, especially when he'd been sitting for so long, as he had now, staring out the window of his hotel room.

He didn't much care for the room, where he'd lived since the accident. He knew it wasn't nearly as nice as the guest rooms. Carl had seen one of the guest rooms once, with its dainty wallpaper, fancy brass bed, and pretty lace curtains. It depressed him to compare it to his own room—the dull walls that screamed for paint, a single cot, a crummy dresser with cracked mirror.

But hell, he thought, it was free. It wasn't a bad deal for only having to sweep out the hotel lobby once a week. You learned to compromise in this life, Carl Irvine believed.

When he finally got up from the rocker, he felt the pain, sudden and cumulative, a delayed reaction to the strain of getting up. It was always worse at night, and he'd decided a long time ago that it would never go away. He tried to stretch his body to a full standing position—a reflex that still survived—but it only made the pain worse.

How he craved to stand completely upright again, not in this forever kind of half-slump. How he wanted his body to be the way it used to be—strong, lithe, masculine, the kind of body a woman liked to watch in motion. When he watched the other townsfolk walk down Main Street, he tried not to feel envious, but it was hard not to. It was especially hard when he saw the teenage boys, the easy way their legs and hips moved, as if on perfect pivots. They looked so proud in their new bodies, walking upright with that effortless kind of strut, so arrogant—like roosters.

Carl noticed that his window was half open. A breeze blew in, fluttering the filthy curtain.

It was cold, he thought. Much too cold for August.

He'd heard the man on the radio say it was going to get down to forty tonight. In *August*! And hell, that's five degrees colder than it was the night before!

It seemed to Carl that the freakish weather was all the people of Wallenberg were talking about these days. Everywhere he went, he heard it: downstairs in the hotel lobby, at the brand-new Safeway, at Ruby's Cafe. He'd heard it a lot over at the Texaco station, where they'd ordered up a special stock of antifreeze.

Carl struggled to the window and pulled it shut. He stood and looked at Odeon, where the ragged line of kids had grown longer, stretching all the way to the Busy Bee Bar.

The big vertical sign flashed *ODEON* the way it always had, but Carl saw that the *D* had burned out, and the *N*, fluttering now, was about to go.

The purple light wasn't as bright as it used to be, he could tell. And yet, he realized, it could still reach all the way across Main Street and touch his face and hands; it could still wink at night across the peeling paint of his room, the bedspread without design or color, the battered table with the hot plate he wasn't supposed to have.

He felt a rage as precise as the pain that worked along his back. He hated Odeon. It seemed more and more that he'd spent his whole life in the bowels of it. Sometimes he imagined the plaster was a skin—hardened and dead, ready to molt. The portholes, he decided, were eyes: They were dark and filled with evil.

At night, alone with his buckets, Carl would feel his anger grow so great that he'd shake his fist and scream out his hatred. He would cry out to the crumbling Gothic arches, the stained murals with the rotting arabesques and the ugly, faded frescoes.

And then, if he listened hard enough, he would hear the rats as they stirred and squealed in all the dusty, unknown places of the theatre, responding to his voice as it rattled throughout the old theatre.

He heard the rats everywhere, as they crawled from hiding places—the million concealments in the crumbling decoration. He watched them squirm from cove-lit domes and leap by the hundreds from side-wall cathedrals. Often, their tiny muzzles would poke up from the cozy nests they had made in the ruined seats.

But Carl never reported the rats to Jack MacGruder. He never put out traps or laced the floors with poison, as a good janitor should. On the contrary, Carl *liked* the rats. He often sneaked them bits of cheese or globs of peanut butter, which he would smear on the armrests before waiting in the dark for the rats to come for it.

Carl liked the rats for a very simple reason: He knew they were Odeon's only enemy. Carl could tell that Odeon hated them, feared them. Carl knew that Odeon found their squirmy bodies an annoyance—the agonized itch of a constant infection. The rats in the Odeon Theatre were like mites beneath its skin.

"You'll never be rid of them!" Carl cried out to his empty room.

But the force of his cry had made him stand up too tall, and the pain hit him hard. It was worse than before. It felt like someone dragged a rake along the lump that was his back.

It hurt so bad he had to double over, searching for his breath in panicked gasps until he was able to stand up. After wiping away the sweat along his face, he stared down at the teenagers, who laughed and jostled in line.

He knew all their names—those rambunctious kids—and he knew it would surprise them if they knew that he did.

Carl even liked them, and he didn't blame them for making fun of him. At their age he too would have mocked such a person—a man with a lump on his back; a man who walked crooked-over, as if in perpetual search for something he had lost along the sidewalk; a man who at thirty-five looked as though he were sixty, maybe older.

No, he thought, I don't blame them. Time made me like this, and he thought of the big mad bear and the honeycomb.

And they *couldn't* know, of course. How could they know that Carl Irvine, who now found it difficult to speak without drenching his lower lip in spittle, had once been handsome?

And how could they know that he'd once been loved by someone beautiful, and that—after all these years—he still loved her? How could they know that he still wished her love, that he still saw her face in every lover's moon that passed before his hotel window—the thousand hopeless moons he had charted above the blue distraction of Odeon.

He turned sharply from the window, for these, the thoughts of love, were the hardest to bear. When he thought these things, they made him think too much of what he'd become, how ugly; it made him think of how impossible it would be for anyone to love him.

After limping to the bed, he sat so that his hands folded neatly into his lap, and he saw how red they had become. Odeon had ruined even them, he thought—his hands, one of the few vanities the accident had left him. All those nights of plunging them into astringents had roughened them, making them hard and red and blemished, like the husks of the pomegranates he'd buy at the Wallenberg Grocery.

Carl reached for his bedside table, which was strewn with his possessions: an ashtray, a dirty comb, a beer can, a dog-eared western paperback he'd been reading for several months. He picked up his pride and joy—a portable radio and cassette player, the thing he'd heard the kids call a ghetto blaster.

Cradling it in his lap, Carl worked the tuner through a blast of static until he had found his favorite: country and western.

He sat with it a long while, his music—sad music; this time, it was a song about someone who'd left someone at a train, and he felt the music vibrate in his lap, so that it seemed to work through the dirty fabric of his denim trousers and settle along his flesh.

As Carl listened, he remembered and he thought. He remained

completely still and quiet until the song reached its final chord. When it was over, he was certain, very certain, that the broken heart the woman had sung about was his own.

Carl wondered what he would do when he lost his job, for he knew the time was drawing near.

He wasn't supposed to know, but he'd heard all the rumors. Carl knew that Jack MacGruder was finding it hard to pay for Odeon's upkeep. It didn't help that Jack's brother, Roy, the projectionist, often ran off with the night's receipts and drank them up at the Busy Bee. Overhead was high; revenue was low. The whole business with the lottery had been a big flop, and all the kids used the armrests to rub off their tickets. Jack was always yelling at Carl for not cleaning up the silvery residue that trailed throughout Odeon along the rotting carpets.

Odeon was a monstrous shrine to its own obsolescence, and Carl knew that even Jack, who loved the old place, had just about given up.

He felt sorry for old Jack MacGruder, but he didn't feel sorry for Odeon.

Hell, I can hardly wait to see you suffer and die.

And Carl knew that it would happen soon, for he was aware that Jack was just about to close a big real estate deal. Mayor Eddie Bendix wanted to tear Odeon down and replace it with a mini-mall. "What the hell," Carl'd heard him say, "people don't wanna go see movies at a big old place like that no more; they can rent 'em just as easy at a video store. We'll put one right there in the mall and, by God, we might even call it Odeon."

But Carl worried, and he was more than a little scared. That's why he kept his nightly vigil; he had a creepy feeling that something bad was going to happen, and the strange cold weather was only making it worse.

But what could he do? He knew they all thought he was crazy—he'd seen their faces. He'd seen the looks they gave him when he said that he thought the theatre was really alive and had a mind of its own.

They didn't believe he could really hear the old place making noises—*living* noises—and old Jack MacGruder was adamant: He absolutely did not want to hear a word about it.

Whenever Carl went on about such things, Jack would shut himself in his basement office and lock the door. Like the time Carl told him that the curtains opened up one night, all on their own, and up there on Odeon's screen, just like a movie, was a picture of Jack as a little boy, downstairs in the bowels of Odeon, staring at a woman who was all covered with blood.

No, sir. Jack don't want me to talk about that one at all.

Carl sat still on the bed, cradling his radio while watching the purple light as it blinked its way across his room. It was more intense than ever, filling the room up slowly but steadily, like water.

Was it getting brighter these last few days?

After carefully putting the radio away on the bedside table, Carl struggled his way over to the window again.

Most of the kids were inside now, and only a few hung around the forecourt. Carl felt worried for them.

Really worried.

But no matter what, he knew he had to keep quiet. He had to keep his temper and stop yelling at the old place night after night. He knew he could secretly taunt Odeon about the rats. He knew he could shake his fist and stick out his tongue at the ugly cherubs, but he had to keep quiet about the wrecking ball.

If Odeon found out about the wrecking ball, Carl knew there'd be hell to pay.

"How come you're so scared of a dumb old movie theatre?"

"It's not the theatre, it's Billy Burnside."

"You're not gonna start in about him, are you?"

"Well, he's always here, Mike . . . He's like . . . well, he just gives me the creeps."

"You're too much, Amy. You're just too much."

Amy Bradley stood in Odeon's forecourt, where she folded her arms defiantly against the cold, watching as her boyfriend, Mike Barnes, swaggered up the terrazzo. At the box office, he took a Velcro wallet from the hip pocket of his tight jeans, tearing it open with a deliberate force that Amy knew was intended as a comment on their argument about Billy Burnside. The sound of fabric ripping from fabric echoed loudly through the huge forecourt, so that it might as well have been a gunshot, she decided.

Mike had got his own way again.

But now she stood and studied him. Odd about that swagger, she thought, and all those blunt and masculine moves Mike made. Sometimes the way he moved made her think he was the sexiest and best-looking guy in the whole world, and if she squinted just right, Amy thought he looked a lot like Matt Dillon. But other times, like now, Amy wondered if Mike wasn't just a caricature of what she wanted, rather than what she needed: a nice guy who'd take her to bed and make gentle love to her for the first time in her life.

Amy was seventeen years old and pretty—too pretty, her father, the local sheriff, always said. She had a high, intelligent forehead, and her eyes were robin's-egg blue, framed by honey-blond hair, which she had recently cut short. Mike hadn't approved of the haircut at all, but Amy, for the first time since knowing him, had defied him, and she had cut her hair the way *she* wanted it.

It annoyed Amy how Mike was always trying to control her, and now she stood in the cold forecourt and wondered if the whole evening with Mike hadn't been a big mistake.

It was supposed to have been a special night—a kind of farewell gesture to summer before she started up at the community college in September. Amy had hoped they could have gone over to Haleyville for a dinner at one of the nice restaurants, then maybe go to the multiplex and see that love story that had just come out.

But Odeon was having a triple bill, a Karate-Thon—two Chuck Norris and a Bruce Lee—and Mike had insisted. So here she was, wondering in the icy forecourt of a crumbling old movie theatre if this was the way it would always be with boys: Did they get their own way all the time?

Worse, his car was broken once again, meaning they couldn't take that walk along the beach he'd promised—Mike's big concession to romance. Mike owned the sort of car that was always filled with tools, which clunked around in the back seat whenever they took those sharp turns he tried to impress her with along North Post Road. Sometimes Amy feared that the car was more important to Mike than she was.

"Carburetor's screwed," he'd said to her in that curt and sullen way of his, as though the lack of wheels had somehow placed a claim on his manhood.

And so it was Amy's father, Sheriff Leo Bradley, who had ended up driving them to Odeon. Annoyed as she was, Amy had nonetheless found a certain pleasure in Mike's discomfort in the back seat of the patrol car—the one place in all the world where he couldn't grope at her.

But Amy had come to notice that cops had a way of intimidating guys like Mike, and she didn't know why, except she suspected that maybe Mike really wanted to be like her father—big and strapping, a gun brushing against his husky thigh whenever he made those trademark masculine strides across a room.

It was Amy's father, in fact, who had started their fight about Billy Burnside.

"Caught that creepy fucker Billy Burnside digging holes again on North Post Road," Amy's father had said.

"Creepy fucker," Mike repeated.

Amy had sat in the patrol car resenting them both—her father for having brought up Billy Burnside, who he knew perfectly well upset her, and Mike for always finding it necessary to mimic her father's swearing. He had yanked the word *fucker* right out of his vocabulary, just to impress him.

"Dad, I wish you wouldn't talk about him!"

"Sorry," her father had said, then explained to Mike, "Amy's scared to death of Billy Burnside. She ran into him out there on North Post Road. He was diggin' those weird holes of his."

"He goes to Odeon every night," Mike had said, then turned to her. "But I'll protect Amy."

And that's when Amy's heart had sunk.

Of course! Billy Burnside will be there! He's *always* at Odeon!

Anxious and upset, Amy had stayed silent the rest of the way to Odeon, while all hopes for a romantic evening dissolved into visions of karate in a musty old movie theatre.

Amy watched as Mike headed back with the tickets. He held them up, fanned and proffered, like a bluff in a round of cards. He approached her in that confident stride, the one that said, I'm a man, and I'm the man you want. It scared Amy that she was attracted to him all over again, as if this whole thing of love only meant that you just kept losing track of who you were and what you really felt or wanted.

"Let's go," he said, taking her arm.

When he touched her, Amy smiled at him—a big and friendly smile, which she genuinely meant, for his touch felt strong and protective.

"You aren't mad no more? About the kung fu flicks, I mean?"

Amy shook her head.

"Colder'n a witch's tit out here," he said, and he moved up closer, wrapping her waist with his dark, muscled arms. She could smell him now—that smoky, masculine smell, mixed with musk, a hint of sweat, and she liked it. He kept pressing up to her until she could feel his pelvis against hers. It was like the whole essence of Mike were closing in on her, enfolding her completely, so that, defenseless now, the only thing she could do with the anger and resentment was let it go.

"Whazza matter mich *chew*?"

Amy froze.

Even before she turned around, she knew who it was. She recognized both the voice—deep and raspy—and that stupid expression; Billy Burnside used it all the time.

He stood only a few feet away, over near the karate posters, and he stared at them both. His eyes were wide behind the thick lenses of his glasses, the crooked frames held together by a soiled Band-Aid. His face was such a mass of angry pimples it was difficult to make out his true features. As usual, he wore a yellow rain slicker, which was crusted with bits of dried mud. When Amy noticed the dirt that marked his hands and thin, sticklike fingers, she wondered if he'd been digging more of those holes out on North Post Road.

"What do you want?" Mike shouted.

Billy kept staring.

"I asked you a question!"

Amy saw that Billy Burnside clutched a paper sack, and it scared her. It was Amy's friend Cindy who claimed that Billy liked to kill little animals just for fun. She said that after he wounded them he put them in a paper sack and carried them into Odeon, where they would suffer and die while Billy Burnside watched the movie.

Now she thought she saw the sack move. "Mike!"

When Mike stepped forward angrily, Billy Burnside grinned and turned away, securing the paper sack beneath his arm and moving up the terrazzo. With a final glance at Amy, he offered up his ticket to Jack MacGruder, then walked inside the theatre.

Amy grabbed Mike's arm. "I want to go home."

"He gives you any trouble, I'll bust his ass," Mike said, then he pulled her up close to him, even closer than before. When Amy looked into his eyes, she forgave him almost everything, for she believed that Mike *would* protect her. "I promise," he added.

And then, arm in arm, they walked into Odeon.

• Four •

KAREN STARTLED AWAKE.

When she raised her head and blinked her eyes, she tried to place where she was. She'd been dreaming, she knew, for she felt disoriented, and the dream, whatever it had been, had left her uneasy. Focusing upon the paperwork that was strewn before her across the familiar surface of her kitchen table, Karen remembered where she was. She noticed the large red blotches that lined her wrists, where her head had lain against them in unexpected sleep.

But now she panicked. What time was it? Had she overslept? Would she be late for the banquet? Just great, the single most important event of my whole career and I go to sleep at the kitchen table and miss it!

But when she turned and looked at the clock above the stove, she saw that it was just five-thirty. She breathed a sigh of relief, for the banquet, at which she would be delivering the keynote speech, was not until eight.

After rubbing her eyes, Karen looked at the stack of index cards, which contained the text of her speech. Already she felt a major attack of nerves, for she hated getting up in front of large groups of people. Worse, the banquet was for the firm's top clients.

Only Karen's desire for a promotion could have motivated her to do such a daring and vulnerable thing.

But now, in spite of her apprehension, Karen felt as though she could go back to sleep. It bothered Karen to feel so little energy, even though she knew why.

In the days since the break-in, she'd been unable to sleep. She wondered constantly: Was it just imagination? Or, much worse: Did it signal the beginning of another breakdown?

Matters were complicated by Karen's constant preoccupation with hearing from the adoption agency. Every moment of her life now seemed measured by anticipating the fateful call from Estelle Hopkins. An irrational part of her believed that, having discovered her past, the agency had now rejected her: *No thanks, Karen—no crazy mothers, please.*

Picking up the index cards, Karen secured them with a rubber band and tossed them into her purse.

If I don't know the speech by now, I never will.

Standing up from the table, Karen glanced out the window toward the pool, where Alan Fitschew's chaise was empty. She sighed long and deep.

There had been no further evidence of anyone having entered her apartment, yet the incident was still unexplained. Nights found Karen sleepless as she lay and waited for sounds that never came. At night, after work, she would ransack her apartment, like a burglar in her own home, yet nothing had seemed out of place.

When confronted, Alan Fitschew had denied everything. While his denial was predictable, Karen nonetheless chose to believe him, for she had long ago found in Alan's lost, sad eyes a single virtue: He did not lie.

Moments later Karen settled in for a long, hot bath. Just as she began to relax, Karen found herself thinking of the boy again—the boy with green eyes. The boy she had loved and lost in Wallenberg.

Why, she wondered, did she think of him after all of these years?

But Karen *did* know why. Her therapist had warned her that attempts to adopt a child would revive his memory. The therapist, in fact, had opposed the adoption: "It will bring everything back. You will start to obsess again. You have to accept the fact that you lost him. He left you, Karen."

But no, Karen thought, he did not leave. He was taken away.

But what did it really matter? What did it matter how or why people left? It still came down to one thing: They were gone.

She thought of that last time they were together—up in the balcony of the Odeon Theatre. The boy had loved horror movies and she had not, and they had fought about it.

So silly, she thought now. Such a trivial thing to fight about.

If only I had stayed with him in the balcony.

If I hadn't left him in the balcony, I might never have been raped.

Karen slammed her palm against the water, for she realized she was doing it—obsessing, just as her therapist had warned. When her hand hit the water, the sudden loud sound was enough to obliterate her thoughts. Water splashed up against her face.

It made her forget that she had started to cry.

Karen looked at the clock and saw that it was almost six forty-five. Realizing it was later than she thought, she dried herself while running from the bathroom to the bedroom.

When she caught her reflection in the full-length mirror by the closet, she paused to check her new haircut. She'd had it cut at a trendy shop on Melrose the afternoon before. The layered, shorter cut favored her large blue eyes, she decided, and she was anxious to see how it would complement the new dress.

Karen slid open the closet door and reached for the dress, but her hand quickly passed through empty space.

The dress was not there.

She tried to remain calm, for she knew the dress had been there that morning. She remembered having admired it before going to work. She had even touched it, lovingly running her hand along the expensive fabric.

Yes, yes. It was there! It was!

Karen searched her way down the length of the closet, pawing frantically through all of her clothes. Hangers collided with other hangers, tossing the rest of Karen's clothing to the floor. The new dress was not to be found.

When she looked at her watch, Karen saw that she had but twenty-five minutes to get ready for the banquet.

And she had that feeling—that sense of reality pulling away, just like before the breakdown.

Karen knew that the last place she should have gone in such a state was the Bonaventure Hotel, and had the banquet not been so important, she would have stayed home.

And yet, she wondered if she could ever be comfortable in that apartment again. A part of her was terribly frightened and *never* wanted to go back.

Arriving at the Bonaventure just before eight, Karen surrendered her car to valet parking and took the escalator upstairs to the lobby, which was futuristic and cold, located within a cylindrical core made up of shiny metal and glass.

The enormous lobby lacked signs, and Karen found it immediately confusing—an unsettling mix of coral-shaded walls, burbling fountains, and concrete skybridges. It took her several minutes to locate the elevators that would deliver her to the top floor and the banquet.

By the time she got inside the glass-bubble elevator, Karen felt nauseous. Her stomach lurched with the rapid, upward motion as she rocketed toward the thirty-third floor, and the sight of the city streets below—seemingly torn out from under her—filled her with dread.

She supported herself against a chrome rail inside the elevator.

Calm down, just calm down.

But now she caught her reflection in the glass. The dress she wore—a blue crepe de chine with bits of pearl beading—was nice, she thought, but nothing like her new dress.

Where in the name of God did it go?

A wonderful dinner was served, but Karen ignored it.

She tried to make conversation with coworkers and friends, but she could not get her mind off the dress. She convinced herself Alan Fitschew *was* the culprit, and she intended to confront him when she got home.

Yes, there is a logical explanation. *I am not having a breakdown*.

"You're very pretty. You here alone?"

Karen turned to the voice, which sounded drunken and obnoxious. She saw that it belonged to a fat man, who was cinched in an expensive but ill-fitting suit. His fleshy face was scarlet, flushed with alcohol, and a sour odor of booze drifted across the table to Karen, aggravating the nausea she already felt.

He introduced himself as chairman of a toothpaste company, which Karen recognized as an important client. Karen hated him on sight, and it bothered her that she felt so utterly incapable of rising to the occasion. If she wanted to make it in this business, she knew she would have to learn the art of being charming with persons she could not stand.

What's wrong with me? What in the name of God is wrong with me?

"Hear you're making a speech," he said, leaning up closer to her. He puffed busily on a fat, smoldering cigar.

"Yes," she said, and she turned away.

Karen looked toward the lectern, where someone toyed with the microphone, preparing for her speech. Dishes clattered in the background while tables were cleared. Her speech would begin in just a few minutes.

Karen felt more and more ill, as though she might have to throw up, and she couldn't get her mind off the fat man behind her. The acrid odor of his cigar overwhelmed her, as though she were slowly being sealed within some foul little cloud.

Karen felt him watching her. And waiting. Waiting for her to make a single wrong move.

All of them were!

Karen shifted the index cards, which felt damp within her sweaty hands. When she looked down to scan the opening of her speech, she saw that the ink had smeared.

A moment later they introduced her from the podium.

Up behind the lectern, Karen tried to smile. As the warm applause began to die, she laid down the index cards, then stared out at the featureless faces in the smoky room.

"I'd like to thank you all for coming," she began, but her voice sounded thin to her and foreign. Clearing her throat, she began again. ". . . here this evening . . ."

Karen realized her attention had drifted to the fat man, who stared at her and grinned. Even though she tried to avoid him, her attention kept wandering back.

But now she knew that she had been silent too long. She was, after all, at a lectern and they expected a speech. She could hear them rustling about in the dark now.

". . . I'd like to thank all of you . . ."

Karen stopped again.

This time, she thought she felt something. It felt as though something had brushed against her leg—something from inside the lectern.

Get hold of yourself, for God's sake!

Aware that her voice was even thinner than before, she began. ". . . very much for being the superb . . ."

It touched her again. Whatever it was felt dry and hard, like something crusted over with mud.

Stop it, Karen! There's nothing under there!

Karen felt herself begin to tremble. She could hear the whispers as they rippled up from the darkened banquet hall: What's wrong with her? Did you see that? Is she all right?

Karen locked eyes with the fat man, who downed another scotch and wiped at his mouth. She saw that he was laughing at her.

Adjusting her index cards, Karen opened her mouth to speak, but before she could form her words, she felt something else.

Now there was pressure against her shin—a stinging sensation, followed by the touch of something damp.

For the love of God, something is biting me!

Barely able to keep from screaming, Karen pulled herself away from the lectern. Her hand bumped against the side of it, upsetting the stack of index cards, which scattered across the floor.

Karen stood frozen. She heard the laughter now—cold, cruel, derisive. "Excuse me," she said, and she knelt down quickly behind the lectern.

Hidden from view, she had a moment to decide what to do. She decided she would tell them she had come down suddenly with the flu and felt very faint. She would make excuses to her colleagues, then drive directly home. If she could just get out of the room without screaming, she figured, she had a chance to save face.

Karen kept grabbing at the cards, which had fanned out in all directions. With her hands groping frantically, she felt like a child playing some silly card game. Now she could hear the audience clearly. They no longer whispered, but spoke instead at full volume.

Beyond embarrassed, Karen feared that indeed it *was* another breakdown.

How stupid to think that it was all over. You don't get over something like that so easily!

And yet, she thought, this seemed so different from before. This wasn't like the breakdown at the supermarket. Things hadn't seemed real that day, and the whole world had felt as though it were slipping away, like in that final swooning moment before sleep.

This was different. It seemed real.

Horribly real.

After grabbing up the last note card, Karen didn't want to stand up, for it would mean she had to face them.

How could she face them again, and now, within her fear and embarrassment, she imagined a chorus of disapproval: *There she is, that crazy woman. Got herself raped once, got herself pregnant, gave herself an abortion. Went bonkers one day in a supermarket. Had the nerve to think she could adopt a child. Now she's going nuts again.*

But Karen knew it was absurd to think she could hide from

them. What am I going to do? Crawl out of here on my hands and knees?

When Karen finally stood up, the room returned to her in a dizzy lurch, and behind a swirl of smoke, she saw the outlines of their faces.

When she was about to speak, another of the index cards fell to the floor. Carried on a current of air, it slipped inside the hollow of the lectern. Fearing they would laugh at her again, Karen knelt quickly to retrieve it. When she looked inside the lectern, she stifled a scream.

The thing inside was coarse and misshapen. It couldn't have been more than three feet tall. The dry skin sprouted long tendrils, which swung dead and useless at its side. Only the huge, staring eyes identified the shapeless mass above its shoulders as a head. The mouth—a crude slit—moved up and down, as though it were trying to speak to her.

She stared at the thing's hand, and she saw that it clutched something. It reached out for her now, offering her what it held.

Karen looked, then she saw what it was.

The thing gripped a wad of fabric—the filthy, encrusted remains of her new dress.

Finally, Karen screamed.

Karen awoke in a room she did not recognize. When she tried to sit up, she felt dizzy, and she was aware of a steady pain in her back.

For a moment she tried to convince herself that she lay in her own bed, and she stared into the room, looking for something familiar. But all she could see were white, blank walls that she did not recognize.

Where in God's name am I? What happened?

The pain throbbed anew in the small of her back.

Did I have a fall?

Now she heard voices—hushed and urgent—and the room came slowly into focus. Squinting against the bright light, she tried to make out who was there.

But I really don't know her that well.

Someone will have to drive her home.

I'm certain she'll come to.

Karen saw that the voices belonged to two women, who stood by the door. One of them was dressed in a nurse's uniform.

"Where am I?" Karen cried.

The two women reacted to her voice, breaking from a conspiratorial huddle. As the nurse rushed to her side, Karen began to remember; the evening returned to her in the frantic bits and pieces of nightmare.

"You fainted," said the nurse, taking Karen's hand. "You're still at the hotel. This is the first-aid room. Do you remember what happened? Can you tell me where you are?"

"The Bonaventure," Karen said, and then cried out, "The lectern! My God, there was something inside . . ."

But she stopped. Her mind was clear enough now to realize she would only seem crazy.

But it was real! I am *not* insane!

Now Karen grew curious, wondering who the other woman was. She looked in her direction, but the woman's back was turned. She was large, middle-aged. Was it someone from work?

"Hello," Karen cried out. "Do I know you?"

When the woman turned around, Karen recognized Estelle Hopkins from the adoption agency.

Miss Hopkins moved to her slowly. "I'm sorry, Miss Webster. I thought . . . well, I thought it would be a good way to view you in a work situation . . ."

Her voice drifted off before her sentence was finished. Karen could tell that the large, officious woman was embarrassed for her.

"I'm sorry," Karen said. Mortified, she turned away, burying her face in the pillow, where she caught the scent of the expensive new perfume she had worn. Now it made her sick to her stomach, and she knew she was going to cry.

"Please," she said, "I'd like to be alone for a few minutes."

Karen felt the reassuring touch of Miss Hopkins' hand on her back.

"Maybe a couple years from now, you could . . . adopt . . ." Miss Hopkins said. "I'm sorry." After a long pause, she spoke again. "Miss Webster?"

"Yes."

"When you were lying on the floor, Miss Webster, you said something . . ."

Karen turned to her. "What? What did I say?"

"Well, Miss Webster, you said, 'My child is in danger. My child is in danger.' You said it over and over, in fact."

Karen looked into the woman's eyes. For a moment she considered telling her everything, but decided it would do no good. "I can't imagine what I meant."

"I mean, you did say that you . . . well, that you aborted your only pregnancy, right?"

"Yes," Karen said, then added quietly, "I really should be alone."

Miss Hopkins smiled. "Of course."

After they left, Karen sat in silence for a long time, pondering what Miss Hopkins had said.

Why *had* she cried out that her child was in danger? she wondered.

My child is dead. I aborted my child. It couldn't possibly have survived.

Could it?

Karen got up from the cot and paced the tiny room, trying her best to reconstruct what had happened at the banquet.

Suddenly, she remembered the thing inside the lectern, and she pictured the monstrous hands as they offered up the dress. In her mind she pictured its hideous mouth. She watched as it moved up and down in its attempt to form words.

Why does it seem so familiar?

Karen thought and thought, possessed by that feeling that came with trying to place something naggingly familiar.

All at once she remembered. She remembered where she had seen that hideous thing before.

She had seen it in a movie.

• Five •

AT EIGHT-THIRTY, in the Nu-Art Theatre, Paul Chesney felt the tingler again.

It was the weekend—that glorious *alternate* weekend, which meant he had Kenny all to himself. Kenny had been released from the hospital a day after his incident, and he had made what appeared to be a speedy recovery.

But at the back of his mind, Paul felt a constant preoccupation: When would Kenny have another episode?

In the meantime, Paul did what he always did when reality had become too much. He went to the movies, whisking Kenny off with him.

What better movie to see, he figured, than one of his favorite old horror films from the fifties?

If you couldn't escape with *The Tingler*, Paul decided, you couldn't escape at all.

When the Tingler appeared on screen, a tiny jolt of harmless current was zapped into each theatre seat.

"Did it get ya, Dad?"

Paul turned to Kenny, whose Dodger jacket was pulled up across his face, an impromptu tent that shielded him from monsters.

"Right in the butt," Paul whispered, "and don't talk in the movies. It's rude."

Up on the screen, the Tingler crawled across the floor of a movie theatre. If you didn't scream, it would snap your spine. A young and black-and-white Vincent Price warned the audience: *"The Tingler is loose in the theatre! Scream! Scream!"*

It occurred to Paul that he hadn't seen *The Tingler* in twenty-five years. Back then, in the dark with his father, it had terrified him, but now it made him laugh.

Looks like a lobster, he decided.

"Scream, Dad!" Kenny cried, hiking the jacket up even further, so that his own scream came from inside the cocoon of fabric.

Paul listened to Kenny's scream—a *fun* scream, not the real and genuinely frightening scream that his illness had so often brought on.

In the dark of another movie theatre in his life, Paul felt the luxury of loving, not fearing, his only child.

While Paul drove them home an hour later, Kenny slept beside him.

Stopped at a red light on Hollywood Boulevard, Paul lit a cigarette, first making certain that Kenny was still asleep, for he knew the boy didn't like him to smoke.

Nothing was worse than that, Paul decided—that moment when you realize your child is old enough to sense your weaknesses and limits.

Guiltily, he took a drag off the cigarette, then opened the window so that the evidence would drift away into the garish, noisy haze of a Friday night on Hollywood Boulevard.

In the distance Paul saw the Shelton Apartments, which was his favorite grisly landmark. In 1963 Auntie Em had committed suicide there. Careful not to muss her brittle helmet of hair, Auntie Em pulled a dry-cleaner's bag across her face, smothering those fine and sensible Kansas features forever. It was not actually Auntie Em, of course, but rather the actress who had played her. But the actress—Clara Blandick—*was* Auntie Em, and that, Paul believed, was the morbid trick of movies.

The light changed to green, and Paul engaged the noisy machinery of the car, continuing ahead toward Silverlake.

When he heard Kenny stir beside him, he quickly tossed his cigarette out the window.

"We home yet, Dad?"

"Not yet, pal. Soon."

Kenny sniffed the air. "You smoking, Dad?"

"Just one."

"Where are we?"

"Hollywood," Paul answered, and he couldn't help but hear a little sadness in his voice.

* * *

Paul lived in an unfinished room behind his video store, which served as both apartment and office. Because of this, the room was filled with odd juxtapositions: a file cabinet next to a small refrigerator; a hot plate pushed to the edge of a desk awash in paperwork.

Paul was embarrassed to bring his son to such a place and call it home, but it pleased him that the boy liked it. Kenny preferred to find within its flimsy spontaneity a child's fascination with the unfamiliar, and he always pretended that he and his dad were in the army together, sharing a barracks, referring to Paul's haphazard stack of canned goods as rations.

After gathering up a stack of videotapes from the store out back, Kenny hopped into the hide-a-bed, which Paul had just turned down.

Paul sat beside him, studying the tapes. "All horror movies again?"

"Sure," Kenny said. "And neat ones too."

As Kenny slipped under the covers, Paul noticed that he was wearing the red pajamas he had given him two Christmases ago. Designed to look like a karate outfit, they were frayed now and much too small, and Paul realized that Kenny wore them just to please him.

"Dad," Kenny asked, "did you see *The Tingler* with Grandpa?"

"Yes," Paul said, remembering his trips to the movies with his own father. His father had worked a graveyard shift, so they usually only saw each other at the movies—preferably the sci-fi/horror that his father loved. Together in a darkened theatre, their whole relationship had formed, witnessed by outsized bugs, the angry victims of radiation that stomped across desert floors. Even now, horror movies could make Paul feel curiously sentimental.

"Did you see all the horror movies with Grandpa?"

"Think so, Kenny."

"Just like us, huh?"

"Yeah, Kenny, just like us."

Paul touched Kenny's hand, working his fingers up the bony wrist until they reached the tattered cuff of his pajamas.

Am I doing the same thing? Will this be all my son remembers of me: a night at the movies?

"What's wrong, Dad?"

"Nothing, Kenny."

Paul could tell that his son didn't believe him, for the boy looked quickly away, as if there were words backed up in his throat—words that he might not ever say. Kenny reached for his videotapes.

"Bet you saw all of these with Grandpa, huh?"

Paul looked at the first cassette, *The Blob*.

"Yup," he said, "and that one, too," pointing to the second cassette, *The Crawling Eye*.

It was the third tape that startled Paul.

He recognized the ad art immediately—letters dripped with blood, and a woman's severed head was gripped by a monster. Blood oozed copiously from dangling strips of torn flesh: *Night of the Blood Beast*.

Taking the tape from Kenny, Paul held it, as if in a sudden trance. He could feel his stomach tightening.

Guilt. It still survived. Why was guilt the one emotion that refused to yield to time?

Kenny could tell that his dad was upset. "You see that movie with Grandpa?"

"No."

"You see it with Mom?"

Paul shook his head, then returned the cassette to the night-stand.

"See it with a girlfriend?" the boy persisted, grinning.

"Just someone," Paul said quietly, tucking the boy into bed. "Someone I knew a long time ago."

Kenny crinkled his forehead. "You see it at that Odoron place?"

Paul smiled. "Odeon," he corrected, and then he kissed his son good night.

Moments later Paul stood alone in the video store. Outside, he heard the rush of gathering wind as the Santa Anas rose up out of heat and dust.

Paul knew a storm was coming, for he could hear it in the trash that skittered along the parking lot. He could feel it in the sudden and exaggerated thump of his heart.

More than ever, he wanted a drink. He wanted the sensation of good booze as it washed down his throat and slammed against his gut. There it would vaporize and fill the soul of him with smooth heat. It would roll up through his body and find the pain, sealing it off.

Paul busied himself by reshelving tapes, which his staff had left undone. Finished, he stood at the sci-fi/horror rack, where he studied the rows and rows of tapes with the lurid cover art: Cities fled monsters; scantily clad women screamed; vampires posed in velvet capes; an overgrown woman grabbed planes right out of the sky.

Why did Kenny have to pick *that* tape? he thought, and he turned away, suddenly feeling sick. It amazed him that the guilt could still be so active inside of him.

He heard the sound again—perfect, like an old recording. It was the sound he had spent a lifetime trying to forget. It was the sound he had heard in countless bars, where he had tried in vain to drown it out with scotch. All these years he had carried that sound into the dark of movie theatres, where he had hoped to leave it behind. But the sound would never go away.

It was the sound of his best friend screaming, and Paul had not been able to help.

Now he stood still in the empty video store, feeling paralyzed, just as he had that afternoon so long ago.

It was seventeen years ago, he realized, but it might as well have happened yesterday. He could still hear the screams—in his mind, the most relentless movie theatre of them all, the screams had grown even louder.

"Dad!"

The cry was sharp and loud and Paul turned instantly, not yet certain if he had heard it.

It has to be my imagination. Kenny's asleep. Safe.

"Dad! Help!"

A new wave of nausea rushed against his stomach as Paul ran to the door that separated him from Kenny. When he tried the knob, it would not budge, as though it were locked from the inside.

But there's no lock on this door! For God's sake, there's no lock!

"Kenny!" he cried. He kept turning the knob, which spun uselessly, greased by the sweat that poured from his hand.

Paul heard a crash from inside and then the unmistakable sound of shattering glass. There was a loud and muffled pop; something imploding. A crackling sound, then silence. Paul knew immediately that the television had fallen to the floor.

"Kenny!" he screamed, backing away from the door. Gathering force, he rammed at it, colliding against the wood with a dull and futile thud.

Suddenly, the room lit up with a flash of clear white light.

Lightning, he realized. The storm had come.

While thunder rumbled all around him, Paul kept charging at the door, pounding with his fists.

But then it swung inward, gently—as though no force had ever been needed. Paul stood stunned for a moment, wiping at the sweat that filled his eyes. Moving into the room, he stared at his son.

The boy sat on the bed, his eyes glazed over with shock. To his side lay the ruined television, which had been knocked from its perch to the floor. It lay within a sparkling sea of broken glass. Beside it, the cassette—*Night of the Blood Beast*.

Paul stood terrified, afraid to look at his son. Please don't be sick, Kenny. Please don't be sick.

When Paul rushed up to the boy, he saw the gash above Kenny's right eye. "Kenny? What happened? Are you all right?"

Blood appeared at the edge of the wound. It trickled down the bridge of the boy's small nose.

But Kenny seemed strangely detached from his wound, and after a puzzled moment he looked at his father.

"It came out," Kenny said. "The monster came out."

While the wound was only superficial, its source was not yet clear.

"Wasn't the glass that caused the wound," said the doctor.

Paul stood with him in the corridor of an emergency hospital in Glendale. Trembling, Paul had not yet recovered from the frantic ride, which had necessitated navigating the sudden rainstorm. Driving through flooded streets, he had kept one hand on the wheel, the other on Kenny. The boy had not spoken the whole way.

"What was it, then?" Paul asked.

The doctor shrugged, as if confused. "Well," he began hesitantly, "I suspect that the shock of the exploding television set might have scared the boy enough to scratch at his own face."

"What makes you think that?"

The doctor paused for a long time. "You see, I think the wound was made by a fingernail."

"A fingernail?"

"Yes."

"But he *is* all right?"

The doctor smiled. "Yes. In fact, you can take him home just as soon as we finish the paperwork."

By the time they started home, the storm had lifted. Driving, Paul thought the streets seemed unnaturally quiet, the only sound that of his own tires as they sliced through the large puddles of water.

He drove slowly, for the boy beside him seemed all at once so fragile. It was if an unexpected bump in the road might suddenly shatter him, so that he would lose him, after all. A thick bandage covered Kenny's wound.

A block from the video store, Kenny turned to him. "It didn't *really* come out of the TV, did it, Dad?"

"No, son. It was an accident. That's all."

Paul reached for him, pulling him gently up to his side. As he drove, Paul heard the fast clicking of bad valves in the engine. He decided they were like a clock gone wild, measuring out the minutes he had left with his son. Paul knew that Rita would blame him for what had happened. She would most likely challenge his custody.

"You knew something bad was going to happen, didn't you, Dad?"

"What?"

"That movie. The blood beast thing. You got so funny about it. Remember?"

"Maybe you shouldn't talk about it, Kenny."

"It sure was a weird movie, Dad."

"I thought you liked them weird."

"But this was *really* weird."

"How so?"

"The guy got pregnant, Dad."

Something skittered along Paul's flesh, and all at once he was back—there within Odeon's forecourt, unable to help as they took away the only girl he had ever really loved.

After he put Kenny to bed, Paul called Rita. Waiting for someone to answer, he stared at the cassette, which he had managed to retrieve from the bits of shattered glass.

He had never been so frightened in his life.

• Six •

DOWN IN THE BOWELS of Odeon, they hid behind a tapestry in the foyer that faced the rest rooms.

"Shhh!" Mike cried.

Terrified, Amy turned to his warning, for she was certain they were going to get caught. Behind the tapestry, it was totally dark.

"You sure it's him?" she whispered.

Mike nodded. "Jack MacGruder always comes down to his office before he closes up the theatre. Just be quiet and we won't get caught."

Amy wished she'd never gone along with Mike's idea. After the movie, he'd suggested they sneak downstairs into the men's room. Since they had no car, it would give them a place to be alone. When they'd reached the men's room door, they heard a noise, and they'd ducked behind the tapestry.

Now they heard him. It was a soft tapping—the sound of his expensive shoes against the concrete steps that led from the upstairs lobby into the foyer.

"He'll only be down here a second," Mike whispered. "He puts the receipts in the safe, then he leaves."

The sound of his footsteps stopped. They heard a door as it opened, then shut.

"His office," Mike whispered. "He'll be in there just a second, then he'll come back out."

Amy was hot and had begun to sweat. Her nose was filling up with the dusty rot of the tapestry, and she was terrified she might sneeze. Through the tattered fabric, she could make out a pattern of light as Jack came out of the office.

"See what I mean?" Mike whispered.

"How do you know all this stuff?"

"My buddy Rick used to work here. He and some guys sneaked down and had an all-night party. He told me how they did it. He knew MacGruder's every move."

When Jack approached the tapestry, Amy was certain he had heard them. She imagined him ripping the fabric away, confronting them, turning her over to her father, who would ground her forever. After what seemed an eternity, he passed them by.

"He's checking the johns," Mike whispered. "In a second he'll turn off the lights."

Amy heard the sound of switches being snapped, and the light vanished beyond the tapestry, plunging them into total, dusty darkness. Holding Mike close, she heard the old man's footsteps as he climbed back upstairs. He closed the door, which echoed through the foyer like a drum.

"C'mon," Mike said.

"We'll get caught."

"No, we won't."

"What about Carl?"

"He always does the rest rooms last."

Inching their way along the crumbling concrete wall, they emerged from behind the tapestry, but it was so dark they still couldn't see. Reaching into his pocket, Mike pulled out a lighter, which he thumbed into action.

The room, visible against the lighter's tiny flame, was a maze of moving shadows. With its dark mahogany walls, stenciled-beam ceiling, and heavy antiques, it reminded Amy of a witch's castle.

"I know where the light switches are," Mike said, moving off with his lighter, so that the shadows flickered all the more.

When the lights came back on, Amy looked at the tapestry from which they had just escaped. It was a hand-stitched scene that featured an Edwardian fox hunt.

"I'll bet that tapestry was beautiful once," she said.

Mike swaggered up to it. "Just an old piece of junk," he said, pulling out his pocket knife. Before Amy could stop him, he stabbed full force, the blade piercing a fox that leapt through high green grass. Pieces of rotten fabric fell in a pile across his sneakers. Laughing, he kicked them away.

"Why did you do that?" Amy cried.

Ignoring her, Mike grabbed her hand and dragged her to the thick mahogany door that opened into the men's rest room.

Pushing it open, he peeked inside, checked for stragglers, then turned to her. "We're going to do it now," he said. "We're going to do it in one of the stalls."

Carl hated Friday nights the most, for the teenagers made a mess he couldn't believe.

As he rolled his buckets into Odeon's auditorium, he felt the pain working into his arms and back. If it got any worse, he figured, he wouldn't be able to do his work.

Carefully, he grabbed his broom, then began his sweep, grumbling as he watched the mountain of popcorn assemble before him. How much popcorn had he swept out of Odeon in all these years? he wondered. A ton? Two tons?

When Carl had finished with the auditorium, he transferred his equipment to the lobby, where he realized the pain was worse than ever before. The lobby, with its maze of intricate detail, was the hardest job of all.

And for what? he thought. For what? Nobody gave a damn anymore.

Now the pain rose up sharply. He cried out and dropped his bucket, the sound of which echoed crazily throughout the lobby.

He couldn't do it. Not tonight.

Carl decided he would skip the lobby and do the rest rooms.

Mike sat in his jockey shorts, his back against the stall. His arm draped the rim of the toilet bowl while a Marlboro burned to a nub between his fingers. He puffed it angrily.

"What's the matter, anyway?" he snapped.

Amy sat opposite, naked from the waist up, her arms folded across her breasts. She saw that she had broken out in red blotches. As big as quarters, they ran the length of her pale flesh. She had never felt so humiliated.

"I'm sorry," she said, and she tried her best to keep from crying. She reached for her bra, which dangled down off the toilet tank.

"C'mon," Mike begged.

"I just don't want to . . . not here, Mike. It's too weird and cheap and . . . I just don't like it, that's all."

Angry, he tossed his cigarette in the toilet bowl. It sizzled as it hit the water. "It's your dad, isn't it?"

Amy shook her head, but she knew he was partly right. The big sheriff had always been overly protective; guys sensed it, she knew, and they got the idea that having sex with her could land them in jail or something.

"I thought you wanted to," Mike accused.

As she worked to untangle the bra, Amy saw that her hands were trembling. "I just don't want to. Jesus, Mike, I changed my mind. Okay?"

Fumbling with the clasp, Amy put on the bra, then stared uncomfortably at Mike. His disappointment had changed him. It had made him into a little boy, pouting there by the toilet, and Amy felt guilty.

"I just don't want it like this," she said softly. "You should know that, Mike."

He crossed his arms angrily. "Forget it."

Amy felt the cold as it gathered along her shoulders, as though she suddenly wore some gown of ice. She reached for her blouse. "Why's it so cold?"

"Who cares?" He reached for another cigarette from the pocket of his shirt, which lay discarded along the tile. Amy saw that he too was trembling.

"What do you suppose he carries in that paper sack?" Amy asked.

"Huh?"

"Billy Burnside. That paper sack. The one he always carries into the theatre."

Mike lit the new cigarette and a grey cloud of smoke formed between them in the stall. "Didn't come here to talk about *that* creep," he said. "Who knows? Who cares?"

"Cindy says he kills things, Mike. Little animals and stuff. All those holes he digs . . . those holes in the ground . . . Do you suppose . . ."

A toilet flushed.

"Mike!"

Amy could tell that Mike was suddenly as scared as she was, and it occurred to her that she had never seen him scared before. All those times he had driven his car so fast around hairpin turns on North Post Road, Mike had seemed fearless. Now the color drained from his face as he signaled her to keep quiet.

Waiting, they listened for the tap of shoes against tile.

"Jack MacGruder?" Amy whispered.

"Maybe . . . or Carl . . . or maybe it just flushed on its own."

Amy leaned forward, so that the icy tile seemed to rip from her flesh. She tried to convince herself that Mike was right—after all, the theatre was old, falling apart; the plumbing *could* do something weird like that.

She touched his naked back. Even though his flesh was cold, she could feel the drops of sweat that had formed with his fear.

Amy heard another sound, which she recognized as the sound of lapping water.

"It's . . . it's just the pipes," Mike whispered, but Amy didn't believe him.

Who's here? she thought, frightened. Who's here?

From where she sat, Amy could see beneath the stall, all the way to the opposite wall, the floor of each stall visible to her the whole way.

Now she thought she saw movement—the delicate flutter of something, a few feet away in the middle stall.

"Mike . . ."

She saw it again, and this time she realized it was a piece of fabric.

Yellow, she could see now.

Yellow!

The rain slicker! Billy Burnside's rain slicker!

"Mike! He's in here . . . God, he's in here."

When Mike turned to speak, the sound of lapping water grew louder, followed by a slamming sound.

"Let's get the fuck out of here!" Mike cried.

They both plunged at the floor for their clothes. Grabbing for her blouse, Amy remembered. She remembered what Cindy had asked her that time, so long ago.

Know what Billy Burnside's favorite movie is?

Who cares, Cindy?

Should be obvious, Amy.

Amy pulled the blouse across her shoulders as fast as she could. She watched as Mike stood up and pulled on his jeans. After yanking up the zipper, he reached for the latch that would open the stall. He pulled at it frantically, but it would not budge.

My God, she thought, we're stuck in here!

Amy stood up, backing away from Mike, who worked frantically at the latch. Glistening with sweat, he banged at the door with all of his strength, but it would not budge. Amy felt the back of her calves as they pressed against the toilet bowl. Suddenly, she felt something cold and moist, like something had nipped at her calf, and she turned around to look inside the bowl.

C'mon, Amy. Try to guess. Billy Burnside's favorite movie is that one you got so scared of . . .

"Mike!"

It's Willard, Amy. That's what Billy Burnside's favorite movie is!

Amy watched as the first one poked its black muzzle out along the rim. Another one crawled out, as if to sniff and test the air, then another.

Another.

Amy screamed and grabbed at Mike, who turned from his work at the door. They both stared into the toilet. The rats, more than they could count, had formed a jet-black line, ready to strike. Their tails—unusually fat and long—whipped the air.

They leapt all at once.

Amy watched in horror as they flew from the rim—a wet, black blur that charged at Mike, swarming along his naked back. She reached out to slap them away, but now there were more—thousands, it seemed—rising up, soaking wet and furious, from inside the toilet bowl.

"Get 'em off me!" he screamed.

"I can't, Mike! I can't!"

She worked crazily at Mike's back, her hands thudding against the warm, wet fur of his enraged attackers. Just as she slapped one away, another took its place—more and more, until she saw them encircling his waist, his legs, his arms, like some hideous coat of moving black fur. All the time she expected them to come after her, but it was suddenly clear that Mike, screaming in agony, would be their only prey.

Horrified, Amy watched as Mike's face disappeared beneath the hungry swarm of bodies. He fell away from her, landing with a cracking sound on the tile. His cries were quickly muffled by the rats that worked at his face.

When Amy heard a snapping sound, she turned to it, just in time to see the stall door fly open.

Now she could hear someone pounding on the rest room door. A voice yelled from the foyer.

Someone's here! Someone can help us!

Amy ran frantically for the door, and she soon recognized the voice as belonging to Carl Irvine. She ran so fast she slipped on the tile, slamming up full force against the door. She lay stunned across the tile. "Oh God, help me!" Amy screamed.

She looked up from the floor and saw the door handle, which

now seemed a million miles away. If she could just reach it, she knew that Carl would help her.

Raising her arm, she felt it fill with a throbbing pain, and she realized it was badly sprained from her fall. But she kept forcing it upward, resisting the pain, until she had finally touched the handle. All the time, she heard the rats, wondering if they would change their mind.

Will they attack me next?

She tried to turn the knob, but it wouldn't move. Like the latch on the stall door, it had frozen, and for a terrible moment she thought she might be stuck there.

"Help me!" she cried. "Oh God, help me!"

Finally, she heard a clicking sound, followed by a slam as the huge mahogany doors flew open.

Amy looked up at Carl, who stood above. Behind her, Amy heard the terrible sound: licking, biting, chewing.

When he knelt to her, Carl touched Amy gently, then pulled her up. The last thing she thought of before she fainted in Carl's arms was Billy Burnside. She thought she could hear him say:

Whazza matter mich CHEW?

• Seven •

THE LAST PERSON Karen ever thought she would invite to lunch was Tyler Briggs. Desperate, she called him up at work, asking him to meet her at a restaurant near the office.

But as Karen drove to Century City, she felt uneasy. A deep, anxious part of her wondered if she was doing the right thing.

Maybe I should just check myself into a hospital, she thought.

She glanced at herself in the rearview mirror, deciding she looked awful. Huge dark circles hung beneath bloodshot eyes, and her new haircut—so smart and neat only the day before—now stuck out in coarse, unmanageable clumps.

But the rumpled version of herself that stared from the rearview mirror did not surprise her. Indeed, she felt exhausted. After the disastrous banquet, she had not slept at all.

Good God, she'd wondered, will that hideous thing still be in my apartment?

In abject terror she had lain in bed, imagining the small sounds of night into preludes to disaster. It had become one of those awful, seemingly endless nights that pitted her against all the fears of her life; memory had risen like some dark and suffocating thing, enfolding her there in the sweat-soaked bed.

Only gradually had she reasoned herself into a state less hysterical: Get ahold of yourself. Of course it won't be there. It's all hallucination. You'll be fine.

But even the morning had not freed her, for it had brought bad news. Her boss had called to say that Karen had been given a leave of absence at full pay. Grateful as she was, Karen still felt as though she'd been fired. Later, Estelle Hopkins had called with even worse news: Karen's application had been denied.

The news, while anticipated, had left Karen devastated, and at first she believed the unthinkable—that she *was* having another breakdown.

But no! I am not having another breakdown. A hallucination, yes, but not a breakdown.

Driving toward Century City, Karen considered the puzzle that had begun coming back to her. All through her sleepless night there had risen up from the swamp of memory a single preoccupation: the hideous thing in the lectern, which she realized was something she had seen in a movie.

Later, she had remembered the most important part of all: She had seen the movie at Odeon, just before she was raped.

But what movie was it? she wondered now, and it was this question that had led her to Tyler Briggs. She hoped that his store of movie trivia would provide her the answer.

Hopeful but still very anxious, Karen tried to think back, hoping that in doing so she might figure out the rest of the puzzle. It was difficult for her to do, because it ran in opposition to her therapy, which had encouraged her to forget.

Good, she thought, I'm glad. I never did think that forgetting was a good idea. Maybe none of this would be happening if I'd faced it back then.

Karen pictured Main Street Wallenberg the way it had been when she was a girl, when she had lived out on North Post Road with her mother, Nell.

A thin, sour-faced woman, Nell was a religious fanatic, and the house in which Karen grew up was a ramshackle shrine to the stubborn details of her faith. Religious kitsch adorned the plain walls: oil paintings of Jesus, crude plastic altars, piles of yellowed pamphlets that heralded a Second Coming filled not with love, but with violence.

The dawn of an attractive girl's sexuality was not to be tolerated in such a house, and Karen learned quickly to keep such delicate transitions in her life a secret, swearing to her mother that such impulses were foreign to her, that her face and figure, unusually mature by sixteen, were denied the boys who desired her at school.

And they were, until she met *him*—the boy with green eyes.

Karen loved him at once, and she knew, without hesitation, that she would love him forever. He was shy, and so was Karen, but it wasn't long until longings were expressed, and Karen remembered the day they first declared a love—a feeling that managed to grow in spite of Nell, who would have locked Karen in her room had she known that the boy had kissed her and touched her breasts, swearing to her that they would marry after high school.

Karen loved the boy with the beautiful green eyes.

But then it happened.

—just lie back, sweetie! Take it easy, bitch!

—no! no! I can't! Please! Please!

—shut up and stay still!

Karen remembered how she had lain beneath him in the dark, her body sliding across the icy tile of the men's room in Odeon. Moments before, she had been up in the balcony with the boy with green eyes, but she had left him.

—talk about this, you little bitch, and I'll see that you die. I swear it!

His voice would haunt her all of her life: a singsong lilt, disguised; a terrible falsetto.

Now Karen gripped the steering wheel as she thought back to that awful day. After all this time, she still wondered why she had left the boy with green eyes up in the balcony.

Only now did she remember that they had fought. They had fought about the movie they were watching.

—it's too scary.

—it's only a movie, Karen.

—I want to go home.

—I came to see it, Karen. C'mon.

But then she saw the monster, the blood beast—huge, coated with mud, tendrils hanging at its side.

Frightened and angry, she left the boy and stalked to the lobby, where she continued down into the rest rooms, her hand sliding across the banister as she moved into the bowels of Odeon. Right down into hell . . .

Karen remembered how he'd grabbed her.

There was a flash of pain as fingers clutched her neck, the hand grabbing her from behind, forcing her through the great mahogany door that led into the men's room. After slamming her down on the floor, he fit a two-by-four in the handle of the door so that no one else could enter. Before Karen could make out who he was, he snapped off the lights. After slapping her repeatedly, he dragged her into the stall, where he tore off her clothes.

When it was over, she lay alone, terrified.

—talk about this, you little bitch, and I'll see that you die. I swear it!

Karen could not tell her mother what she had done, and to Karen it *was* something that *she* had done. After all, hadn't *she* been the one who entered Odeon—Satan's Church, as Nell called it—against her mother's will? Hadn't *she* been with a boy? Hadn't *she* desired him?

Karen remembered walking all the way home out North Post Road, then lying to Nell, telling her she had fallen on the way home. Upstairs, she scrubbed it all away, inch by inch: She stuck the sponge as far up as her vagina as it would go. Gone then it was; the terrible, filthy, sticky fluid he had placed there.

But *who*?

Karen knew it could not have been the boy with the beautiful green eyes. No, she had thought, he was far too kind for such a thing, and besides, she loved him and she knew that he loved her. But when he apologized to her at school for their fight in the balcony, she had spurned him.

Oh God, she'd thought, I'm not worthy of him now. I can't look him in the eyes, I'm so ashamed.

The pregnancy came to Karen like one of Nell's promised demons. She tried to will it away, but the symptoms, like those of some fatal disease, were clear. The baby would grow in her womb like cancer.

Karen gave her terror a shape, a force. It was as if she had constructed a demon from the scraps of Nell's guilt.

It would come to her at night and sit at the edge of her bed, where it would watch her, filling up the room with the stink of it—a rot as putrid as that which she felt inside: the decay of her own damned soul.

When it stared at her through the darkness, a flutter of curtain would throw moonlight across its face. It stared with ugly, piercing eyes, night after night, all through those weeks that her secret shame grew full in her belly. It would sing to her—a hideous, obscene lullaby. Finally, she gave her demon a name.

Odeon.

When Nell found out about the pregnancy, she cursed Karen and kept her away from school, so that Karen was forced to lie alone in her room all day, feeling ashamed and banished.

And all the time, Karen wondered what had happened to the boy with green eyes. When she begged her mother to see him, Nell insisted that the boy didn't really love her, finally producing a note that she said the boy had left for Karen. Unfolding it, Karen read its neatly typed message: The boy with green eyes told her he didn't love her anymore.

Two weeks later Karen's class graduated from high school and Karen decided to approach him on the night of the ceremonies. Ashamed to face her former classmates, Karen waited in the parking lot, where she wept and trembled in the night air. When he finally appeared, he was with another girl. Karen watched the two of them kiss before they got into his car and drove off.

All alone, Karen felt her world blow apart. She imagined atoms as they burst away from each other, whirling into space, so that shape and substance all fell away. When she started home, her body heavy with her child of horror and guilt, she decided it must die, and she knew it must die where it all began.

Karen remembered waking to the blurred confusion of voices, the scent of medicine; pure, antiseptic air. The voices were those of Nell, Dr. Phillip Matson, and a heavyset nurse named Cora. Matson informed her that the coat hanger she had used to kill her child had almost killed Karen as well. He told her how foolish it was to attempt an abortion so late into term. She had hemorrhaged, blacked out, and they had taken her up from the bowels of Odeon on a gurney. And then the worst part: She had damaged herself irreparably; the soft and secret place of her womanhood, that which had bloomed inside of her body only a short time ago, would now be lost to her forever. She would never conceive again.

Certain they were disgraced, Nell decided they would move to Los Angeles, where she had a relative they could stay with until they had a place of their own.

"We cannot stay here," Nell had said. "We've been shamed now and it's all because of you."

Karen would never forget the night they left Wallenberg. At midnight, near the railroad tracks outside of town, Nell stopped the car so they could pray. Karen looked up into the rearview mirror, where she saw the sign: *ODEON,* which loomed enormous out of darkness. Even then, she knew that the blue neon light, indistinguishable from the moon, seemed too bright; she knew that the things they tried to leave behind would follow her.

Always.

When Nell died two years later, Karen supported herself through college, soon becoming a woman who was proud of her independence. Things went well. Until the breakdown.

Until now.

Pulling up to the restaurant where she was to meet Tyler Briggs, Karen prayed that he would know the name of the movie.

To Karen Webster, the title of an old horror movie had become the most important thing in her life.

"Rumor is you got fired," Tyler said. While Karen poked at a spinach salad, he devoured a hamburger ravenously.

"They gave me a leave."

How they must be talking about her today, she thought, picturing them in the office kitchen, where they would drink coffee and discuss what had happened: *Poor thing. Did you hear? Went off her rocker.*

"I don't want to talk about last night," she said.

Tyler saturated a tangle of french fries with catsup. "Sure," he said, "so what is it you *do* want? Can't imagine I finally got lucky."

"Tyler, you know more about movies than anyone I've ever known."

Grinning, he sipped his chocolate shake. "Thanks," he said, "it's nice to be appreciated." He frowned suspiciously. "But hey, I've been trying to get you interested in movies for half my natural life. What gives all of a sudden?"

Karen pushed away her salad and folded her hands. "There's this movie, Tyler. Something I saw a long time ago. I need to know what it was."

He shrugged. "Shouldn't be too hard. Tell me about it."

"Well, it was one of those old science-fiction movies. From the fifties, I think."

"Perfect!" He laughed, rubbing his hands together. "My specialty." He yanked a cigarette from the pocket of his Hawaiian shirt. "Mind?"

Karen watched as Tyler lit his cigarette, her attention drawn to his lighter, which was the oddest she had ever seen. A large glass cylinder, it was decorated with enormous blue fish. Karen decided that only Tyler Briggs would own such a thing.

"So," Tyler said, exhaling a column of smoke, "tell me about the movie."

"I can't remember it too well . . . except that it scared me a great deal. I left in the middle of it, actually. I don't like those kinds of movies much."

Tyler frowned his disapproval.

"Anyway, there was this astronaut, you see. He came back from outer space. There was this monster . . . an alien."

Tyler drummed long fingers against the table. "There were lots of those, Karen. You just described half the movies made in the fifties. *Sputnik* started it, you know." He leaned back and stroked the ragged little patch along his chin that he currently passed off as a beard. "Let me see. How about *The Creeping Unknown*?" Before Karen could answer, he grimaced. "No, no. That was a British movie." He looked at her. "Wasn't one of those limey pix, was it?"

Karen shook her head.

"Didn't think so. Well, let me see. There was *First Man into Space*. This astronaut comes back to earth, you see, and he turns all gooey, starts sucking the blood out of cattle and stuff." Tyler stopped, stared at the french fry in his hand, then tossed it to his plate in disgust. "But then, there really wasn't an alien. *He* was the alien." He thought for a long time. "Hey," he said, snapping his fingers, "I've got it!"

"What?"

"How about *Night of the Blood Beast*?"

Karen reacted to the title, which she knew had touched something deep in her memory. "Tell me about it, Tyler."

"It was one of those cheap AIP jobs. American-International, I mean. Fifty-eight, I think. This alien pumps all its cells into this astronaut's blood, see, and"—Tyler laughed—"something really *bizarre* happens."

"What?"

"It makes the guy pregnant."

A chill gathered along her neck, as though an icy draft had worked through the crowded, noisy restaurant.

"What did you say, Tyler?"

"I said this guy gets pregnant." He smiled. "Did I say something right?"

Karen sat in silence.

"Guess I did, huh?"

"That's the one," Karen said, remembering her breakdown in the supermarket.

All that work, she thought, all that work by her therapist—the time, the pain, the emotional dead ends. Now she had been given the beginnings of an answer, and it had cost her a burger, shake, and fries.

Tyler smiled and blew at his fingernails, buffing them along his shirt. "I figured it out, didn't I?"

"Yes, Tyler. You did."

"Hey, I'm the best."

Karen leaned forward. "Look, Tyler, this is very important. Is there any way I could see this movie?"

"Maybe on late-night TV. That's about it."

"Couldn't I rent it? On tape or something?"

"Doubt it. The old AIP stuff's hard to get."

"Please, Tyler. It's important."

Tyler snapped his fingers. "Wait a minute!" he said, whipping a pen from his pocket and scribbling across a napkin. "Check this place out. Video store over in Silverlake . . . near where you live, right? Guy's got the best collection of horror and sci-fi in town."

When he handed her the napkin, he shrugged. "So," he asked, "why's this such a big deal anyway?"

Karen smiled. "You've convinced me, Tyler. I think I like horror movies, after all."

• Eight •

PAUL CHESNEY SAT IN HIS CAR at the bottom of the hill, staring up at the house that mocked him. Huge and sprawling, the envy of a hot real estate market, the house belonged to Rita's second husband, symbolizing to Paul his own failure as husband and father. As he watched, he smoked, so that the car windows fogged, and he felt that it all might be happening within some strange and paranoid dream.

Rita had done precisely what he had feared. Blaming Paul for Kenny's accident, she had implied to the authorities in charge that Paul might be drinking again. She had managed to stir up enough suspicion concerning his character to get a restraining order; Paul would not be able to see the boy until after a hearing.

He glanced at his watch, realizing he'd been sitting in the car for over an hour, hoping for a glimpse of Kenny. Looking up, he studied the pattern of lights as they snapped on and off within the house. When a light popped off on the second floor, replaced by another two doors over, Paul decided the boy had taken his bath and gone to his bedroom, which was fully in view.

Come to the window. Come to the window and let me see you.

Car headlights flared behind him and he ducked down in his seat. He had been careful to keep a lookout for security, which combed the exclusive hills above Coldwater all night long. He knew that Rita would call them if she saw his car, for she had already implied that Paul, given the chance, might kidnap the boy. The idea amused him. How could you kidnap your own son? he wondered. It sounded so illogically reflexive, like giving yourself your own germs.

The headlights disappeared up another road that wound through mountains, and Paul relaxed. Taking another cigarette from his pack, he turned once again to look at Kenny's window.

But it was too late.

The boy's light had gone out.

When Paul got back to the video store, he decided to make a pot of coffee. Certain that he faced another sleepless night, he brewed the maximum ten cups. While measuring out the coffee, he found himself thinking of Kenny, whose essence still filled the video store.

Would it always be this way? he wondered. Would everything remind him of the boy? He suddenly felt less a father than he did an obsessed lover, who treasured all that the beloved had touched, endowing it with a kind of magic.

And why *that* movie? he wondered. Why did Kenny have to pick *Night of the Blood Beast*?

Paul turned on a desk lamp, then searched the shelf behind the counter, where he had left the cassette of *Night of the Blood Beast*. When he picked it up, he saw that the cassette was badly damaged; a corner of the black plastic case was cracked, and a curl of magnetic tape hung limply from inside.

He noticed a blue card attached to the cassette. The card, a device used in Paul's rental system, indicated that a customer had reserved the tape by telephone. In this case, the tape was being held for repair.

Curious, Paul removed the card from the broken cassette. He flipped it over, then held it beneath the desk lamp, so that he could make out the customer's name.

Paul drove as quickly as he could, guided by the address on the blue card.

It was all too much to be a coincidence, he thought. It *had* to be her. All these years Paul had wondered what had happened to Karen Webster. He had lain awake so many nights, wondering where her pain had taken her.

As he drove, Paul remembered the hot pops of light from the ambulance that had come for her. He pictured her as they placed her on the stretcher. Blood saturated the sheet that covered her, and he remembered the drops that formed a scarlet trail out of Odeon, along the terrazzo, where they all stood to watch.

—*is she dead?*

—*what happened?*

—*they say she tried to give herself an abortion. In a movie theatre? Can you believe that?*

–she was going to have a baby? Whose baby? Whose?

Paul drove faster, overcome once again by a flood of memory. He had run away from all of it—away from Wallenberg, his guilt—as though the town that had nurtured him no longer held a claim. His flight from Karen Webster had caused him to change his life; it had caused him to marry the wrong woman. Time and distance had failed him, because he had tried to do the impossible: He had tried to escape his heart, all that he had ever really loved.

When he reached the apartment complex, he checked its address against the blue card. This was it, he realized, and getting out of the car, he moved to the mailboxes, where her name was embossed in black labeling tape.

But all at once, he seemed to freeze up. Just the sight of her name on the mailbox—concrete evidence that, yes, Karen Webster does live here—paralyzed him at the gate.

Am I doing the right thing? he wondered.

Worse, he wondered if he had the nerve to do it at all. What if she rejected him?

But now he remembered Kenny's bedroom light; he watched as it went out, so sudden and beyond his control; and he remembered the pain of it. In his car, alone, the world so vague beyond the steamy windows, banished from all those in the world he loved, he had felt a perfect aloneness. But now he realized he had a rare chance—a chance to undo the past.

How many lights in his life would have to go out before all hope was gone? he wondered.

He pressed himself suddenly forward, walking quickly through the courtyard. Long legs tripping up the stairs, he took them two at a time, afraid that if he faltered, he might turn back.

At Karen's door he stopped, waited, held his breath, finally raising his hand and poising it to knock. After a slight hesitation, he brought it up hard against her door.

"You lookin' for Karen Webster?"

Paul turned to the voice.

"Name's Alan Fitschew. I'm sort've the manager."

"Yes," Paul said to the man with the muscles, "I am looking for Karen."

"Left town."

"Where?"

"Don't know. Kind of spur of the moment, I think. She loaded up her stuff like she'd just robbed a bank or something."

"She didn't say anything?"

Alan shrugged his huge muscular shoulders. "She did say home. Yeah, she said something about going home."

When Karen reached the exit into Wallenberg, she considered turning back. She had come to this crossroad a thousand times in dreams, only to be stopped by the remembered warnings of Nell: *Don't ever go back! They'll hate you!*

But now she was determined. She would defy Nell once and for all. With a deep breath she summoned up her new resolve and made the turn.

The distance between the turnoff and Wallenberg was ten miles, and Karen drove the dark, empty road as if in a dream. Her decision to come had been so spontaneous it didn't yet seem real.

By her watch, she saw that it was nearly eleven o'clock; the narrow road before her was illuminated only by the harsh white streaks of her headlights. The silent glide of country, blanketed by darkness, offered no landmark, making her feel disoriented. She could have been anywhere in the world, she thought, not necessarily on the road into Wallenberg—her hometown, her past.

When she turned onto Main Street, Karen slowed the car, almost coming to a stop. The town, as familiar as yesterday, unfolded out of darkness, bit by remembered bit. Ruby's Cafe, the Wishing Well Bookstore, Joe's Collectibles: The neat line of shopfronts looked the same as ever. The familiarity of it troubled her, for she thought she had left it all behind.

Karen looked to her right, where she saw the town square, a patch of land that the locals called Wall-Park. An old set of swings and a rusted slide stood in its center, and Karen wondered if they were the same she had played upon as a girl.

A half block later, Karen pulled up to the Wallenberg Hotel, whose plain, two-story wooden structure also had not changed. The sign, which Karen recognized as the original—*Clean and Economical Rooms*—still swung on rusted chains above the porch of battered wooden slats.

Karen stopped the car, then shuddered, aware of how terribly cold it was. She sat still, unable to move. Shivering there in the car, Karen realized what was wrong. She didn't want to look at the theater across the street.

Face it, she thought. Face it all.

When she turned to it, Karen expected the brightly lit facade of memory. But now she saw that Odeon, like herself, had changed. The theater was utterly dark and still. Suddenly, a pile of paper and debris whipped up through the forecourt, borne by a new stir of wind. Karen watched as they slapped against the empty box office.

Looking up, she read the marquee: CLOSED UNTIL FURTHER NOTICE.

Moments later Karen carried her single bag to the hotel porch. The wind still blew out of Main Street, rocking the wooden sign, so that the chains that held it groaned.

Why is it so cold? she wondered, still shivering. She felt the shock of having come from the heat of Los Angeles to a night as chilly as winter. It was as if her journey had allowed her to skip a season.

But hadn't it still been hot at the turnoff? she wondered. How could it get so cold so suddenly? The thin white blouse and cotton pants she had worn—summer clothes she had deemed appropriate—afforded her no protection at all. She felt the prickly bite of cold along her flesh.

Karen moved to the thermometer, a large replica of a Coca-Cola bottle cap, at the hotel entrance. The thermometer's detail had been devoured by rust, yet the thin red line was clearly visible. Karen saw that it registered an unbelievable thirty-six degrees.

Pushing open the door to the hotel, Karen tried to remember if an August night in Wallenberg had ever been so cold.

Inside, the lobby was large, but dim and shabby, its walls adorned by western murals that were cracked and fading. A small black-and-white television buzzed unwatched in the corner beside a cluster of worn furniture. Two old vending machines bordered an ancient elevator.

When Karen walked up to the desk, an elderly clerk put down his newspaper, coming to sleepy attention.

"I'd like a room for the night, please."

"Yes, ma'am," he said, turning away with a loud yawn. With long, nicotine-stained fingers, he reached for a registration card and key.

Wondering if the old man recognized her, Karen felt a vague, unsettling paranoia. She smiled and filled out the registration card. "It's awfully cold," she said.

"Got all the way down to thirty last night," he said, "a record. Even got us a mention in the *San Francisco Chonicle*."

She gave him the card, which he examined with obvious suspicion. Karen decided that in Wallenberg a single woman checking into a hotel alone would still seem odd. She would have to readjust herself to such things, she realized. Karen picked up the key. "Why's the theatre closed?"

"Trouble. Coupla kids got in a pretty bad scrape over there."

"Oh?"

"Rats."

"Rats?"

"Attacked 'em. The boy got himself killed. The girl—she's the sheriff's daughter—got herself pretty shook up, I'd say."

"How horrible."

"Yeah." He took a seat behind the desk. "Course, some folks say they shouldn't've been down there in the first place."

"*Down* there?"

"Yup," he said, picking up his newspaper. "It happened down in the rest room. In one of the stalls."

As Karen reached for her bag, she felt another chill. Only this time she knew it had nothing to do with the strange August weather.

After arranging her clothing across the large brass bed, Karen held up the single jacket she had brought—the top to a blue cotton pantsuit—and she knew its flimsy fabric would be worthless against the cold. The room clattered with the sound of pipes along the radiator, which she had turned on moments ago.

Karen carried her clothing to a large armoire, which she recognized as a genuine antique. The room, with its tasteful blue wallpaper, rich wooden moldings, and other fine pieces of furniture, had been a pleasant surprise.

After making a cup of instant coffee, Karen sat at a small writing desk beside the bed. There she took a piece of stationery and jotted down a list of all that she intended to do the following day.

Her first stop would be the office of Dr. Phillip Matson, who had attended to her after the abortion. She would find out everything she could about the incident, including whether a death certificate had been filled out for her unborn child. If nothing else, she would ask the sex of her child—an important piece of information that Nell had claimed not to know.

Next, she would visit the sheriff, asking to look through old records. It had occurred to her that other young women might have been attacked and raped about the same time. Surely, she thought, such a maniac would have struck more than once. Perhaps he had been caught and punished. Regardless, Karen knew that any information regarding her attack would be helpful.

But it was the third item, she knew, that would be the most difficult. Once and for all, she intended to find out what had happened to the boy with green eyes. If she found him, she would ask why he had written her that final letter of goodbye.

And she would tell him, regardless of how foolish it might seem, that she still loved him.

So much to do, she thought. So much unfinished business. God, why didn't I come back years ago?

Karen studied her list, then grinned ruefully. It seemed ironic that all the traumas of her life could be reduced to something as simple as a grocery list.

She was about to fold it when another errand occurred to her, and she jotted it down quickly: *Find out more about what happened to those two kids at Odeon. If possible, talk to the sheriff's daughter.*

Folding the list and putting it in her purse, Karen felt the room as it began to fill with heat, and she realized how exhausted she was.

When Karen moved to draw the curtains on her window, she could not help but see the theatre, which sat so dark and still across the street. She could make out a portion of the vertical sign: *ODEON*. The letters were unlit.

They were closed, she thought, like eyes.

One floor above, Carl Irvine's room filled with music.

He sat on his bed, holding the radio in his lap, imagining that the music, the mournful refrains of lost love, played only for him.

She's here! She's here!

Carl Irvine had dreaded this. Ever since the night those kids were attacked, he had suspected something like this would happen; he had feared Odeon's trick might go this far.

Now he stared angrily at the darkened sign. All you needed was to have Karen back, didn't you, Odeon! Well, to hell with you! I'll fight you yet! You'll see!

When Carl stood up, he felt the pain, and the way it rolled through his body made him think of that pinball machine he liked to play at the Busy Bee. The pain careened along the sharp points of his nerves like that little glass ball, he thought—wild, hard, aimless.

Carl moved slowly to the dresser, where he caught his reflection in the mirror. Studying his image, he tried to view himself as she would. No matter how hard he tried to convince himself that he wasn't ugly, the reflection was irrefutable proof that he was. He knew that he couldn't let her see him.

Panicked, he pulled open the top drawer of the dresser and took out his shoe box filled with treasures. After struggling to the bed, he sat down and opened the lid, gently moving through the contents until he found the photograph.

Carl picked it up and stared at it, this awful and mocking piece of the past: The two of them stood posed beside his car. Karen's arms were wrapped around his body, the way it once had been—strong and perfect.

Searching further, Carl found the other souvenir: a napkin from Ruby's Cafe, a flower Karen had worn in her hair, a frayed piece of ribbon.

Finally, he came to the envelope, which had been stuffed way down at the bottom of the box. When he picked it up, a piece of the yellowed paper broke in his fingers. He opened the envelope and withdrew the letter, reading it for what he knew must be the millionth time.

Dear Carl,

I hold this pen in my hand, but it does not want to move across this paper. I hope that I never have to write a letter as painful as this again in my life. I do not love you anymore, Carl. There is someone else. I am going to have his baby. If you truly love me, you will stay away from me. Forever. This is my choice, and you must honor it.

Sadly,

Karen

Carl stared at the letter, which he had long ago memorized. Even after all this time and pain, it still did not make sense to him.

Why? What did I do to make you stop loving me? I would have loved you, Karen. Always. We could have been happy.

Gently, he returned the letter to its envelope, then stared out the window, his eyes narrowing with anger as they focused upon Odeon.

He stood up from the bed, not caring about the pain that the sudden movement caused him. Moving angrily to the nightstand, he picked up a pencil and a piece of paper.

Biting his lip in concentration, Carl began to write. He pushed his pencil with the exaggerated purpose of a child, working his way through letters that all went to large and hesitant loops. Finished, he read what he had written: "Gett out. Gett out beforr to later. The theetur nose you and mus be stopp."

After carefully crossing all of his *t*'s, Carl folded the piece of paper as neatly as he could, then stood up from the bed and struggled his way to the door, which he opened quietly.

When he was certain no one was looking, he began the long and difficult journey to Karen Webster's door.

• Nine •

ROY MACGRUDER SAT IN A BOOTH OF WORN LEATHERETTE at the Busy Bee Bar. He sipped his fourth Wild Turkey, smoked a Lucky, and listened to Patti Page. While a part of him wanted to yield to the jukebox—this dreamy ditty about old Cape Cod he had played for his girlfriend—anger gathered up inside of him like heartburn, and he felt the impulse for sentiment fade away, like the tiny bits of ice that melted along the top of his drink.

Disgusted, he reached into his glass, plucking out one of the cubes, which he studied pointlessly before flicking it away.

Roy stared at his hands and the long, thin fingers that were coated with patches of nicotine stain. He saw the pattern of liver spots—must be a million of them by now, he grumbled to himself. He reached up and touched his face, which he decided must be as old and worn as the leather booth in which he sat.

Time gets by too fast, he thought, and he finished his drink with a greedy gulp. Time's getting by and my brother Jack and that goddamned theatre are standing in the way of everything.

Roy looked toward the black upholstered bar, where other drinkers gripped their glasses, most of them staring at a television, which hung on chains beside a stuffed marlin affixed to a slab of plywood.

The reception was bad and some old western played out within a flurry of electronic snow.

Squinting, Roy finally recognized Audie Murphy, and he wondered if he'd ever projected the old movie at Odeon.

Who knows? he thought, for after a while the thousands of movies he'd projected began to blend together: Audie Murphy or Cary Grant, it didn't matter.

And besides, he never really got to *watch* the movies he'd projected, stuck as he was in that hellhole of a projection booth.

Now he caught sight of Emma Burnside, his girlfriend, and she distracted him from the TV. Filling up her tray with drink orders, she puffed on a cigarette and made idle chatter with the bartender.

Roy got jealous the way Emma got on so well with everybody. While he knew there was nothing between Emma and the bartender, it still bothered him, made him feel inadequate. And besides, Emma hadn't looked at him yet tonight.

He studied her, deciding once again that Emma Burnside was the sexiest woman he had ever known. He liked the uniform she wore—a black taffeta, like a maid's skirt—for it showed off her long legs, which stuffed a pair of nylon net stockings.

Not bad legs for a sixty-year-old woman, he thought.

But now he wondered what she was going to say when she learned that the deal with Odeon was off.

Is that why she hasn't looked at me yet? Does she already know?

When Emma started toward him, Roy's spirits lifted, for halfway across the bar she blew him a kiss, which leapt like fire from scarlet Kewpie lips.

But happy as he was, he could only respond with a weak grin.

She put down his drink. "What's the matter with you?" she asked, her voice low and throaty, telling of booze and cigarettes.

"Nothin', Emma."

"Bullshit, nothing," she said, sliding into the booth. She batted at her hair, a lacquered beehive. It was a gesture that always signaled to Roy that she was mad. "I mean, you've been lower than a monkey's balls all night," she said. "What gives?"

"It's my damned brother."

"Jack?"

"Of course, Jack! How the hell many brothers do I have, for chrissake!"

"Well, 'scuse me for living!" she said, sticking a hand to her hip.

"Sorry, Emma. I'm just in a stew is all."

"I'm sick of that damned theatre," she said.

"You and me both."

"I mean, the sheriff claims my Billy was down in that stall when the rats showed up. What would *Billy* be doing down there anyway?"

"Don't know."

The mention of Billy Burnside made Roy uncomfortable, and he hated it when Emma mentioned her son. How could they ever get married with a creepy kid like that around? When he pictured them making love, the boy always got in the way. It was bad enough seeing that goofy kid night after night at Odeon, let alone live with him under the same roof.

"Sheriff's coming by to see me tomorrow," Emma continued. "His daughter's filled his head with lies, as far as I can see. I mean, it's sad and all what happened to those kids, but I don't like the idea that it's somehow my fault . . . *Billy's* fault. They pick on him, you know. All the time, those kids pick on him."

"Goddamned theatre!" he spat.

He watched as Emma lit a cigarette. She was angrier now, he knew, and something happened to her face when she was angry that Roy didn't like. The eyes, usually large, narrowed into tiny slits, and the pretty face seemed to lose its shape—the gentler lines becoming suddenly hard. Roy thought she got angry like a man, and he didn't like it.

"So what's the deal?" she asked. "We going to Vegas or not?"

"Of course!" he cried, even though he wasn't sure if they could anymore.

When it was decided they would sell Odeon, Jack had promised Roy they would sell some of Odeon's artifacts at an auction and Roy, in turn, had told Emma he would use the money to take her to Las Vegas. But now Jack had changed his mind, deciding that the things inside of Odeon were too sacred to sell in such a way. And besides, he now had this idea for a closing-night show: He would run the same movies that had opened up Odeon sixty years ago, and he would let the whole town in for free.

After Roy had spilled out the whole story to Emma, she sat quietly for a long time. Finally, she picked up his Zippo lighter, flicking it on and off in front of his face.

"Don't you have a say in all this?" she asked.

"Jack took care of that too!" he said angrily. "He put the deed in his name only. And, hell, we bought the place with money we inherited from Mom and Dad."

Roy's resentment for Jack flared anew.

He had never got along with Jack—the pampered brother. How Roy hated his brother's obsessive love for the movies. How he hated Odeon, the projection room, the miles of film he had threaded up and projected in all these years. How he hated the way his brother banged on the projection room door, screaming at him for allowing the picture to slip out of focus.

"Sorry, Emma," Roy said. He searched her face for the kind of pity that would get him some sex later on at the Starlite Motel up the 101, but all he could see was contempt. He knew she'd be angry with him all night, and women had a way of letting their anger hang in the air, he thought, like bad perfume.

She flipped the Zippo two more times. "More than one way to skin a cat, Roy."

"Huh?"

Emma flicked it again, then again—over and over, each time bringing it closer to his face.

"What's goin' on, Emma? Do you wanna cigarette?"

Emma rolled her eyes, then tapped him on the forehead, digging one of her long red fingernails into his flesh.

"Christ, Roy," she said, "ain't there anything up in that head of yours besides a lot of old booze?" She clutched at his hair. "Ain't there nothin' under this bunch of old dead straw, Roy?"

Watching her work the lighter again, he stared at the flame. After a few seconds he got the idea. He grabbed the lighter and flicked it himself.

Emma watched him. "That's right!" she purred. "You got it now, don't you, babe!"

Roy held the lighted Zippo until the metal grew intolerably hot. With a tiny yelp he flicked it off and laid it down.

"Why not?" he said, grinning, and felt awfully stupid that he'd never though of that great big fire insurance policy his brother had bought.

Roy's plan was simple. An hour later, as he drove along North Post Road to the house he shared with Jack, he rehearsed it in his mind.

He would leave the car a few blocks from Odeon, then work his way through Wall-Park and across Main Street to the theatre. Slipping down an alley that ran along the theatre, he would enter through the fire door, which would place him directly behind the screen. There he would dump gasoline across a jumble of boxes, which Jack had so carelessly stored.

All that crap!

The clutter backstage was the sum total of Jack's collection of movie trivia—those things too large or plentiful to drag home: thousands of one-sheets, press kits, eight-by-ten stills. Forty of the boxes contained 3-D glasses, which Jack insisted would make a comeback someday.

How perfect his timing was, Roy thought, for only a month ago the fire marshal had warned them to move the boxes.

Steering the car unsteadily, Roy maneuvered onto North Post Road, feeling the booze as it pumped through his brain. In his fantasy he could already see the boxes as they burst into flame.

When he got to the house he shared with his brother, Roy killed the engine and tiptoed up to the garage, where he intended to get the two cans of gasoline they used for the tractor.

Inside, he groped in the dark, for he didn't dare turn on the light. Jack might see him from the house and his plans would be ruined.

Roy stumbled toward the workbench. It was there he had last seen the gasoline.

Roy worked his fingers the length of the workbench, brushing against tools, paint cans, and a scattering of screws and bolts.

Where the hell are the cans? he wondered, and he worried that they might not be there anymore. It would be just like Jack to have put them somewhere else, he grumbled to himself. Another damned attempt to tidy up.

After searching the entire workbench, he reached for the small shelf above. When his hand bumped suddenly against the cold metal surface of a gasoline can, he grinned. He felt a second can next to that.

Gathering them awkwardly in his arms, Roy moved out of the garage.

Fifteen minutes later Roy drove carefully down Main Street, making certain he didn't weave or cross the dividing line. Still drunk, he feared being stopped by Sheriff Bradley or Deputy Travers.

Roy parked the Oldsmobile on Ivy Street, which was a half block from Wall-Park. After slipping out of the car, he looked up and down the street, checking for movement, but everything was still. Just as he had figured, Wallenberg had closed up for the night.

Roy opened his trunk, took out the two cans, then closed the trunk as quietly as he could. When he clutched the cans to his chest, he realized they weren't going to be easy to carry.

Roy stared into Wall-Park, where a sliver of moon illuminated the trees and playground equipment. Satisfied the park was empty, he started off.

The cans proved immediately awkward, sliding about within the uncertain cradle of his arms. Worse, it was colder out than Roy had imagined, so that he could feel his hands as they welded to the freezing metal.

Now he smelled a strong odor and he realized the gasoline had begun to ooze from the spouts. He felt the liquid penetrate his jacket, all the way down to his chest.

Goddamned stupid cans! he cursed to himself, each new whiff of gasoline increasing his rage. He had begun to tremble, and his head ached with a dull, relentless throb.

He looked down at his shoes. Gasoline had fallen on them, leaving veiny, purple blotches across the leather tongues. He could feel the gasoline rolling down inside, soaking his freezing feet. He decided he needed to sit down and rearrange the cans. At this rate, he figured, they'd be empty by the time he reached Odeon.

Roy noticed the children's slide up ahead. He waddled up to it and sat at the bottom of the chute, feeling the icy grab of metal at his butt. The gasoline fumes were making him steadily nauseous.

Roy worked with the two cans, trying to regroup them, but his arms were slick with gasoline, making it difficult to get a grip. His fingers were so cold he could barely move them. In the icy air they fumbled uselessly, as if they were connected to someone else's hands.

"Would you kindly get out of my way?"

Roy sat up sharply, stiffening with dread.

Someone was there. Someone had seen him. His plan was ruined.

Roy tried to determine where the voice had come from. He stared into the park, but he saw no one, only trees, their branches looking heavy, drooping in the cold night.

"I'm up here!" the voice said.

Roy panicked. This time the voice sounded exasperated, and he also detected a slight British accent.

"Up here! At the top of the slide!"

Roy turned slowly, his heart pounding. He really didn't want to see the man at all. He didn't want to see the man who had spoiled his plan. Frantic, he concocted excuses: Car ran out of gas, you see, over on Ivy Street. It sputtered and died right there in the middle of the intersection.

Sure, Roy thought, I really haven't done anything wrong yet. There's no law against carrying gas cans through a public park.

Craning his neck, Roy looked up the metal chute, which was like a sheet of reflective ice in the moonlight. He squinted against the glare, trying to make out the form at the top of the slide. Whoever it was stood in silhouette and looked enormously fat, wearing an ill-fitting suit and a derby.

"How do you expect me to come down this slide if you are going to sit there at the bottom?" the man asked indignantly. His cadence was overemphatic, each word spoken with a peevish lilt. A tiny smudge of a moustache twitched along the fleshy face.

"Who . . . who are you? Why are you dressed up like . . ."

". . . I'm just a private citizen trying to use the public park," he answered. When he spoke, he fit a thumb to his index finger, the remaining fingers opening in a splay from the swollen fist. Roy felt his rump as it bonded to the slide.

The fat man scowled. "My friend and I came here to play, my good fellow."

"Friend?" Roy asked, swallowing.

"Why, yes." The fat man smiled. "He's over there."

Roy looked across the park. There, on one of the swings, sat a thinner man. Roy saw that he was dressed identically to the fat man. Swinging only barely, he let his shoes drag lazily along the dirt. With a little grin he waved at them.

Roy turned to the fat man. "What the hell is this? A costume party? Is that it? Huh? You guys comin' home from a . . ."

"Whooooaaa!"

Roy watched as the fat man hurtled down the slide. The bottoms of his shoes looked all at once enormous and Roy saw they were headed directly for his face.

Roy tried to shift position, but he couldn't move quickly enough. The fat man's shoes crashed into his back, sending him in a sprawl to the ground. Lying there winded, he saw that the gasoline cans had tumbled to each side of him. He turned over and stared into the fat man's face. "You big fat sonofabitch!"

The fat man grimaced, his moustache twitching displeasure. He shook a plump finger and spoke. "Why, that wasn't a very neighborly thing to say!"

Roy sat up, but he felt too weak and dazed to stand. His back ached, as though he had been hit from behind by a truck. He looked at the gasoline cans, then turned to see the thin man approaching. His movements were awkward—the gangling lope of a child in a man's body. "What's the matter?" the thin man asked.

"Did you hear what this fellow said to me?"

The thin man squinted his confusion. "No. You see, I was over there on the swing and I . . ."

"Never mind!"

Roy stared at them. "Why the hell are you dressed like that? What the hell are you doing?"

"Dressed like what?" the fat man asked. His manner seemed all at once grotesquely courteous.

"You know what the hell I mean!"

Roy reached for one of the gasoline cans.

"What have you got there?" the fat man asked.

"Nothing!" Roy said. He whimpered from the pain as he struggled to his feet.

"Looks like gasoline to me."

"Yeah, so it is."

"Gasoline could be dangerous."

"Ah, fuck you!"

The fat man gasped, then poked at Roy's chest. "Didn't your mother teach you not to use such language?"

"Don't touch me," Roy yelled, slapping away the fat man's hand. "You crazy bastard."

Roy knelt down and retrieved the second gasoline can. When he turned to move away, the fat man lunged at him.

"Hey!" Roy screamed, but the enormous mass of weight took him all the way down, so that Roy's cheek smashed against the ground. Turning, he realized that the fat man was sitting on his legs, confining him. "Get off me, you fucking lunatic."

The fat man turned and glowered at his friend. "Will you *please* try to help me?"

"What do you want me to do?"

He pointed to the gasoline cans. "Pick those up!"

"No!" Roy cried, but he could tell that the thin man didn't hear him, or at least had no intention of doing what Roy said. Instead, the thin man knelt and picked up each cap obediently. When he stood, one of the cans fell from his grasp. The cap popped off and gasoline gushed from the open spout, flooding along the grass, right up to the edge of Roy's face.

"Now look what you've done!" the fat man accused.

The thin man knelt again, reaching for the can. He managed to get another grip, but it was unsteady. It tumbled from his arms, like some huge unwieldy fish.

Roy watched in terror as cups of new gasoline roared from the spout. He felt it splash across his body and his face. It soaked through his shirt, gathering along his torso.

"Jesus Christ!"

"You'll have to find that cap!" the fat man cried.

"But it's so dark out here!"

"Use this," the fat man said.

The fat man reached into his jacket pocket, withdrawing a box of wooden matches.

"Nooo!" Roy screamed. "For God's sake, no!"

The fat man looked at him. "Don't you see? We are trying to *help* you."

Taking the match, the thin man stared at it, as though he did not know what it was for. After a moment he stood on one leg, striking the match to the worn sole of his shoe. When it flared in the icy night, he bent toward the ground, holding the match as he searched for the cap.

Roy watched helplessly, his mouth filling up with gasoline. He tried to scream, but all that escaped his lips was a frothy mass of purple bubbles.

"Ouch!" the thin man cried.

Roy stared at the match, which had burned to the tips of the thin man's fingers. Roy watched as it fell to earth.

"*Whoooaaa!*" screamed the fat man, rolling off Roy's legs.

Roy heard the gasoline ignite, a sound like roaring wind. It formed a flaming trail to his face. He tried to move, but he knew it was too late. He could already sense the sudden heat along his body.

"Look what you've done!" the fat man howled.

The thin man began to bawl. "What are we going to do?"

Roy looked up at the fat man. *For Christ's sake, help me!* he tried to scream, but he knew it was no use. His lips were scalding hot, blistering, unable to move. He watched as the fat man considered a course of action, finally taking off his derby and waving it as a fan against the flames. *Damn fools!* Roy cried to himself. *Damn fools! Pull me out of here! Do something!*

"Let's get out of here!" the fat man cried.

Roy lay helplessly as the flames moved across his body. He watched as the two men ran away through Wall-Park. They were jumping up and down now, the fat man slapping at his friend with the derby.

Roy tried to move within the center of the flames that consumed him. His nostrils filled with the smell of his own burning flesh. He pressed a flaming hand to the grass and tried to push himself up to a kneeling position.

Just as he got to his knees, he heard the other can explode.

The impact knocked him on his buttocks—the last movement of his life a kind of pratfall.

• Ten •

IT WASN'T JUST THE NIGHTMARE that woke Amy. Lying in a half-sleep, she felt the touch of someone's hand—icy cold and dead. It pressed against her face until she could no longer breathe.

"Mike!" she screamed.

Bolting up, she stared into darkness, expecting to see whoever it was that had just touched her, but what she could see of her bedroom—tidy and familiar in a crooked shaft of moonlight—appeared empty. A clock ticked noisily on the nightstand. Grabbing it, she saw that it was not even four.

Amy sat in darkness, gasping for air. The dream had left her breathless, like that time she had almost drowned. She remembered the greedy gulps for air as water covered her lips; the awful guttural sounds she'd made, like some other language, as she slowly slipped beneath the waterline, unable to scream for help. But this, she knew, had been worse.

Amy shivered now. The thick blankets had fallen away, exposing slender, naked shoulders. Trembling in her bed, she looked across the room, where even the window looked ominous. It was a black, foreboding rectangle beneath fluttering curtains.

It was the eye of some huge monster, and Amy knew that it was the only thing that separated her from the night—all that moved there.

Watching, Amy wondered when the horror, at last, would come for her, just as it had come for Mike. She wondered when she would see his face—Billy Burnside's face—pressed to the window. She imagined his fat lips as they flattened along the pane, thick and grey, like worms; his fingers, caked with mud, would beckon her to come with him.

In her nightmare she had watched a thousand hungry rodent mouths nibble away at Mike's flesh. Only this time they had turned away from Mike and come for her. No amount of comfort from the sheriff would ever convince her she had escaped. She knew that, sooner or later, regardless of what her father said, Billy Burnside would come for her.

It was only a matter of time.

Stop it! Stop it!

And yet, as much as he protected her, it was hard for Amy not to blame her father. It was he, after all, who had not trusted her. It was her father who had treated her like a child, thus making growing up a thing not of difficult transition, but of hostile rebellion. Why else would she have considered surrendering her innocence in a manner that so disgusted her? That she had even considered making love to Mike in the stall of a movie theatre men's room now filled her with shame.

She glanced about her bedroom, which formed out of darkness as her eyes readjusted. It was a little girl's room—a place of gingham curtains, dainty decorations, fussily appointed dolls, and stuffed animals.

Let me grow up, Daddy!

She loved the big, strapping sheriff with all her heart, and she knew that he loved her, but she desperately needed a life of her own.

Amy slipped out of bed, clutching herself against the cold as she ran to the window and looked out. All seemed quiet and still along the acre of property that fronted the huge, dilapidated barn.

She worried about Dandelion. The pregnant heifer lay in the barn, swollen and uncomfortable in these last few critical days before giving birth. Amy had checked that afternoon with Dr. Ohfers, the veterinarian, but he assured her the heifer would survive the unseasonable weather. "Ever been in a North Dakota winter?" he'd asked her. "This is nothing, Amy."

But this isn't North Dakota and it isn't winter, she'd thought, and his remarks had only slightly buoyed her spirits.

Eventually, she talked herself into believing him, for indeed she worshipped Dr. Ohfers. The old doctor was her mentor and Amy had already signed up for her first year of college with a major in veterinary medicine. The doctor was delighted that she wished to follow in his footsteps, especially a girl of such extraordinary promise.

Still concerned, Amy pressed up against the window. Was

Dandelion warm enough? Would the unusual weather trigger an early birth?

More than anything, she wanted to check, but she was frightened. Nothing in the world could convince her to walk the distance from her room to the barn, not even her love for Dandelion.

Out there in the dark, Amy reasoned, Billy Burnside was *certain* to get her. He would grin at her and bare his teeth in the moonlight, carrying her off to make her his own.

When a sudden gust swept across the property, Amy pulled away from the window, which seemed to buckle in the wind. At the mouth of the barn, a loose-hung door rattled in the night.

Yes, yes, he's coming for me. I know he is.

The sheriff stood just outside his daughter's door. Clutching a can of Budweiser, he waited. He had heard the telltale sounds—a cry in the night, the thrash of bedcovers, her feet as they hit the floor—and he knew that she'd had another nightmare.

Let me help you baby, he thought, and he raised his hand to knock.

But just as quickly, he stopped it in midair, remembering his daughter's words. Amy had made it clear that she could take care of herself.

Where was that point when you stayed back, no matter how much you knew they needed you?

It was the worst part about being a father, he decided: not knowing when or how much to help.

Sometimes he worried that he'd been too protective, and he hoped she realized that his protectiveness had risen up out of love.

Bradley believed that if you loved something, you protected it at all costs.

Now he pressed an ear to her door and he heard the soft pads of her feet against the old oak floor. He knew that she was pacing about inside; she always did after a nightmare.

Worried about the heifer, he figured.

While the sheriff ached to knock and see if she was all right, he kept his resolve, allowing his fist to unfold slowly, finger by finger, so that the knuckles barely brushed the wood.

In the kitchen Bradley grabbed another beer. Sitting at the kitchen table, he took half of it in a single gulp, his fourth beer that evening. He promised himself he would start his new diet tomorrow.

Bradley fingered the swell of belly that pressed too tight against his khaki uniform shirt. At fifty-five he wasn't happy with how his body had gone. It seemed to thicken day by day beneath his uniform. His thighs had begun to chafe, and his waist invited seams to rip. He often felt heavy and inefficient, like a bag of stones.

He missed the body he had lost, and now he shunned his image in the mirror. Gone forever was the muscular young man who had played all-star high school football. Captured by his good looks and charisma, all the girls had fallen in love with him, and the hidden, naive part of Leo Bradley had imagined such days would go on forever. It didn't seem fair to end up like this: a paunchy widower at a kitchen table drinking beer by himself in the middle of the night.

When the telephone rang, Bradley knew right away it was his deputy.

"Yeah," he answered, "what's up?"

"Better get down here, Sheriff. Right away."

They still didn't know it was Roy MacGruder. The mass of charred flesh and bone that lay before them could have been anyone. Black clouds of foul-smelling smoke hissed in the cold air.

Sheriff Bradley knelt to the remains with Dr. Phillip Matson, each with a handkerchief pressed to his face. Matson poked at the remains with a stick. "Only clue we're going to have here is dental records," he said.

Bradley scowled, then grabbed Matson's stick. He used it to tap at what remained of the gasoline cans, which lay a few feet from the remains. The ruined metal crumbled inward.

He turned to Matson. "What sort of crazy sonofabitch would be carrying gasoline cans through a freezing park in the middle of the night?"

"Damned if I know," Matson said. He was short and stocky, a bullish sort of man. Officious horn-rimmed glasses covered cold grey eyes that seemed immune to the horrors of death. "People die in stupid ways, Leo. Remember when old man Bitts took a bath in Clorox? Thought it would take off his tattoos, remember? Damned fool didn't realize it was just like drinking the stuff. Seeps into your pores, you know."

Bradley stood up. "Well, someone's bound to turn up missing. When they do, we'll get the call." Wearily, he turned to the small crowd that had formed behind them to gawk, most of whom had stumbled up from the Busy Bee. "Go home," he ordered, "there's nothing to see." Mumbling among themselves, they moved away.

When Bradley turned to Dr. Matson, he saw Jack MacGruder, who ran toward them across Odeon's forecourt.

"I know who it is!" Jack cried.

"Who?" asked Bradley.

"My brother," he said, choking back a sob.

"How do you know?"

"I woke up in the night. Saw him leaving the garage with some cans of gasoline. It finally hit me what he might be doing."

Bradley spoke. "What *was* he doing?"

"He was going to burn her down."

"Burn *who* down?"

"Odeon," Jack said. "When it hit me, I went there to stop him, but he never showed up." His voice cracked. "I heard the sirens."

"You're sure about all this, Jack?" Matson asked.

Blowing his nose and nodding quickly, Jack pointed at the smoking remains. "He had a big old heavy key chain, shaped like elk antlers. Bet you'll find it in there, if you poke around."

Bradley nodded at Matson, who prodded the black ash with his stick. Sure enough, he bumped up against something hard. When he pulled it out, they saw that it was the key chain.

"I'll need a statement, Jack," said Bradley.

Nodding, Jack turned away and moved off quickly for Odeon. He felt sick to his stomach.

Now he was old and falling apart, and so was his theatre.

Jack MacGruder stood in Odeon's lobby. He felt cold and numb, not yet certain how he should react to his brother's death. The part of him that craved to mourn clashed violently with that which felt betrayed.

He stared up at the domed ceiling, all of it cove-lit and metal-leafed. It was still brilliant, even in the semidarkness.

You were going to destroy it all! he thought, and he was suddenly so angry at his brother that he paced a pointless circle across the lavish chenille rug. One little match, he thought, and it all would have vanished.

It was bad enough that they would soon take a wrecking ball to Odeon—that alone had caused him endless grief—but Jack didn't think he could have stood a fire. A fire would have disfigured Odeon.

Horrified, he imagined smooth cherub faces turning into dead, carbonized rock, mighty festoons becoming useless rags. He pictured walls as they surrendered to fire; they would melt into hot and putrid puddles.

Now it occurred to him that Roy might have sabotaged the theatre in other ways. Moving to the central switchbox, he flooded Odeon with light, deciding he would have to search the theatre from top to bottom.

He began in the maintenance room, which was eighteen feet beneath the stage floor. With its enormous, twisting labyrinth of dense grey metal pipe, it had always reminded Jack of a ship's engine room.

Two huge boilers dominated, each with the power to process thirty gallons of oil. Farther back, a water storage tank loomed, capable of shooting three hundred gallons of water a minute into an intricate fire hose system.

Jack knelt down and scanned the several dials, checking the setting of each. He knew that Roy could easily have set them within a range capable of causing an explosion. Relieved, he saw that each dial was in its proper position.

Crouching low, he moved through a series of catacombs that led to the ventilating system, which was located beneath the orchestra floor. As he struggled along, Jack felt the strain of old muscles, stretched to the snapping point throughout his back; they ached from the awkward position necessary to navigate the mazelike network of Odeon's guts.

He reached the huge ventilating fan, then knelt to check where each needle was set. The fan, equipped with lengths of metal duct, could blast one hundred thousand cubic feet of air into Odeon's auditorium in ten minutes, releasing the stale air into Main Street.

Again, the dials appeared untouched. Encouraged, Jack doubted that Roy had ever set foot into these massive, hidden rooms. He might not even have known they existed.

He concluded his search in the projection room, where, as expected, he felt overcome with feelings for Roy. The air still smelled of cigarettes—the countless Lucky Strikes that Roy had smoked there in hostile silence.

Jack moved up to the workbench, where everything seemed in order. Bottles of film cement formed a neat row beside a large Griswold film splicer.

No sabotage here, he thought, and he turned to leave.

When he reached the thick fire door, Jack noticed a can of film that seemed at once out of place. Propped against the wall, it was conspicuous to Jack in its brand-new silver can.

Odd, he thought, for he himself was responsible for coordinating film deliveries and he wasn't expecting anything right now. Picking it up, he noticed that the can was unlabeled, and when he withdrew the reel of film, he saw that it too had no markings.

Jack carried it to one of two large Simplex projectors, threading it as fast as he could.

Where could the film have come from? Could it have been delivered while he wasn't there?

He had, after all, contacted a film distributor in Berkeley who specialized in hard-to-find 35mm prints. The same distributor had helped him locate a 35mm print of *City Lights* for the closing-night show.

After firing up the arc light, Jack engaged the projector's motor, then dropped the fire gate and dowser. Hitting a switch that operated the curtains down below, Jack peeked through the porthole, watching as a series of numbers popped across the elegant sweep of drapes.

A speaker above him in the projection room produced the hiss of a blank soundtrack, followed by the beep of a sync pulse. For several seconds the screen was totally black, and Jack began to wonder if there was anything on the film at all.

But suddenly he heard music—a scratchy hurdy-gurdy that he recognized immediately.

Jack watched the screen, where there suddenly blossomed a familiar title: *Stan Laurel & Oliver Hardy*.

• Eleven •

THE SIZE OF THE ROOM surprised her. Karen had expected Dr. Matson's waiting room to be as huge and intimidating as she remembered it from childhood. Instead, the room seemed small and drab.

When Karen entered, a reception window slid open noisily. "Can I help you?" asked a small and elderly woman in a nurse's uniform.

Karen was surprised, for again she had expected the past. She had expected Cora Grady, whose severe and humorless manner had frightened the young Karen. By contrast, this nurse appeared pleasant, her eyes twinkling behind harlequin-framed glasses. She extended a tiny hand. "My name is Emily Joslin."

Karen smiled at her. "I expected Cora Grady."

"Oh, Cora's been retired for years," Emily said, frowning and shaking her head. She drummed her fingers across the ledge that separated them. "Cora had a stroke. Several years ago. Totally paralyzed . . . she's over in Haleyville, poor thing. I visit her whenever I can."

"I'm sorry," Karen said, and a part of her felt guilty that she didn't really care. She still resented the nurse who had been so cold to her. When Karen came to see the doctor after the abortion, Cora Grady had been cruel and accusatory, playing into her guilt and sending her home in tears.

"Are you Karen Webster?" Emily asked, checking her appointment log.

"Yes."

"What is it you'd like to see the doctor about?" she asked, pulling out a clipboard. Her manner was warm yet efficient.

"I was a patient of his several years ago. I guess you'd call this a follow-up." Karen paused, suddenly embarrassed. "A seventeen-year follow-up, to be exact."

Emily arched her eyebrows. "I see," she said. "I'll get your file."

"There's *still* a file?" asked Karen, the prospect filling her with hope.

Emily blanched. "Well, of course . . . I mean, I would *think* so, Miss Webster." Handing Karen the clipboard, Emily gently slid the reception window closed.

Karen moved to the small couch and filled out a form attached to the clipboard. When she finished, she looked about the room, once again surprised by its size. She decided that the disparity had to do with childhood fears. In those days the doctor's office—filled with the prospect of pain and humiliation—had loomed before the frightened girl like the anteroom in the castle of an evil wizard.

The reception window slid open and Emily called to her. Karen walked up and presented the clipboard, noticing at once that Emily's mood had changed. This time the friendly smile was gone and her cheeks were flushed. Karen glanced at Emily's hands, which were clenched in anger. Clearly, she had just argued with the doctor.

"The doctor will see you now," Emily said, only barely disguising her fury.

A few minutes later Dr. Matson entered the small examination room, where Karen waited tensely.

"How nice to see you, Karen."

Karen smiled and returned his greeting. Unlike his office, the doctor seemed exactly as she remembered. With his imposing, stocky body and deep voice, he intimidated her every bit as much as he had before.

"Sorry about Nell," he said, taking a seat on a stool. "Your mother was a fine woman."

Karen nodded quickly. She had focused her attention upon his right leg, which jiggled nervously up and down.

All at once he yawned, tapping his mouth with a large, bejeweled hand. "Sorry," he said, "but I was up all night. That business in the park, you know."

"What business?"

"Some poor fool got himself burned up last night . . . right there in Wall-Park."

Karen startled. She had noticed the ribbons of yellow police tape on her way to the doctor's office. Snapping in the cold air, they had reminded her of crime sites in Los Angeles; it was a vision she hadn't expected in Wallenberg. "Who was it?" she asked.

"Roy MacGruder. Projectionist over at Odeon."

Karen stirred uneasily in her chair.

Dr. Matson leaned forward. "Something wrong?" he asked.

Karen shook her head quickly. "If you don't mind, I'd like to get right to the point, Dr. Matson."

"Please do."

Karen told him all that had happened since the abortion, including a detailed account of her breakdown and subsequent therapy. Finished, she watched his bushy eyebrows arch, signaling his deep disapproval—a gesture that Karen remembered all too well. His look of loathing on the day he confirmed her pregnancy would haunt her forever.

"I'm sorry you've had such difficulty, Karen," he said, "but I'm not certain how I can help you."

"I want my medical records, Doctor."

The doctor flinched. "They were sent to your doctor in Los Angeles, Karen. It was all arranged through Nell."

"They never arrived."

"Impossible!"

"When I had the breakdown, my doctor had no file. I understand that they contacted you. I understand further that you were less than cooperative."

Matson shifted uncomfortably on the stool, then pointed his finger at Karen. "Forgive me, but I can't help but pick up an accusation in your tone. I have since the moment you walked in here."

"I'm sorry you do. But I can't imagine, Doctor, why a simple request for medical documents should be considered an accusation."

"If the medical records were lost, it is not my fault. Clearly, it was the fault of the doctor to whom they were sent."

Karen smiled. "Fine, Doctor. In that case, I'm certain you have a copy."

Karen watched as a few beads of sweat formed along his upper lip. She saw it as a good sign, for she figured that the more nervous he became, the more likely he was to let something slip.

He snapped at her. "What good would medical records do you after all of this time?"

Karen glared at him. "Then I take it you're saying that you have no copies?"

"Don't put words in my mouth, young lady! I asked you a very simple question. What good would it do?"

Karen stiffened in her chair, years of accumulated rage coursing through her. "All right, Doctor, I'll tell you what *good* they would do! I went through *hell . . . seventeen years of hell* that still aren't over. A large portion of that hell, Doctor, was a direct result of never knowing the full truth of what happened to me!"

"You aborted your child. What else is there to know?"

"Is there a record of what happened once I got to you? Is there a record that proves the fetus was destroyed?"

"I'm sure your file is somewhere!"

"Where, damn it?"

Matson shot up from his stool, looming suddenly enormous above her. "I've had enough of this, Miss Webster!"

Karen stood. "I've only begun, Doctor!"

"Leave my office!"

Karen ignored him. "Was it a boy or a girl?"

"I don't remember."

"I don't believe you."

"I don't care if you believe me or not."

"What did Nell have to do with it?"

"*Do* with it?"

"Whenever I asked my mother about the baby, she was always strange about it. She never wanted to discuss it."

Matson glared at her. "Perhaps, Karen, she was ashamed."

"Oh, I know that very well, Doctor. I know how ashamed she was. I spent those months locked in my room. I was suddenly the town leper. I know a *great deal* about being treated with shame, Doctor."

Matson moved swiftly to the door. "We're getting nowhere this way," he said, gesturing that she should leave. "I'm sorry that the incident left you incapable of conceiving a child. Unfortunately, some actions in life exact a terrible price."

"I'm not here for your damned absolution!" Karen shouted. "I'm here for information."

"*What* information?"

"Are there medical records or not?"

He pulled a handkerchief from his pocket, which he used to mop his forehead. "I would have to . . . well, there are a great deal of files to go through . . ."

". . . fine."

"How long are you going to be in Wallenberg?"

"Until I have answers."

Matson fixed her with a stare of utter contempt. "This is so typical."

"Typical?"

"Typical of you girls . . . the ones who get themselves in trouble. You do it all to yourself and then it's up to the rest of us to get you out of it. No one forced you to take a coat hanger to your unborn child!"

Karen had guessed he would say such a thing. She looked in his eyes and spoke simply. "Doctor, I've spent the better part of my life in guilt. A day hasn't gone by that I haven't regretted what I did. Do you *really* know what it's like to live with such a thing? I've kept track of the child's age, you know. I've invented a life for it. If you intend to dissuade me with guilt, then I'll tell you something. I've done the job quite well myself."

The doctor turned away, walking to the window, which flooded him with grey morning light. Karen gathered up her things and moved to the door.

"Once you have gathered up the records in question," she said, "please contact me at the hotel."

Karen turned and walked to the waiting room, where Emily Joslin stood at attention.

"Well?" the old nurse asked.

"Frankly, I didn't find out a damned thing," Karen said, still emboldened by her confrontation with the doctor. "If you'll forgive me, I don't feel that you work for a very nice man. He insists there *are* no files."

"I'm sorry about this," Emily said, looking away.

Karen could tell that the woman's concern was genuine. "Thank you."

Emily took a deep breath. "Miss Webster, I hate to tell you this, but I think the doctor is lying to you."

"Oh?"

"When you called for your appointment, I gave your old files to the doctor."

Karen moved to her excitedly. "Then there *are* files?"

"Yes," Emily said. Her face had turned scarlet and she

suddenly spoke very quickly, as if afraid that she might suddenly lose nerve. "After you arrived this morning and I asked where they were, he denied they existed. Later I found them on my own. He seemed upset that I had. Now they've disappeared."

"Go on," Karen said, furious.

"It wouldn't be such a big thing, Miss Webster, except . . . well, I could get fired for telling you this, but this has happened before. *Other* files have turned up missing, you see."

"Thank you," Karen said, touching Emily's hand. "I know how hard it is for you to say these things."

The nurse smiled. "I'll try to help you."

"You already have," Karen said, then turned and left the office. She felt a new rise of confidence—the sort that came with having found an ally.

• Twelve •

IT WAS A DAY FOR DOING THINGS he didn't want to do.

First, he had to convince the City Council that opening up Odeon—even if for a single evening—was the stupidest thing he'd ever heard of.

Then he had to tell Emma Burnside that the precious son she considered incapable of doing anything wrong might be involved in a grisly death in the theatre's men's room.

And if that weren't enough, he wasn't certain if Emma knew that her boyfriend, only the night before, had burned to a crisp in Wall-Park.

All in all, not a terrific day, Sheriff Bradley thought as he strode into the Wallenberg City Council chambers at just after ten.

He grabbed a folding chair and slid it up alongside Jack, who was dressed in a tuxedo. The sight of it annoyed the sheriff, for it reminded him of the fanciful kind of thinking that had led the old man to insist upon a closing-night ceremony for Odeon in the first place.

"Real sorry about your brother," Bradley obliged, removing his hat respectfully. From habit, he ran a hand through thick, unruly hair. "You sure you're up to this?"

Jack nodded. "Yes, Leo. Thank you."

"Okay, but I'm telling you, I'm gonna keep you from openin' up that theatre of yours if it's the last thing I do."

"I'm sure we can have a lively debate," Jack offered.

"Buried the Barnes boy last week," Bradley snapped. "So many rats got to him, Doc Matson couldn't tell at first what sex he was. Debate *that* for me."

Jack shuddered away from Bradley and they both turned to the dais, where Mayor Eddie Bendix sat with the other members of the Wallenberg town council—Dr. Matson and Joe Rydell, owner of the local appliance store. Eating their breakfast from a box of doughnuts, they examined a sheaf of paperwork, brushing away sugar and glaze.

"You gonna start this meeting, Eddie, or stuff your face with doughnuts?" Bradley shouted.

"Hold your horses," said the mayor, looking down at the sheriff over the tops of wire-rimmed glasses, which he now pulled off indignantly. "We'll begin when we're ready."

Bradley waved away the mayor and sat back with a mumbled curse, for he knew already that he was licked. Bradley knew it was Mayor Bendix who had negotiated the deal for Odeon's property, intending to use it for a mini-mall, so it was highly likely that he would rule in favor of MacGruder.

Angry, the sheriff pulled out a cigarette.

"No smoking in chambers!" Mayor Bendix cried, rapping his little gavel.

Bradley flicked away his match. "You make the laws around here, Eddie. You change 'em. I'm having a smoke!"

After scowling at the sheriff, the mayor rapped his gavel again. "I hereby call this special session of the Wallenberg City Council to order. Jack MacGruder has petitioned this council for permission to open the Odeon theatre for a closing-night ceremony this coming weekend. Approval of the council had been unanimous, but Sheriff Leo Bradley has protested the event, citing the possibility of general health and safety violations within the theatre."

"Damned right!" Bradley cried.

The mayor ignored him and gestured to Earl Zweibach, who sat to the side of the dais. "Council has asked Earl Zweibach, an exterminator from Haleyville, to testify."

Nervous, Earl Zweibach cleared his throat, staring at the floor as he spoke. With his large nose and small eyes, he resembled the critters that he eradicated for a living. "I have searched the theatre thoroughly, and it is my conclusion that there is not an extraordinary infestation of rats."

"Ah, for Christ's sake!" Bradley bellowed.

Bendix shot Bradley a warning look, then turned to Zweibach. "What do you mean by an *extraordinary* infestation?"

"Hell, Eddie," he said with a shrug, "all theatres got rats."

"They do?"

"Sure. You see, there's no other structure that allows them a better opportunity for survival. A theatre's got unlimited space for burrowing and nesting. It's dark most of the time, it's filled with all those nooks and crannies, and it's full of forageable food—popcorn. The rats will often build their nests in the seats."

Mayor Bendix wrinkled his nose in disgust. "They will?"

"Look, Earl," said Bradley, "isn't it true that they came up through the shitter?"

"Bradley!"

"Ah, come on, Mayor! This ain't the PTA. Let's call a spade a spade." Bradley stared at Zweibach. "Well?"

Zweibach considered. "Rats've been known to work their way up through the plumbing, yes."

Mayor Bendix consulted his notes. "Carl Irvine said there were thousands."

"Thousands?" Zweibach smiled. "Up through the sewers? Impossible."

"Just how many rats *did* you find?" Bradley asked.

"None."

"None!" Bradley shouted. "Bullshit!"

Bendix worked his gavel. "Sheriff Bradley, you are out of order!"

Bradley stood up sharply. "Look. I've got a little girl at home in a state of grief. She can't eat and she can't sleep. I hear her in the bedroom at night, crying. Later, she wakes up screaming from nightmares. Don't tell me there aren't rats in that damned theatre!"

"No one's denying the tragedy, Sheriff," Bendix said. "The problem here is this: Do we have sufficient cause to deny Jack MacGruder his closing-night ceremony?"

Bradley shook his head. "I don't believe it. I really can't believe this sudden streak of sentiment in you, Eddie. Could it be you'll get a better deal on the property if you kiss up to Mac-Gruder . . ."

"That's entirely unnecessary," Bendix warned. "One more crack like that and I'll ask you to leave."

Bradley sat down in the flimsy chair with a great crash. Folding his arms, he glared at Jack, who stood up slowly.

"Gentlemen," he began, "I'm most upset by what befell those two innocent children. No one more than I wants to make certain that Odeon is a safe place to watch the motion pictures. I want the record to show that I stand very firm on that. What happened to the boy makes me ache inside, and I know how much Amy means to Leo. I can understand the feelings here.

. "As you know, I've spent most of my life at Odeon. I worked there as a boy, managed it during the forties and fifties, then was lucky enough to buy it with my brother back in seventy-one."

The mention of Roy brought a series of mumbled condolences from the dais. Accepting them with a gracious nod, Jack continued.

"All of you might wonder, in fact, why I'd come to this meeting this morning—on account of what happened to my brother last night, I mean. But, you see, Odeon's very important to me. I love it deeply. But these are very financially troubling times. Maintenance was a fortune, and *insurance* . . . well, you can imagine what my premium would've been after an incident like that . . . I just couldn't support the old place anymore. I had to sell. I guess a man has to keep up with the times."

As he grew reflective, he scanned their faces, smiling at each. "You all came to Odeon as boys. I remember each and every one of you. You came in for the Saturday matinees, and . . . well, it was an important place in your youth. Whether you realize it or not, Odeon taught you a few things about life. The way you one day lived it. All I'm asking, given the old gal gets a clean bill of health from Earl, is a final moment of glory for a place of dreams."

After he sat down, the chamber fell into a long silence.

Mayor Bendix finally turned to Zweibach. "So, Earl? What do you say?"

"I say we let him do it."

"So be it," the mayor said, smacking his gavel.

Bradley sat in silence, shaking his head. After a moment he stood up, turning to Jack. "I'll fight this yet, old-timer," he said.

After the sheriff left, Jack sat perfectly still, bristling at the name he had called him. *Old-timer*. It made him think of Gabby Hayes or Smiley Burnette, the stock movie hermits—grizzled old coots in the desert with a mule and a geiger counter.

Mayor Bendix smiled. "You and I are going to have to have dinner real soon, Jack."

When Jack looked up, he noticed the broad smile on the mayor's face.

"Yes," he said pleasantly. "We should."

When Bradley pulled up to Emma Burnside's house on North Post Road, it occurred to him he hadn't visited for three years.

Switching off the engine and staring at her ramshackle farmhouse, he wished it didn't have to be for three years more.

He stayed in the car, where he stalled his unpleasant errand by lighting up a cigarette. Opening the door, he sat so that a husky leg angled out the car, his boot scratching across the dirt driveway in front of her house.

Bradley remembered his last visit with Emma Burnside and the terrible scene they had had. That time, he had caught Billy out in front of Drummer's Liquor. Sitting on a cinder block with his pants down, the boy had his hand on his penis, blithely stroking it in public.

When Bradley forced the boy to pull up his pants, Billy fought him like something wild, and later Billy giggled the whole way home. Bradley would never forget the boy's high-pitched giggle—eerie for having been so inappropriate. When Bradley dumped the offending Billy on Emma's doorstep, she insisted that Billy couldn't do such a thing.

Now Bradley stared at Emma's plain, one-story house. Flimsy with neglect, it swayed to one side and most of the paint had peeled away. A sofa and its ripped-out guts were strewn about the front lawn. Garbage rotted in piles beneath swarms of noisy flies.

With a flick of his cigarette Bradley approached the house, stepping around heaps of garbage as he worked his way to the porch, which was nearly hidden by a tangle of untended shrubs.

When he took the first step, he felt something shatter beneath his boot. He looked down and saw a piece of pink plastic; a tiny replica of a human arm, it was the mottled remains of a discarded doll.

Bradley pushed his way through the branches that dipped through the porch, blocking his way. To the left of the front door sat a group of Mason jars, forming a crooked row to the end of the porch. Bradley saw that each was filled with a creamy-looking substance. Patches of furry rot floated inside.

Suddenly, he heard the familiar giggle—a flutter of high-pitched sound, followed by a honk, like that of a goose. It had come from the end of the porch.

"Billy!" he cried, spinning to it, but it was too late. There was another burst of giggling, followed by the dull thud of someone crashing against shrubbery as he ran away.

Cursing, Bradley maneuvered himself through the clutter to the end of the porch, where he caught sight of Billy Burnside, dressed in his yellow rain slicker, as he loped into the backyard. There,

knee-deep in grass and weed, the boy jumped up and down,
howling and giggling until he became a blur of yellow. Finally, the
scrawny legs lost their footing and he fell to the ground with a
strangled little yelp.

"You're late!"

Bradley turned to the deep voice. Emma Burnside had stepped
from inside the house.

Bradley apologized and removed his hat, moving back down
the porch and joining her.

"S'pose you're looking into what happened to my Roy," she
said.

"Then you know."

"Course I know."

"We'll do everything we can," Bradley said.

He studied the woman, struck again by paradox. Whereas he
might have expected an old crone to emerge from such a house,
the opposite was true. In a robe with flowing drifts of pink chiffon
that wrapped a slender body, she was actually attractive, the
sheriff thought. Especially for her age. The only thing he didn't
find appealing was the oddly inappropriate beehive hairdo, which
never seemed to change, as if constructed out of hard plastic upon
the woman's head.

"Emma," he added awkwardly, "I hate to bother you at a time
like this, but . . ."

"Freezing out here," she interrupted. "Let's go inside."

The living room was as much of a surprise as Emma herself,
and Bradley found the room pleasant. Tall bookcases were filled
with fine leather volumes that were neatly shelved, and the plump
backs of velvet chairs were covered by homey antimacassars. A
fire crackled in the fireplace.

"First time I've ever made a fire in August," Emma said.
"Weatherman says it's going to freeze again tonight." She sat
down without gesturing Bradley to do the same. "How's your
daughter?"

"Amy's doing the best she can," Bradley said. "May I sit?"

"I suppose."

Bradley sank into the large chair. "Amy has nightmares," he
said.

"Hardly a surprise. Terrible thing that happened. I sent flowers
to the boy's family. Don't know why I did it, though. Mike Barnes
was cruel to Billy. Always was. Some people think it's all right to
torment the afflicted."

"How *is* Billy?" Bradley asked.

"You saw him. You know how he is. It never gets any better, I guess. Someday they'll put him away, you know. I'll hold on as long as I can."

She reached for a cigarette from the package on the coffee table. Bradley pulled out one of his own and he lit them both.

Emma thanked him and took the smoke in deep. "Is Amy still going to college in the fall?" she asked.

"Oh, yes." Bradley smiled, at once the proud father again. "In fact, she's already started some early classes. Was afraid the whole thing with Odeon might have affected her plans, but she's a strong girl. Real strong."

"What does she want to do?"

"Veterinarian. Fixed up the barn out back all by herself. She's got herself a pregnant heifer. Calls her Dandelion. Boy, she sure dotes on it."

Emma inhaled again on her cigarette. "Sheriff, I can't imagine you came here to talk about a pregnant cow."

Bradley stiffened. "No," he said, "I didn't."

"What is it, then? What did Billy do now?"

"I told you that Amy was having nightmares. You see, she doesn't seem to remember all that happened that night, and I haven't pressed her. The other night I heard her screaming. I went into her room and she told me she was . . . well, her nightmare was about Billy. She told me he was there that night. Down in the rest room with them before it happened."

Emma glared at him. "What are you suggesting now, Sheriff?"

"Well, I'm not really suggesting anything, Emma, it's just that . . . I thought Billy might have seen something. I thought he might be able to . . ."

"Billy will have nothing to say," Emma snapped.

"I don't think he has a choice, Emma."

"What?"

Bradley stood. "Look, I've tried to be polite here, but I don't have to be. I'm an officer of the law, Mrs. Burnside, and if I want to talk to your boy, I'll talk to him."

Emma stubbed out her cigarette and stood, gathering the robe about her with an extravagant move. "Very well," she said.

After putting on a heavy jacket, Emma led Bradley through the small kitchen to the back porch, where there were stacks of junk. Bradley saw that they were broken bits of things—table legs, coils of rusted bedsprings, pieces to a broken ceramic lamp. He saw the arm to another doll.

Everything had been sloppily swept to the side of the porch, where it all lay in the corner, like the pieces to some enormous, unassembled mosaic.

When they reached the backyard, Emma cried out for Billy, her deep voice resonant in the cold morning air. They waited for several minutes, but the boy did not answer.

All at once Bradley felt something, and he jumped in the ankle-high grass. It had felt like something skittering across the top of his boot.

Embarrassed for having jumped, he looked at Emma. "You feel that?"

"Critters," she said. "Everywhere there's critters."

Now she moved to the side of the house, and the sheriff followed. "You probably frightened the boy off," she accused.

Bradley stared at the ground where a hole had been dug. It was fresh, not far from the steps, and he knew it hadn't been there before.

"Billy likes to dig holes," Emma said.

"I know," Bradley said, feeling angry, for the hole reminded him of Amy's incident with the boy, the one she'd been upset about the night Mike Barnes died.

Emma looked at him sadly. "Sometimes he puts critters down there, I think."

Bradley nodded. "I'll be calling again," he said, then walked to his patrol car as fast as he could. After starting up the engine, he looked back toward Emma, whose attention remained along the ground.

With her body bent down, she studied the ugly, gaping hole that her son had dug.

• Thirteen •

EVEN THOUGH SHE HAD NOT SEEN HIM in seventeen years, Karen recognized the sheriff immediately; she didn't even have to get a look at his face. The body was thicker—maybe about twenty-five pounds' worth, she figured—but it didn't matter: Karen Webster knew Leo Bradley just by the way he stood.

"Hello, Leo," she said, standing as yet unnoticed in the center of his office.

Bradley turned around from a file cabinet, where he was stuffing reports into a folder. Startling when he saw her, he slammed the drawer shut and approached her, his hand outstretched. "Karen," he said, taking her hand.

Their handshake was quick but friendly, and afterward Bradley introduced his deputy, Ron Travers, a young man who looked enough like Bradley to be his son. The deputy went into another room to make coffee, leaving the two of them alone.

"Please sit down," Bradley offered, and he quickly tried to tidy up his little desk, first removing a stack of papers from the chair, indicating Karen should sit there.

"Congratulations," Karen said. "The last time I saw you, you weren't even deputy yet."

Bradley shrugged. "It's been a long time . . . Jesus, how many . . ."

"Seventeen," she said.

Karen was barely able to believe that so much time had passed by. Bradley was several years older than Karen, but they'd shared one of those tacit relationships that a younger child often has with one much older. Strong and silent as a boy, Bradley had been destined for police work, for even then he was vigilant and protective, watching over the younger children. He had seemed like everybody's big brother.

Bradley shook his head, studying her. "My God, but time does get away."

"Sure does." Karen smiled. "How's the wife?"

"Passed away," he said quickly, like he always did, as though he preferred getting it said and over with. "Had that damned rheumatic heart, you know."

"God, I'm sorry, Leo," Karen said, genuinely shocked. An image of Bradley's wife flashed through her mind. Karen hadn't known her at all, but the memory she had was of someone strong and hardy, not the sort to be struck down prematurely by a heart attack. "When did it happen?"

Bradley shifted nervously in the swivel chair, which creaked beneath his weight. "Actually, it happened about the time you left."

Karen remembered that Bradley's wife was pregnant at the same time that she herself was. She remembered it because she'd envied her so; after all, she had thought, Mrs. Bradley's pregnancy was legitimate.

She hesitated. "What about . . . the baby? Wasn't your wife . . ."

Bradley stood up sharply. "I have a beautiful daughter," he said. "Name's Amy. Starting up college, in fact. Gonna be a veterinarian." He turned to her, his manner all at once less polite. "So how can I help you?"

Wearily, Karen related her long story yet again. This time, for the sheriff's benefit, she stressed her attack in Odeon's rest room, asking him to check the files for other incidents that might have occurred about the same time. "I also intend to look up Carl."

She watched as the blood drained from Bradley's face. He plopped down in the chair with such a force she feared it might break beneath him.

"What's the matter, Leo?"

"Amy," he began, expressionless, "a few days ago, in the same stall . . . she and her boyfriend were attacked by rats. The boy died."

A chill gathered along Karen's back. "My God, that poor girl . . . it was *your* daughter?"

"You know about it?"

"The clerk at the hotel told me, right after I got here." She leaned forward. "Leo, I'd love to talk to her."

"No!" he cried.

"Why not?"

"I want her to forget about it! She has nightmares!"

"*I* had nightmares," Karen cried. She added softly, "And let me tell you, the best thing to do is *face* the fear."

Bradley got up and strode across the room, grabbing his holster and gun. "I got a lot to do, Karen," he said, snapping the holster into place around his thick waist. "I'll check out the files like you want."

Karen moved up to him. "Why don't you want me to talk to your daughter, Leo?"

"I told you!"

"Could I at least meet her?"

"No!" he said, then moved to open the door. "I got myself enough headaches, Karen, without taking this on."

"Very well," she said, and started out.

"How long'll you be here?" Bradley called after.

"As long as it takes," she said, then left his office, slamming the door behind her.

When she got back to the hotel, Karen hesitated before she stepped up on the wooden porch. Her encounters with the doctor and sheriff had left her angry and unsatisfied. In particular, she felt hurt by the incident with Bradley, for she had expected the cooperative boy of her youth. It was yet another piece of the past that had fallen away.

Frustrated, Karen turned around, facing the theatre once and for all. While it was old and so much less grand than she remembered, Odeon was still imposing.

And yet, she thought, it looked so comically out of place on the sleepy little street.

There was no use putting it off any longer, she realized: She had to go inside. Looking down through the forecourt, she saw that the tall bronze doors that led into Odeon's massive lobby were wide open, ready for her to enter.

She walked up to them. "Anyone here?" she said, poking her head inside.

A wind whipped up through the forecourt delivering a pile of paper and debris to her feet and she turned around to look. Leaves skittered along the fading squares of terrazzo as Karen hugged herself against the cold. The wind howled through the forecourt like air through some gigantic reed, producing an eerie whistling sound.

"Mr. MacGruder?" she cried, turning once again to stare into the enormous, darkened lobby.

I'm actually *here*.

Karen thought of all those years in therapy and her insistence that she would never set foot inside of Odeon again.

Karen made the first move, her foot sliding confidently into a lush pile of chenille carpet.

I'm inside. One more move and I've done it. I've faced it.

When she was completely inside the theatre, Karen felt a curious exhilaration. She was proud of herself for having done something that others swore to her she could not.

"Mr. MacGruder!" she called once more, wondering where he was. She knew he was in the theatre, because she had noticed his signature blue Cadillac parked in the alley alongside Odeon. Like the theatre, the car had become a relic, and Karen remembered how excited they got as kids when they saw it coming down Main Street; the big car meant a show would soon be starting. Jack MacGruder's dedication to Odeon was legendary. He and his theatre had become inseparable entities, like two members of an eccentric couple.

Karen walked the length of lobby, stopping at a familiar set of red velvet drapes. How well she remembered them, for they led into Odeon's basement.

Karen pulled them back, revealing a circular stairway, and she looked down the carpeted steps that spiraled away into darkness, thinking of that night—the night she had aborted her baby. Turning and twisting into the bowels of Odeon, the stairway signified everything to her now.

I have to go down there! I have to face it!

Karen took the first hesitant step, and there rose up inside of her an almost irresistible impulse to flee, but she knew she had to keep going. Emboldened with every step, she still heard Nell's warning. It mumbled in her head like the buzz of a trapped, persistent bee: *Don't go back. You can never go back. They hate you there!*

Now she stood in the foyer opposite the rest rooms, her foot pressing against the same carpet of seventeen years ago, and she remembered. The same, thickly sweet odor of disinfectant drifted through the air, and when she looked around the room, she saw the same heavy antiques, hulking in the dusty corners like monsters.

A movie, she thought. It was only a movie that had sent her running to the foyer, and all this time she had wondered: How different would her life have been if she had stayed up in the balcony with Carl?

Don't worry. A man cannot get pregnant. Don't worry!

Karen stood looking at the mahogany door that led to the men's room. It was as imposing as before, its bulky lintel carved with a row of scowling gargoyles. Silent and judging above the mammoth doors, they were the same gargoyles that had witnessed her deed seventeen years ago.

I didn't mean to do it! she cried to herself, and for the countless time she felt a spasm of guilt.

Now she decided what she needed to do. Facing the room, she would cry out her grief and hope that her guilt, thus exorcised, would abandon her life forever.

And then I'll locate Carl Irvine!

If she was ever to face her past completely, Karen knew that she would have to know the fate of the boy with green eyes. No matter how long it took or how painful it might be, she would run the risk of his final rejection.

Karen, like all unrequited lovers, had invented scenarios for him, and by now she had invented Carl Irvine into a life much happier than her own: He loved someone wonderful and worked at a job that gave him pleasure. He had fathered children who were healthy and happy.

But where? she wondered. Where had Carl gone? What city? What country?

Moving toward the men's room, Karen knew it was love that pulled her forward—love for Carl and the baby she'd never known—and as she paused before the door she felt a strange exhilaration. Puzzled, she soon realized that the joy she felt came from testing the limits of her pain.

Yes, yes. I should have done this long ago.

Karen had grown weary of loneliness and guilt, and she had made the mistake of believing that because of what she had done she had no right to life or love. It was Nell who had taught her the destructive lies she lived by, the worst being that life offered up no second chances.

Now she reached out to open the great mahogany door; its large brass knob was icy to her touch. Turning it slowly, she heard the bolt working delicately within the fine old wood. The heavy door then swung open with an ease that surprised her.

Karen moved cautiously. Her heels clicked against the tile, reporting off the hard walls, and again the sound was familiar, filling her with anxiety.

Karen stopped at the row of gleaming white basins, where she suddenly felt hot and uncomfortable. The room was thick with a humid mist, which clung to her face and arms. Before her, the mirror had gathered steam, obscuring her reflection. Deciding to douse her face with water, she reached to turn on the tap.

The faucet—the sculpted head of a pensive griffin—was familiar to her, yet she saw the years of corrosion in its detailed carving. When she touched it, she felt suddenly afraid, and she retracted her hand.

Of course, she realized, this was where she had stood after the attack, trying to cleanse away her shame and guilt.

Slowly, Karen turned away from the basin, taking in the whole room, which spoke to her of the past and regret.

Regret. Such a useless and stupid emotion.

Why hadn't she gone back to him? she wondered. Why hadn't she gone back to Carl in the balcony? Why hadn't she told him that she'd been attacked?

God, he loved me. He would have understood.

Karen moved toward the row of stalls, stopping when she noticed that the door of the last stall was shut, as if it were in use.

But there's no one here, she thought, the fear returning, so that the huge rest room, with its countless squares of tile, seemed as ominous as it had that awful day she was attacked.

"Is there someone here?"

Her voice slammed against the tile walls, returning as a rapid volley of taunting echoes.

No, there can't be anyone. *I won't* be afraid. That's why I came back to Wallenberg in the first place, to *stop* being afraid.

When she stepped closer to the stall, she heard a sound, which halted her, as if her fear had suddenly rooted her to the tile.

No, I'm not afraid, I'm not afraid!

Just as she stepped, she heard the sound again.

This time, she knew it was a voice.

A young girl's voice.

—Mommy! Oh, Mommy, help me!

Karen felt her stomach churn, but she stifled an impulse to cry out; instead, she stood there listening to the voice.

—the rats, Mommy! the rats!

It's hallucination again.

This isn't really happening.

It *can't* be!

Only the stall door stood between herself and her sanity, and she stared at it, crying out defiantly. "There is no one here!"

—the rats, Mommy! They killed him . . . they killed him, Mommy!

Karen moved all the way up to the stall door, as if she might suddenly press forward and break it down. Once and for all, she would find the horror that waited on the other side.

—Mommy!

"No! No! No!"

Karen turned and ran, just as she knew she should have done those seventeen years ago. And as she ran, she heard the awful words—*Mommy, Mommy, Mommy*—which still shrieked from the stall behind her.

When she reached the foyer outside, the child's voice had grown fainter, but Karen kept on running, knocking over a standing wrought-iron ashtray as she dashed for the stairway that would lead her back upstairs.

The lobby seemed brighter than before, as if additional lights had been turned on.

"Mr. MacGruder!" she cried, but the enormous lobby swallowed up her voice.

Now she heard a sound coming from the auditorium, revealed to her by one of the massive aisle doors, which was flung open wide. Beyond the downward rake of seats, she caught a glimpse of the bloodred curtains that masked Odeon's face.

Suddenly, she heard sound, as yet indistinguishable, as it crackled full blast out of Odeon's speakers.

Could there possibly be a movie starting? she wondered, and she moved swiftly to the door, entering the massive auditorium. It seemed cavernous without people to fill the thousands of plush red seats, and it occurred to her that she'd never been all alone in the huge auditorium before.

Karen moved warily down the aisle. "Is there anybody here?" she cried. Spots of gentle rosy light from fixtures alongside the seats guided her way.

When she was halfway down the aisle, Karen turned and looked toward the projection room. Shielding her eyes against the glare, she tried to see if someone was inside the booth, but it appeared empty.

She thought of Roy MacGruder and what she had learned about his death the night before, and it filled her with dread.

Why was there suddenly so much death involving the old theatre?

Something snapped, startling Karen so that she turned abruptly and faced the drapes. She watched as they parted gracefully across a square of white projected light.

She spun around and looked again at the portholes, where a column of light poured forth.

My God, they're showing a movie!

"Who's up there?" she cried, but her voice was suddenly drowned out by the sound that blasted forth from the speakers, and she turned back to the screen.

Karen tried to make sense of what she saw. As yet, it was only movement—random bits of steely light that would not lock into form. She saw something that looked like a man, but she couldn't make out a face. It was only a vague form—light upon light, colorful lines that wavered in a kind of dance across other colorful lines.

But this time the sound was clearer, so that she could make out bits of muffled dialogue.

—you don't have the nerve!

—go to hell.

Karen saw a vague shape projected upon Odeon's screen. She saw it was two young men, and it was they who spoke the dialogue that now blasted throughout the theatre.

—all you do is talk, Paul. If you want to have sex with a girl, you just gotta decide to do it.

—she's not that way.

—the hell she isn't!

Karen kept her eyes on the screen, where the image grew steadily clearer. Just as she thought, the two boys were Carl and Paul, looking the way they had the day they all went to the movies together—the day she was raped.

"What is this?" Karen screamed, and then she saw that Carl and Paul were walking down into the foyer outside Odeon's rest room.

"No! This can't be happening!" she cried, and she watched in terrified disbelief as her two old friends moved about on the huge screen, as if they were appearing in some ludicrously extravagant home movie.

—if you don't fuck her, I will.

—do it and you die, Carl.

Karen reacted to the utterance of Carl's name—the final confirmation.

But it can't be! It can't!

Another hallucination?

Charging down the aisle, she watched as her two old friends loomed impossibly large above her, their faces marred by bits of film grain.

"Stop this!" she screamed. "You can't be there!"

–Karen's just a prick-tease, Carl. Don't you understand?

"Stop it!"

Suddenly, the image shifted, as if the film were spliced, and one image slammed rudely into another. Karen recognized the white tiles of the rest room below.

Now there was another image up on Odeon's screen: her own.

It was the same day—the afternoon of the attack—and it was just as she remembered it. Karen watched the screen as a hand grabbed her and dragged her into the men's room stall.

How could this be? How?

And now, after all these years, Karen could see it from a different angle, from *outside* the action, and she strained to see who it was.

For the first time, she looked into the face of the man who had attacked her.

But it's me up there! Me! The way I was!

Even in her fear, it occurred to her that now she would be able to see who it was. At last, she would know who attacked her. Staring up at the awful image, Karen looked at the face of the man who ripped off her clothes.

"No!" she cried, recognizing Carl Irvine. "It wasn't Carl! It wasn't Carl! I know it wasn't!"

Frantic, Karen looked for a way to get to the stage, for a part of her believed she could run up and physically rip the image right off the screen.

Karen knew she had to stop this. The sight of her rape appalled her; the sounds of her screams were shrieking from the massive speakers like some horrible stereophonic memory.

But when she made a move to run for the stage, the image stopped, vanishing as fast as it had appeared. The light from the projector snapped off, and the sound slowed to an incoherent garble, quickly groaning into silence.

Karen looked up at the portholes.

Someone has to be up there!

Karen ran up the aisle, feeling her way in the dark. Even the aisle lights had snapped off. "Why are you doing this to me?" she screamed. "Why?"

But something slammed up against her and someone touched her.

"No," she screamed, lashing out with both fists, "don't do this to me! No! I won't let you!"

Two strong hands grabbed hers, resisting her efforts to fight until she had no more strength. She could feel the heat of him now; he was pulling her up against him.

Oh my God, don't hurt me!

After a moment he loosened his grip, and she could tell that he wasn't going to harm her. The auditorium filled slowly with light, so that Karen could see his face. She knew immediately who it was.

He spoke. "I know it wasn't Carl who attacked you, Karen."

Karen looked into his eyes. "Paul? Is it you?"

"Yes," he said. "My God, Karen, are you all right?"

"I don't know," she said. It occurred to her suddenly that this—her latest hallucination—might have had a witness. "Did you see it? Did you see what was up on the screen?"

Paul Chesney nodded and Karen caught his look of fear in the rise of light. She could see the beads of sweat along his forehead, further proof that the incident had frightened him as much as her.

"How do you know it wasn't Carl?" she asked him.

"Because I saw someone. That day it happened, I saw someone else coming downstairs into the rest rooms."

• Fourteen •

IN THE BARN behind Sheriff Bradley's house, the whole world had stopped. Everything was suspended in the moment that preceded miracle.

"Tie it tighter, Amy, tighter!" the old doctor cried. He was down on his knees now, firing out orders to Amy, who was tying a rope to the two hooves that protruded from Dandelion's vagina.

"You can do it, Amy. That's it!" Dr. Ohfers said.

The birth, a breech, was difficult—the hooves were coming first. The new life had wedged far up inside the birth canal. Amy and Dr. Ohfers would have to pull it through with the rope, thereby completing the process left in limbo by nature.

Dr. Ohfers studied the knot Amy had tied, then tugged it a couple times to test its strength. "Good, Amy. Good," he said. His suit jacket lay discarded beside the heifer, and his shirt sleeves were rolled to the elbow, and while he was ready to take over at any moment, he wanted to guide Amy through the whole process.

Neither of them noticed Sheriff Bradley, who had pulled in just a few minutes before. Noticing the doctor's car, Bradley had known something was going on with the heifer and he'd come into the barn, where he now stood quietly in back, watching as his daughter and the old veterinarian struggled to bring a new life into the world. The sheriff had never felt so proud in his life.

Amy wrapped a loop of rope around the hooves, which had slipped out another inch or two from the cow's uterus.

"Concentrate!" Dr. Ohfers yelled, and the girl pulled harder, so that a few more inches of the calf's feeble legs were revealed. "It's coming!" she cried to the doctor. "It's coming!"

A thrill went through Bradley, who was so concerned he might interrupt them he was afraid to breathe.

"Reach inside," Dr. Ohfers ordered.

Amy looked at him, hesitating before she pressed her hands through the vaginal opening, which was soaking wet. Grabbing the spindly legs, she tried to pull them through. "They won't move."

"The hell they won't!" cried the doctor, and the old man took the rope in both hands, settling back on his haunches and pulling with all his strength.

Now they both pulled with all their strength, harder and harder, until with one final effort, the calf washed out in a spew of black fluid.

Scrambling over to it with a towel, Amy wiped it free, then knelt before the motionless animal with Dr. Ohfers. They waited for a stir of life.

"Please!" Amy prayed aloud. "Please!"

Just as the sheriff walked up and placed a reassuring hand on Amy's shoulder, the girl saw the first sign of life: A hoof jerked free of the sticky torso, trembling in the air.

"It's alive!" the girl whispered, and she began to cry, burying her face against the sheriff's thick chest.

An hour later Bradley sat at the kitchen table. The heater had gone out, leaving the old ranch house so cold that Bradley wore his heavy peacoat. Two electric space heaters glowed from opposite sides of the cluttered kitchen.

"You don't suppose it's going to snow, do you, Daddy?" Amy asked. Showered and fresh, she pulled a casserole from the oven and ladled up a portion for her father's dinner.

"Course not," the sheriff said, taking another swig of his Budweiser.

But looking out the window, he wasn't sure at all. He had lived in Wallenberg all of his life, and he had never seen anything like this.

Snow in August? Impossible.

After setting his plate in front of him, Amy walked to the window, where she stared out toward the barn.

Bradley saw that she was concerned. "Dr. Ohfers said they'll be fine," he said, stabbing at the mound of casserole with a fork. It occurred to him he hadn't eaten all day, and he was ravenous. "Aren't you going to eat, honey?"

"No," she said. "I'm not hungry."

Walking back to the table, Amy sat opposite him. Bradley noticed that the look of joy he had seen in Amy's eyes while she birthed the calf was already gone.

"How do you feel, baby?"

"Tired."

"Not sleeping?"

"No."

He lay down his fork and wiped his mouth, cracking open another Budweiser, which he used to quench what seemed a sudden and desperate thirst. "I wish you'd talk to me about it, honey."

Amy looked at him. "Nightmares, is all. Every night, there are nightmares. Terrible ones, Daddy."

"I know," he said. "I hear you sometimes. You cry out things in the night, baby."

"What things?"

Bradley hesitated. All this time he had wanted to talk about it, but now, given the chance, he felt a strange shyness. He ran a finger down the folded lip of metal at the edge of his beer can, then shrugged and spoke. "You cry out the theatre's name, honey. You cry out the name *Odeon*."

Amy stared into a glass of Diet Coke. Nervously, she fingered the top of the liquid, flicking an ice cube so that it pinged against the side of the glass. She looked up at the sheriff. "I see this thing," she said. "Every night I see this thing. It's like . . ."

"What, honey?"

"A monster, Daddy."

For a long time he just looked at her, a part of him wanting to reassure her that everything would be fine. But somehow he couldn't, and he figured it was because he had too many unanswered questions of his own.

"Nightmares, honey. You said so yourself."

"No, Daddy, no! It's . . . it's like it's real! It comes to the side of my bed!"

"What?"

"This monster comes to the side of my bed and stands there in the dark, looking at me!"

"Amy!"

"It does!" she cried, pressing her hands to her face. "And Daddy, sometimes it *sings* to me. Like this weird lullaby."

Bradley felt his hunger vanish. Pushing aside his plate, he took Amy by the hands. "I went to the Burnsides' today."

"Daddy, you promised! You promised you wouldn't!"

"He's not after you, baby! He's just a poor retarded kid, that's all!"

"He wants to kill me!" Amy shouted, pulling away from him.

The sheriff was startled by her sudden emotion, but he sensed that the best thing to do was to leave her alone. In the silence that followed, he watched as she sat and trembled, and his inability to comfort her made him feel stupid and inadequate; more than ever, he wished his wife were here. He knew how much Amy needed a mother.

After several minutes had gone by, he spoke. "There ain't no way that Burnside kid's coming after you. Ain't no way."

Reaching out, Amy touched him and smiled. "I'm sorry," she said.

While her touch soothed him, the sheriff still worried. He worried because, at some level, he couldn't shake the feeling that his daughter was right. Crazy as it seemed, he had the feeling that Billy Burnside *was* going to come for her.

And it scared the hell out of him.

• Fifteen •

It was as if he had stepped from some vivid dream of a distant past. When she opened her eyes and saw him, he seemed no more real than he had upon Odeon's screen.

"How are you feeling?" he asked, and his voice—smooth and deep—was comforting.

"Better," she said.

Karen sat up on the bed in her hotel room, squinting and adjusting her eyes, as if to accustom herself to the light. But in fact it was because she could not yet believe that Paul Chesney was with her.

"My God, Paul, how long has it been since we've seen each other?"

"A long time."

"You still live here?"

"No. In fact, I live near you. Silverlake."

"Why didn't you ever call?"

"I didn't know we were neighbors until yesterday."

"*Yesterday?* Paul, did you follow me here?"

"Yes."

"Why?"

Paul sat down gently upon the bed. He took her hand and laughed. "I think we'd better have a long talk, don't you?"

After he told the whole story, Karen sat in silence. She didn't know whether to feel relieved or more uneasy.

"Something very odd is happening," she said finally, then proceeded to tell him what had happened to her with the same movie, *Night of the Blood Beast*.

Finished, she looked at him, long and hard. "You remember, of course, what happened that day . . . the day we saw that movie . . ."

Paul nodded, for indeed he would never forget it, not the longest day he lived. Even now, he couldn't picture in perfect detail how he and Carl Irvine had competed for Karen's attention.

"I was so jealous," Paul said, blushing, and it amused him that something that happened so long ago could still affect him that way. "I had a terrible crush on you," he added, his tone, even now, heavy with confession.

"I guess I knew," Karen said, "but I was so in love with Carl." She remembered the horrible images up on Odeon's screen. "You saw them too, didn't you, Paul? You saw what I saw on the screen?"

He nodded.

"It isn't possible," she said. "I was certain it was another hallucination, but if you saw it too . . ."

Paul stood up. "There must be a logical explanation. I'm going to find Jack MacGruder. Maybe *he* knows something . . ."

Karen got up from the bed and walked to the heater, for it seemed that the room was growing colder with each passing moment. Turning up the radiator, she stood before it with her hands outstretched, the pipes clanging noisily in the bowels of the hotel.

"Paul?"

"Yes?"

"It wasn't Carl who attacked me. I don't know how or why his image was up there on the screen, but it's a lie. It *wasn't* Carl." She turned to him. "Just before I fainted, you said you saw someone else coming down into Odeon's rest room. Who did you see, Paul?"

"Jack MacGruder."

"Jack!" she cried, surprised, for she had never even considered Jack before. When she thought of Jack MacGruder, she always pictured a kind, if eccentric, man whose whole world revolved around a movie theatre. With his natty appearance and love of elegance, he seemed to her incapable of violence. "Are you sure? I mean, his office was down in the same foyer . . . couldn't he have been headed *there*?"

He answered quickly. "I suppose," he said, "except that he was coming down about the same time you . . . cried for help."

Karen stared at him incredulously. "My God, Paul, you heard me?"

Paul felt his stomach contract; this was the confrontation he had been dreading for seventeen years.

"It isn't like it sounds, Karen. I heard your cries, then I saw Jack. I thought he would help you. I ran up the stairs and left him there. For some reason, I was scared."

"My God," she said, her voice surprisingly steady, "do you have any idea what I've been through because of that day? If you had come in, it might not have happened."

"There hasn't been a day I haven't thought about it, Karen . . ."

"Why were you there in the first place?"

"I knew that you and Carl had quarreled . . . I wanted the two of you to break up . . . I was so jealous, Karen, I just wasn't thinking straight. When I saw you get up and stomp out of the balcony, I followed you . . . Later, when I heard you were pregnant, I just assumed it was Carl's baby. That's why I didn't visit you in the hospital after the abortion. I was still so jealous, Karen . . . I couldn't think straight. And all this time . . . I felt such terrible guilt . . ."

Karen was quiet for a long time, but suddenly the rage took hold of her, and she turned to Paul and screamed for him to leave her alone.

When he had left the room, Karen regretted her outburst. It was as if she had fired at him with a gun she did not know was loaded.

Turning to the window and pulling back the curtain, Karen stared down at Odeon.

The theatre was dark now, as quiet as the night she had arrived. Another pile of paper and debris fluttered in a swarm up the old terrazzo, rattling ominously in the night.

None of this can be happening. It just isn't possible.

And besides, she thought, the theatre was closed now. Nobody would go there anymore.

Why, nobody in his right mind would go into Odeon now.

Billy Burnside *wasn't* in his right mind.

His eyes snapped open from a deep and unbidden sleep, and he did not recognize where he was.

Reaching around behind him, he poked at his back. It felt stiff beneath the yellow rain slicker, like it was strained and sore. Groggy, he moved his head, so that it lobbed about like that of a rag doll. He realized that he couldn't see properly; the lights before him were fuzzy and indistinct. They were blurred and they spun about, reminding him of the video games he played.

Where am I? How did I get here?

The last thing he remembered was seeing the sheriff in the backyard. Frightened, he had taken off for town, and that's the last thing Billy Burnside remembered.

He felt about until he found his glasses, which had fallen into his lap. He figured they must have slipped off his nose while he slept.

When he got them up to his nose, he saw that they were broken: The Band-Aid that held them in place had come loose, dangling along the side. He worked the soiled plastic strip with his thumb until it edged up along the frame and curled into place, securing the glasses. Convinced they were okay, he slid them on.

With the glasses back on, Billy Burnside recognized where he was. It made him happy, and he grinned.

Glancing up excitedly, he looked at the ornate poster frames, but he was disappointed.

Where are the pictures?

The poster frames were all empty, and it puzzled him. There were *always* pictures. He liked the pictures in the ad frames, because they let him know what movie he was going to see. He especially liked the posters that didn't have many words. If there was lots of action in the photographs, Billy believed, it meant the movie was going to be better.

Befuddled, he sat on the terrazzo, squinting and wrinkling his nose, like some rat awakened from sleep.

He had come to the show, but now there was *no* show.

What's going on?

Then he remembered. He had sat down to wait a long time ago, propping his back against the bronze doors. There he intended to wait until the box office opened.

Furious, Billy stood up, and he started jumping up and down.

"When you gonna open up?" he yelled, and he turned and ran to the row of doors behind him, where he pounded on the etched leaded glass with his nose pressed flat against it.

Inside, he saw that the lobby was dark and empty, which made him all the angrier.

"If you don't open up this door, I'm gonna be awful mad at you!"

His reflection, which loomed suddenly before him in the glass, startled him, and he jumped back.

Billy hated how ugly he was, and he usually avoided looking at himself in the mirror, but now he stared at the reflection with a numbed fascination, studying the rotten teeth and discolored tongue. The hair was a ghastly tangle; bits of it poked up in thatches that were coated with old grease. He saw the countless pimples, their angry centers swelled and ready to burst.

Disgusted, he looked away, but his eyes darted to his hands, which also disgusted him. The bony, misshapen fingers remained a filthy black, the result of having spent the afternoon clawing at the dirt.

My paper sack!

Frantic, he turned to the terrazzo, looking for his paper sack. He knew he'd had it with him before he had gone to sleep.

Could I have left it somewhere? But Billy knew how careful he was with it. Someone must have taken it while I was asleep.

Growing more upset, he made grunting sounds, slapping at his sides while turning in a constant circle; his heart raced crazily beneath the yellow rain slicker.

Finally, he spotted the paper sack. It was in the middle of a pile of trash, beneath one of the empty poster frames.

As Billy spotted it, a new rise of cold wind blasted through the forecourt, so that the stiff paper sides of the sack began to rattle, and the sack started to blow away.

But the weight inside the sack acted as an anchor, keeping the sack secure to the ground. Billy ran to it and snatched it up, holding it possessively to his chest for a long time.

He turned angrily to Odeon.

"It's way past six forty-five! You're late with the show!"

He saw the sign on the box office, and he moved up to it, squinting at the letters he could not make into words:

CLOSED UNTIL FURTHER NOTICE.

"Where are you! It's time to sell the tickets!"

Billy considered the empty forecourt, which had been bugging him for a long time: There hadn't been any pictures in the poster frames for several days; worse, there hadn't been any people coming to see the show.

A sound startled him—something electrical. He looked both ways, then upward, where light flashed beneath the marquee. Billy shaded his eyes as a thousand bulbs snapped into life, illuminating the scrollwork design that looped along the marquee soffit.

"It's about time!" he cried, his face breaking into a huge and self-satisfied grin.

I did it! I made it open!

Billy looked down the terrazzo, which suddenly sparkled as it never had before. All around him he could hear the buzz of neon, and he watched as it crackled into life—tube after brilliant tube.

Now he watched as the bronze doors—full and wide—opened up all by themselves.

Confused, he turned to the box office, which was still empty. There was no one to sell him his ticket.

He bounded forward toward the entrance, then stopped; he was all at once afraid he would get in trouble, for he knew he shouldn't go inside Odeon without a ticket.

If Jack MacGruder finds me, he'll throw me out for sure.

Billy stood, considering his dilemma. *Could I just lay my money down? Wouldn't that be the same as buying a ticket?*

But now his thoughts were interrupted by the sudden whir of machinery—delicate and precise—and the sound of it lured him forward to the box office.

There he saw that the ticket machine was moving through its cycle, finally spitting out a bright orange ticket, which slid down a shiny metal chute and landed upon the box office sill.

Should I take it?

Billy grabbed it quickly, after first looking cautiously in all directions. It was stupid to think anybody would catch him, he knew, for there weren't any people around.

Billy scuttled up to the bronze doors, where he faced yet another dilemma. He had his ticket, but now there was no one to take it from him. Usually Jack MacGruder would tear it in two and drop it in the receptacle, but the old man was nowhere to be seen; the huge forecourt still hummed with an emptiness that seemed ghostly.

Could Mr. MacGruder be setting some kind of a trap? the confused boy wondered. *Or maybe the sheriff?*

Angered by such thoughts, Billy tossed his ticket into the receptacle and walked into Odeon.

If I got my ticket, then I can go into the theatre!

The great bronze doors slammed shut behind him. "Hey!" he cried, turning, banging his fists on the heavy glass. "What's going on?"

He was about to bang his fists again when he smelled something good—it was popcorn, he realized, fresh and buttery.

Billy turned to the refreshment stand, whose chrome arabesques had never shone brighter.

Place has gotta be open. And just for me!

On the gleaming glass countertop to the refreshment stand sat a box of popcorn—the large size, Billy's choice—and he could tell by the smell that it was drenched in butter; beside it, a king-sized Coke and a jumbo box of JuJubes, his favorite movie candy.

Billy ran to the snack bar, snatching up the treats greedily.

Maybe I've won some kind of a prize, he thought, and worked to arrange it all around his paper sack. When it was all securely cradled against him, he walked to the aisle door, where he peeked inside, noticing that the auditorium seemed unusually dark.

When he saw it was completely empty, he felt spooked again.

The boy moved cautiously down the aisle, careful not to drop any of his treats or the paper sack, and as he got up closer to the curtain, he could see the bits of colored light that played across the sequined fabric.

But the tiny bits of light, which danced across the curtain, were the only illumination in all of Odeon, he realized, which was why he could barely see to work his way over to a seat in the middle of the row.

Taking a seat, he organized his treats in his lap, feeling about the floor so that he could set the big cup of Coke beside his feet.

Content, Billy tossed a handful of popcorn in his mouth, enough to make his cheeks bulge, and he slurped at his Coke. Tossing in a couple of JuJubes, he sloshed it all together in his mouth, swallowing it like some great sweet river.

A few minutes later the lights along the curtains began to dim, draining away slowly until the whole auditorium had sunk into blackness.

Billy waited eagerly for the curtains to part, but nothing happened. Annoyed, he turned around and looked up at the portholes, but no projector light was shining through.

"Where's the show?" Billy yelled, turning back around to the screen. He squinted, wishing he could see something. In the dim, knifelike light that leaked through the auditorium, he could tell that the curtains still hadn't moved.

Once he'd been at Odeon when the curtains hadn't worked. When all attempts to get them open had failed, Roy stomped down from the projection room and worked the curtains manually with two huge ropes at the side of the screen.

Angered, Billy made a move to stand, but right away he found that he couldn't.

"Hey!" he cried, struggling to get up, but he was stuck in his seat, immobile; it felt like something huge and heavy had sat on his lap, pressing him there with its force.

All at once he felt a jolt of pain—deep and cutting, as though he'd been stabbed.

"Ouch!" he screamed, and the bucket of popcorn tumbled from the armrest. Kernels scattered across the concrete floor.

The pain hit him again; two quick jabs that felt more intense, pulsing throughout his entire body.

"Help me!"

The pain quickly gathered force, until it became unbearable, matching the wild, panicked beating of his heart. It felt like his body had been packed full of hot coals, and Billy decided that his blood must be on fire.

He tried to cry out again, but now he couldn't—his tongue felt thick—*it was too thick to move*.

Billy clawed at the air with both arms, knocking the cup of Coke to the floor, where it poured across his sneakers, seeping way down inside and bathing his toes. In his agony Billy imagined sound—the sizzle of icy liquid as it touched white-hot flesh.

He tried to scream again, but now the tongue was so large it would not move at all. It lay in his mouth like something huge and dead.

Billy felt himself begin to bloat. It was that feeling he'd had when drinking too much water, only a thousand times worse—as though gallons of liquid had been poured down his throat. A tremendous pressure now gathered beneath his flesh, and he could feel himself expanding.

What's happening? What's happening?

Billy stared at his right arm, which moved in a series of strange, spasmodic jerks. Suddenly, he watched in horror as the flesh began to move—a bizarre kind of undulation.

Billy pulled frantically at the rain slicker, exposing the full wrist. Horrified, he watched as a jagged line formed along his arm—a deep and bloody scratch.

Helplessly, he watched it grow larger, deeper, until one layer of skin pulled away from another, forming a crevasse.

No! What's happening to me! No!

The lips of torn flesh now spewed out blood and sinew, exposing cords of red-slicked muscle. Released from the ruined arm, they dangled and twisted, glowing within the dim light of Odeon.

Unable to scream, Billy sat in horrified silence. The only sound now was that of the bones in his arms as they began to shatter. They snapped with the puny insignificance of dry and brittle sticks. Folds of flesh opened up, the strips of skin falling away like husks that were ripped from corn.

In the place of his arm came a new arm—a stronger, fresher limb. Tight and muscular, it flexed itself, as if beyond the boy's control, and he watched as fingers that were not his began to curl, as though testing a fist.

Billy winced with a new and sudden assault of pain, and soon he felt the same awful burning sensation in his left arm.

His right leg.

His left.

It gripped his chest.

Then his back.

His face.

Flesh pulled from flesh again as new limbs formed, clawing their way out from the center of blood and pulp.

The relentless force continued—the steady emergence of another body: a body more perfect and strong and beautiful than Billy's own.

Watching in horrified silence as long as he could, Billy soon felt all consciousness drift away.

Moments later the new body fought to survive, gradually struggling outward from its filthy cocoon—the yellow rain slicker—until finally he loomed up full: a handsome young man, naked, his arms glowing with sweat.

When he had tossed aside all that remained of Billy Burnside's clothes, the Kid reached up and grabbed an armrest, pulling his perfect body up into a half-crouch.

He touched himself, gently, an inquisitive exploration of what he had become, and a smile of delight formed at the edges of his lips as he ran strong arms along his nakedness, feeling the damp heat of golden skin still slick with Billy's blood.

And his new eyes opened.

Sheriff Bradley was fifteen minutes into the Letterman show when the telephone rang.

"Yeah?"

Deputy Travers sounded upset. "Better get down here, Leo."

"Ah, Christ, Ron, I'm just getting settled. What's going on?"

"Found a kid. Seventeen or so. He was running out of the alley by the movie theatre."

"So?"

Travers was quiet so long Bradley started wondering if the line had gone dead. Finally, the deputy spoke. "Leo, he was stark naked."

Bradley sighed wearily. "Look, it's probably one of the college boys . . . one of those hazing pranks. Tell the sonofabitch to get lost or we'll throw his naked ass in jail."

"But that's not all, Leo."

"What do you mean?"

"Leo, he's covered with blood."

• Sixteen •

THE KID WAS UNUSUALLY HANDSOME, and that was the first thing
that Bradley found odd.

He had expected a real screwball. After all, the kind of kid that
would run around naked at midnight with blood streaked across
his body would *have* to be a screwball, Bradley thought, and he
liked to think he'd become pretty good at predicting such things.
In any event, he certainly wasn't expecting the blond, tanned Kid
who stared at him with blue eyes set in a perfect face. Moving up
to him, Bradley decided the Kid would be more at home on a
surfboard in southern California than the streets of Wallenberg.
The Kid sat in a holding cell, a six-by-eight cubicle with a tiny
cot, toilet bowl, and sink.

Bradley could tell the Kid was nervous, which was always a
good sign. Real criminals weren't that nervous, he'd learned. The
Kid sat hunched forward, his hands folded together and held tight
between his thighs. He was dressed in jail-issue grey slacks and
shirt.

Bradley was surprised that there wasn't any blood on the Kid,
for after hearing Deputy Travers' description, he'd expected the
cell to look like the setting of an axe murder.

"Travers!" he shouted, summoning his deputy, who came
bounding into the room.

"Yes, sir!"

"Where's all this blood you were yappin' about?"

Travers breathed in sharply, so that his barrel chest swelled
beneath his uniform shirt. "Made him shower," he said.

Bradley couldn't believe what he'd heard. "What the hell did you do that for? I mean, Christ, Ron, I would like to have seen the evidence, you know!"

Travers considered this for a moment, then shrugged. "Searched him for drugs, too," he said. "At least there weren't none."

"Good job!" Bradley snapped, then turned to the Kid. "Deputy here says you were covered with blood, fella."

The Kid looked away. "Yeah, I was."

"Look at me when I talk to you, damn it!"

The Kid startled, then swung his head to meet Bradley's eyes. "Yes, sir."

Bradley decided they were the bluest eyes he had ever seen. "Wanna explain yourself?"

"I'm really embarrassed, sir."

"I'd say you oughtta be." Bradley moved up closer. "Look, I'm not famous for tolerating bullshit, so you'd better give it to me straight, okay?"

The Kid nodded. "I go to college over in Haleyville. It was this dumb prank, see. These guys . . . well, I'm new and all, and they . . . well, they dared me to do stuff." He swallowed hard. "Stupid stuff, sir. They dared me to take my clothes off, smear myself with this . . . uh"—his face blushed—"chicken's blood, sir. And well, they dared me to run down Main Street that way, and, well . . ."

When the Kid finished, Bradley stood silent, a trick he always pulled after a suspect had rattled off an alibi. He'd discovered that a liar, feeling compelled to embellish, usually couldn't keep his mouth shut during Bradley's silence.

But the Kid kept quiet, passing the little test, and Bradley continued his interrogation.

"Where'd these guys go?"

"That's the pisser, man. They were supposed to wait for me there . . . you see, their car was right by that big old theatre, and . . . well, I feel pretty stupid, sir, because when I got to where the car was supposed to be, they'd taken off . . . just left me."

"Left you buck naked, huh?"

The Kid shrugged his shoulders, which were wide and well built beneath the ill-fitting jail-issue shirt. "Embarrassed? I'll tell you, sir, I was just trying to get to a phone booth when the deputy found me."

Bradley found it hard not to laugh. He knew it wasn't the first time a college prank had got him up in the middle of the night, and he did find it a little satisfying to see one of these arrogant college kids taken down a peg or two. "What's your name?"

The Kid paused.

"You have to think about it?"

"William, sir. William Burns," he said, and he smiled so that Bradley could see the row of perfect white teeth. "But I go by Bill, sir."

"Where are you from originally?"

"Haleyville, sir."

"How long you say you've been at the college?"

"Just got there, sir. Just moved into the dorm, in fact. I'm starting as a freshman in the fall."

"What's your major?"

"I'd like to be a veterinarian, sir."

Bradley smiled. "So's my daughter. Name's Amy Bradley. Know her?"

"Don't think so, sir."

Bradley turned to Travers. "Did you manage to print him?"

"Sure did, Leo."

He turned again to the Kid. "Are you aware you have broken the law?"

The Kid's face, as perfect as that of a model's, grew a deep scarlet. "I am, sir, and I probably caught myself one hell of a cold too. It's freezing out there, man. I thought it was supposed to be summer."

"Anybody see you out there? See you naked, I mean. Other than the deputy?"

"Don't think so. Hope not anyway."

"Indecent exposure carries a fine."

The Kid shrugged.

"This is the first offense?"

The Kid laughed. "Hell, sir, I'm not a nudist, if that's what you mean."

"Think you've learned a lesson here?"

"You bet."

"What happens the next time they ask you to pull a prank like this?"

"I think I'll beat the crap out of them, sir."

"That sounds like a good idea. Need a ride back to the school?"

The Kid paused. "Well . . . sure."

• • •

When they reached the campus of Haleyville Community College, the Kid jumped out of the patrol car, feigned gratitude for the ride, then watched as Bradley turned the car around and started back toward Wallenberg.

The Kid breathed a sigh of relief. He hadn't expected the offer of a ride back to the college, and he hadn't been able to think fast enough to get out of it. He wished now that he'd told the sheriff he had a friend that would pick him up, but now he decided that things had probably worked out for the better. It probably wasn't a good idea to tell too many lies, he figured, as the more you told, the more likely you were to get caught. The last thing he wanted to do was antagonize the sheriff, who he decided was probably a lot smarter than he looked.

Worse, the sheriff had kept talking about his daughter, Amy, how she went to the same college, and he'd asked the Kid a lot of questions about teachers there and other things that a real student would know. The Kid had had to fake all the answers, and he wasn't sure that the sheriff wasn't just testing him anyway. He worried that maybe he'd made a gaffe or two and had given himself away.

But now he was frustrated. Here he was fifteen miles from Odeon, and he was conspicuous in his jail-issue clothes. He'd told Bradley that he had plenty of clothes back at the dorm, but the truth was, he didn't even know where the dormitory was.

The Kid walked along the campus lawn, where the air, in contrast to Wallenberg, was heavy with summer heat. Up ahead was a clock, and he saw that it was almost two-thirty, the time everybody would start coming back from the local pubs and bars. The thing to do, he figured, was look for someone crazy enough to be up at such an hour, and if he was *real* lucky, the person would be wearing clothes that were close to his size.

It wasn't long until the Kid saw someone off in the distance, about a half mile away, up across a large hill and near a huge replica of the Liberty Bell.

Cornball stuff, he thought, and he tried to imagine the type of student who went to such a dumpy little college. He tried to picture the sheriff's daughter, and he figured she was squeaky-clean and dull, just like her father, who had bored the Kid with lame stories the whole ride from Wallenberg to Haleyville.

Gonna be tough, the Kid thought, but he did look forward to the girl. He was certain Amy was a virgin, and he liked virgins best.

He liked that feeling you had with them—sort of like you were bursting into their bodies and their minds forever, and no matter what happened, they just never ever forgot you.

"Colder'n a witch's tit, huh?" the Kid said to the young man who approached alone.

Christ, I'm in luck, the Kid thought, sizing up the other guy's clothes, for he had to be pretty close in size, and, hell, all he needed was something to get him back to Wallenberg without too much suspicion.

"Sure is," the young man said, stopping. He smiled at the Kid. "You go to school here?"

"Yup," said the Kid, and his face was boyish enough to muster up a smile that was both winning and manipulative. "But guess what?"

"What?"

"You're gonna laugh at me, man, but, shit . . . stupid thing, I'm locked out. Roommate won't be back until morning. Can you believe that? And I don't even have my wallet, so I can't call security. Stupid!"

The Kid hissed his displeasure, shrugging and shaking his head, starting away with a little wave that suggested he considered the whole thing his own problem and that he didn't need any help. He hadn't gone ten feet when the other young man called to him.

"Hey, you can use my phone if you want. I mean, if you need to call security and stuff."

The Kid turned to him. "That's really nice of you."

When they got to his place, the young man moved into the kitchen for a couple beers. The Kid hung back and checked out the apartment, which was a small studio with two single beds in the corner.

"Pretty small," the young man said, "but I'm lucky right now. My roommate flunked out, so I've got it to myself right now. By the way, name's Rick."

"Hello," the Kid said, and it occurred to him he still didn't have a name. He gave Rick the same one he'd given the sheriff. "Name's Bill."

Rick came back into the front room, where the Kid was leafing through a *Road and Track* magazine he'd found on the coffee table.

"Into cars?" Rick asked.

"Kinda."

Rick shrugged, then pointed to the telephone. "There's the phone."

"Huh?"

"You said you were gonna call security . . . You were locked out, remember?"

"Oh, yeah," the Kid said, then picked up the receiver. It occurred to him that he didn't have a number to dial and now Rick was looking at him strangely, like he was suddenly suspicious. The Kid punched out seven random numbers, and then, when Rick wasn't looking, he tapped the switch hook, disconnecting the line.

There was a long uncomfortable pause while the Kid decided what he should do.

Kill him? he wondered.

A good idea, but it was kind of risky to kill a kid right here in his dormitory room, he thought, and he didn't want to kill anybody if he didn't have to. Not that he cared at all, but he didn't think he should kill any more people than he actually had to, for it just upped his possibility of getting caught. Holding the receiver, he listened to the dial tone as he tried to figure out what to do.

Finally, Rick moved off toward the bathroom. "Excuse me," he said, "gotta take a piss."

As soon as Rick closed the bathroom door, the Kid slammed up the phone and ran to the closet, flinging it open and pawing through Rick's clothes. He found a suitable pair of jeans and a clean shirt.

Tucking them under his arm, the Kid started for the front door, hoping to get out before Rick came back, but he was too late.

"Hey!" Rick cried. "Where the hell you goin' with that stuff?"

But the Kid just kept on running. He ran and ran until Rick's cries had faded away behind him.

By the time he reached the highway, he had managed to slip out of the jail-issue clothes and into the new ones, which fit him better than he had hoped.

Now he was laughing. He wondered what the stupid jerk must have thought when he came out of the bathroom. Why would a guy come into his house in the middle of the night and steal a pair of pants and a shirt?

Fucker's lucky to be alive, the Kid thought, and then he started walking back toward Wallenberg, a solitary figure in the moonlight.

He was already planning the day ahead.

A busy one.

• Seventeen •

EMBARRASSED, KAREN WAITED a long time before knocking. When she finally heard the familiar voice on the other side, she found it difficult to speak.

"It's me," she said, then waited, listening to chains and locks as they came undone and bounced noisily against the heavy oak door. After a moment Paul's face appeared. He was smiling at her.

"How can you smile at me?" she asked. "I was so terrible to you last night."

"You had every right."

"Ruby's Cafe used to make a good cup of coffee," Karen said. "Would you like to check it out?"

Ruby's Cafe had not changed at all. Even the selections on the jukebox seemed the same, and you still made your choice from a remote chrome and red plastic coin-op at each of the linoleum-top tables. Karen flipped through the old songs, wondering how many times her fingers had pushed those same buttons to summon up the sad love ballads that she had always liked the best.

Odd, she thought, that a child could like a heartbreaking love song, even though the child had yet to be in love. What was it about that aching feeling of lost love that was so instinctive?

Ruby appeared and took their order, scratching it down on a pad while she stared at them over the top of her glasses. Karen wasn't certain if the skinny old woman recognized her, and she decided not to introduce herself, letting her sprint away with their simple order of two cups of coffee. Karen's memory of the cafe wasn't pleasant, and with a shudder she thought of her Friday nights there with Nell, who would mumble prayers over chicken fried steaks, filling the young girl's head with fears about sex and love.

"I didn't come here much," Paul said.

"You were lucky."

Karen toyed nervously with a package of Sweet 'n Low, tearing off the top and pouring the contents in an ashtray.

Paul reached out and touched her hand. "It must be so hard for you," he said.

Karen smiled. "I suppose it's hard for everybody." Ruby brought their coffee, slamming it down before them. When she was gone, Karen continued. "I'm sorry I said those things to you. I didn't give you much of a chance to explain."

"If I'd have known what was going on, Karen, then of course I would have come inside the rest room."

"I know," Karen said, stirring her coffee. She had lain awake until three o'clock, finally coming to the conclusion that Paul was incapable of hurting anyone.

After they shared more details of the lives they had lived since last seeing each other, Karen brought up the subject that most frightened both of them.

"That movie, Paul. *Night of the Blood Beast*. The thing I saw. The thing your son Kenny saw. What in the hell is going on? And why were those awful images up there on the screen?"

Paul opened a new package of cigarettes, crumpling the cellophane with a shrug. "It's more than coincidence," he said, then pointed his finger at her emphatically. "And you're *not* having another breakdown," he said. "You didn't imagine those things. You're all right."

His words affected her strongly, and it occurred to her that no one had ever said that to her before. While the doctors had always pretended an optimism, Karen could sense their basic mistrust of her.

"Tell me about your boy, Paul."

"He was fine . . . until a while ago."

"What exactly is wrong?"

"We don't really know. They call him schizo-affective."

"What's that?"

Paul laughed ruefully. "Kind of the schizophrenic Little League, I'm afraid."

"What did he do?"

"He acted out things . . . strange things. Still does. The doctors say that's a symptom of the disease. Kind of a ritualistic behavior, I guess. Anyway, he spoke in these voices, like he was playing characters."

"Anyone you recognized?"

"Not really. The one about the funeral was *really* bizarre."

"Funeral?"

"Yeah. Started out when we went to the Glendale Mall one night. Kenny saw this yellow rain slicker there. He really wanted it . . . became obsessed with it, really. I bought it for him and soon he wanted to wear it all the time. Anyway, this last time, he was acting out this funeral. I think it was an old man who had died of cancer. In his fantasy, my son acted out the grief part. He was playing the old man's son, I guess, carrying him off to an imaginary grave and everything. Weird part is that Kenny did cry out 'Wallenberg.' I figured he'd just heard me mention where I was from and the word had stuck in his mind. The last part was really strange. Kenny actually pretended to throw himself on the grave. He cried so hard he was sick."

Karen considered what he had said. "Maybe he was referring to *Mr*. Wallenberg," Karen said.

Paul put down his coffee cup so that it smacked loudly against the saucer. "What?"

"The funeral that Kenny acted out. Mr. Wallenberg died of cancer. Don't you remember all your town lore?"

Paul shook his head, interested. "Go on, Karen."

"Nell said there was quite a scandal. Mr. Wallenberg's wife died suspiciously and Mr. Wallenberg was never the same after. Died of cancer a couple years later."

"I knew that part," Paul said. "She died on Odeon's opening night. But what does that have to do with Kenny's spell? They didn't have a son, did they? Who was Kenny acting out?"

Karen shrugged, trying to call back the countless stories that Nell had told her about Wallenberg.

"Wait a minute!" she cried. "Maybe it was Forbes Carlton."

"Carlton? The architect who designed and built Odeon?"

"Sure."

"What makes you say that?"

"After Mrs. Wallenberg died, Henry Wallenberg treated Forbes Carlton like a son."

Paul shook his head, confused. "Lotta people say Forbes Carlton *murdered* Mrs. Wallenberg."

"Never proved it," Karen said. "Anyway, Forbes Carlton lived with Mr. Wallenberg until the old man died. I mean, he *must* have gone to the funeral. Perhaps it was Carlton who threw himself grief-stricken on the grave . . . just like Kenny acted out."

Paul considered it, shaking his head. "Whatever happened to Forbes Carlton?" he asked.

"Nobody really knew," Karen answered, finishing her coffee. "Mother said he just disappeared after Mr. Wallenberg died. Surprised everybody too, because they thought for sure he was just hanging around for the old man's money. He had no heirs and he'd left it all to the city anyway."

They were silent for several minutes, each considering the ramifications of what they had just said.

"Gives me the creeps," Karen finally said. Then she looked Paul in the eyes and asked the question he had dreaded. "Paul," she began, "do you have any idea what happened to Carl Irvine?"

Karen could tell by the look in his eyes that something was wrong.

"Paul!" she cried loudly, forgetting the crowd of chattering townsfolk that surrounded them in the tiny cafe. "What's wrong?"

Paul spoke quickly. "Carl had a terrible accident, Karen. He's crippled. I'm afraid there was also some brain damage."

Karen closed her eyes, and in that strange and muffled moment of shock she pictured the boy with green eyes—strong, handsome, posed so proudly beside his car.

Her voice was barely a whisper. "How?"

"The theatre," he answered. "It was shortly after you moved away. Carl was despondent. We *both* were upset when you left. One day he tried to kill himself, Karen . . . by jumping off the balcony . . ."

Karen opened her eyes, blinking away tears. "Odeon?"

"Yes," Paul said, and his deep voice trembled as he continued. "I was with him, Karen. It was after the last movie and I'd gone down to the rest room. When I came back up, he wasn't in the lobby. After I checked outside, I went back in, walked up into the balcony. I got there just as he was standing on the rail. He looked at me, just for a second, and then he jumped."

Karen saw how upset he was and she reached out and took his hand.

"He was so in love with you," Paul said. "I don't think he got over your letter."

Karen pulled her hand away. "What letter?" she cried. "I didn't send Carl a letter."

Paul stared at her. "But I saw it, Karen. He showed it to me several times."

"I didn't send him a letter, Paul. My God, *he* left *me*!"

But now she considered the most horrible possibility of all: It hadn't been real. After all of the pain she had been through, Carl might have loved her all along!

Her words tumbled out carelessly now. "He sent me a note, Paul. It said that he was ashamed of me . . . that he didn't love me anymore. My God, it's what led me to do the awful thing that I did . . . the abortion!"

"But Carl showed me *your* letter, Karen. It broke his heart. For God's sake, Karen . . . it was in his hand when he jumped!"

Now her whole body trembled. "My God," she said, "it was Nell."

"What?"

"Don't you see? It was my mother. Nell didn't want us together. It was Nell who wrote those letters . . . to each of us!"

"Oh, Jesus . . ."

"Where is he?" Karen demanded. "He's in town, isn't he?"

Paul nodded. "At the hotel. One floor above you. I was going to tell you today. I swear to you."

He reached out to comfort her, but she was already going through her purse, gathering up change to pay the bill.

Now he was *really* scared. When he saw her walking down the street with Paul Chesney, he knew that Odeon was going to go through with it.

"Damn you!" cried Carl, and he raised a fist and shook it toward the old theatre.

But why hadn't she found his note? He worried that he hadn't stuck it far enough under the door. That nosy old clerk probably found it and threw it away.

Carl moved about his room as quickly as he could, assembling the few things he would need. He had already decided that he couldn't let her find him, that he had to stay hidden as long as she was in town, and he had to decide what to do.

Convinced he had everything he needed, Carl reached for his radio, which he secured under his arm. Finally, he unfolded a small piece of paper and read over the note that he intended to leave for Karen: "Theetur Evill. Theetur wants too kil your babee!!"

He sat up, grimacing at the pain that the sudden movement caused along his back.

Too fast. Gotta watch it now.

Limping to the bureau, Carl opened the bottom drawer and reached far back inside, pulling forth an old file folder. From inside he pulled out a thatch of old yellowed newspaper articles.

Certain they were in order, he attached his note to Karen, then taped the edges of the file folder so that the contents wouldn't spill out.

Finished, he grabbed his things and left his room.

When they got to the desk, the clerk handed Karen a large manila envelope. Without even looking at the label, she asked if Carl was in.

"Just left," he said.

"Where did he go?"

"Didn't say. Carl never does."

Karen looked at Paul, then moved to a nearby chair. There she opened up the manila envelope, which she saw was from Dr. Matson.

She read the enclosed papers, all of them official-looking, then handed them to Paul.

"What is it?" he asked.

"Proof," she said. "My medical records. The ones I asked for. Proof that my baby is dead."

• Eighteen •

HE WAS ALREADY SCARED, for he'd never done anything quite so dangerous in his life.

But she loves me, Tyler Briggs thought to himself, his big hands gripping the leather-wrapped steering wheel to his father's black Corvette. She really *does* love me, and when you love someone, you'll do *any*thing for them.

With that, Tyler Briggs seized enough courage to keep speeding along Highway 101. Ever the movie buff, he started feeling like Janet Leigh in *Psycho*.

Yeah, he thought, hunched at the wheel, thinking of the scene where she fled Arizona with stolen booty for her lover—forty thousand dollars' worth. What was her name? he wondered, and then it came to him, bubbling up from that peculiar vat of movie trivia that was a major portion of his brain. Yeah, yeah, it was Marion Crane, and now as he drove he could hear the scary strings of Bernard Herrmann's music score.

Only in this case, he thought, the booty's not forty thousand dollars, but a videotape of an old Grade Z sci-fi flick from the fifties, *Night of the Blood Beast*.

When they told him *Night of the Blood Beast* was temporarily unavailable at the video store in Silverlake, Tyler was desperate. After all, he'd pledged himself to coming through for Karen, figuring if he gave her the tape, she'd go out with him. He'd finally located it by calling up all his movie-buff pals and putting out the word. That led him to a kid in the Valley who had taped it off commercial TV, Channel 5's "Movies to Dawn." That meant it was loaded up with car commercials that featured some manic guy in a cowboy hat, but, he figured, it was better than nothing. Karen would have her movie.

Tyler glanced to the side of the highway, where a sign flew by in a blur: Wallenberg was only fifteen miles away, and he'd be coming up to the turnoff in just a couple of miles.

Of course she loves me. She just doesn't know *it yet, that's all!*

And in fact Tyler Briggs *did* believe that Karen Webster loved him. He could tell by the way she avoided his eyes, and he could tell that she really liked that glass ball paperweight he'd given her. Besides, he thought, hadn't Karen called *him* when she needed help with that old movie?

Oh, yeah, yeah, she's in love with me, all right.

It was for that reason he'd decided to be a hero for her. That was why he'd decided to do something unthinkable: He had borrowed his dad's black Corvette without permission. He'd driven it right out of the garage while his dad was away on a business trip.

What the hell. After all, it was just sitting there, a great big expensive car gathering dust. His dad was *always* away on business trips, Tyler decided, and it made him mad.

Yeah, Tyler thought, *stick around a bit, pops, and maybe we could negotiate stuff like this.*

Besides, he hadn't intended to go this far—all the way from Los Angeles to Wallenberg. He'd originally planned to deliver the tape to Karen at her apartment, but she wasn't home. It was then he'd run into that bozo with the muscles out by the pool. It was that guy who'd led him to Wallenberg, a place Tyler had heard of but had never been to.

Now he opened up the side window so that he could light up a cigarette. Flicking his lighter, he thought of the way Karen always commented on its funky design, and it made him smile, because to Tyler that was just one more bit of proof that, whether she knew it or not, Karen was crazy in love with him.

With that thought in mind, he blew his smoke out the window so as not to befoul his dad's expensive leather upholstery, then flicked on the stereo, filling the fast car with the throbbing sounds of U2, his very favorite group.

What a life, he thought, and he reached out and stroked the videocassette, which sat in a case beside him—his key to Karen Webster.

The Kid needed a name.

He stood on the stretch of 101 just before the turnoff into

Wallenberg, sweating in the heat. It was a big switch from Wallenberg, where he heard the temperature had slipped below thirty-five.

He wore the clothes he had stolen the night before, and he kept his thumb out, poised to hitch a ride. Meanwhile, he was careful to keep an eye out for Sheriff Bradley's car. If the sheriff caught him, he figured, his plan wouldn't work at all. And he *had* to get a name.

When he saw the tall, goofy-looking guy in the great car, he knew he was in business.

The Kid depended upon the fact that most kids stop for kids, and he was right.

"Need a ride into town?" Tyler cried from inside the Corvette, ducking and leaning awkwardly across the seat so he could look up and see him.

The Kid leaned down and poked his head into the Corvette, smiling. "I sure would appreciate it," he said, careful to keep some humility in his voice. He then ran his finger along the car's shiny finish. "Nice!"

Tyler almost told the truth, but then decided it would be more fun to lie. "Got it last month," he said, an arrogant lilt in his voice. "C'mon. I'll give you a ride into Wallenberg."

"Really?"

"Really," Tyler said, then he popped all the locks with a flourish.

"Thanks, man," said the Kid, getting inside. "Bet this mother goes, huh?"

Tyler answered by gearing down fast, gunning the Corvette so that it left the shoulder in a spray of gravel.

"Aw right!" cried the Kid.

Tyler smiled and shrugged. "What's the matter? Did you have car trouble?"

"Yeah," said the Kid, picking up his cue immediately. "Blew a rod. Couple miles back."

"Funny," Tyler said, "I didn't see it." He reached for his lighter and cigarettes. "Cigarette?"

The Kid shook his head. "Neat lighter, though," he said, and he was immediately taken with it: He couldn't keep his eyes off the blue plastic fish, which seemed to bob to and fro with the motion of the car.

Just as they took the turnoff into Wallenberg, the Kid moaned and grabbed at his stomach.

"What's the matter?"

"I don't know, man," said the Kid, doubled over, "I'm afraid I don't feel so good."

"You aren't going to puke, are you?" Tyler cried, panicking. He imagined himself trying to scrub the smell of vomit out of his father's car.

"I don't know," cried the Kid, and he hunched over, releasing another long and distressful moan. Gagging, he cupped a hand to his mouth.

"Jesus!" cried Tyler, turning the wheel with a mighty force and slamming on the brakes. "Hurry!" he cried, and he popped the locks and pointed outside. "Come on, man . . . I'll wait."

The Kid looked at him. "You will?"

"Sure, man. Just don't puke in my car, okay?"

"Never been this sick," the Kid moaned before stumbling out of the car.

Tyler watched as the Kid walked up to the edge of the road, where he stumbled over a mound of gravel and started down the other side. There was a sound of spraying gravel, followed by silence.

After a few minutes Tyler began to worry. Christ, what if the Kid was *really* sick? He'd have to take him to a hospital, maybe pay for his treatment. He slammed his palms against the steering wheel, then waited, rewinding U2.

Fifteen minutes later he still sat. He looked at his watch, turned off the cassette, and drummed his fingers on the dash.

Hell, I'll just leave, he thought, but he was quick to feel guilty. He knew he just couldn't leave the poor guy sick in the woods.

Christ, what if he died?

Stepping from the car, Tyler walked to the edge of the ravine. He cupped his hands and shouted into the tangle of brush below. "You all right?"

He listened for an answer, but all he could hear was a light wind that whispered up the ravine, rustling the trees and shrubbery.

"Where the hell are you?"

Concerned, he stepped down off the shoulder, all the time crying out for the Kid, and soon he was knee-deep in the thicket himself.

When he stopped, he realized how utterly quiet it was. The only sound was the distant thrum of cars along the highway.

"Can you hear me? Are you all right?"

After walking for several minutes he realized he had lost his way. Even the sound of traffic had disappeared, and Tyler felt panicked. Turning back, he decided that the best thing to do was call the Highway Patrol.

But as he thrashed his way through the tangle, he had the terrible feeling he wasn't going the right way. The sound of distant traffic had still not returned. Meanwhile, his hands were badly scratched, bloodied from the thicket.

Now he had reached the steepest stretch of all. When he grabbed a vine to pull himself forward, it snapped in his hand, and he fell backward, tumbling down the ravine.

When he landed, his head struck full force against a jagged rock, and he could feel the blood as it trickled out from his scalp and down the back of his neck.

Stunned and scared, he realized he couldn't move.

"Hey!"

He lay there listening to his voice, which returned to him in that eerie, flat echo that told him he was completely alone.

"Help me!"

He tried to sit up, but all the energy in his body seemed drained away. Even his fingers wouldn't move, and he stared at them with horror, as if they now belonged to someone else. Tears streamed down his cheeks and he worried that he might pass out. If he did, he feared he would lie unconscious until he was dead.

And then he heard the sound—a sputtering sound, like motor noise.

At first he thought it was a car. It gave him hope, for it made him think he was close to the highway, after all.

"Over here!" he screamed. "I'm over here!"

He heard it again—a little bit louder this time, and he decided that the sound was too tinny for a car engine.

Rasping.

Closer.

"Help me! Please, somebody. Help me!"

The sound increased.

It became a roaring sputter, like a crude motor.

And someone moved—someone big and heavy, for he could hear the crash of branches as someone bounded through them.

Suddenly, he recognized the sound.

"For God's sake, help me!"

When he stared upward, he could only see the smallest patch of sky—a broken piece of yellow sun in a gap between the tops of trees.

Then the light was gone.

It was cut off, blocked by the enormous man that stood above him. A halo of yellow sun splintered behind the man's head, like the fogging on a film, and it obscured his face. And all the time, the awful sound—louder, faster, until Tyler could smell the heat of the motor.

He squinted, trying to make out detail, and he soon realized that the man's thick, stocky frame was dressed in a blue suit; his face was covered by a mask, which was blank—hideously without feature.

Tyler watched as the man leaned down to him, bringing with him the origin of all that terrible sound that vibrated throughout his body.

The sound came from the man's weapon—the awful, sputtering chain saw.

And it severed the arm that tried to push it back.

An hour later the Kid pulled the black Corvette onto Main Street, feeling so happy that he whistled a tune.

After all, he had a car.

And he had a name.

• Nineteen •

JACK MACGRUDER WAS NOT AFRAID of the ladder anymore. As a boy, he had been terrified to climb the twenty feet necessary to change Odeon's marquee.

But now he sat fearlessly, his thin legs straddling the ladder's head step as he fished through the cardboard box of plastic letters.

Finding the appropriate letter and polishing it with a chamois cloth, Jack clicked it into place. When he had secured it within the parallel slots of the marquee, Jack sat back as much as he could in order to proofread his work, which he checked against an index card in his hand.

CLOSING CEREMONY TOMORROW NIGHT 8:00
CITY LIGHTS STARRING MR. CHARLIE CHAPLIN
PLUS LAUREL & HARDY SHORT, MOVIETONE NEWS

Once he was certain it was perfect, Jack felt a strange letdown, and for a long time he sat perfectly still atop the ladder, so suddenly depressed that he couldn't find the energy to move.

It bothered him that he felt so little satisfaction about the special show he had planned. Before the death of Roy, he had managed to feel *some* enthusiasm about his closing-night show—his joy stemming primarily from a slavish dedication to reproducing Odeon's opening night, right down to the expensive formal programs that he'd had printed up in Haleyville.

Now the whole thing seemed obligatory to him, and not in the greatest of taste. Even worse, he felt as if he had no choice.

"You think anybody's gonna come to your damned show?"

Jack looked down at Sheriff Badley, who leaned out of his patrol car, pointing at the marquee.

"Don't know," Jack said, starting down the ladder. "Guess we'll just have to wait and see."

When he reached the sidewalk, he started to gather up his things.

"Won't be anybody there who listens to *me*," Bradley said, then leaned away from the window and gunned his engine.

Jack watched for a few moments, until the patrol car had disappeared around a corner.

He wanted to be mad at the sheriff, but a part of him couldn't blame him.

Why am I having this show?

Turning back to his ladder, the old man folded it up and carried it back inside his theatre.

Karen knew immediately that she was not welcome.

"She's studying," the sheriff said, stepping out on the porch and shutting the door behind him, so that Karen couldn't see into the house. "Amy takes her studies very seriously."

"I'm sure that she does, Leo. It's just that I think I can be of some help."

"Help?"

"Leo, I might be able to convince Amy that it's possible to get over things like what happened to her at the theatre. After all, I went through some pretty terrible things there myself."

Defensive, Bradley reached into his shirt pocket and yanked out a cigarette. He then began searching the rest of his pockets for matches. "Maybe the best thing to do is forget about it!"

Karen bristled. "That's the *worst* thing she can do!"

"I'll be the judge of that!" he cried.

Suddenly, a gentle voice spoke from behind them. "Why don't you let *me* be the judge of that?"

With her hand extended to Karen, Amy walked up the porch. "My name's Amy. You wanted to see me?"

"Why, yes," Karen said, taking her hand, which felt warm and impossibly soft.

The sheriff shuffled awkwardly, so that his large uniform boots scraped the old wood planks of the porch. "I thought you were studying, honey."

"Went out to check on Dandelion."

"Dandelion?" Karen asked.

Amy tugged her hand. "Come on," she said, "I'll show you."
Following the girl's lead, Karen stepped off the porch.

"Guess I have no choice," Karen called out to Bradley.

The sheriff nodded perfunctorily from the porch, but he did not smile back.

Watching as Amy stroked the calf, Karen felt an uncanny affection for the girl. Amy had already described every detail of the difficult birth and how she had assisted the veterinarian.

"You used to live in Wallenberg?" Amy asked.

"Yes. Years ago. Not far away. In fact, I had to pass my old house on the way here."

It had been painful for Karen to see the old house, even though it had been remodeled extensively by its young new tenants. Sitting there in the car, Karen had shuddered nonetheless, for no amount of remodeling could blot out the awful memories.

"Must be weird," Amy said. "To come back, I mean . . . after all these years." She looked Karen in the eyes. "Why did you leave?"

Karen wondered if she should answer Amy's question. While a part of her felt compelled to pour out the whole story, she still felt ashamed. "Some bad things happened. When I was about your age."

"It's not easy to be this age."

"No."

Karen smiled at the girl, hoping that she would bring up the incident with the rats, for she felt presumptuous bringing it up herself. If I can't tell *my* story, how can I expect Amy to tell hers?

But after looking away nervously, Amy spoke. "Some bad things happened to me too. My boyfriend was killed. I was there when it happened. It was just a little while ago, in fact."

"I know," Karen said. She had felt such a splendid intimacy with the girl, she couldn't lie to her. "I heard about it at my hotel."

Amy looked shocked. "You mean, somebody who just got to town hears about it right off?"

"No," Karen said, "you misunderstand. You see, I had my troubles at the theatre too. Naturally, when I mentioned Odeon, I heard about what happened to you."

"I see."

Karen squeezed Amy's hand. "I'm glad that you told me."

Amy looked away abruptly, so that Karen couldn't tell if the girl was angry. But then, without warning, Amy burst into tears, burying her face against Karen's shoulder. "It was so terrible! I have nightmares every night. Nobody understands!"

Karen held her tight. She could feel the young girl's tears as they soaked against her shoulder. "Get it out, Amy . . . that's it . . . get it out. It's good for you."

And she could tell that Amy had not yet revealed even a small portion of her fear and guilt.

It's so important. How different things would have been if I had been honest from the beginning!

The moment between them was broken by the sheriff's voice from outside. "What in the world's going on here?"

Karen looked up at the barn door, where Bradley's silhouette loomed enormous in the golden light of sundown, and she thought of a cowboy appearing at a swinging saloon door.

Embarrassed, Amy pulled away, busying herself with the nursing calf.

Bradley looked at Karen. "Could I see you?"

"Of course," she said, then turned to Amy. "You all right?"

Amy nodded—a quick nod that suggested she wanted to be left alone.

When Karen and Bradley got outside the barn, he turned to her angrily. "That's the last thing I want, damn it!"

"I'm sorry, Leo, but it wasn't as bad as it may have looked. She just needed to express herself, that's all."

"I can take care of my daughter!"

"I'm sure you can, Leo. But I also think she needs the attention of a woman."

"I try to do both."

"But you can't, Leo. You're only one person."

Bradley lit a cigarette. "That may be true, Karen, but what I don't like is someone messing her all stirred up."

"Stirred up?"

"Crying like that. In the barn."

"She was unloading, Leo."

"That's the first time I've seen her cry since it happened."

"Leo, believe me. It's when she *doesn't* show her feelings that you should worry."

Bradley shook a huge finger in her face. "Don't give me all that psychological mumbo jumbo! Not all of us were dragged off to the nuthouse, you know!"

Karen slapped him so fast that for a moment it didn't seem to her that she'd actually done it.

"I'm sorry!" she cried at once, watching as a huge red welt blossomed along his cheek.

Bradley rubbed his face. "Forget it," he said, then turned and headed toward the house.

Karen pursued him up the porch to his door. "Leo, why didn't you tell me about Carl yesterday? When I told you I wanted to find him, why didn't you tell me he was here in Wallenberg?"

Bradley's eyes went suddenly softer. "Couldn't find the heart for it, I guess. Figured you'd been through enough." He looked away, all at once self-conscious. "You gonna look him up?"

"I already tried. I knocked on his door this morning but he didn't answer."

Bradley reached out and took her gently by the shoulders. "Karen, has it occurred to you that maybe it's best for a lot of people—Carl included—not to stir these things all up?"

She shook her head. "You just don't get it, do you?"

Exasperated, he pulled his hands away. "I can't stop you from seeing Carl, but I sure can try to keep Amy away from you."

"What are you hiding from me?" Karen cried.

But Bradley had already entered his house, slamming the door behind him.

For a moment Karen considered going back to Amy, but she could tell that the girl had been deeply embarrassed, and she didn't want to push too hard. Besides, she didn't want to come between her and her father at such a delicate emotional time.

Deciding she'd call her later, Karen walked back to her car, the ground so cold that the grass and weeds snapped and broke beneath her feet.

Just as she got to her car, Karen noticed another car as it pulled into Bradley's driveway. It aroused her interest immediately, because a new black Corvette was not the sort of car you expected to see in Wallenberg, especially out on North Post Road.

When a young man stepped out and started walking toward her up the drive, Karen studied his face, noting that he was handsome enough to be a teenage heartthrob. Were she casting a commercial, she decided, she would cast him on looks alone.

"Hello," he said as he walked past her toward the barn. An unlit cigarette dangled from his lips.

Karen studied him, inexplicably fascinated, watching as he

stopped and pulled his cigarette lighter from the pocket of his leather jacket.

Looking up, he saw that she was watching him, and he nodded, waving with the hand that grasped the lighter. Embarrassed for having been caught staring, Karen waved back and then moved quickly to her car and drove off.

It was only after she'd driven halfway back to town that she remembered where she'd seen that huge, peculiar cigarette lighter before, the one with the electric blue fish.

When Karen parked the car in front of the hotel, she saw something that first amazed her and then filled her with dread.

There, on her windshield, in the middle of August, she saw a perfect snowflake.

• Twenty •

"COULD YOU KEEP TRYING the number?"

While angrily stubbing out another cigarette, Paul strained to hear the operator, whose voice grew dimmer. He imagined her voice a weak bit of electricity that struggled through frozen phone lines. Outside his window, snowflakes sputtered above Main Street.

"I can't hear you!" he said.

Again, he tried to make sense of the tiny voice that spoke beneath the static, but it was useless and he hung up.

Sipping a cup of instant coffee, he looked at the snow that fell with such a bizarre defiance of season. The news on the radio was filled with reports of the freakish snowstorm that had struck only Wallenberg. If you drove out of Wallenberg, the temperature went up thirty degrees just as soon as you got back on the 101.

Meanwhile, it bothered Paul that he couldn't reach Kenny. Tensing at the window, he followed a snowflake all the way to the ground. He felt intensely lonely, for the distance between himself and Kenny now seemed without hope—a void made up of anger and misunderstandings. He imagined Rita tearing apart what remained of his image as a father; his son would hear tales of incompetence and drunkenness.

Beyond the flurry of snow, Odeon stood like some arrogant assertion of Paul's childhood, for it was Odeon that linked him to his own father.

Paul's father took him to the movies, plucking him right out of school for Wednesday matinees. This made Paul feel special, for you weren't supposed to go to the movies on weekday afternoons.

Returning to class the following day, he would act out the movies he had seen there.

At the window, staring out, his efforts to reach his own son thwarted, Paul felt memory as it rose up inside of him. He saw himself at Kenny's age, standing with his father at the box office.

Paul's father—handsome, dressed neatly in a suit—would count out change for their admission, flirting with the cashier as she handed them their tickets. A day at the movies with his father was a chance to love the man, if only for the running time of the movie.

The phone rang and Paul picked it up.

"Your call is ready," said the operator, her voice, this time, crystal-clear.

Rita sounded angry, even before they had said much.

"No, you can't talk to him," she said, the telephone emphasizing her crisp style of speech.

"Why?"

"I told you that yesterday."

Indeed, Paul had called her from a pay phone along the 101 on his way to Wallenberg, hoping that Kenny would pick up the phone. But Kenny *never* answered the phone at Rita's, and it made Paul suspect that the boy didn't consider the house in which he lived his home.

"Where are you?" Rita demanded.

"Wallenberg."

"Why?"

"The Pope is stopping here."

Rita's silence reminded him that she had no sense of humor.

How could he have married someone without a sense of humor? he wondered, but in fact he knew why. He had married Rita for the simple reason that, at one time in their lives, she had adored him. Believing in his talents, she had exalted him through frequent and breathless praise, making his meager gifts seem greater than they were. Paul had used her, he realized now, as a vanity mirror. How could such a relationship, however noble its intentions, end in anything but contempt?

"You won't win this case," he said, momentarily forgetting his lawyer's advice: Never sound threatening. "I won't let you do this, Rita."

The line went dead immediately, in its place another wave of popping static.

Paul tapped the switch hook, summoning back the operator.

"Your party voluntarily disengaged, sir," she informed him, and as he hung up the phone he found the word so ironic: *disengaged*.

There was a sudden and thunderous knocking at his door. He opened it immediately and found Karen, who walked right in, waving a manila envelope. "Carl left these," she said, moving to the bed, where she spread out the contents, a thatch of yellow clippings.

"He left them for me at the desk."

"Then he knows you're here."

"Yes."

Paul moved closer to examine the clippings. "Have they found him yet?"

"No," she said, then reached for his cigarettes.

"I didn't know that you smoked."

"I don't," she said, "except when I'm afraid."

"You are now?"

"Terrified."

Karen lit the cigarette, taking the smoke in full. It was so long since she had smoked it made her slightly dizzy. She pointed to the clippings. "Go ahead. Read."

Paul looked down at the first newspaper clipping, which he saw was dated May 1929. The photograph that accompanied the article made him immediately uncomfortable, as it featured the pale countenance of Forbes Carlton.

Both Paul and Karen began to read about the strange-looking man who stared at them from so many yellowed photographs.

The details they read regarding Forbes Carlton were disturbing—in particular, an entry that Paul had found. Resembling a précis from *Who's Who*, it provided an accounting of Forbes Carlton's life. Clearly, Paul decided, Carl Irvine had clipped it from a book that dealt with the occult:

Forbes Carlton   b. 1875, Chicago, Ill., d. 1931(?), only son of George Bennet Carlson, Chicago architect, and Vera Raines Carlson, socialite; graduated summa cum laude, Harvard, 1905; worked intermittently as architect and stage magician in vaudeville; supervised several digs in Mayan ruins in 1928; is believed to have organized coven in San Francisco, circa 1930, which included the sacrifice of animals and—although proof was never found—human

children; experimented widely with Specta-Graph, patented
by Forbes Carlton, 1927, a scientific precursor to laser
photography and holograms; attempted construction of
Specta-Graph theatre for purposes of displaying effects, but
was denied proper permits pending investigations into alleged cults and sacrificial ceremonies. . . .

Paul looked up from the clipping, holding it out to Karen. "Did
you see this?"

She nodded quickly, signaling her discomfort. "About the child
sacrifices?"

"Yes."

Karen pored through several other clippings, handling them
carefully, so that the yellowed paper, as brittle as parchment,
wouldn't break in her hands. Finally, she located the one that she
wanted, handing it over to Paul. "Here," she said, "look at this."

Paul took the clipping, which he saw had come from a 1930
issue of a San Francisco daily newspaper:

While several of Carlton's followers testified that indeed he
had sacrificed children at his Market Street temple in San
Francisco, no clear evidence was ever uncovered. The body
of the alleged victim—Claud Dagel, age eight—was never
found. Carlton insisted throughout his testimony that he
himself was the victim of jealous colleagues within his peer
group of alleged mystics, psychics, and magicians.

"So who was this character?" Paul asked. "He sounds like a
barrel of laughs."

Karen handed him another article, this one from a 1929 issue of
the local Wallenberg paper. Paul saw the headline, "Famous
Architect to Build Movie Dream Place in Wallenberg."

Beneath the headline was a photograph that featured a beaming
Henry Wallenberg. Dressed in suit and tie, he stood with his arm
around Forbes Carlton, who glowered into the camera. They were
posed before a massive hole in the ground, which would later
become the Odeon Theatre, a fact extolled by a large sign behind
them. To their right stood Edith Wallenberg.

Paul decided that she looked uncomfortable. "Mrs. Wallenberg's death was quite a scandal, wasn't it?" he asked Karen,
handing her the photograph.

"Most hush-hush thing that ever happened in Wallenberg," she answered. She smiled wryly. "With the possible exception of me."

"What else do you know about the Wallenbergs?" he asked.

Karen assembled a few more articles, handing them to Paul like a lawyer with exhibits. "By reading all of these things," she began, "I've kind of pieced their life together. Henry was a bachelor, well into his thirties, I guess. He loved the stage and he often traveled to San Francisco, where the better vaudeville troups appeared. It's there he met Edith Atwater."

"She was an actress?"

"A show girl, really . . . beauty was her major gift, I guess. There's a whole article about her career somewhere," Karen said, shuffling through the papers. "Here it is."

Paul looked at the article, which was clipped from the Wallenberg newspaper. Clearly, he decided, it was a puff piece commissioned by Mr. Wallenberg himself. A huge photograph of Edith Wallenberg dominated the page.

"Beautiful, wasn't she?" Karen asked, but then continued before he could answer. "Anyway, it was there—up in San Francisco—that the two of them had a kind of whirlwind courtship. They married in the summer of 1927."

Moving further through the clippings, Karen found an article that had been cut from an old magazine. "Here's where it gets interesting. This is clipped from one of those scandal magazines from the forties. Seems the story got a bit of national attention, actually . . . owing to her mysterious death and all. Seems Edith didn't exactly like having given up her theatrical career for Henry. I guess when all was said and done, Henry was kind of a dull guy. When she wasn't appeased by trips to Europe and South America anymore, Henry built her a theatre. Edith wanted it modeled after all the lavish stuff she'd seen on her travels."

"Hence, the clash of styles," Paul said, looking at the article, which featured large photographs of both Henry and Edith. To the side of the page was a photograph of Forbes Carlton, who, as usual, did not look pleased. "What about Carlton?"

"Rumor is, he and Edith had an affair."

"They met while he was here building the theatre, huh?"

"Nope," Karen said. "Remember now . . . Carlton had his controversial church up in San Francisco. Also, he was basically a performer—a stage magician, principally. He and Edith met on the same bill of a vaudeville show. Both of them played the Orpheum circuit."

"So what was the deal? She died opening night, right?"

Karen nodded. "And guess what?"

Paul shrugged.

"Edith Wallenberg was found dead in one of the men's room stalls. The sheriff's daughter and her boyfriend were attacked in one of the stalls, too. Awful lot happens down there, wouldn't you say?

Paul nodded slowly. "The boy was killed, right?"

"Yes."

Paul thought back to his boyhood fascination with the Odeon, trying to remember some of the things he had learned about the grand old place.

"It was Jack who found her body, wasn't it," he said, "when he was a little boy?"

Karen bristled. "I didn't know that. It's not mentioned in any of this."

"I'm sure of it. Thing is, it was all so secretive. Some people say she committed suicide, others say she was murdered."

"I've got another theory," Karen said.

"What's that?"

"I think she tried to abort her baby . . . just like me."

Paul turned to her, startled. Moving closer, he touched her gently along the face, which was flushed and hot. "Are you all right?" he asked. "This must be upsetting you terribly."

"The closer I get to the truth, the better I feel. After all, it's why I came here. Frankly, I think the doctor and the sheriff would like me to leave. I think they expected me to leave right after they gave me that envelope full of papers."

"You think Matson forged those papers? He destroyed the originals?"

"I didn't say that."

"I could play devil's advocate, Karen. I could say that it might be wishful thinking on your part. That you want the child to be alive so much you'll deny everything to the contrary."

With a small nod Karen agreed.

Paul worried that he had gone too far. "Don't be angry," he said.

"I'm not angry. You cared enough to follow me here. It meant a lot to me, Paul. It did."

Looking her in the eyes, Paul felt the old feelings stir up again. .

Wasn't it funny how you never totally fell out of love with someone? he thought. With a single gesture the beloved could remind the lover what had possessed him so.

At once self-conscious, Paul withdrew his hand. "Why do you think Carl left you these clippings?"

"As a warning. A warning to *me*."

"And he's still not in his room?"

"I've called every half hour. The desk says he's been gone since last night. He must have left the envelope before he took off . . ."

"What about Jack? Have you tried to contact him?"

Karen nodded. "Several times. He's never home. Or at least he doesn't answer his phone."

"He's pretty shaken up about Roy, I think," Paul said, still sifting through the old clippings. "He might be able to shed some light on things, particularly about your attack. I mean, we know he was on his way down there that day."

Karen hesitated, then handed Paul a piece of paper. "Look at this," she said. "It's a note from Carl. It was in with all the clippings."

Paul read Carl's note aloud, then looked at her. "It wants your baby? The theatre? Is that what he means?"

Walking up to the window, Karen clutched herself against the cold, startling when she looked across Main Street.

"What is it?"

"Look at the marquee," she said.

Paul walked to the window and looked at Odeon's marquee, which had collected a huge mantle of snow. Feathery white powder had nestled along the swooping arabesques of copper. If it wasn't so unsettling, he decided, it would be pretty.

"So?" he asked. "What is it, Karen? What am I supposed to be looking at?"

"The marquee," she repeated. "Look at what it says."

Paul read closer, and this time he saw what Karen meant. Jack's carefully chosen letters—CLOSING CEREMONY TOMORROW NIGHT— had changed. In their place was a new message: GRAND OPENING TOMORROW.

"Why, it has to be a mistake," Paul whispered. "The old man got confused."

"But that's just it," Karen said. "It wasn't that way this morning. Just before I came in here, I looked. Paul, it changed *itself* . . . the marquee *changed on its own!*"

• • •

It wasn't hard for the Kid to get past the desk.

Old fart, he thought, can't stay awake to do his job, and he kept his eyes on the desk clerk until he reached the stairway. The old man stayed asleep, his head cradled in his arms, a thread of saliva rolling out of his mouth and onto the desk.

The Kid dashed up the stairway, taking three steps at a time. He felt strong and good about the new, thrusting sense of power in his legs, and he was happy that his body was as perfect as his face.

It pleased him now to get those looks from the girls. He'd noticed them on Main Street—they'd stood in a giggling cluster, watching his every move. He loved how they looked at him twice, how they sized him up as he got in and out of his new black car; there was a power that came with beauty, he learned now, just as there was an impotence in being ugly, like Billy Burnside.

When he reached Carl's floor, the Kid looked both ways before he left the stairwell and entered the narrow, badly lit hallway. The hallway smelled dusty and old, just like the lobby had, and it depressed him as he stood at the door and jimmied his way into Carl's room.

Whole place smells like old people smell, he thought, that creepy smell, sort of the way wet cardboard smelled, he decided. The Kid hated everything about old people—the crabbed way they stooped through life, the drag they put on things, the way they expected young people to carry them along, like they were runners who couldn't keep up with the race anymore.

Oughtta kill 'em when they get to be sixty. That's what he'd do, if such things were his to decide.

Now the Kid worked fast, rifling Carl's shabby little chest of drawers as he looked for a piece of paper and pencil.

If the hotel depressed him, Carl's room made him feel even worse, what with the drab paint and the insistent odor of old cooking grease. The room made him want to gag.

See, he thought, groping through Carl's stuff, what's an old guy like this allowed to live for? What good does he do anybody else? What the hell good can he do *me*!

He found a piece of paper, which looked like something Carl would use. It was a cheap little pad of the type you bought at the dime store, most of the paper ripped out, so that the blue rubber lip flapped down across the two or three sheets of paper that remained.

The Kid found a pencil, which was embossed in raised gold letters: *Rydell's Appliance Shop*. Moving up to the bed and sitting down, he started to write. He gripped the pencil just the way Carl would, making certain that his script was uncertain and appropriately shaky:

> *Karen,*
>
> *I cannot liv withe mysellf no morr withis hole thing. I was the one hoo tackked you that day down in the theatre. Pleese try too forgive mee!*

The Kid read it over, grinning with satisfaction when he was done, for he knew right away that he had done it precisely right.

Convinced that the note was a perfect evocation of Carl Irvine's feeble mental processes, he folded it over twice and into sloppy quarters, making certain that the crease was crooked.

After sitting up from the bed, he moved across the little room to Carl's dresser, where he stuck the note. He arranged a few articles around it, purposely askew, so that it would have the look of genuine clutter.

When he finished, the Kid was whistling, but he quickly stopped himself.

Can't be too confident. Anybody hears me, I'm in trouble.

He opened the door carefully, grimacing at the sound of a sudden squeaky hinge. Certain the hallway was empty, the Kid shut the door, and after pausing to make sure he hadn't forgotten anything, he headed back downstairs for the hotel lobby.

• Twenty-One •

JACK MACGRUDER SQUINTED TO SEE. While the windshield of his Cadillac El Dorado was coated by a hard shell of ice, he had managed to chip away a peekhole before driving into Wallenberg and parking along Main Street. Now that he could see his theatre, he couldn't believe his eyes.

GRAND OPENING TOMORROW, the marquee proclaimed.

It just isn't possible!

Jack sat shivering in the front seat of the big old car, trying to figure out what had gone wrong. He specifically remembered checking and rechecking the message before getting off the ladder.

What in the hell happened?

He stared at the marquee again, just to make certain that he wasn't having some kind of weird daytime dream, but indeed the message had changed. All mention of *City Lights*, the Movietone News, and the Laurel and Hardy short subject were gone. His own message had been completely preempted, and Jack was left with the eerie feeling that someone else was in charge now.

But who?

Gathering the collar of his fur coat around his neck, Jack stepped from the car and walked up the terrazzo. He moved carefully, for the ice had formed a treacherous black sheet all the way up to the bronze doors.

No, I *did* put up the right letters!

But no matter how much he told himself that, he was still unconvinced. There was simply too much going on that he couldn't explain.

Inside the lobby Jack stopped, puzzled again.

The lobby was warm—almost hot, the sudden contrast in temperature flushing his face.

Odd, he thought, for the heat hadn't been turned on since February. It was a bit of economy that Jack, ever mindful of Odeon's escalating upkeep, had insisted upon.

Jack pulled off his huge winter coat, which he folded neatly across his arm. Walking to the snack bar, he saw that its glass countertop had steamed over. Boxes of candy, in neat rows beneath beclouded glass, looked as if they were underwater.

Why in the world was there so much heat?

He moved up to one of the aisle doors, checking inside the auditorium to see if it was hot there too. Indeed, the enormous room, illuminated by a dim rosy light that spilled from cove-lit domes, was comfortably warm, almost hot.

Stepping forward, Jack saw something in the aisle—a piece of material, it looked like—yellow and slick, lying in the center of what appeared to be a crusted brown pool.

Closer now, he knelt and studied it, grimacing at the unpleasant sight of it. All at once, he recognized it as a piece of yellow plastic raincoat.

Billy Burnside's!

Strange, for the theatre had been closed up for several days, and Jack was certain the Burnside boy hadn't found a way inside.

Besides, it occurred to Jack that Billy Burnside would never part with his rain slicker; it was as ubiquitous to the boy as that crazy leering grin of his.

But wait! Hadn't he heard a rumor that the Burnside boy had been involved in the incident with the rats?

Yes, of course. It was one of several things that Bradley was looking into.

Once again, he thought of his brother, and of Emma Burnside, that dreadful woman Roy had loved. How Jack had shuddered at the thought of having her for a sister-in-law.

How terrible *that* would have been! he thought, wincing when he imagined family outings—he, his drunken brother and the slatternly Mrs. Burnside with her idiot child loping along beside them.

Kicking at the piece of yellow material, Jack worked it across the floor until he reached one of the side doors that led to the alley.

Suddenly, he felt guilty. He realized he shouldn't think such things about his brother and the woman he had loved. After all, it was Roy's life, not his, regardless of how Jack might have disapproved.

I'm so controlling!

He got that hopeless feeling he always got when pondering the defects in his character: in this case, his lifelong need to control others. He knew it was why he had stayed alone, why he had never made friendships that lasted. Eventually, he figured, people wearied and left.

What better thing for a controlling person to do, he figured, than run a movie theatre? There he could assemble people in the dark, decide what they should experience or when they should laugh or cry. There was a godlike gesture to such an interest in organizing the emotional experiences of others.

When he opened the side door, a blast of cold air hit him. Ice had formed along the telephone wires that stretched above the alley in which he stood; bits of it fell, shattering like glass beside him. Shuddering, he grabbed the piece of yellow fabric and tossed it into a trash can.

Depressed and tired, Jack moved quickly to his basement office, whose solitude usually soothed him. Inside, the heat was thick and uncomfortable, so that he felt almost feverish. Tossing down his jacket, he loosened his collar and sat at his desk, where he switched on a small fan. A drop of perspiration slid down his cheek and landed upon his desk blotter, spreading quickly into a stain the size of a quarter and warping the cardboard.

All at once he heard something.

"Carl?" he cried.

He was certain it was someone walking across the foyer, coming toward his office.

"Carl?" he cried again, but his voice only bounced off the hard walls of his office.

Frightened, Jack felt his face soak with sweat. His heart was beating faster than he could ever remember.

"Who is it?" he cried once more, this time angrily. "The theatre is closed!"

And then the boy's face appeared—a smiling vision of handsome innocence that seemed to float to him out of the murky light of Odeon's basement.

"Hello, Jack," said the Kid.

"Hello," Jack said stiffly, for he wasn't certain yet how he should react. He knew that he hadn't seen this boy in town before, as all the teenagers had come to Odeon at one time or another and he would certainly remember such a strikingly handsome face as this one. "What is it you want? The theatre's closed."

The Kid offered his hand up to Jack. "Howdy, Mr. MacGruder. My name is Tyler Briggs."

Jack managed a smile. "Pleased to meet you." He shook the boy's hand, finding it odd that the hand was not cold. How long had he been inside? Jack wondered.

"I'm new at the college," the Kid said. "The one over in Haleyville, I mean."

"What is it you want?"

The Kid stared at him. "I was sorry to hear about your brother."

"Oh?"

"Yes."

"Thank you for your concern."

"Guess you'll be needing a projectionist, huh?"

The question caught Jack off guard. "A projectionist?"

"For the closing-night show tomorrow."

Jack was surprised. "Oh, yes."

Indeed, it hadn't even occurred to him yet that Roy's death meant that Jack himself would have to run the projectors. The weather was far too bad to bring in a projectionist from Haleyville. To his knowledge, no one else in Wallenberg knew how to run the two 35mm machines, which were both complicated and temperamental.

"You know how?"

"Sure do." The Kid smiled.

"Show me."

Up in the projection room, the Kid threaded up the first reel of *City Lights* as though he had done so every day of his life.

"Where did you learn to do that?"

"Spent a couple of summers working at a theatre my dad owned." He fired up the arc light, then reached for the lever that would slowly dim the house lights. Engaging the projector's motor, he worked the dowser, then tapped the button that would part Odeon's drapes. When everything was humming along efficiently, he turned to Jack. "I'm a little rusty, but I didn't do too bad, huh?"

Impressed, Jack shrugged. "You did just fine."

"Do I get the job?"

"Well, there isn't much of a job. It's just one night, you know."

"Fine. How about fifty bucks?"

"I have a rather intricate schedule planned for tomorrow night."

The Kid laughed, then touched his forehead, offering up a mock salute. "I'm at your command, boss," he said.

Jack smiled. "You know, the whole issue is most likely going to be a moot one anyway. With the weather and all, I doubt that we'll have very many customers."

The Kid looked at Jack with an intensity that unnerved him. "Don't worry," he said, "there'll be people here. I promise you that."

Irritated, Bradley pushed aside his plate. When he looked at Amy across the kitchen table and signaled with his eyes that he wanted to talk, she looked away.

"Mad at me?" he asked, picking up his cigarettes.

Amy shrugged. While she did manage a faint smile, the sheriff knew that things weren't good between them.

"Is it that boy?" he asked.

Amy looked at him, her blue eyes flashing. "I just wish you weren't so protective, Daddy. I'll be in college next month. Isn't it time I had a little independence?"

Bradley knew she'd be mad when he told the Kid he couldn't see her. If only he'd done it faster, she might not even have seen him, he thought. When he saw the Kid approach the barn, he ran after him, stopping him before he could get inside. It was only the noise of that flashy new car starting up that had brought Amy running out of the barn to see.

Great, he'd thought. First Karen Webster shows up and gets her all upset, then this kid. And what the hell's a freshman in college doing with a car like that? Bradley thought, feeling guilty for acting like such a sheriff when it came to Amy's friends. Maybe she had a right to be angry, he thought. Maybe he *did* try to police his daughter's life.

"I mean, what was the big deal, Daddy? If he came to see me, then why couldn't he?"

Bradley hadn't told her yet what had happened the night before—the Kid's naked run through the streets of Wallenberg with blood on his body. He figured that any mention of blood might trigger bad memories for Amy.

"Who is he?" Bradley asked. "Do you know him from school?"

"I don't *know* who he is. And how will I if you don't let me talk to him?"

"He says he goes to the college."

Amy's eyes narrowed suspiciously. "You sure did talk to him a lot."

Bradley realized he had almost given himself away, and he shifted in the chair and stubbed out his cigarette. "Look, honey, I'm sorry if I look like I'm trying to run your life. I'm not, really."

"I know it!"

All at once, Amy began to cry and Bradley made a move to comfort her.

"No," she said, gently gesturing him away. "I know you love me, but you have to understand how hard it is for me. You have to let me grow up!"

Bradley sat silent. While a part of him wanted to rage at her, he was grateful for her honesty.

Just as he was about to speak, someone knocked at the kitchen door. Surprised, Bradley moved to the door and opened it. There, in a swirl of snow, stood the Kid.

"Hello, Sheriff."

Stunned, Bradley only nodded.

The Kid stood trembling in the cold. "I was passing by. Wanted to thank you again, sir."

Wind swept through the night and up along the porch, so that Bradley was doused by a cold flutter of snow. He knew that the Kid had come to see Amy.

"For God's sake, come in," he said, for he knew that he could not keep this boy from his daughter any longer. If he sent him away now, Amy would be furious.

When they were inside and the door was shut, the sheriff stared at him without smiling. "This was nice of you, but you didn't have to thank me again."

Amy approached. The Kid smiled at her.

"This is my daughter, Amy," Bradley said, embarrassed, for he knew that Amy would discover his dishonesty now. He hated appearing to his daughter as anything less than heroic. He looked at the kid. "Sorry, but I've forgotten your name."

"Tyler," the Kid said, "Tyler Briggs."

"Huh?" the sheriff said. "I thought it was Bill. Yeah, I'm sure it was Bill."

The Kid shrugged and shook his head. "No."

Amy moved to him and took his hand. "Nice to meet you."

Bradley gestured to the sound of wind, which howled from outside. "How the hell did you get here in this mess?"

"Was lucky. Happened to have a pair of chains in my trunk."

"Oh. Would you like a Coke? A beer?"

"Beer would be nice, sir."

Amy moved off to the kitchen, where she got the Kid one of Bradley's beers. It occurred to the sheriff that she hadn't appeared so sprightly since the incident at Odeon. Not even the birth of Dandelion's calf had so completely revived the sweet girlish enthusiasm he missed so much.

"Want a glass?" Amy smiled.

The Kid nodded.

"C'mon," Bradley said, leading the Kid into the front room, which was warmed by a small fire that crackled in the stone fireplace.

"Warm in here," the Kid said. "I understand most of the heat in town is off."

"Christ! It's off here too. Damned fire and a few space heaters is all we got."

Amy returned with the glass. "Here you go," she said, handing it to him.

Bradley noticed the clear connection between them as he thanked her and took the beer. It bugged him about the Kid's name. "I could have sworn you said your name was Bill."

The Kid shrugged. "Always been Tyler, sir." He patted the pocket of his pants. "It's on my ID anyway."

Amy shot her father a warning look. "Daddy, stop being a policeman."

Bradley let it go with a nervous smile. "Tyler's a veterinary student too, Amy."

"Really?"

"Yeah." The Kid smiled, taking a sip of the beer.

"I helped birth a calf. It was a breech. Real hard. It felt great. Helping life come into the world like that."

The Kid looked at Bradley. "You must be proud, sir."

"I am, son."

The Kid looked back at Amy. "Bet your mother's proud too, huh?"

"My wife passed away," Bradley said.

"Oh, I'm sorry."

"She wasn't my real mother," Amy said.

"Oh?"

"Daddy adopted me."

The Kid shrugged. "Sorry about your wife, sir."

"She had a rheumatic heart. Died when she was thirty-six. Amy saved my life. The most beautiful baby God ever put on this earth."

"I can tell."

With his eyes on Amy, Bradley watched the way she looked at the Kid, and he recognized the look on her face.

Already, she was falling in love.

The bottle smashed against the mirror behind the bar, shattering it. Ducking, the bartender avoided the huge shards of glass that clattered noisily to the floor. When everything was quiet again, he swallowed hard and looked at Emma.

"Emma," he cried, "settle down now, girl."

Emma Burnside had thrown the bottle, releasing a rage the bartender had seen building up all night. Now she sat utterly still at the bar, lighting up another cigarette. She puffed it dramatically, batted away some hair from her huge, overly made-up eyes, then apologized to the only customer, an elderly man who looked at her with his mouth agape.

"Sorry, babe," she said, "I'm really sorry."

"Maybe you oughtta go home," the bartender said. He was already picking up the shards of glass, handling each one delicately so as not to cut himself. "This thing with Roy's got you all screwed up, honey."

"I know it," she said, and she took another puff of her cigarette. "Billy's gone too."

"Billy?"

"That's right. Don't know where the hell he is."

The bartender was careful when it came time to talk about Billy to Emma, just as everybody in Wallenberg was, for it was too easy to slip and call him a name in front of her. It wasn't just embarrassing but also dangerous, for the bartender, after all, had just seen an example of Emma's temper. If the truth were known, he didn't much care for the woman, and if he weren't just a little bit scared of her, he'd fire her. Emma Burnside had always rubbed him the wrong way, and he never could see what it was that attracted old Roy MacGruder to her. This wasn't the first time he'd seen her vicious temper.

"Tell you what, Emma. There's nobody here 'cause of the weather. Why don't you go home? Get some rest?"

Emma stared at him for a long time. "You sure, babe?"

"I'm sure," he said.

When she had gathered up her things and left, the old man at the bar turned to the bartender.

"Emmie's in a bad mood," he said.

"Yeah." The bartender sighed, kneeling down to sweep up the glass. "Tell me about it."

In her bedroom Amy stood in the darkness. Staring out the window, all the way back to the barn, she watched and she waited.

Amy knew that her bed was just a little over a hundred feet from the stables. She knew the distance because, having worried so obsessively about Dandelion, she had actually paced it off once, just to see how close she really was.

But tonight she was not thinking of Dandelion. Tonight she waited for him: the beautiful boy named Tyler Briggs.

When he was talking to her father, Amy had seen the signal—it had passed between them unseen by the sheriff, like the unspoken words of lovers.

Meet me in the stable!
Yes, yes, I will!

And now she could see him, as he moved in front of the barn, coming to a stop and looking her way. Even beyond the shimmering curtain of snow, he was visible, as if he were possessed of a special light, and Amy realized she had never beheld anyone so physically beautiful.

Certainly, he was as gorgeous as the boys in her secret cache of teenage fan magazines—the teenage idols who posed provocatively, their doe eyes staring balefully up at her from the slick pages: *Take me, Amy, I'm yours!*

Now, in the distance, he beckoned to her, and she watched his fingers, so long and elegant, gesturing to her that she should come at once.

Amy moved quickly, for she was already dressed in her heavy coat and boots—she had been since an hour ago, when she first started to wait for him.

Gently, she opened her bedroom door, listening for her father, then sneaked down the hallway. She had never sneaked from the house at night before, but she knew the house well—its noises and eccentricities—so she knew where to step. More important, she knew how deeply her father slept.

The sleep of the dead, he'd told her once, that's me.

Once in the living room, she saw the mess, the several empty cans of beer, which indicated that her father, having drunk himself to sleep again, would sleep even more soundly.

When Amy stepped out on the porch, she slipped, her foot sliding across a patch of ice. She braced herself, but her fall was broken by the Kid, who grabbed her and held her in his arms.

"Careful," he whispered, and they walked together up to the barn, entering and shutting the big door behind them.

While it was cold inside, it was not nearly as cold as Amy had expected. Dandelion and the newborn calf were in a corner, barely visible in the high thatches of hay. Dr. Ohfers had told her to stack it that way to help keep them warm. When they entered, the calf made a soft mewing sound, while its mother rustled in the dark.

"Amy!" the Kid cried, and he pulled her toward him.

Amy buried her face in his leather jacket, touching him all over his body.

He started working at the buttons of her blouse. "I want to fuck you," he said.

"Yes!" Amy cried, helping him with the blouse.

When they were naked together, he took her by the shoulders. "It's going to hurt," he said.

"I don't care."

He watched as her hair, a natural gold, fell across pale, creamy shoulders. He touched the small but firm breasts, caressing them until the nipples hardened beneath his fingers.

"I want to," she said. "I want to."

"I know . . . I know . . ."

When it was over, they quickly dressed against the cold.

"You liked it, didn't you?" he asked. "You like to fuck, don't you?"

"Yes," she said, kissing him once again; she sucked at a patch of skin along his neck, biting it gently.

"You'll come to the movie with me tomorrow night, won't you?"

"Yes."

The Kid groaned with pleasure, then looked over at the calf, which was only a few feet away. Its new face filled up with curiosity as it watched them.

"You like me a lot?" he asked her.

"More than anything," Amy said.

"You going to stay with me?"

"Yes."

"Always?"

"Of course."

"Will you prove it?"

"Yes."

The Kid reached to his side, feeling about the pocket of his leather jacket until he felt the bulge of the hunting knife. When he pulled it out, he handed it to her.

"See this?" he asked.

Amy nodded.

The Kid pointed to the calf, which still stared at them. "See your friend over there?"

Amy nodded once again.

"Kill it," said the Kid.

Amy took the knife.

Without hesitation she obeyed.

• Twenty-Two •

IF EMILY JOSLIN HAD LEARNED a single grim fact in all her years of nursing, it was that people who were dying had a certain smell. It was a subtle smell, yet one she had always noticed, often recognizing it even before the patient had been diagnosed as fatal.

Now Emily stood at the bedside of her friend Cora Grady, and she smelled it—subtle as always, like the vague odor of something dusty—and it made her sad.

"How are you?" she asked, leaning over Cora's bed.

Cora had lost so much weight she was barely visible within the tangle of bedding, and she offered nothing more than a long, phlegm-filled moan.

But Emily had asked the question only out of habit, for she knew that Cora would never speak to her again. Cora Grady hadn't spoken since she had the stroke two years ago.

"Are they treating you all right?" Emily asked.

Emily ran a finger along Cora's forehead, which was cool yet damp. Reaching for a towel, she dabbed it dry, then watched as Cora's fingers curled just slightly in response.

In all these weeks of visiting, Emily had come to recognize such subtle reactions; she could read her tiny movements as though they were part of a secret code.

"Dr. Matson's still a slave driver," Emily said, noticing that the fingers relaxed. This signaled that Cora was pleased with what she had heard.

Emily was careful when she mentioned Matson, for she did not share her friend's admiration for the man. Emily, in fact, had always suspected Cora's infatuation with the doctor.

"Weather's the biggest news in town," Emily continued, then

stopped, deciding it was best not to mention the freak summer snowstorm. It was, after all, difficult enough for those in the best of health to deal with. Why worry Cora about it?

The weather, in fact, had almost prevented Emily's weekly visit to her friend. If not for Emily's nephew, a truck driver who had been leaving Wallenberg that morning on a long haul, she would not have made it.

Emily sat silent for a moment, unable to think of anything to say.

She thought of what happened at Odeon. "They closed down the old movie theatre," she said.

Cora's hand twisted, the thumb moving rapidly from side to side. Emily recognized this as a signal that Cora didn't like what she had heard.

Odd, she thought, for she hadn't known that her friend cared very much about the theatre. As far as she knew, Cora had never even gone there.

How I wish we could talk. How I wish we could just sit down and have one of our good old chats.

Emily stared hopelessly into the cold, dead eyes that she could not hope to penetrate.

How I wish I could convince you, Cora, that the good doctor might not be so good!

Emily had been in a quandary about the doctor's affairs for some time now. On many occasions she had actually decided to quit, and she'd gone so far as to write up lengthy, detailed letters of resignation, always losing her nerve when it came time to deliver them.

No matter what anyone says, Emily thought, the doctor is a frightening man.

But several things had bothered her lately about the doctor, especially the incident with Karen. When Emily first heard that name—Karen Webster—an alarm had gone off. She was certain she had heard the name before. Even more important, she was certain she had heard *Cora* mention the name.

And damn it, she thought, the doctor *did* replace Karen's records with phony ones! What was he trying to hide? Was Karen right? *Did* the baby survive?

Emily leaned forward, close enough to study Cora's face. Once pretty, it had lost its delicate set from all the weight loss; the flesh now hung in loose folds along the cheeks, and the mouth, once full and sensual, had become a thin, frowning line.

Leaning down even closer, so that her lips almost touched the old woman's ears, Emily spoke. "Karen Webster came to the office. She was asking about her old medical records."

Cora's eyes grew wide within the deep sockets. She closed her right hand, squeezing it tight, so that it soon became a tiny wrinkled fist.

At once Emily recognized it as one of the old woman's signals: She was deeply upset.

"I want into his room!" Karen demanded of the elderly desk clerk.

His old eyes darted to Paul, who stood behind Karen and shrugged.

"Not policy to let people into other folks' rooms."

"I understand that," she said, "but no one's seen Carl lately. He might be sick."

Paul stepped forward. "Might have had an accident in his room, see . . . slipped in the tub or something, maybe shocked himself on the faulty wiring. Could be a lawsuit."

After considering what Paul said, the clerk turned to the row of cubbyholes behind him, grabbing a set of keys.

As they all moved to the elevator, Karen whispered to Paul. "Why is it men only listen to *men*?"

"That's because women worry about people," Paul whispered back. "Men worry about litigation."

At Carl's door the desk clerk fumbled with his keys, working his way through several until he found the one that fit. Before opening the door, he turned to Karen and Paul.

"Haven't seen him for a few days," he said. His eyes narrowed. "Sure you knocked hard enough? Old Carl kinda gets in a dream world from time to time."

"Yes," Karen snapped.

Scowling, the clerk turned the key, and while Karen looked furtively to Paul, the door creaked open noisily.

Once inside, they all reacted at once to the terrible cold.

"Like a freezer in here," the clerk said, his breath forming a quick stream of vapor before him.

Karen and Paul eyed the bed, which was empty. Glancing at each other, they shared a moment of relief, for their worst fear had been finding Carl sprawled dead across the blankets.

Paul opened the single closet and found it empty.

Relieved as she was, Karen was suddenly overcome with

sadness. "How long has he been in this room?" she asked the clerk.

While rubbing his hands together to make them warm, the clerk shrugged. "Oh, guess about fifteen years or so."

"Why is the room substandard?" she asked. "It isn't nearly as nice as mine."

"Difference between the permanent rooms and the transients," the clerk said, defensive.

Karen thought of all the years in which she had tried to invent a life for Carl. At no time had she envisioned such despair.

Karen continued through the room, touching his things—the pitiful markers of his life. On the chipped bureau, across a yellowed newspaper, lay a comb with thatches of hair trapped in its teeth. Next to that was a glass filled with filmy water, beside it an uncapped tube of toothpaste. Her hand stopped at a soup can, its lid standing up, coated by a dry crust and mildew.

Paul walked up to her. "Shall we go?"

Karen nodded.

Just as they reached the door, she saw the note, which she picked up and read at once. As she finished, her face went pale with shock.

"What is it?" Paul asked.

Karen handed it to him slowly. "A confession," she said.

"What?"

After reading the childlike message himself, he looked at Karen. "My God, Karen, it just can't be."

Karen felt in a daze. Walking slowly to the window, she stared down at Main Street, which was covered by a blanket of snow.

She saw the hand-painted sign in the Chevron lot: TIRE CHAINS NOW AVAILABLE!

"They have chains now," she said, turning to them.

"Got 'em in from Haleyville," the clerk said, "but you'd better hurry."

Karen started for the door.

"Karen!" Paul cried, watching her leave.

He followed her to the elevator, where she punched several times at the call button.

"Where are you going?"

Karen spun to him. "You heard him! If I'm going to get chains, I'd better hurry. I'm leaving here, Paul. Once and for all, I'm leaving here!"

The elevator doors shuddered open and Karen stepped inside.

"But what about your child?"

Karen was crying now, and she made no attempt to wipe the tears that flooded from her eyes. "I don't have a child. I killed my child. Seventeen years ago."

When the doors began to shut, Paul jumped into the elevator with her. He held up Carl's note as they started downward, the old elevator creaking in its shaft. "There's something wrong with this, Karen."

"What?"

"Remember the last one? The one we found with all the clippings?"

"Yes."

"In that note he spelled the word *theatre* wrong. He spelled it *t-h-e-e-t-u-r*."

Paul pointed to the new note.

"See? In this one he spells it right. Funny, don't you think? Almost all the other words are misspelled, so why did he suddenly spell *theatre* right?"

"What are you suggesting, Paul?"

"That Carl didn't write this note. That maybe somebody else did."

"Who?"

"Somebody who wants you to leave. The doctor, maybe . . . or the sheriff."

As Karen stared at the note, the elevator lurched to a stop at her floor. Wiping at her eyes, she looked at Paul. "Maybe it's all best forgotten," she said. "Maybe I *should* have left things well enough alone."

"I can't believe you mean that. The truth is, I think you're just getting onto something."

After stepping out of the elevator, Karen flared with anger and turned to him. "What makes *you* the authority on the brave thing to do?" she cried. "You weren't so brave down in the foyer that time, were you?"

Karen regretted her outburst the moment it left her lips. "I'm sorry," she said.

Paul folded the note and handed it back to her. "Take it," he said. "He wrote it to you."

The doors to the elevator closed and Karen turned and walked to her room, where she intended to pack her things and leave Wallenberg forever.

• • •

It looked like a monster.

Deputy Travers grinned. "Pretty swell, huh?"

Bradley watched as his deputy slipped into a seat atop the snowplow.

"You know how to run that thing?"

Travers glared at him, then consulted a small instruction manual. After a moment he examined a group of buttons and levers, yanking the largest.

"Whoaa!" he cried as the snowplow shook into sudden, noisy life.

"Just be careful!" Bradley cried.

With a lurching motion the snowplow sputtered and started down Main Street while Deputy Travers, glancing at the instruction manual, yanked at levers and pressed buttons.

Shaking his head, considering any number of disastrous scenarios that might await the huge machine and its inexperienced driver, Sheriff Bradley walked inside his office.

The first thing he did was dial home, for he'd been unable to reach Amy all morning, getting the busy signal each time he tried.

Amy had been worse than ever at breakfast—rude and abrasive, actually cursing at him when he asked if she was all right. To the sheriff it was as if his polite, responsible daughter had become someone else.

After dialing he waited anxiously, but once again he heard the irritating pulse of the busy signal.

Hanging up, Bradley considered driving home, but he decided he didn't have time. The town was jumping with activity, given the continuing storm, and he had his work cut out for him. Bradley had only barely avoided the media, which had set up shop at Ruby's Cafe, intent upon chronicling the freak storm for the national news.

Deciding he would distract himself with paperwork, Bradley poured a cup of coffee and walked to his desk, which spilled over with the sort of bureaucratic tasks he hated.

Sipping coffee from a thick mug labeled *The Boss*, he reached for a group of forms that needed his attention.

One of the forms caught his attention immediately, for he realized it was the result of the fingerprint check he had ordered on the Kid.

Bradley unfolded it at once, eager for the results, for he was still suspicious of the Kid. He didn't trust him and he didn't like the connection he was making with Amy. Maybe if he had some proof, his daughter wouldn't hate him for keeping them apart.

But when Bradley looked at the report, he was puzzled. He looked twice and then again, checking to make certain he hadn't made a mistake.

Fuming, he realized that Deputy Travers had made one of his classic blunders.

After all, he thought, how else could the Kid's fingerprints have come back identifying him as Billy Burnside?

"You sure your parents know where you are?"

Kenny looked at the Greyhound bus driver and met his gaze direct. His dad had told him that the best thing to do when you were scared of someone was to look them right in the eyes.

"Yes, sir," Kenny said.

The driver stood just outside the door of the huge bus, which was loading up for the rest of the journey up the coast to Haleyville. To Kenny, the driver seemed a hundred feet tall. While he had already taken Kenny's ticket, the driver hadn't torn off the little receipt yet, so the boy still worried that he was going to get caught.

But after looking at Kenny suspiciously for a long time, the driver smiled and tore his ticket. "Okay," he said, handing Kenny his receipt. "Get on board, son."

"Yes, sir."

Scrambling up the steps and rounding the corner as fast as he could, Kenny moved all the way to the back of the bus, where the only people seated were a couple of soldiers, who were sound asleep, their long legs stretched across their duffel bags. Kenny squeezed in between, being careful not to wake them.

So far, so good, for he had planned on sitting in the back of the bus anyway. He'd taken a long bus trip with his grandmother once, and he remembered how the driver never bothered people much in the back. "That's where all the criminals sit," his grandmother had warned, but Kenny hadn't believed her.

After all, he thought, that's where the sleepy soldiers sat and the women with the babies that cried all night and made too much noise. The people who sat in the back of the bus were the ones who didn't quite fit in for some reason or another.

And that's exactly how Kenny felt.

When the bus finally started up, knocking forward with a hiss and a lurch, Kenny felt a pang of instant relief. He'd never done anything quite like this before, and he kept conjuring up the vivid scenes of punishment that would be inflicted upon him once he was caught.

What'll Rita do?

He pictured his mother as she discovered he'd lifted fifty dollars from her purse.

Would she call the cops?

Maybe she won't want me anymore!

After a moment the thought of not having to live with his mother anymore actually comforted him, which made the boy feel guilty, and he slumped down in the sticky bus seat and folded his arms.

It wasn't that he didn't like his mother, it was just that he needed his dad so much more. Try as he could, Kenny couldn't explain that to anyone and he was too embarrassed to try. Besides, he couldn't understand why he couldn't live with Paul and help him run the video store.

Kenny felt the bus pulling forward, the seat vibrating beneath him, and as the bus moved out of the station, the boy was frightened, for the sheer magnitude of his act was hitting him now. Watching the seedy downtown streets of Los Angeles pass by, realizing they were now a part of the world he faced and not just something he watched from the protection of his father's car, Kenny felt like crying. He found himself wishing that grown-ups would consider the consequences of their acts once in a while.

If they did, he thought, I wouldn't be in a mess like this.

The night before, he had heard his mother talking on the phone, and even without knowing his dad was on the other end Kenny could tell by his mother's angry voice that she was talking to his father. When it came to his parents' fighting, the boy had become a kind of unofficial expert.

Later, when his mother told him that he couldn't see his father for a while, not even on the alternate weekends he had become accustomed to, Kenny felt a rise of panic that was stronger than anything he had ever felt before.

In his nightmare he was certain he would never see his dad again.

The whole thing with the exploding television set had made him feel bad enough, but now it bugged him that his dad, who hadn't done anything wrong, was getting all the blame.

Why were adults like that? They were always yelling at kids, but then they always *acted* like kids.

And besides, his dad was the only one who'd seemed to believe him, he thought, and in fact he couldn't help but think that his dad was having some kind of trouble with that stupid *Blood Beast* movie too.

Kenny couldn't forget how scared his dad had looked when he told him about it.

Thing is, Kenny figured he had to get to his dad and help him out, and besides, he knew that Rita and her husband were fixing to send him to another one of those psychiatrist guys.

I hate it! I hate it!

When they sent him to that last one, Kenny got so scared it almost seemed worse than the thing that had sent him there in the first place.

He couldn't ever exactly remember the little "spells" they said he had. That's what he'd always heard his mom and dad call them. All he knew was that he woke up from them really scared—sometimes he was even shaking.

Whenever possible, he tried to hide anything the slightest bit strange from his mom and dad, for he was afraid that it would only worry them and that they'd send him to another one of those doctors.

Kenny had never told them, for instance, the real reason he'd got so obsessed—that was the word they used—with the yellow rain slicker over at the Glendale Mall.

He'd never told them that the real reason he wanted to buy it was that a voice had come to him telling him that he *had* to buy it. That he'd *better* buy it.

Now Kenny felt a little scared, for thoughts like this *always* scared him.

Had he done the right thing?

Sure, sure, I have to help Dad, have to help my daddy, and I have to get that guy with the yellow rain slicker out of my head!

I can't stand him! I can't stand him!

And that's what had scared him most—that skinny, ugly, pimple-faced kid in the rain slicker, the one who'd come to him night after night.

He'd come to him so often, in fact, that Kenny felt a weird sort of relationship to him, as though he were some nuisance of a brother that he didn't like much or something.

In the seat beside him, one of the soldiers stirred, causing Kenny to jump with surprise.

Kenny looked at his eyes, which were still shut in sleep. He watched the mouth as it started fluttering and twitching at the edges, as if the soldier might suddenly wake up.

Guys that age scared Kenny, for they made him think of the creep in the yellow rain slicker, who'd been coming to him so long in his nightmares.

And last night, Kenny had woken up in the worst panic he'd ever experienced, and this time he had felt something different—instead of just scared, he felt mad.

He was mad that they were all trying to keep him from his dad. He missed his dad, and he thought he ought to be able to see him whenever he wanted and whether they wanted him to or not.

When Kenny called up the video store and found out from one of the clerks there that his dad had gone to Wallenberg, and when he'd finally got up the nerve to steal the money from his mother's purse for a ticket, he wasn't even exactly sure where Wallenberg was.

Except that he did sort of remember it was where that theatre was.

What was the name of it? He wondered, sitting there on the bus and trying to remember.

It was a funny name. He had always mispronounced it.

Oh, yeah . . . Yeah, it was called Odeon.

• Twenty-Three •

PAUL DIDN'T BLAME her for wanting to leave. The memories were simply too painful. Maybe it did no good to stir up the past like this.

He walked to the window of his room, pulling back the curtain so that he could see the Chevron station, where she sat in a little room off the service bay. She waited with several other citizens of Wallenberg, all of them trying to get chains. Meanwhile, their cars were parked akimbo along Main Street, some with the doors flung open, as if abandoned. To Paul it looked like some perverse Christmas card.

Maybe I should leave too.

What was there to do, after all? When Karen left, he had no reason to stay. If it hadn't been for Karen, he wouldn't have come at all.

But everything that had happened continued to bug him. He knew that the theatre was somehow involved, and he suspected that Jack MacGruder knew a lot about what was going on.

Paul looked at the theatre, hoping to get a glimpse of the man. The terrazzo was invisible now, totally obscured by snow, which blew in great steady blasts up off the sidewalk. The forecourt acted like a wind tunnel and there was a constant, mournful moan.

Eager to talk to Jack, Paul had called his house several times, and on two occasions he had gone over to the theatre, where he had pounded on the brass doors, but the old man was not to be found.

Most of all, Paul wanted to ask the old man some questions—more important, he wanted *Karen* to have the opportunity to ask

Jack questions, specifically whether the old man had seen her attacker.

What was the old man doing down there the day of her rape, after all?

Had he seen anyone?

Or had Jack MacGruder himself attacked Karen?

No, he thought, impossible. Jack may have been many things, he decided, but a rapist was certainly not on the list.

But now, as Paul watched the snow that fell above his hometown street in the middle of August, he realized that what was and was not possible had little to do with what he believed.

Just as he was about to turn away from the window, he saw him. The old man was walking up Main Street, his arms thrust deep into the pockets of his huge wool coat. After stomping his feet, the old man walked into Ruby's Cafe.

"Time was you got soup *and* salad with dinner," Jack said. "Now you only get one or the other."

Even when Jack complained, his voice remained soft and modulated. After gently putting down his fork and wiping his small mouth, he spoke again.

"It really is wonderful seeing you, Paul. I've thought about you often over the past few years."

As the old man buttered a piece of bread, Paul watched his hands, which still seemed impossibly small and delicate.

"I've been trying to get ahold of you for a couple of days, Jack."

"Sorry. It's been a terrible time. I'm sure you heard about Roy."

"Yes," Paul said, stung by sudden embarrassment, for he hadn't thought to offer his condolences. "I'm really sorry."

Ruby arrived with a coffeepot. Two bracelets clattered on her wrist as she refilled their cups.

"Sorry it's so cold," she said, as if the weather were her fault. "Heard there's not a heater working in all of Wallenberg."

"That's right," Jack said. "Except at the theatre."

"That so?" Ruby asked, then scuttled off into the busy cafe.

"Is it true?" Paul asked. "Does Odeon have the only working heater?"

Jack took a small portion of his mashed potatoes, dabbing it into his mouth with a nod.

"Odd, don't you think?" asked Paul. I mean, we're talking

about heaters of all types—electric, gas, steam. Right? The hotel, for instance—they've got steam heat, and it's out too. If it were just the gas heaters, I'd understand . . . but everything?"

"Everything seems odd, wouldn't you say, Paul?"

Paul nodded.

"So what did you do with your life, Paul? Didn't you go off to Hollywood to make movies?"

Paul flushed with embarrassment. "Didn't quite make it."

"Few do, I guess. I never had the nerve to try it, even though I wanted to. Hard down there, I suppose."

"Very."

"Family, Paul?"

"Wife. Son. Divorced, though."

"Sorry."

For a moment Paul felt a kinship with Jack MacGruder, for certainly there had never been two boys in Wallenberg who had loved the movies more than they had. It was Paul's father, knowing how much his son loved movies, who had conned the old man into allowing Paul a glimpse of the projection room. It was the biggest thrill of his childhood, for to a movie-crazy child a projection room was a magic place.

"You love the theatre, don't you, Jack?"

The old man nodded, then lifted his cup. After blowing gently on its steaming surface, he sipped.

Paul was silent for a long time, for he hated asking his next question. "What's wrong, Jack? What's wrong with the theatre?"

"Wrong?"

"You know what I mean. All these things that have been happening."

"City Council said there aren't rats," Jack said.

"You don't believe that, do you?"

"Of course I do."

"And you're really going to have this closing ceremony tonight?"

"Yes."

"In this awful weather? Why? Why not wait?"

"I can't . . . they won't let me."

"Who?"

Jack cleared his throat, then reached for his collar, which he tugged away from his neck. Nervous, he began to sweat. "I meant the Mayor and the council," Jack said. "I arranged for tonight, so it has to be tonight."

Paul remembered Karen's theory. "What about Mrs. Wallenberg, Jack? The night of Odeon's opening."

Jack's eyes grew wide. He suddenly looked terrified, like an animal trapped in car headlights. "What about Mrs. Wallenberg?" he asked indignantly.

"I understand she died the night Odeon opened. I understand that you found her, Jack."

"Why, everyone knows that!"

Paul hated to pursue the old man so aggressively—he could see the fear and pain in his eyes—but he felt he had no choice.

"Mr. MacGruder, did Mrs. Wallenberg try to abort her child?"

"Yes!"

Embarrassed, the old man slapped a hand across his mouth, for the word had seemed to escape unbidden. Now he released a strange sound—a desperate, muffled whimper—and he looked away from Paul, staring at his empty plate.

Before Paul could speak, he heard Karen's voice and he turned to her. She moved toward his table, followed by Emily Joslin and her truck driver nephew, a large, burly man with a beard.

When all introductions were made, Emily spoke first. "I think I have proof that Karen's child survived."

"Her friend," Karen said, "the nurse who attended me. She's still alive."

Jack shot up from the table. "No!" he cried, then took Karen's arm. Noticing the heads that had turned to him in the tiny cafe, he lowered his voice and whispered to her. "Go home! Leave it be!"

With that, he turned and ran out of Ruby's.

Emily looked at all of them. "It's awfully cold," she said. "S'pose we could talk over a shot of whiskey?"

Like everywhere else in Wallenberg, the Busy Bee was freezing. While two space heaters glowed in the center of the dark room and provided some heat, it was still cold enough to see Emily's breath as she spoke to them.

"I was upset from the moment Karen came into my office," she began. "For years I've been suspicious about the doctor . . . It might mean my job, but I'd rather see justice done. I knew for a fact that he'd destroyed some of the old files. Further, I knew that something funny was going on with Karen's file in particular."

Karen and Paul waited while Emily took a sip of her Irish coffee. Her nephew sat beside her, drinking a glass of draft beer.

"Cora was my friend," Emily continued. "We talked about

things . . . had confidences. I knew that she had a crush on the doctor back when she was his nurse. At that time I worked for another doctor over in Haleyville. Cora used to talk about a case involving this young girl. I have a good memory, see, and I remember that the girl's name was Karen Webster."

Smiling, Emily reached for Karen's hand and squeezed it affectionately. "But, you see, I *remember* seeing Karen's file. When she came in the other day, I knew it existed. When I asked the doctor about it, he said it didn't exist. He lied to me. We quarreled about it that day, in fact."

Emily looked Karen in the eyes. "Honey, it really bothered me the other day to see how upset you were . . . I didn't sleep that whole night because something was haunting me . . . something *really* bad."

Now Emily turned to Paul. "You see, Cora told me once that this young girl . . . a high school student . . . had tried to abort her child and had passed out and gone into shock in the process. But Cora told me that the baby *lived*. She told me that the girl's mother and the doctor sold the baby to someone in Wallenberg who desperately wanted a child. Meanwhile, the girl was told that her baby had died."

"Who took Karen's baby?" asked Paul.

Karen answered immediately. "It was Sheriff Bradley," she said. "Amy is my daughter. I know it."

Paul looked at Emily. "Is it possible?"

"Yes," she said, "Amy *was* adopted. I do know that."

"Then we'll go to Matson," Paul said.

Emily bristled. "You will *not*! How would you explain where you heard this?"

"Of course," Paul said, embarrassed. "How stupid of me." He looked at Karen. "No use going to Bradley without proof. I mean, it's likely he didn't even know about the deception. We need to talk to somebody who was there that night."

"Precisely," Emily said. "That's why I tried to communicate with Cora in the first place."

"Is there any way you can communicate with her further?" he asked.

Emily sighed deeply, then looked at Karen. "I have a feeling that if Karen herself were to ask, it might trigger the response we need."

"It's worth a try," Karen said.

Paul thought of the storm. "But how can we even get over there?"

Emily's nephew, until that moment utterly silent, spoke in a deep voice. "I'll drive ya."

"Good boy," Emily cried, downing the rest of her drink.

Paul signaled for the check and Emma Burnside arrived, locking eyes for a moment with Karen. When Emma went away to get change, Paul could see that Karen was troubled.

"You all right?"

Karen turned to him and smiled weakly. "Of course," he said.

But she immediately looked back in the direction of Emma, who was up at the bar and getting their change. The odd angles of the woman's face were struck by the ambient glint of neon from the gaudy jukebox.

As she returned with Paul's change, Emma noticed that Karen was staring at her.

Setting down her tip tray before Paul, she turned to Karen. "Can I help you, miss?"

"No," she said, looking away.

Dr. Matson was thinking about money—lots of it.

He tried to picture the cash he'd get from the Odeon mini-mall deal, once he worked out his cut with the mayor. He imagined the money spread across his bed, or stacked in bundles inside a valise, the way it always was in movies that had a kidnaping theme.

Now he pulled at the chains along the front left tire of his Chrysler New Yorker, checking his handiwork. Squatting in his garage, he examined the tires and burped the indigestion that came with having too much bourbon with his lunch.

There, he thought, checking the other three tires. No use paying the Chevron to do it when I can do it myself. Matson prided himself when it came to areas of thrift.

He moved to a small sink in the garage, where he flooded his large hands with water, then scrubbed them with Boraxo, working the lather thoroughly up to his elbows, just the way he would before surgery. Back inside the house, he checked the thermostat and saw that his heater was still not working.

Cursing, he started to wrap himself in a blanket when the telephone rang.

"Hello!"

There was a long pause at the other end.

"Doctor?"

"Yes, who is this?"

"This is Sheriff Bradley . . ."

Matson hesitated before answering, for it didn't sound to him like Bradley, whose deep, gruff voice was usually recognizable at once. Instead, the voice was high-pitched, even soft. It had what he decided was a singsong lilt to it.

"What's wrong with you, Leo? Got a cold or something?"

"We need to talk," the voice said, ignoring his question. "It's about Karen Webster."

Matson's stomach turned.

He had tried to ignore the problem with Karen Webster, but their scene together had upset him a lot. "What is it, Leo?"

"She knows!" the voice said.

"Knows what?" Matson demanded.

"Meet me and I'll tell you."

"Meet you where?"

"The cemetery. Near the main vault."

"The cemetery! Christ, Leo, why the cemetery! For God's sake, there's a damned blizzard out there."

"You have chains!" said the voice.

"How did you know that?" he asked, but it was too late. Whoever had been on the other end of the line had hung up.

Matson kept his eye to the road as he drove to the cemetery.

With its sudden sharp turns and steep rise, the road was difficult under the best of circumstances, let alone in a snowstorm that had left it nearly invisible. Meanwhile, the clatter of chains beneath the Chrysler unnerved him.

It was only his memory of the road that led the doctor to the large, rusted gates that marked the cemetery. Flung outward and hanging loose at the hinge, the gates were shaped like angels.

Matson idled the car, so that soon he was surrounded by a cloud of vapor. He looked through the thickening mass for the sheriff's patrol car, but he saw nothing. Even worse, he wasn't exactly certain now where he was.

Under normal circumstances, Matson knew the cemetery well, but now, blanketed by snow, it confused him; it lacked the usual landmarks provided by recognizable clusters of tombstones.

Wiping at the window, Matson squinted against the white glare, finally making out the vault where Bradley had told him to meet him.

What the hell does he wanna meet in this mess for? he thought, then switched off the engine. Gathering his coat collar to his neck, he opened the door and stepped out, reacting to the loud crunch of ice beneath his weight.

Up on a rise, the vault was of a heavy Gothic design, crumbling beneath a weeping willow whose boughs sagged all the way to the ground with snow and ice.

Matson approached, all the time watching for Bradley, but there was still no sign of him. Furious at what he decided must have been a practical joke, Matson trembled in the cold and he rubbed his gloved hands together. His face ached with cold and he knew that before evening fell he'd be sick in bed.

"Bradley!" he screamed.

His voice was a brittle echo in the cold air, followed by silence.

A few minutes later Matson started back for the car. Furious and chilled to the bone, he no longer cared if Bradley was coming or not.

While waiting for the car to fill with heat, Matson looked in the rearview mirror.

Odd, he thought.

A man approached. He had come out from behind the vault that Matson had just left. It was not Bradley, he realized, but a much older man—much taller and skinnier than the sheriff. Dressed in a loose blue suit, he looked emaciated.

Matson looked away, reflecting.

Who the hell could it be? Who else would be dumb enough to walk through the cemetery in weather like this?

The caretaker! he thought, relieved.

But out in the snow?

Dressed in a suit?

Looking up, Matson saw that the man had moved closer, and it was obvious that the car was his destination.

The man's eyes—so dark they seemed but empty sockets—stared intently, and he walked in a shambling motion; sticklike arms waved above his head. His face was pasty white, its expression blank and dead.

Matson started the car and released the brake, but when he tried to drive, the engine died and the car came rolling to a stop. The man was only a few feet behind him now.

Matson turned the key, grinding the starter, but the engine only sputtered and died again, its final droning noise traveling through icy air, leaving in its aftermath a deadly quiet.

Matson was frightened. He could not bring himself to turn and look out his window, as he feared that the strange old man might be standing there, looking in at him.

Slam!

Jumping at the sound, Matson looked to his left, where the old man had brought his hand up hard against the window. He hit it again. And again.

"Get away!" Dr. Matson screamed, trying in vain to start the car again.

Now the old man pressed his face to the window. His lips, dead and grey, moved up and down, passing across rotten teeth. The look in his eyes was desperate, and Matson knew where he had seen that look before: in the eyes of something wild and starved.

The old man pulled away with an angry snarl, frustrated by his failure to gain entrance to the car. After bending to pick up a rock, he held it in huge, bloodless hands and slammed it up against the window.

It did not break.

Frantic, Matson slid across the seat, reaching for the handle to the other door, figuring he would jump out and run as fast as he could to North Post Road, where someone was bound to see him.

But suddenly he heard the sound of exploding glass.

Matson turned just in time to see the million gummy shards as they spewed from the force of the rock and showered into the car, followed by the old man's arms, which groped about greedily. The arms were long and revoltingly pale.

In speechless horror Matson sat still.

Until the old man's hands found his throat.

After getting out of the truck, Karen and Paul followed Emily up the walk to the hospital in Haleyville. Inside, Emily moved up to the nurse's station.

"We're here to see Cora," she said.

The nurse glanced at a doctor, who approached them down a hallway. He took her hand with a friendly greeting, but they all sensed something was wrong.

"What is it, Doctor?" Emily asked.

He looked at Karen and Paul.

"They're friends," Emily said.

"Well," he began, "there's never an easy way to say this, so I won't even try. Cora passed away. About an hour after you left."

Emily looked at Karen, who turned away.

When Paul moved to comfort her, Karen gestured him away with a gentle rise of her hand.

• Twenty-Four •

HE KNEW THEY WERE going to come for him.

When they pounded on the brass doors and threatened to call the police if he didn't talk with them, Jack let them into his theatre immediately.

Paul stared at him. "Look, Mr. MacGruder, I don't mean to be an asshole, but if that's what it takes to get information out of you, then I will be. Believe me."

Karen entered behind him. "Mr. MacGruder, I've been through a lot. If you know something, you have to tell me now."

Surprisingly, Jack did not act defensively. On the contrary, he appeared relieved, inviting them into his theatre with a gentle beckoning motion.

"Come in," he said, "where it's warm. The *only* place where it's warm."

"What in the hell's going on, MacGruder?" snapped Paul when Jack closed the great brass doors behind them. Indeed, the lobby was warm, almost hot. "Why did you run out of the cafe like that?"

Karen stepped in front of Paul. "Forgive us, Mr. MacGruder, but we're ready for the truth."

Jack nodded. "I'm sorry. I should have talked to you as soon as I knew you were in town."

"Have you been hiding from me, Mr. MacGruder?"

"Yes," he admitted to her.

"Why?"

Jack gestured them forward. "I think it's best if we begin downstairs. Right where it all began."

• • •

The first thing he showed them was the tapestry that Mike Barnes had defaced with his knife.

"You see this?" he asked, looking at Karen. "How old would you say this was?"

Karen walked up and touched the fabric, gently rubbing it between her thumb and forefinger. Perplexed, she looked at Jack. "Has it been replaced? It seems brand-new."

"No. It's as old as the theatre."

"Impossible," said Paul, touching it himself.

"The boy who was killed by the rats cut into this tapestry," Jack said.

"What are you talking about, Mr. MacGruder?" Karen asked.

Jack looked at them both. "The theatre is regenerating itself."

"What?" Karen cried.

Jack released the tapestry from his grip. "You know how a snake sheds its old skin? Well, that's what Odeon is beginning to do. The tapestry revitalized *itself*. The morning after the boy's death, I found it this way."

Paul and Karen exchanged a look.

Jack smiled. "I don't blame you for being skeptical."

"It's not skepticism," Karen said. "What you see is impatience. I want to know how this involves my child!"

"This way," Jack said gently, moving off toward the rest rooms. Karen looked at Paul, who took her hand as they followed him.

Inside the men's room, Jack's voice echoed off the sea of white tile.

"The night of Odeon's opening, I was standing right at the basins there, changing from my usher's uniform into my regular clothes. I had been fired for watching the movie. When I heard a moaning from the stall there, I approached it. I knew it was a woman in trouble."

Karen spoke softly. "The same one where I . . ."

"Yes," he interrupted gently. He walked up to the stall. "What I found there was a horror. Mrs. Wallenberg was a beautiful young woman. Some, including myself, felt she could have been a movie star in her own right. As you know, I found her dead. As you know further, the manner of her death was always hushed up."

Paul spoke. "She aborted her child, didn't she?"

Jack paused, then shook his head. "I'm afraid it wasn't that simple."

"How do you mean?" asked Karen.

Jack turned and looked at them. His face had drained entirely of color. In the bright light of the huge tiled room, it seemed as though he had no face at all. "She truly aborted her child, I'm sure, but then . . . I think someone carved the fetus right out of her womb!"

Karen moaned, crossing her hands against her stomach.

"I'm sorry," Jack said.

She looked up at him. "Who would do such a thing?"

"No one ever knew, except for me."

"Who did it?" Karen asked.

"Forbes Carlton," Jack said. "After it was over, I ran all the way up to a little hill that overlooks Wallenberg. It was kind of a secret place that I had as a kid. He followed me there."

Jack felt a curious rush of excitement as he spoke. In all the years since it happened, he had told no one about his experience with Forbes Carlton, and there was a sense of relief now as the words flooded up from inside.

"In the moonlight he looked monstrous, and I had never been so frightened . . . have never been that frightened since. He was carrying a carpetbag. When I looked, I saw that it was soaked along the bottom with blood. He opened it up and forced me to look inside. It was there, in the carpetbag, the remains of the little baby . . ."

"My God!" Karen cried.

"What did you do?" asked Paul.

Jack stopped pacing. After clearing his throat, he looked at them. "Nothing. I told no one. He told me he would kill me if I did. He knew how much I loved the movies, you see . . . more than life itself. He knew that I loved Odeon more than anything else on earth. And it is so very, very beautiful . . . Odeon is."

"Why didn't you report him?" Karen asked.

"I was frightened," he said, then studied each of them. "How much do you know about the man?"

After Paul related what he and Karen had read in the clippings, Jack nodded. "Yes, all of that is true . . . the child sacrifices, the Church of Satan. All of it and more! He was capable of changing his shape . . . he could become other people."

"Where is he?" Paul demanded.

Jack paused. "But don't you see, the real question is, *Who* is he?"

Karen looked at him accusingly. "Who attacked me? Did you see who it was?"

Jack's old eyes fluttered with confusion. "Attacked? When were you attacked, dear?"

Karen explained what had happened to her that day.

"And you were coming down the stairs just before it happened," Paul said, not bothering to hide the accusation in his tone.

"My god," Jack said. "Is that what you think? Of course, I didn't see anyone. If I had, I would have done something.

"This way," he said, leading them out of the rest room and into his office across the foyer, where he flicked on an old tabletop fan made of olive-green metal. It clattered noisily as it pushed stale air across the tiny room.

"If I was coming downstairs during a matinee," Jack said, "then most likely I was coming to my office. I've had this fan for thirty years. As you can see, it's very noisy. When I'm working in here with the fan on, I can hear nothing."

Paul considered this, then looked at Karen, who sighed and looked at Jack. After a moment she spoke. "I believe you."

The old man sat in his desk chair, folding his hands pensively before him. "And of course, Karen, I'm assuming that the baby you tried to abort was . . . the product of this attack."

Karen nodded.

Jack grew thoughtful for a moment, then looked up. "But of course I think I know who attacked you."

"Forbes Carlton?" Karen asked without hesitation.

"Yes," Jack said. "You see, I believe that the theatre is still controlled by Forbes Carlton, wherever he is and whoever he's become. I believe that the theatre is touched by the same unspeakable evil that characterized Carlton's church in San Francisco."

Paul spoke. "The sacrifice of children."

"Yes. Mrs. Wallenberg's baby. Karen's . . ."

Karen leaned down to him. "Why did you run out of the cafe like that? What do you know about my child? Do you know where my child is?"

"No!" he said. "I honestly do not. I'd tell you if I did, I swear it! But I know that if indeed your child is alive, Carlton intends to sacrifice it to the theatre."

"But why go on with this show tonight?" Paul demanded. "Why not just lock up the place and be rid of it?"

"Because I'm frightened!" he cried. "I'm afraid of what he might do. You've seen the terrible evil he's already perpetrated. That poor boy . . . the rats!"

Swallowing hard, he tried to regain his composure, continuing more calmly.

"When it happened, I tried to pretend it wasn't true. I had

convinced myself that it was just an unfortunate accident . . .
the rats had come in from the sewers or something, and the
loathsome things had crawled back where they had come from. I
convinced myself that it *wasn't* the theatre. I went on with my
plans for a closing-night show, because . . . well, you must
understand that I do love this place. I wanted it to go out with
style. But always, in the back of my mind, I wondered . . .
about Carlton . . . if he intended to . . ."

"Sacrifice another child?" Karen asked.

"Yes! And then, at the cafe, when I heard about your child, I
realized it was true! Carlton intends to sacrifice another child!
Don't you see? The tapestry I showed you. If he can re-create what
happened opening night, then the theatre will renew itself!"

Karen considered what he had just said. "But in all the incidences
of child sacrifice," she said, "all the ones I read about in Carl's
clippings, it was the *mother* who took the child's life. And wasn't that
the case with Mrs. Wallenberg? Didn't she abort the child?"

"Yes," Jack said, "and that's why I think the theatre declined
over the past seventeen years. Because you weren't successful.
Your child survived!"

"But don't you see?" Karen cried. "How can it happen? Even if I
find out who my child is, there's no way that I would take its life!"

The old man grabbed her hands, holding them tightly. "I know,
Karen. I know. That's what I'm praying is true."

When they reached Karen's room, they stood in silence for a long
time.

"Do you believe it?" Paul asked.

"Yes," Karen said, "I do."

Paul nodded. "We'll talk to Dr. Matson, then to the sheriff. We
have to find out if Amy is your child."

"I know she is. And the worst thing is, I feel she's in danger,
Paul."

Karen walked up to the window, then looked across the street at
the marquee.

"Look," she said, her vice so low that Paul barely heard it.

He moved up alongside her and stared across Main Street at the
marquee.

Only four plastic letters comprised its message now.
HEAT.

• Twenty-Five •

IN THE DARK of her bedroom, Amy lay beneath the covers, hearing her father's voice as he called to her from the front room.

"Amy, are you home?"

When he opened her bedroom door, she startled against the light that suddenly silhouetted the sheriff in the doorway.

"It's still afternoon. You okay? Why are you in bed? Sick or something?"

"No, Father. I'm fine."

He stepped in further, his heavy boots thumping against the wood flooring.

"No!" she cried when he reached to turn on the light.

"What's wrong?"

"Nothing!"

"It's the weather, right? That's why you're in bed so early? 'Cause it's so cold?"

"Yes," she said, "that's it. That's why I'm in bed."

"Okay," he said, "but how about Dandelion? How about the calf?"

"What about them?"

Bradley tried to ignore her defensive tone. "I noticed the barn door wasn't closed all the way. Have you checked on them?"

"Yes, Father," Amy said, trying not to sound too impatient, for she didn't want to raise his suspicions. "Just an hour ago. Guess I forgot to close up. I'll get it later."

"Okay," he said, then stepped out of the room, closing the door behind him.

When he was gone, Amy giggled, for she could feel the Kid's tongue as it passed across her thigh, tickling her.

Now the Kid rose up from inside the covers. He wrapped her

nakedness with his own, then nibbled at her neck as he whispered. "Scared you, huh? Thought we were gonna get caught, didn't you?"

"Yes!" she cried, feeling excited all over again; the danger of almost getting caught had aroused her.

"Want me to do it to you again?"

Amy nodded.

"Harder this time?"

"Yes!"

"You like it, don't you?"

"More than anything," Amy cried, burying her face in his chest and kissing him.

"First you gotta help me," the Kid said.

"Anything . . . anything . . ."

The Kid smiled. "You'll like it," he said. "It'll be fun. More fun than the calf!"

After a moment he added, "We'll make him scream!"

"Yes!"

Bradley knew she was lying. He had noticed the barn door flung open that morning, just before he left for work. When it came to the calf, Amy was so conscientious, but now, lying in bed in the middle of the day, she hadn't seemed concerned about its safety at all. It was just the latest in what seemed to him a bizarre change in Amy's behavior.

Downing a Budweiser, he listened to the musical interlude on the other end of the line, which meant he was on hold. He had called up the college in Haleyville, asking to check up on a student, and he hadn't expected so much bureaucracy. When would he ever learn? There was bureaucracy everywhere.

"I'm sorry, Sheriff," said the woman's voice that came back on the line, "but we don't have a Tyler Briggs registered here."

"You're absolutely sure?"

"Yes."

Bradley thanked her and hung up the phone. He dialed his office immediately.

"Travers," he ordered his deputy, "I want you to put out an APB right away."

"What's the name?"

"Tyler Briggs," said the sheriff.

There was a long pause at the other end of the line.

"Something wrong?" he asked.

Travers came back on the line. "Since when've you started reading minds, Leo?"

"Huh? What the hell're you talking about?"

"Tyler Briggs? Is that the name you just said?"

"Yeah."

"Just got a call from Haleyville. Couple hikers found a body over there. Pretty gruesome, I guess. Chopped up with a damned chain saw's what I hear. Anyway, guess there was a credit card slip in his pocket. Identified him as Tyler Briggs. L.A. We got ahold of his dad there. He'd been looking for him. Seems this Tyler Briggs guy had 'borrowed' his dad's car for the weekend. If you know what I mean."

Bradley was afraid to ask the next question.

"What kind of car was it?"

"A black Corvette."

Bradley told his deputy to be on the lookout for the Kid until he got back to his office and then he hung up the phone. He felt a slow and gnawing fear unlike anything he had ever felt before. A part of him wanted to rush into Amy's room, snatch her up from the bed, and carry her away to safety.

But no. That's why she resents me in the first place. Too strict with her.

Bradley stood up and walked to his bedroom, which was just down the hall from Amy's. The room was furnished sparsely with a bed, a small dresser, and a single chair, and there were no decorations to speak of. All the little touches of his wife, the things she had placed there so lovingly throughout their marriage, had long ago been removed by Bradley. He hated it that the living got stuck with all that crap that makes you so sad to see.

How he missed her now, when Amy was in trouble. How he wished that he could go to his wife and admit that yes he was confused and scared and did not know what to do.

Bradley slipped out of his uniform shirt, letting it drop to the floor, and opened his closet, where he pulled another one off the hanger.

There were six of them, all in a row, each wrapped in plastic from the cleaner's. Sometimes it all seemed so horribly predictable to the sheriff: life, an endless journey through a terrible sameness.

Before he put on the shirt, he remembered that he had not showered the night before, and he grimaced when he sniffed at his armpit. Pulling off his clothes as he walked, Bradley moved to the bathroom.

By the time he was naked and had turned on the shower, he was shivering in the cold.

Incredible! he thought, maneuvering himself into the shower tub. It's August and it's cold enough to worry about freezing pipes!

With that, he surrendered to the spray of water, which he had turned up full blast, thinking that the needles of water would function like a massage.

When he turned his back to it, he let the water play full force along his flesh.

Amy's closet door opened slowly and the Kid stepped out, the woman's dress hanging loosely about his body.

The wig—foolishly fake—threatened to fall from the Kid's head, yet as silly as he knew he looked, he kept a straight face, refusing to laugh.

What he was about to do, he would do very seriously.

Amy stood nearby. She held a butcher knife, which she had just found for the Kid in the kitchen.

"Good," the Kid said, taking the knife, lowering it so that it brushed up against the wretched floral pattern of the ill-fitting dress that met him at mid-calf.

"We'll make him scream!" Amy said, her eyes wide and glassy.

"Shhhh!"

Walking down the hall, the Kid stiffened his posture, so that his back was perfectly straight. He kept his arms totally still and at right angles to his body as he moved in measured strides, the knife pointed forward.

Amy padded down the hallway behind him, trying not to giggle. When they reached the bathroom door, she covered up her mouth and pressed it with her hands, trying to keep from laughing aloud, which she knew would spoil everything.

Inside the bathroom, water pounded down upon the metal tub while Bradley sang.

The Kid opened the bathroom door as quietly as he could, but before he stepped inside, he turned to Amy.

"I want you to watch!" he whispered to her, and she nodded and stepped up to the door's threshold, watching as the Kid approached the shower curtain. Bradley's silhouette moved behind the plastic as he soaped his body and continued his song.

After waiting for a second, the Kid turned to Amy to see if she was watching. When he saw that she was, he raised the butcher knife.

Amy watched as he grabbed the shower curtain.

And she saw her father's startled face, just before she saw the violent flash of red.

• • •

When it was over, Amy sat on the lid to the toilet, gazing ahead into space as the Kid finished wrapping the sheriff's body in the shower curtain.

Just before he folded a flap of curtain across the man's face, Amy looked at her father's expression.

He was staring at her, she thought—that big, judging eye she had resented so much still watched her every move.

He had fallen hard, his face smashing against the tile, breaking one of his front teeth. Blood had flowed copiously, forming tiny rivers through the grout of baby-blue tile.

The Kid, who was dressed now in jeans and a blue cotton shirt, looked up from his work.

"Help me," he ordered.

His body was heavier than they expected. Dragging it across the backyard, which was now adrift in snow, they left a rust-colored trail behind them from the house.

While Amy watched him, the Kid dug a hole in the ground with a shovel he had taken from the barn. But the ground was hard, resisting his attempts to dig, and it almost bent the shovel's blade.

A half hour later he had dug a hole deep enough to hold the body. Kneeling to it, he pulled at the remaining dirt with his bare hands.

Amy watched, impressed by how fast he was able to dig with his hands. The dirt flew up every which way, and she could see that, regardless of the cold and the exertion, he was enjoying himself.

It reminded her of something.

Yes, she thought, and she remembered the time she'd come across Billy Burnside out on North Post Road. She remembered how he clawed at the ground with his ugly, sticklike fingers.

The Kid stood up, then pushed at the body with his foot. Bradley's corpse rolled easily, the plastic shower curtain that enfolded him skating smoothly across the snow.

Squatting on her haunches now, Amy held out her hand to catch the snow that fell from the sky. When her hands grew full, she squeezed, watching the snowy powder ooze through the spaces between her fingers.

Hearing her father's body drop into its icy grave, Amy began to sing.

She played in the snow and danced with delight.

It was the damnedest thing he'd ever seen in his career.

Joe Rydell had been repairing television sets in the back room of his Wallenberg appliance store ever since they were invented, but nothing had prepared him for this.

What the hell is this? A television set plague?

Irritated, Joe Rydell tossed down his screwdriver, scowling as he examined the innards of a nineteen-inch color portable, which were spread across his workbench. He had torn the television set apart twice, obsessively searching for the reason it wouldn't work, but he'd found nothing.

Meanwhile, his shop was filled with broken televisions. They were lined along the walls, often three deep, but he couldn't fix any of them.

The door opened and his wife entered, carrying another nineteen-inch portable.

"This one just came in," she said.

"No picture, no sound."

"You got it."

Joe sighed. "Put it with the rest," he said, then added, "Far as I can tell there isn't a single operating TV in all of Wallenberg. Time was, this would have been a business bonanza, now it's just a damned frustration."

"You looked at the theatre marquee today?" she asked.

"No. Why?"

"Marquee says 'Heat.' I checked it out with Deputy Travers. Guess the only place in town with a heater working is Odeon. It's the only warm place in town."

"So?"

She looked at him. "I was just thinking. Rats or no rats Jack's show tonight is sounding better and better."

When the Kid showed up with Amy at Odeon, the old man was not surprised.

"Hello, Amy," Jack said cordially, holding open the bronze door. Just moments before, the Kid had tapped on the glass, and Jack, sitting patiently in the lobby as if expecting them, had answered immediately.

Now he smiled at Amy. "Didn't expect to see you here again, honey."

Amy said nothing, but instead walked across the lobby to the refreshment stand, where she immediately began stacking paper cups.

The Kid looked at Jack. "I'll work the projectors," he said. "Amy'll handle the refreshment stand."

"Very well," Jack said, nodding sadly.

• Twenty-Six •

FOR THE THIRD TIME in an hour, Karen listened to the stern recorded message on Dr. Matson's answering machine, which informed her that the doctor could not be reached.

She hung up and looked at Paul. "I'm glad one of us isn't seriously ill," she said, getting up and moving to the window of her hotel room. She looked down at Main Street, which was completely covered with snow.

"What did Emily say when you called her?" asked Paul.

"She hasn't heard from the doctor either. She called every number she has. Nobody's seen him."

Paul considered what it might mean. Between the two of them, after all, they had turned over a number of rocks that he imagined some would prefer had been left alone.

"He could be hiding," Paul suggested, "but it's doubtful. With so many people to screen his calls, he wouldn't have to abandon his practice just to avoid you and me."

Karen nodded in agreement. "I have to find out for certain if it's Amy," she said.

"Guess it's time to talk to Bradley."

"I know," Karen said, putting on her coat, "and it's not going to be fun."

When they walked into the sheriff's office, Karen and Paul found chaos, all of it a result of the weather.

Deputy Travers sat at Bradley's cluttered desk, where he argued with someone on the telephone while sifting through a stack of messages.

With the other two lines on his telephone blinking, the deputy gestured them to a pot of fresh coffee.

They were halfway through the first cup when Travers finished with his last call, slamming up the receiver with a curse. Jotting down a message, he spoke to Karen and Paul without looking up at them.

"So how can I help you folks? If it has to do with chains or towing, forget it."

Karen stepped forward. "We need to talk to the sheriff."

"You and me both," the deputy grumbled. "Been trying to get ahold of him all afternoon. There's no answer up at the house. Funny, but the operator says the number is workin' all right, but no one answers. Not even Amy."

Travers finished scribbling a note, which he speared onto a bill file. He turned to them in the swivel chair, his thick, unhandsome features narrowing with suspicion. "Might I ask what it's regarding?"

"Old business."

"That's a relief," Travers said. "Sick of this damned weather, I'll tell you that."

He picked up the receiver and dialed the sheriff's number, letting it ring a half dozen times before he hung up. "Mighty damned funny."

"Car trouble?" Paul asked.

"Could be, but he's got a radio."

Travers stood up and moved to a coatrack, where he grabbed his overcoat and holster. "Wanna come out there with me?" he asked.

"Sure do," Paul said, and they followed Deputy Travers out the door.

Outside, the sun was about to set. Odeon's vertical sign flashed on and off, while neon arabesques danced in a circle about the marquee. It advertised heat, not movies.

They were heading down Main Street when Deputy Travers spoke.

"Hope nothing's goin' on with that Tyler Briggs character."

Karen took a quick sharp breath. "Tyler Briggs?"

"Some weird kid's in town," Travers said. "Sheriff's bent out of shape about it, 'cause he thinks he's after his daughter."

Karen's mind raced with scenarios, all of them absurd. Was *her* Tyler Briggs in town? If so, why would he be following Amy? How would he even *know* Amy?

"Weird thing," the deputy continued, "but now a guy named Tyler Briggs has turned up murdered in Haleyville."

Karen pulled away from Paul. "Oh my God!"

"What's wrong?" Paul asked.

Karen remembered the boy she had seen approaching Amy in the barn.

"This kid," she asked Travers, "nice-looking? Blond hair? About eighteen years old?"

"That's right," Travers said. "You seen him?"

Karen thought of the cigarette lighter.

Tyler Briggs *did* have the only one like it.

"Faster!" she cried. "Oh my God, go faster!"

When they got to Bradley's property, it was almost dark, for Deputy Travers was no more used to driving across snow and ice than anyone else in Wallenberg. Even with chains, the ride was erratic and dangerous. Twice they almost skidded off the ravine that ran along North Post Road.

"There's his patrol car," Deputy Travers said, pulling the car to a stop.

When he stepped from the car, his leg disappeared in snow all the way up to the top of his motorcycle boots, and it was hard to walk. He turned to help Karen, but Paul had already taken her hand.

It took them several minutes to trudge their way up to the porch, where they found the front door open. Travers, immediately suspicious, gestured them back and reached for his gun. They all saw the rust-colored splotches of blood that led out from the house and down the porch.

Karen held Paul tight. "My God!" she whispered.

Travers slogged through the snow and up to the porch. Listening intently, he stood there for a moment, then cautiously mounted the five steps that led up to the door.

Holding his gun before him, Travers kicked at the door, which flew open the rest of the way and snapped violently on its hinges. In the silence that followed, he gripped the gun with both hands, aiming it into the house.

"Sheriff!" he screamed. "You in there? Amy!"

When no answer came, he motioned for Paul and Karen to stay back while he moved into the house.

Karen spoke softly. "If anything's happened to her . . ."

Gently touching her lips, Paul stopped her words. They stood together in silence, listening to the new wind that rose up from the freezing land. It howled about them as it circled through the small enclosure of the sheriff's porch.

Suddenly, Deputy Travers ran out of the house, a look of horror on his face. Standing at the porch railing, he swallowed hard and fought back an urge to scream. After wiping at his face, he bounded down the porch steps.

"What is it?" Paul cried.

Travers stood breathless. "Bradley . . . Jesus Christ . . . maybe Amy too . . . Somebody . . . somebody's . . . There's blood all over . . . In the shower, for Christ's sake!"

Karen felt the sort of fear that ached along her back, and for a terrible moment she thought she might be paralyzed and could not move. "Amy!" she screamed finally, lunging toward the porch.

But now Travers saw that the rust-colored trail led off toward the barn.

"This way!" he yelled, holding his gun before him as he started off. Paul and Karen followed.

The trail became a series of rust-colored spots the size of quarters, which, after a hundred feet, gave way to a large muddy brown patch.

Travers fell to his knees with a cry. "Oh my God! I think somebody's buried here!"

When he dug frantically with his bare hands, Paul knelt down to help. Karen knelt too, brushing away the snow that accumulated from their furious dig.

It did not take them long to reach the sheriff.

"Leo!" Travers screamed.

Paul tried to comfort him, but the big deputy pushed his hand away. Tears streamed down his face as he kept digging.

Horrified as she was, Karen felt an intense relief.

The sheriff had been buried alone.

As he drove them back to town along North Post Road, Travers did not speak. With his big hands gripping the wheel, he kept his eyes on the snow-covered twist of road that snaked before them. Paul and Karen were silent too.

When they reached the larger road that would deliver them to town, the deputy finally spoke.

"If that kid didn't kill the sheriff, then I have me a suspect."

"Who?" Paul asked.

"Local boy named Billy Burnside."

"A boy?" Karen asked. "What makes you think a boy could do something as horrible as that?"

" 'Cause he ain't no boy, that's why. He's the local creep, the kind they used to call the village idiot. Scares the bejesus out of most folks, especially the girls. Fact, it's alleged that he was down in the rest room when Amy's boyfriend was killed by those rats."

"Where does he live?" Paul asked.

"That's just it. Not too far from the sheriff. You might've seen him. Can't miss him, really . . . always dressed in that filthy yellow rain slicker, carrying that damned paper bag all the time."

Paul looked at the deputy. "Rain slicker?"

"That's right. Never seen him out of it."

Karen could see Paul tense. "What is it?"

"Nothing," he said, looking away and out the window.

But his mind now filled with images of Kenny in the yellow slicker. He remembered how obsessed the boy had become with it that night at the mall in Glendale.

And hadn't the deputy just said that Billy Burnside always carried a paper bag?

With a shudder Paul recounted to himself Rita's description of Kenny's most recent episode: The boy had stood in his rain slicker, clutching the paper sack in the bathroom.

Paul was scared. He had that lost, sinking feeling he'd had after the monster came out of the TV, the night his son told him about *Night of the Blood Beast*.

How could Kenny have known about any of this? he wondered, all at once sickened by the possibilities.

When the three of them saw Main Street, they reacted with shock. It was dusk. A dozen townsfolk, dressed in their winter coats, had formed a ragged line in front of Odeon.

"Imagine that," Travers said. "Imagine anyone wanting to go to that place."

"It's the heat," Paul said quietly. "They're going inside the theatre for heat."

Paul and Karen exchanged a quick look, which they hid from Travers. After all, they decided, the deputy had no idea how much they blamed Odeon for all that was suddenly wrong with Wallenberg.

"Gonna put out an APB on the kid and Amy," Travers said, stumbling out of the car. "If he hasn't done something to her, I suspect he's kidnaped her."

As he spoke, a cloud of vapor formed around his face, following him as he started across Main Street. Plodding his way through the deep snowdrifts, he slipped several times and almost fell before he reached his office door across the street.

Karen and Paul turned and entered the hotel lobby, moving right up to the desk, where the elderly clerk, wearing a stocking cap and muffler, greeted them curtly.

"Did Dr. Matson call?" Karen asked at once.

"No," he said, then turned to Paul's box and pulled out a message. "Woman named Rita down in L.A. Called you twice. Urgent, she said."

Anxious, Paul dialed her number, feeling as though his veins had filled with ice water.

Rita answered after the first ring.

"Rita? What's wrong?"

"Where is he?" she demanded. "Where's Kenny?"

Oh god, Paul thought, it's all going to be true. Please, God, not the little boy. Take *me* if you have to, but not the little boy.

"So help me, Paul, if you've kidnaped Kenny I'll make sure that you never see your son again. Do you understand me?"

"He isn't here!" Paul cried.

But in his heart he suspected that he was.

Somewhere.

"I'm calling the police," Rita said, slamming up the phone.

When Paul put down the receiver, he was ashen. Karen moved to him immediately.

"What is it, Paul?"

"Maybe it isn't Amy," he said.

"What?"

"Maybe Amy's not the child that Carlton wants."

"Your son?"

Paul ran for the door.

"I gotta find him!" he cried. "I gotta find my son!"

• Twenty-Seven •

THE SOLDIER HAD GOT OFF THE BUS two hours ago, leaving Kenny alone in the back seat. The boy had taken a liking to the soldier, who had talked to him and played cards. Instead of chips, they used matches, which the soldier kept tearing from their books. Now the matches lay scattered along the floor at Kenny's feet, reminding Kenny of his absent friend.

Now that he was alone, Kenny felt scared, for it occurred to him how weird this was, his running away from home to see his dad. It scared him to consider that maybe once he got to this strange new town called Wallenberg his dad wouldn't be there. Then what'll I do? After all, I'm only eight years old!

In all his young life, Kenny had never been so desperately aware of his age and how vulnerable it made him. All those stories his mother had told to him—about people who might want to do him harm—rushed through his head, so that as he sat alone in the back seat, listening to the thrum of the motor beneath him, he felt more and more nervous, even slightly sick to his stomach.

When they stopped in Haleyville, the driver approached him in the back of the bus.

"Where you going, son?"

"Wallenberg," Kenny said, looking up at him. He seemed ten feet tall.

" 'Fraid we aren't going there," the driver said.

Kenny felt panic. "How come?"

"Weather's bad there. Can't get in. Is there someone to pick you up?"

He was worried now as well as scared. He felt like one of those criminals in the TV shows he watched. He knew he had to answer his questions carefully or risk going to prison for stealing his mother's money.

"My dad lives there!"

The driver looked at him suspiciously.

"Okay. Then let's go try to call him up."

Kenny slipped off the back seat, picking up the little suitcase he had sneaked from his mother's closet, then followed the driver down off the bus and into the tiny depot, which was filled with people moving back and forth as they tried to decide how to get where they were going.

"Do you know his number?"

"No, sir."

"What's his name?"

"Paul, sir. Paul Chesney."

The driver moved away toward a small office, where he picked up a telephone book. Kenny waited, trying to figure out what to do.

"Little boy!"

Kenny turned abruptly to the voice, which belonged to a person with the palest skin he had ever seen.

"Your daddy sent me."

"How did he know I was here?"

"Your mother told him."

Kenny looked away, embarrassed. "Am I in trouble?"

"Only if you don't come."

Kenny turned around and looked toward the driver, who sat with his back turned away from him, talking into the telephone. The boy imagined that the driver was talking to his mother.

"You sure my dad wants me?" Kenny asked.

"I wouldn't lie to you," Emma Burnside said, then took his hand and led him off toward her car at the back of the bus depot.

When Paul ran out of the hotel and reached the snow-covered street, he realized he didn't have a clue as to how he would find Kenny. If he went off hysterically, without purpose or direction, he would lose time, which would end up harming the boy. Deciding to swallow his pride, he returned to the hotel and called Rita.

"How much money did he take?"

"I'm not sure. Fifty. Sixty."

"You say he talked about visiting me?"

"For God's sake, Paul, then he *isn't* with you?"

"Of course not!"

Rita paused for a long time. "The bus!" she cried suddenly. "He always liked the ads on TV about the bus. He said he was going to go on a bus trip someday."

"It's worth a try," he said, hanging up and calling the Haleyville bus depot. After waiting through a series of clicks on the line, he was connected to a man with a deep, reassuring voice. "You the father of the little boy? Blond. Eight or nine? Traveling alone from L.A.?"

"Yes! Is here there?"

"He was. I went to call you and when I turned around he was gone."

"How long ago was that?"

"Hour or so!"

Frightened as he was, Paul felt renewed hope. "Then maybe he's still there, huh?"

"Don't think so."

"Why not?"

"Someone saw him get into a car with a woman."

"Woman?"

"Older woman, I guess. I take it you don't know her?"

Paul thought frantically. "No . . . of course not. What else? Did the witness describe anything else?"

"Said she had her hair piled up in one of those do's, like the sixties . . . Beehives, I think they used to call them."

Paul was suddenly more baffled than frightened, for the description hardly sounded like Kenny had fallen into the hands of a typical kidnaper.

"Oh," the driver added, "we know she came from Wallenberg because there was snow on the car."

Paul was silent as he tried to assemble this bizarre information into something that made sense.

"Nobody you know, huh?" asked the driver.

"No," Paul said, frightened, experiencing the escalating fear that came with not knowing where your child was. The world was suddenly a looming place of a million dangers.

After thanking the bus driver, he hung up and called the Haleyville police.

It was the creepiest place he had ever been. The room was like a baby's room, only the old woman kept talking about her seventeen-year-old son.

"My Billy's the sweetest boy in the whole world," Emma said, leading Kenny into the tiny, stuffy room. "It's just that nobody understands him. You know, it's hard to be an outsider . . . 'specially when you're a child."

When she looked at him, she squinted her eyes accusingly, so that the thick mascara caked into a wad. A piece of it broke off, fluttering silently to the floor. "You don't make fun of people less fortunate than yourself, do you?"

Kenny shook his head. "Where's my daddy?"

"Coming."

"Who are you?"

"Your friend."

"No, you're not."

He looked at the baby's bed, which sat eerily out of place in a corner of the room. It had tall, cagelike runners along the side, which were designed to keep a baby from falling out. Kenny remembered when his own bed had such a contraption, and it gave him the creeps to imagine a grown boy asleep with such a thing surrounding him. He pictured long arms groping at the rails.

"Doesn't Billy get uncomfortable?" Kenny asked.

"Never," she said, reaching for his face, placing a finger beneath his chin so that she could look into Kenny's bewildered eyes.

"How do you know my daddy's coming?" he asked in a voice that trembled in that instant before tears.

"Because I can *make* him come," Emma said. Her voice had softened, losing some of its husky rasp.

"How can you make him come?"

"By thinking thoughts," she said.

"That's impossible. How could he hear your thoughts?"

"You're a very literal little boy."

"A what?"

"Practical. You believe only in things you can see and touch."

Kenny frowned, as he always did when he was confused. All of a sudden, he felt scared and wanted his father. "When's he gonna get here?"

"Soon!"

"I don't believe you. You can't make people do what they don't want to do!"

"Yes"—Emma smiled—"I can . . . little boy. I can do anything I want . . . I can be anything I want."

And before the boy could cry out his protest, Emma began to

laugh so that her whole body shook, her skin color changing, the ghostly white flesh growing steadily more pale. "See, little boy," she cried, "look at me!"

As he watched the old woman changing before his very eyes, Kenny's mouth opened wide. He watched her flesh grow so utterly pale as to become translucent. Light shone through it, as if the flesh had suddenly turned to gauze.

"What's happening to you?" the boy screamed, and he thought that he was going to cry.

The woman just laughed, and as she laughed her voice sounded less real; it had a tinny sound, devoid of the lower registers. As with her physical self, her voice seemed all at once lighter than air.

Artificial.

"Look at me, little boy!"

Kenny stared at the vision before him, which was now completely transparent. From inside the moving shape of light came a voice that grew steadily more shrill.

"Recognize me!" the voice cried.

Kenny watched as the bizarre cartoon rabbit hopped about the room, as if projected there.

"Th-th-th-th-that's all, folks!"

But as quickly as the cartoon had assembled out of nowhere, so then did it suddenly disappear, replaced by a tall, gaunt man with jet-black hair.

"Who are you?" Kenny cried.

"My name is Forbes Carlton, and I can be anybody I want. I can let you see whom you want. Little boy . . . I have the power."

"Where's the lady?" Kenny demanded. "Where's the lady named Emma who brought me here?"

"Gone," Carlton said, then laughed. "Until I need her again."

"Where did she come from?"

Carlton had to stop and think. "From some old movie . . . I can't think of which one now."

"A movie?"

When Carlton moved swiftly out of the baby's room, Kenny followed him into the hallway, where Carlton's laugh filled the house as he ran to a closet, yanking it open and pulling out a long, dark coat.

"Where are you going?"

"To the movies," he cried. "To Odeon. For its opening night."

At the mirror he fussed with the great winter coat, then pulled it across the tuxedo.

"What about Daddy?" cried Kenny, his face now smeared with tears, which he wiped away with quick swipes from the back of his hand.

"He'll be here soon," Carlton said. He glowered at the boy. "And you should go back to your room!"

"*My* room!" cried the boy, horrified that the creepy room had been referred to as his own. "I don't wanna go in that baby's room!"

"You will!" Carlton snapped, advancing upon the boy with great strides. "And right now!"

Before the boy could protest, Carlton pushed him into the room, locking the door behind him.

Kenny pounded on the door with all his might, screaming to be let out, but Carlton finished with his coat and stalked from the house immediately.

Outside, he got into Emma's car with its newly installed chains, then headed for Odeon.

The long wait alone in her hotel room was growing more difficult for Karen. Ever since Paul left to find Kenny, she had paced back and forth, waiting for the phone to ring. She wanted to be there if there were any message concerning Kenny.

Occasionally she would move up to the window and look down at the theatre, where townsfolk stood in a cluster about the box office, buying their tickets for the closing-night show.

Now she stared at the marble walkway, which sparkled in the light from thousands of bulbs throughout the forecourt. The forecourt looked brighter to Karen than she had ever seen it before. A great purple light reached up from inside of it and across the street, throwing patterns of flecked light in an eerie shimmering dance throughout the hotel room. And all the time, snow streaked the night before it.

But soon the wait had become unbearable. The events up at Bradley's had left her numbed, as if in a mild case of shock. She had never been at a murder site before, and she doubted that she would ever forget the image of blood, crusted into cakes, as it formed a trail through the newly fallen snow.

But her darkest thoughts turned to Amy.

Where was she? Had the Kid harmed her? If they had dug deeper, would they have found her body too?

Even more unsettling, she wondered if Amy had anything to do with her father's death.

Someone knocked on the door and Karen opened it, relieved to find Deputy Travers. He pulled a videocassette from the pocket of his coat and handed it to her. "Found this near the scene of the Tyler Briggs murder."

Sickened by the mention of Tyler's murder, Karen took the cassette. She looked at the label, which was written in longhand: *Night of the Blood Beast.*

"He was bringing this to me," she said.

Deputy Travers removed his stocking cap, brushing sweat-dampened hair from his forehead. "Why would somebody bring you that?"

Karen walked to the window and looked at the theatre. "Because of Odeon," she said.

"How do you mean?"

All at once, Karen gasped and pressed her hands to the windowsill.

"What is it, Karen?"

"It's Amy!" she cried, dashing to the bed, where she grabbed her coat. "I just saw her walking up to the theatre!"

And as Deputy Travers followed Karen out of the room, he patted his gun.

• Twenty-Eight •

JACK MACGRUDER STOOD before the bronze doors. He wore his tuxedo, just as he had a thousand nights before, standing at attention beside the ticket receptacle, where he would greet the customers who strolled up the sparkling terrazzo.

But tonight it was different. The customers, wrapped in their heavy winter coats, bolted up through the forecourt without looking at the ad frames to the left and right of them. While stomping snow off their feet, they presented their tickets perfunctorily.

"Enjoy the show," Jack said to Joe Rydell, who was there with his wife and teenage daughter.

"Don't care a damn about the show," Joe snapped back. "It's the only damned place in town where there's heat."

"And all the TVs are broke," added Mrs. Rydell. "Just ask Joe."

Jack smiled faintly as they walked past him into the lobby. Frightened as he was, it still hurt his feelings that the whole town had come to his show only to escape the cold. All the trouble he had gone to in locating the old 35mm prints and he realized that they couldn't care less. He figured they would have been happy just to sit inside with no movie at all, their eyes focused on the white expanse of a great blank screen. It was hardly the sentimental closing night that he had planned.

Looking at his watch, he saw that it was almost time to start the show and he quickly took the tickets of the few remaining customers, all of whom were as indifferent to the ceremony as Joe Rydell.

Jack thought of the Kid, who was up in the projection room.

What in the world did he have planned?

The old man closed up the ticket receptacle and placed it inside the lobby. He pulled the bronze doors closed behind him so as to block out the steady blast of arctic air.

For a second the old man's thoughts went back to that ancient August night when Odeon first opened. He remembered his joy in the streets as he stood behind the barricade, watching the great doors open upon his dream for the very first time.

Inside, Jack stood in the lobby. For a moment he was able to forget that the whole evening had lost its meaning. The lobby was filled again with adults, reminding him of the old days, and he moved about the lobby greeting them, bowing to each with a charming smile.

Oh, it should have stayed this way, he thought. You should have kept coming here to Odeon all those years. You shouldn't have deserted us. We could have dreamed together in the dark forever.

Jack watched as they examined the lobby, as if to reacquaint themselves with some piece of a forgotten past. Jack realized that most of them hadn't been inside the theatre since they were children.

Now he watched as Mrs. Bendix, the mayor's wife, gestured approvingly toward one of Odeon's more audaciously ornamented surfaces. She seemed particularly taken with the dazzling Verona marble at the base of the grand staircase.

Others were similarly impressed, standing transfixed by the great domed and coffered ceilings. An elderly man shook his head in wonderment, grabbing others and asking them to look upward to behold the splendid vision of metal leaf, the arrangement of cove-lit domes.

Jack sighed as he watched them, for he knew what they were thinking. They had forgotten that the theatre was so beautiful and they wished they hadn't left it all behind.

Karen and Deputy Travers reached the bronze doors just after Jack had shut them. When they realized the doors were locked, they walked back to the box office kiosk, where a fat young girl emerged with a box of unused tickets.

Travers didn't recognize her. "You live in Wallenberg?"

She shook her head, making it clear by her expression that she had no intention of revealing anything further about herself.

Travers pointed to the box of tickets. "Thought the show was free."

"It is free," said the strange fat girl, "but Mr. Carlton wanted formalities observed."

Karen reacted. "Mr. Carlton? Don't you mean Mr. Mac-Gruder?"

The fat girl swallowed. "Of course. Slip of the tongue."

"We want in," Karen demanded.

The girl waddled up the terrazzo and slipped a key into the lock opening the bronze doors. "Lucky you ran into me," she said to Karen and the deputy as they entered the lobby, which was empty now.

"We're looking for Amy Bradley," Karen said.

The fat girl screwed up her face and pointed to the refreshment stand. "She was supposed to be over there."

Both Karen and the deputy turned and looked at the empty refreshment stand. Amy was nowhere in sight. When they turned back to the fat girl, she was gone.

Whether they wanted to hear it or not, Jack intended to make a short speech before the show. It didn't matter to him that they cared nothing about what he had to say or that he himself felt so foolish and used. What mattered to Jack was that he had something to say about the theatre he had loved all his life.

It was never Odeon's fault, he thought, and he remembered the fiendish stare of Forbes Carlton that awful night so long ago.

Now he would make his triumphant walk into his theatre. Reaching the center aisle door, he pulled it open, adjusting his bow tie before making his entrance.

Halfway down the aisle, he heard them applaud.

Startled, he realized that it was not just polite applause, but a genuine demonstration of respect and affection.

When it had died down, Jack described to the audience how wonderful Odeon's opening night had been.

"This was *your* theater," he said, "but you left it and stayed home. You stayed home and watched a dull little box and called it the movies."

Jack was aware of their silence, and he knew they were probably offended, but he did not care. It was what he had to say.

"Isn't it odd," he concluded, "how much the movies make up our past?"

Now that he was finished, Jack held up his hand and signaled to the projection room, where the Kid waited patiently, staring down from a porthole.

"And so," Jack cried out to them, "I bid you now return with me to a warm summer night in 1931 when Odeon was born." He signaled again to the Kid, who hit a switch that began to dim the lights. "Ladies and gentlemen," Jack announced, "Odeon lives!"

When the lights had dimmed away to darkness, Jack crept his way down the steps at the edge of the stage, guiding his way by pressing his hand to the wall. Up on the great screen, he saw the logo for Movietone News; the drapes across Odeon's face parted smoothly beneath it.

Good boy, Jack thought, pleased thus far with the Kid's timing. He had known enough to open the curtains at the second the logo was over—a subtle piece of showmanship that Jack was never able to teach Roy.

But now, just as he stepped down from the stage to the aisle, a hand grabbed at his arm. "Where is she?" Deputy Travers demanded, trying to be heard above the triumphant chords that accompanied the old newsreel. "Where is Amy?"

The old man froze, then looked at Karen, as if to apologize. "It's too late!" he cried. "You can't stop it now!"

"What?" Travers demanded. They were moving up the aisle, toward the doors that would take them to the lobby. As they passed, heads swung in their direction as confused members of Odeon's final audience wondered what was going on.

"You have to help us, Jack," Karen said. "You have to let us try to save the girl."

They were in the very back of the theatre now. "Will somebody tell me what's going on?" Travers demanded. "What do you mean . . . save the girl? What's all this horseshit about the theatre anyway?"

Jack was about to speak when the screen went completely dark, the shimmering silver image of the Movietone News vanishing, so that the theatre was left in total darkness. The three of them turned to the screen and stared. In the audience everyone shifted and mumbled in the darkness.

"Everything will be fine in just a moment," Jack cried out to all of them, but in fact he had no idea if everything would be fine or not—it was simply an attempt to calm them down.

Suddenly, a flash of light lit up the screen, and an image appeared within a swirling mass of color. At first, it was difficult for them to make out what the image was, but it was soon horrifyingly clear.

What appeared to be a thousand rats were gnawing away at a young boy's body.

Karen turned away in horror while the audience reacted with cries and voiced protests.

"What the hell is this?"

"This some kind of awful joke?"

Jack waved his arms in the darkness, his movements illuminated only by the flesh-colored flicker of light from the screen, where Mike Barnes' body was devoured by rats.

There were close-ups now. Mouths as they closed upon bits of flesh.

Tearing.

Chewing.

But then it was gone, as fast as it had come, and the screen became dark again, so that those who were fleeing their seats suddenly stopped in the darkness.

Karen looked up at the screen, where a new projected image had formed—a wide shot of a living room.

My room! My God, it's *my own front room.*

Karen stared disbelievingly at the screen, where her own living room was blown up to enormous proportion. All was still, just as it usually appeared to her.

But then something darted by—something small, fast, nimble, just out of sight at the bottom of the frame.

Karen grabbed hold of Jack's arm. "That's my living room!" she cried, then stared with morbid fascination at the projected image.

Now she could see what moved there—the thing she had seen behind the lectern, the monster from *Night of the Blood Beast.*

Skittering across the floor, it suddenly lost its footing, so that it slipped and bumped up against the wicker chair by the window.

That's how it happened! I'm seeing how the chair was moved!

Then a glass fell, shattering on Karen's living room floor.

Suddenly, the thing looked at her from the screen, where, in close-up, Karen watched as crusted lips pulled apart, forming a crude smile.

"No!" she screamed.

"What the hell *is* this, Jack?" someone cried from the audience.

Now the image on the screen changed again: Karen was at the

banquet. She had just dropped the index cards and was bending down to pick them up.

Karen swung her head toward the projection room.

"Who's up there!" she screamed.

Deputy Travers looked at Jack. "Mighty damned expensive practical joke!"

"It isn't a joke!" Jack said.

Karen tried not to look at the screen, where a projected image of herself crawled about the banquet room floor looking for index cards. She turned to Jack. "Who *is* up in the projection room?"

"Some new kid in town. Young fellow."

Karen and Travers exchanged a panicked look.

"Friend of Amy's, in fact," Jack said.

Karen ran up the aisle toward the exit doors, where a cluster of people had formed, all of them trying to escape the disturbing images on Odeon's screen. Deputy Travers joined them, using his big hands to help pry open the door.

When the door was finally open and they spilled into the lobby, Karen heard a sound as it shrieked through Odeon's speakers and filled the auditorium behind them. It was a woman's scream—her *own* scream as she beheld the hideous monster at the company banquet.

While Karen and Deputy Travers ran toward the staircase that would take them up to the projection room, the rest of the audience moved in an angry mob to the bronze doors.

Joe Rydell tried to open the first door, but it would not budge. Several of the men began trying the other doors, but none would open.

Jack appeared, sweat pouring off his face.

Joe Rydell spun to him angrily. "Hey, MacGruder! Open these damned things. Unlock them!"

Jack looked at him, his expression one of hopeless panic. "But, Joe," he cried, "they aren't locked!"

While Joe Rydell and the others gathered up everything they could in an attempt to smash down the doors, Karen and Deputy Travers ran for the projection room.

But as they mounted the stairs, Karen turned and saw the Kid. He stood across the lobby with his arm around Amy. With a grin that was directed clearly at Karen, he grabbed at the girl, pulling her down the stairs that led to the rest rooms.

"Deputy!" Karen screamed, and they turned and followed the Kid and Amy, pushing their way through the frantic crowd.

The deputy held his gun in a firing position.

Inside the rest room, the Kid pulled out his hunting knife. Kneeling beside Amy in the same stall she had shared with Mike Barnes, he held the knife to her throat.

"You said you'd die for me?"

The girl's eyes were blank. "Yes," she cried, but her voice was so weak and low it barely reverberated off the thousands of pieces of tile that surrounded him.

He pressed the knife closer and whispered. "Now you know the hell of things!"

"Amy!"

Karen and the deputy burst into the room, pushing the door so that it slammed against the wall.

"Let her go or I blow you away!" Travers bellowed, squatting into a firing position, both hands gripping the gun.

Grinning, the Kid kept his knife poised at her throat. "Give me a break! You won't do shit as long as I've got a knife on her."

Karen looked into the girl's eyes, which were eerily blank. "Are you all right, Amy?"

The Kid laughed. "She's fine."

"What are you going to do?" Karen asked.

"Kill her. And you're just in time to watch."

Travers took another step forward. "You got five seconds, pal."

The Kid stared at him. "You mean it?"

"Never meant anything more in my life."

Tossing back his head, the Kid laughed derisively. "Oh God, he's turning into a veritable John Wayne, for chrissake! That it, Deputy? Wayne your hero? I'm sure you saw a few John Wayne movies here at Odeon, right? You craved being a man, didn't you?"

"Shut up!"

The Kid looked at Karen. "And who did *you* want to be, Karen? Let's see . . . I'd say a kindhearted girl with hidden moxie, right? Sort of an Olivia De Havilland, maybe? No, I don't think so. Not with a gun. Olivia was too sweet to pack a rod."

He thought for a long time, then laughed. "Of course, you're a lot like Olivia was in *The Snake Pit*. Remember? When she cracked up and they had to put her in the nuthouse?"

Karen smiled, shaking her head. "It won't work. If you're trying to get to me, it won't work. I have nothing to hide anymore, so you can't do that."

The Kid smiled, his perfect teeth shining like the tile. "Very good. I'm proud of you, Karen."

He looked at the deputy. "So how about you, Deputy? Feel like a man, finally? After all these years, do you finally feel like something more than a cowardly little, mealy-mouthed fake!"

In an instant the deputy lunged forward. His plan was to strike out at the Kid and push him away from Amy, as he figured he'd have a chance to get the Kid into his gun sight.

But the deputy's movement was awkward, overcalculated, and as he grabbed for the Kid, his big arms groped at the air and he fell, landing hard on the arm that held his gun, which slid across the floor.

The kid stared at him, his eyes huge, insane. "Do that again, fucker, and I'll cut out the bitch's heart and eat it in front of you!"

Karen looked at the gun, which was only a few feet away from her on the floor. Petrified, she realized that with the deputy out of commission, everything was up to her. She knew that the gun was her only hope.

But I've never shot a gun!

Karen remembered the clicking sound as they ran down the stairs to the foyer, so she knew that the deputy had cocked it: The gun was ready to shoot.

Now the Kid held up the hunting knife, laughing in a mad cackle while he stared at the deputy. "Coward!" he screamed. "Coward!"

The deputy spoke in a deadly whisper. "You'll never get away with this! The town's locked in with the weather. You don't have a chance!"

The Kid held the knife at Amy's throat. "You deserve to have her die! You know that?"

The knife's blade touched the pale flesh of Amy's neck, but the girl's eyes remained fixed in space, as if she had no idea what was happening. Karen looked again at the gun.

She had to. She had to.

Suddenly, Deputy Travers made a move, as if he might try to leap up from the floor.

"Stay right there!" the Kid screamed.

Karen was moving in steps so small they were invisible, so that inch by inch she neared the gun. The Kid kept his attention on Travers, who continued to cry out threats.

"I got an APB out on you!"

"They'll never catch me, you stupid fool!"

Karen reached down, bending to the floor so slowly that she was barely aware of movement. Jerking her eyes between the gun and the Kid, she reached out for the gun.

"Even if you get out of town, they'll catch you!" Travers cried. From the corner of his eye he saw what Karen was doing, and now he tried to keep the Kid distracted as long as he could.

"Such idiots you all are!" The Kid laughed. "You don't understand what's going on, do you?"

The gun was in her hand now. Crouched over, she prayed that the Kid wouldn't look her way.

But she was scared. The distance between herself and the Kid was farther than she realized. With her lack of expertise with guns, she didn't trust herself to fire. She was afraid she might hit Amy by mistake.

"Why'd you kill the sheriff?" Travers cried suddenly.

"He was in my way!"

"You'll get the death penalty, you bastard!"

Karen moved closer, hoping to work herself into a point-blank position. Her hand trembled and her heart pumped a vile, metallic taste to her mouth, for she feared the Kid might turn to her any second.

Laughing at the deputy's threat, the Kid moved the knife into position at the base of Amy's throat.

"I'm gonna kill the bitch," he said.

And Karen fired the gun.

Blood spewed across the wall, carrying with it bits of flesh and brain.

The noise of the shot deafened her, and its impact sent her reeling to the floor.

Karen lay still, the sound still ringing in her ears.

The sound that came with killing the only child she would ever have.

• Twenty-Nine •

BY THE TIME PAUL reached Emma Burnside's porch, he could barely walk. His feet were so cold they no longer felt attached to his body. He had never known such cold—a throbbing ache, as though something huge and monstrous had clutched his legs and would not let go, squeezing out all feeling.

While he had managed to borrow a car with chains from Deputy Travers, it had become useless the farther out North Post Road he got. Eventually, the car hit a snowdrift, burrowing itself inside.

Crawling out of the stalled car, he had walked the remaining way on foot. Fortunately, it had turned out to be but a quarter mile.

But what brought me here?

Paul had heard something in his head, a buzzing drone, like a bad telephone connection in which another conversation had drifted into his own. All he knew was that he had to get out on North Post Road. He had to keep driving until he saw the house. It was a house he remembered from his youth—one of those huge, wood-framed farmhouses that had fallen into grim neglect.

Now he tried the door, which he was surprised to find unlocked, and he walked inside. He called out for Mrs. Burnside, but the huge musty rooms were empty and silent.

Frustrated, he moved to the hallway, which faced a row of doors on either side. He decided he would open each door and search every room; it might be futile, but he could not escape the overwhelming sense that Kenny was somewhere here on the premises.

He had only reached the second door when he heard the pounding and muffled cries at the end of the hallway.

"Kenny!" he cried, working his way down, throwing open doors as fast as he could.

When he opened the final door, he knew he had the right room, for the muffled voice was clearer to him now, recognizable: It was Kenny's.

"I'm here!" Paul cried. "Daddy's here!"

He ran into the room, stopping short when he saw the baby bed and the dusty, unused toys. There was a dreadful unpleasantness about the room that struck him immediately; it was a room that celebrated not birth, but death.

Hearing that Kenny's cries came from behind the closet, Paul ran to it, but he could not force open the door. Kenny's cries grew more hysterical.

Frantic, Paul ran into the kitchen, rummaging the drawers until he had found a hammer and a screwdriver, using them to knock the hinge pins out of the closet door.

The boy ran into his arms at once.

"Kenny . . . Oh my God, are you all right?"

The boy buried his sobs in his father's chest, so that soon Paul felt the damp warmth of tears as they soaked through and drenched his shirt.

Paul knelt down to him. "Who locked you in here?"

"The lady," Kenny choked.

"Emma?" Paul asked. "Was her name Emma Burnside?"

"Sometimes."

"What?"

"She was different people. She was this lady, then she was this man. Sometimes she was this cartoon, Daddy!"

Paul pulled Kenny to him tight, for all at once it occurred to him how much danger his son had been in.

"Did she ever say a name, Kenny? Did she ever mention the name Forbes Carlton?"

Kenny nodded. "That's who she was . . . she was him!"

Paul considered the strange drone he had heard—the distant drift of words that had led him to this house of his past.

Why had Carlton made it so easy?

Paul glanced at his watch. It was after eight, and he realized that the show at Odeon would have already started. If all was true, the theatre would claim its victory before the night was over. A child would die, thus providing Forbes Carlton another several years.

But whose child?

"Are you okay?" he asked Kenny.

The boy nodded and Paul stood up.

It occurred to him now that the whole thing might have been a trick. If Kenny had been in genuine danger, then why had it been so easy to save him? Why had Forbes Carlton sent Paul direct messages that told how to get to his son?

"Where did he go?" Paul asked his son.

"I don't know. He just left, Daddy."

Paul realized they had to get back to town. If anything was going to happen, it would surely happen at the theatre tonight.

Now he was convinced that Karen's intuition had been correct: Amy Bradley *was* her daughter. If anything happened to the girl, and especially if it happened as a result of Karen's own hand, Forbes Carlton would triumph.

"Come on," Paul said, taking Kenny's hand. "We have to go back into town."

He knew they would have to make it back to the car. He figured that by using one of the shovels he had seen outside Emma's house, they could get the car free of the snowdrift.

When they reached the entryway, they passed a row of coats that hung from pegs, one of them a yellow rain slicker.

Kenny brushed up against it and screamed, as if he had suddenly been burned by fire. He started to back away, emitting a sharp, whispering sound, almost a hiss, then fell to the floor.

"Kenny!" Paul cried, then looked at the yellow rain slicker, realizing it had triggered Kenny's sudden attack. Looking at his son, Paul saw that familiar fluttering look in the boy's eyes—that awful vacant stare that Paul always dreaded, the look that signaled he was about to have one of his spells.

Recoiled there on the floor, the boy looked as frightened as anyone Paul had ever seen. Already, Paul knew that Kenny was about to speak in another voice.

"How come there's nobody there to sell tickets?" Kenny cried.

Paul had heard the voice before, for he recognized it as one of the boy's frequent characters. It was familiar to Paul as a character from one of the movies he had seen over and over.

Paul knelt to his son. "What, Kenny? What?" he cried, all the time wondering what Kenny's connection to all this could possibly be.

Paul grabbed Kenny by the shoulders. "Who are you?" he demanded.

Kenny's eyes stared into his, but they were somebody else's eyes, those of someone frightened and disturbed. It terrified Paul to realize that for this tiny second in time his son's eyes looked like those of someone totally insane, as if to stare into the eyes of his own child was to stare into hell itself.

"What is your name?" Paul screamed.

"Billy Burnside!"

"Your name is Billy Burnside?"

"Yes, yes . . . Let go of me!"

"Where is Amy? What have you done with her?"

"Nothing!"

"Are you sure?"

"Yes!" screamed the boy, twisting about in Paul's tight grasp, moaning in pain as he tried to escape.

It hurt Paul to see his son in such pain, but he knew that for this second in time Kenny was someone else.

Oh God, forgive me, Kenny, but it isn't *you*! If it were you, I wouldn't make you go through this!

Paul knew the question he had to ask.

"If you're Billy Burnside, then who is your mother?"

Now the boy who looked like his son grew still, his little body going limp in Paul's arms. He looked up at Paul and stared at him for a long time, then answered.

"Karen Webster," he said finally. "Karen Webster is my mother."

With that the boy's eyes changed. The madness vanished, as if an image projected upon a screen had been replaced by another, the eyes finally rolling back in his head before the lids fluttered shut completely.

Paul clutched the boy to his chest, and knew he was his son again. He kissed him gently on the forehead, several times, until the boy's eyes reopened, focusing upon his father.

"Daddy!"

But Paul was already carrying him to the door. "We have to go," he said. "We have something to do."

Karen figured the best thing to do was to keep moving. Holding Amy close to her side, she ran out of the rest room and headed for the stairway up to the lobby. The memory of blood left her feeling sick and unsteady, and the overwhelming sound of the gunshot still rang in her ears. Meanwhile, she had to get an ambulance for the deputy, who still lay in shock on the rest room floor. Karen had been unable to rouse him.

But as they reached the stairway, Karen wondered why Amy

had not yet reacted. Was the girl in shock? she wondered, for the girl's eyes were completely without life or expression, as if she were lost in a trance. She had hoped that the death of the Kid would release her.

"Amy!" she cried again as they started up the stairway, but the girl would not answer. As Karen guided her along, she felt as if she were nudging forward some heavy, lifeless doll.

But now Karen felt something beneath her hand as she slid it up the rail. Looking down at the teak rail, she saw that the wood was moving. It buckled and snapped, then peeled itself completely away. In a matter of seconds another layer of wood formed—a fresher layer, like a snake that was shedding its skin.

After leaving Kenny with the clerk in the hotel lobby, Paul worked his way across Main Street to the sheriff's station, where he intended to return the keys to the car he had borrowed.

As Paul trudged his way through the snow, he glanced at Odeon, noticing that the great marquee was as bright as it had ever been. The purple light bathed the lumps of snow in the street, so that particles of ice sparkled like tiny discarded diamonds. Paul wondered how the show was going.

Reaching the sheriff's office, Paul expected to find the same chaos he had found there before, but when he opened the door he found the office empty.

"Deputy!" he cried, but the only sound in the room was the constant bleeping of the telephone. All the lines flashed and went unanswered.

Paul stepped back outside and looked at Odeon, which he knew was brighter than ever before.

The great facade was brighter than the full moon. The vertical sign that climbed into the night blazed with a thousand times its normal brilliance; a bright and lurid light lay across all of Main Street, from the edge of the terrazzo to the tips of Paul's shoes.

But now he focused on the bronze doors at the end of the terrazzo. It was difficult to see from across Main Street, but Paul thought that he could make out faces pressed to the glass.

He stepped off the curb, stumbling through the snowdrifts, which were so high he could barely walk. Each time he stepped forward, he would sink to his waist, so that it took several minutes to reach the other side of the street.

When he stepped into the forecourt of Odeon, he was momentarily blinded. The light was so intense it was like staring into a searchlight; the forecourt flooded with clear, perfect light.

Shading his eyes, he moved closer to the bronze doors, certain now that he could make out people behind them. They were trapped inside, their hands slamming up hard and frantically against the glass, which was thick with chunks of ice.

But now something snapped beside him, like a huge flash of errant electricity.

Paul jumped back, almost slipping on the icy terrazzo, then looked up as a bolt of blue light shot down from beneath the marquee. It looked like a miniature piece of lightning.

Paul backed away as yet another bolt slammed against the forecourt in a fast, sizzling arc, leaving a column of black smoke.

My God! The theatre is trying to keep me away!

Paul looked helplessly at the bronze doors, where he tried to make out faces. He knew they could see him, for the hands pounded more frantically along the glass now.

Moving up as close as he could, he saw the face he was looking for. Karen stared at him from behind the glass, and even with the ice half obscuring her face, Paul could see her look of panic.

"Damn you!" he cried, raising his fist to the theatre.

Paul ran forward, hoping to get to the row of bronze doors, but he was stopped by another flash of light. It was larger, more powerful this time, and the force of it knocked him backward and off his feet, so that he flew the length of the forecourt, landing in a snowdrift along the sidewalk, which cushioned the impact.

Stunned, he looked up.

My God, the theatre tried to kill me!

He stood up and brushed away the huge patches of snow that clung to him. He was soaked through to the skin and freezing. His hands throbbed with cold, even beneath the heavy gloves. Staring at the bronze doors, he tried to decide what to do.

Could he go in through the back entrance? he wondered, but he knew that even under the best of circumstances it was difficult to enter the old theatre from the back and sides. Any kid who had grown up in Wallenberg and had tried to sneak into one of Jack's shows knew the futility of such an idea—Odeon had been built like a fortress.

Desperate, he looked back at the sheriff's station, hoping to catch sight of Deputy Travers or one of the volunteer firemen—

someone who could help him—but the little office still looked empty, its two parking spaces in front unused.

It was then he saw the snowplow.

Inside the cab of the snowplow, Paul stared at the controls, which were as foreign to him as those of a rocket ship. His first attempts at pressing switches were unsuccessful. Hydraulic lines engaged and the snowplow's enormous nose moved up and down, but Paul had no idea yet what he was doing. He practiced, tried, failed, then tried again.

"Here goes," he said finally, and he started up the engine, shifting gears that whined and caught within the blur of his inexpertise.

All at once the truck started moving forward, but it quickly lurched and died.

Sweating, Paul played with the gears long enough to learn their order, then tried again. This time the motor caught, producing a gentle purring noise, and he shouted aloud with joy.

Paul maneuvered the snowplow into reverse. The motor remained engaged this time, and his shifting was smooth. Correcting and working the cumbersome gearshift over and over, Paul gradually angled the snowplow so that it faced Odeon from across Main Street.

As if the snowplow were some enormous gun with the movie theatre in its sights, Paul aimed it, bringing the snowplow in line. Its heavily treaded tires gripped the ground, whining as they dug greedily at the snow. A thick, dirty white spray shot back from the wheels.

When Paul hit first gear, he felt the machine move forward and he gently shifted into second. With Odeon's forecourt looming before him, he pushed forward, hitting the first snowdrift along Main Street with a thud. It collapsed against the powerful plow.

Once inside the forecourt, the snowplow gripped the icy surface. Paul floored the accelerator, so that it clicked into its highest gear.

Hurtling forward, the snowplow crashed into the box office. As the kiosk exploded, fragments of gold leaf and glass flew through the air, like huge pieces of confetti.

Bolts of electricity shot from beneath the marquee, bombarding the plow, and for a terrible second Paul thought that they might stop the huge machine, but the plow kept pushing forward.

With the doors but a few feet away, Paul blinked the headlights and honked the horn. "Get out of the way!" he screamed, then braced himself for the crash.

The snowplow slammed against the entrance so hard that the bronze doors buckled with its impact. Glass shattered, spraying throughout the terrazzo, and the bronze sills bent into grotesque shapes.

Dazed for a second, Paul sat in the cab of the plow, which had wedged itself in the door frame. Dust and steam swirled around the windows, so that he could barely see.

Jack MacGruder stepped from the crowd and up to the snowplow. "Oh, God, Paul . . . what have I done? I'm so sorry. What have I done?"

Paul leapt out of the snowplow. "Help me get everyone in the truck," he ordered Jack, pointing to the truck behind the cab. "And watch out for electricity. Stay out of the forecourt."

Now Paul looked for Karen, trying to locate her face in the crowd that came at him through a swirl of smoke.

"Paul!" she cried suddenly, running up to him, throwing her arms around him. "She's all right!"

Paul looked over and saw Amy, whose face was utterly without expression. She stared ahead as if nothing had happened. Even the Kid's grisly death had not affected her. She had watched it dispassionately. She had watched it like a movie.

"It didn't work!" Karen cried to Paul jubilantly. "It wanted me to kill my child, but I didn't!"

Paul took her by the shoulders. A part of him wanted to spare her from the horrible truth that Kenny had taught him. "What happened to the Kid?" he asked.

"He tried to kill Amy," she said. "Oh my God, Paul, I shot him!"

"Is he dead?"

Karen nodded quickly.

"Oh Christ!" Paul said, his stomach tightening.

He turned and stared into the grand lobby, where the plaster and wood seemed to vibrate, as if in the grips of a small earthquake. He watched as the older pieces fell away, replaced by other pieces—*newer* pieces—and he understood why the lights of the marquee had never seemed brighter.

Odeon was regenerating itself.

The theatre had tricked them.

"What is it, Paul?" Karen asked. "What's wrong?"

He didn't want to tell her, but he knew that he had to. It would be a terrible cheat if she continued believing that Amy was her child. He was about to speak when he thought he saw Kenny running through the lobby. Looking closer, he saw that it was.

When Paul cried out to him, the boy looked up, panic in his eyes, like a small, startled animal, then ran up the grand stairway toward the balcony.

Paul turned to Karen, who had also seen Kenny. "Get in the truck!" he cried. "Take Amy and get in the truck!"

The elderly desk clerk wandered up to them, out of breath from having run across Main Street. "I'm sorry, Mr. Chesney!"

"You were supposed to watch him!"

"All of a sudden, he just started running, right out of the hotel and across the street. Kid was playing some fool game. Said he was the Burnside boy!"

Paul felt a horrible and abiding panic, and he bolted from all of them, tearing across the lobby and mounting the grand stairway where Kenny had disappeared.

When Paul rounded a corner at the mezzanine level, he saw the boy run the remaining distance to the balcony level. There the little boy looked back at his father, his eyes filled with horror. He turned and ran toward one of the aisle doors that accessed the balcony.

"Kenny!" Paul cried, as he bounded up the stairs and ran through the aisle door.

Inside the balcony, Paul came to a dead stop, recoiling in horror when he saw what his son was doing.

The boy stood atop one of the balcony rails, his body rigid, as if he were making no attempt to balance himself there.

It was exactly where Carl had stood.

Paul's heart thumped within his chest, and he could barely find the voice to call out his son's name.

"It's all right, Kenny," he said finally, careful to affect a tone of calm, for he did not want his little boy to hear how scared he was.

The boy looked at him, more confused than frightened, and it wasn't long before the dreaded expression crossed the little boy's face: He was having one of his spells.

"Who are you?" Paul asked gently.

"Billy," Kenny said.

Paul moved in small, measured steps. He smiled as he walked, but inside he felt sick with dread. He could not keep his eyes off

the boy's sneakers, which were poised so precariously upon the
balcony rail. All the time he remembered Carl.

Oh God, please, take me, not him. Don't make an innocent
little boy suffer for things he never did.

Paul was closer now—close enough to leap forward and swoop
the boy from the rail, but he decided it was still too risky.

"You're not Billy!" he said, moving ever closer.

"I am! I am!"

Kenny was trembling now and Paul stepped forward. He was
about to reach out for him when he felt a vibration along the
balcony floor. Terrified, he watched as the balcony rail began to
shift, moving beneath the boy's sneakers.

God, the theatre was changing again, he realized, and he
watched in horror as the rail began to buckle beneath the boy's
flimsy shoes.

"Kenny!" he cried, for now, in a split second, he saw the shoes
as he lost his footing along the rail. The boy screamed—that
horrible, unforgettable scream that is a child's—and the boy
was suddenly no longer in contact with the rail, but hovering there in
space, suspended above the cavernous auditorium below.

But to Paul it was as if all time had stopped. In that millisecond
it took to realize that his son was about to fall to his death, or
worse, slip into that awful, feebleminded netherworld that had
been his best friend's—Carl Irvine's—Paul leapt forward through
the air.

First, his arms groped in space, then wrapped around his son's
torso, which felt so small as to be nearly insignificant.

"Kenny!" he cried, then yanked back, pulling with all of his
might, not yet knowing where they were in the huge space of the
movie theatre of his childhood.

All at once, he knew they were falling.

For an instant Paul felt himself soar back in time, a journey that
accompanied their sudden rush through space. In his dream of the
past, he had now saved his best friend, Carl, who would be spared
his life of humiliation and pain. The battle for Karen's love had
been won.

But now the fantasy snapped off, and he fell to the floor of the
balcony. It took a second, but he quickly realized that they were
all right. They had not fallen into the auditorium below.

But the vibrating continued, stronger now.

Paul sat up and grabbed at his son. As he tried to stand, he saw
that the huge dome within a dome on the ceiling above them had

begun to shift. Turning, it looked like some enormous telephone dial.

Instinctively, Paul pushed his son away from him. "Run!" he screamed.

The boy fell backward, just as one of the aisle doors at the back of the balcony was shoved open.

Karen and Joe Rydell ran in from the mezzanine. When the floor began to buckle beneath their feet, they stopped, watching as the little boy ran up the stairs toward them.

"My daddy!" he screamed. "My daddy!"

While Karen ran to Kenny, Joe Rydell looked up in the air, spotting the dome, which was about to crash down upon Paul. Yelling out a warning, he started forward.

But the dome fell almost immediately.

Those who witnessed it from the back of the snowplow as they pulled away from the theatre said it looked like a cartoon. They said that Odeon just healed itself up like a film run in reverse. The bronze doors, shattered glass, and ruined box office simply regenerated themselves.

And the light—all that blazing neon—just got brighter.

And brighter.

• Thirty •

AT LEAST IT WASN'T COLD ANYMORE.

That thought kept Karen going as she waited for news in the same Haleyville hospital where she and Paul had tried to talk with Cora Grady. She waited for news on the condition of Amy and Paul.

Moments after Paul's accident the Haleyville police had arrived, followed by emergency vehicles equipped for the weather. Paul had been taken to the Haleyville hospital by ambulance. Karen had asked that the doctors look at Amy as well, for the girl was yet to emerge from her strange trance, and Karen suspected that she might be in shock.

A door opened and a doctor walked in, young with wire-rimmed glasses, which he removed to rub at red, exhausted eyes. Putting them back on, he smiled at Karen. "I'm Dr. Schumacher."

Moments later they sat at a small table, each with a cup of coffee from the vending machine. Dr. Schumacher blew at the coffee to get it cool. "Mr. Chesney is still serious but guarded," he said, "but I think he'll pull through."

"Thank God. But what about the girl? What about Amy Bradley?"

"Are you a relative?"

Karen hesitated, then decided not to tell the doctor what she suspected. "No."

"I'm not certain how to diagnose this," he continued. "There seems to be no physical problem and yet she's . . ."

For the first time, Karen realized that the pleasant young doctor had brought bad news. His expression had grown suddenly grave.

"What is it, Doctor?"

"I'm afraid she's slipped into a coma, Miss Webster."

An hour later they let Karen into Amy's room. The machines that monitored her life were noisy, chattering and wheezing within the tiny space. Approaching, Karen could barely make out the girl's face, which was lost behind a tangle of clear blue plastic tubing that linked her with the equipment.

"She can't hear you," a nurse said.

Karen tried to imagine what Amy must be experiencing now. Was it like being asleep? Or did she feel pain?

"Does she respond to touch?" Karen asked.

"No." The nurse checked one of the dials on the machine that controlled the respirator. "She's in a coma, dear . . . there is no sensory reception whatsoever."

The nurse was large and efficient, seeming in perpetual motion, as if activity distanced her from the misery she observed from day to day. She busied herself now with the fluffing of two pillows.

"You a relative, dear?"

"No."

The nurse tossed down one of the pillows and picked up another. "I wonder if it's the same girl."

Karen looked up at her. "*What* girl?"

"Well, it's a strange thing, but seventeen years ago there was a terrible accident. Over on the 101 it was. The worst kind of accident too, because there was an infant in the car."

Karen felt a sinking anguish. "An infant?"

"Yes. The poor thing's mother and father were killed instantly. A miracle, really . . . someone said it was the way the mother held the child that saved her. Cushioned her, really. Anyway, the baby was on life support for several days. The sheriff over in Wallenberg's the one who responded to the accident."

Karen found it difficult to locate her voice, like the night she had begun her speech at the banquet. A part of her did not want to hear the rest of this story, for she had finally convinced herself that Amy was her own.

The truth. I came here to learn the truth!

Karen forced herself to ask the question. "What happened to her?"

"Sheriff Bradley adopted her."

A moment of grief overwhelmed her. "And what about Dr. Matson?" she managed. "Have you heard of him?"

"Of course. Everyone has. It was Dr. Matson who took the little baby back to Wallenberg."

"The doctor arranged the adoption, didn't he?" Karen asked. "He arranged other adoptions too, isn't that right?"

The nurse turned away. She was all at once defensive, as if she knew she had told too much. "That's all I know," she said, turning away and grabbing up Amy's chart. With a curt nod, she left the room.

Karen turned and looked at Amy.

"It's all right," Karen said aloud, "I'm still going to take care of you. Don't you worry."

Paul was heavily sedated, so that when Karen touched his hand, there was no response. The dome from Odeon's ceiling had collapsed, landing upon Paul's left side, fracturing the pelvic bone and breaking two ribs. Miraculously, he had escaped both death and paralysis. His legs had gone virtually unharmed.

While Karen stroked his forehead, a feeling of love welled up inside. And yet, as before, the love was that of a friend, not a lover.

Strange, she thought, how blurred the line between such feelings.

But now she worried, for Karen realized that Paul might know the secret of her lost child. She had seen that strange look in his eye after he smashed into Odeon: It had come over him when she mentioned Amy. She had recognized the unmistakable look of a friend who wished to protect her from truth.

What is it, Paul? What were you trying to tell me?

Even before she spoke to the nurse, Karen suspected that Amy might not be hers, after all. When they pulled away from Odeon in the snowplow, watching as the theatre grew steadily brighter, Karen had wondered: If they had thwarted Carlton's evil plan, then why was the theatre regenerating itself?

Touching Paul's face, she spoke aloud, pretending that he could hear her through the haze of medication. "It's all right, Paul. I know you want to protect me, but it's all right. I *want* to know. I *want* the truth. If there's anything I've learned, it's that."

A child's voice spoke behind her. "Is my daddy going to die?"

Karen spun around to Kenny, who stood in the doorway, his face streaked with tears.

Instinctively, Karen moved to him, hugging him tight. "No. He's going to be fine." Holding him, she remembered that night by the dumpster, when she held that unknown child who had wandered up to her, so alone in the hot, smoky night, and she understood now, as she had then, the overwhelmingly mitigating force that came with loving a child. Indeed, in a world that thrived upon paradox, a child was evil's opposite.

Only the most monstrously evil killed children, she realized, and she thought of the horrible things she had read about Forbes Carlton, the ghastly allegations of child sacrifice.

"Are you all right?" she asked Kenny, looking into his eyes. They were bright red from crying. Kenny nodded. "My mom's coming down to get me. She'll take me away from daddy. She will."

Karen felt his desperation. "You'll see him," she said, trying her best to comfort him. "I promise you will."

"It's all my fault," Kenny cried, "all because I said I was that boy."

Karen held him away for a moment, so that she could look again in his eyes. "What boy, Kenny?"

"That boy. Billy Burnside."

Karen remembered what Paul had told her about his son, the symptoms of his disorder, his need to act out things. She thought of the chilling parallel between the incidents that had led them each to Wallenberg.

"What do you know about Billy Burnside?" Karen asked.

"He's a bad boy."

"How do you know?"

" 'Cause sometimes I heard him."

"Heard him?"

"In my head. Sometimes that happens. It makes Mom and Dad scared. But I can't help it."

"What does he say when he's in your head?"

"Stuff."

"What kind of stuff?"

"Weird stuff. Like how he's going to dig these holes and things . . . how he's going to kill stuff and put them in his paper sack."

"What else?"

"How he's going to hurt that girl."

"Amy?"

Kenny nodded.

"*Did* he hurt Amy?"

"In the dream, he did."

"Your dream?"

"Uh-huh."

"What did he do, Kenny? What did he do in your dream?"

Kenny looked at her quizzically. "What'd you say your name was?"

"Karen Webster."

Kenny crinkled his forehead.

"What's the matter, Kenny?"

"Guess I don't understand how come you're asking me about Billy Burnside."

"Why not?"

The boy paused for a long time. " 'Cause Daddy said he's your little boy."

Karen sat perfectly still before Amy, watching as Dr. Schumacher leaned over the girl with his stethoscope. After a few moments he looked up at Karen, his expression grave again.

"The fever's worse."

At just after midnight an alarm had sounded on one of the several machines that monitored Amy's life. After a group of technicians and the doctor had worked with her for nearly an hour, Amy began to stabilize, but now her vital signs were decreasing. Worse, the coma had now been joined by a new and insidious ally: an inexplicable fever that had quickly moved within the critical range.

Karen looked away from the doctor, for she did not need to hear in words what she saw in his face. Amy's turn for the worse had come only moments after Kenny had provided her the horrifying answer to her question: Billy Burnside was her child.

The theatre had tricked her, after all. Without knowing what she had done, Karen had taken the life of her only child.

Feeling suddenly nauseous, she hunched over in her chair.

"Are you all right?"

She looked up at the doctor. "Will she make it?"

"I have a feeling you want the truth."

She nodded quickly.

"Frankly, Miss Webster, I'd be surprised if Amy makes it through the night. I'm sorry."

Standing over his bed, Karen made a final attempt to communicate with Paul.

"I know what's happening," she said, her lips only inches from

his ear. He slept so deep that it seemed to alter the features of his
face, his mouth stretched tightly to the side, drawn into a frown,
his breathing labored, each inhalation followed by a raspy sound
deep in his throat. When she touched his face, the skin felt cold
and lifeless.

"I know that Billy was my child. Carlton tricked us,
Paul . . . I have to do something. Amy's so sick. I have a
feeling that if we went there and confronted him, she'd be all
right."

Karen watched, hoping for a flicker of expression in his face,
but there was none.

If only you could help me, she thought, but she knew that Paul
would be incapacitated for a long time, perhaps for a week or
more. She knew that if Amy was to be saved, she herself would
have to make the attempt.

And she would have to do it tonight.

When she started the car, she prayed they wouldn't hear her. She
feared they might stop her and keep her from going back into
Wallenberg, where travel was currently restricted. Fortunately,
she had driven her own car back to Haleyville, anticipating the
difficulty she might have in retrieving it later. She had followed
the caravan of cars back to the hospital.

But how can they stop me? I have a perfect right to go where I
wish.

But even as she thought the thought, a flashlight flared in the
parking lot opposite the hospital. A security guard stepped
forward.

"Hello," Karen said, smiling.

He smiled back. "Just checking," he said, recognizing Karen
from earlier. It was, after all, nearly three o'clock in the morning,
that time of night when all movement appeared suspicious,
especially in a small town.

Driving a few blocks west, Karen hooked herself back up to the
101, which at this time in the morning was deserted except for
small clusters of trucks. As she drove the ten miles to Wallenberg,
she listened to the news. While the bizarre weather was a fairly
important story, there was no mention at all of the movie theatre.

It occurred to her that there might not ever be. After all, nothing
that had happened thus far could actually be proven. Even the
images cast upon Odeon's screen would surely be written off as
the collective hysterical reaction of an audience. Authorities in

Haleyville had already implied that their imprisonment in the lobby had less to do with the supernatural than it did with rusted locks.

Taking the turnoff into Wallenberg, Karen ignored the row of orange construction cones placed there to discourage entrance. A roadblock held a sign that said, ROAD CLOSED. Karen simply stopped her car and let it idle, got out, and pushed the roadblock to the side. Now she could only hope that her car would make it through the narrow strip that the snowplow had managed to clear into town.

But the drive went more smoothly than she expected. Keeping her speed down, she tried to remember that when you drove upon ice you simply had to adjust all your driving habits; you had to remember that your vehicle was suddenly more like a sled than a car, and all the usual principles of braking did not apply.

When she turned the corner and saw the town, Karen gasped audibly. All of Wallenberg was locked within a huge, silvery mass of ice.

But the eeriest thing was Odeon.

The lights of the great facade—now seeming ten times as bright as they had when she drove away the night before—were the only source of light in the entire town. All of Main Street was dark, except for the purple light; the marquee throbbed with power, snapping with arcs of electricity, as if some wildly arrogant display of dominance.

The theatre had become the town.

Frightened, Karen brought her car to a stop when Main Street became impassable. Snow still fell, so the path formed by the snowplow was already disappearing. She got out of the car and trudged forward.

Halfway down the block toward Odeon, Karen thought she saw someone duck into the Busy Bee. She moved up the street as fast as she could in the snow, then walked inside the bar.

The bar was illuminated by a single candle, which flickered at one of the leather banquettes where a man sat drinking. Karen moved closer and saw that it was Jack. Even in the darkness his exhaustion was evident, the deep creases in his face revealed by the dancing rosy flicker.

"Why did you come here?" he demanded. "You had a chance to escape. Why did you come back?"

"I have to save her. I have to save Amy."

"You can't!" He took a swig of his drink. "Want one? You can help yourself. Whole town's either gone or locked in their houses."

Karen stepped forward. "How much did you know all along, Mr. MacGruder . . . about me . . . about Billy Burnside?"

"Billy? What about him?"

"That he's my son."

He shook his head wearily. "I knew nothing. You have to believe me. It might seem to you and Paul that I know everything about Odeon, but I don't. This is all a terrible mystery to me too."

Karen sat opposite him at the banquette, choosing to believe the old man. For one thing he looked too sad for a man who was lying or who wished her any harm.

"Why do you say I can't save her, Mr. MacGruder?"

"It's too powerful! I just came from inside! You won't believe what's going on in there now. Carlton is there . . . howling with joy over his victory. The images on the screen are worse than ever. My God, Karen, every bad thing that's ever happened in this town is up there . . . a constant barrage of moving pictures . . . husbands having affairs, betraying one another, stealing, beating their children, abusing them . . . It's all up on that screen like some horrible, endless movie!"

"Why didn't you leave with us?" Karen asked.

The old man stared into his empty glass. "I can't. Crazy as it seems, Karen, I still don't blame the theatre. It's Carlton, not Odeon. It's still the grandest showplace ever built. I want to stay with it. I can't leave it, you see . . . it's my whole life."

A cold draft blew through the bar, causing the candle to dim. Outside, the wind howled.

"I have to save the girl," Karen said.

"You can't! He's too powerful! He's had power over me my whole life long."

The old man was drunk, and he began to cry, laying his arms across the table, burying his head in the cradle they formed. His sobs were deep and racking. Karen knew that he could be of no help to her.

When she got back to Main Street, it was colder than before, as if somehow the theatre knew she was coming and had geared up for her. The purple light was brilliant, so that Karen was forced to shade her eyes as she trudged through the snow toward the forecourt. She thought of that feeling she had as a child, when in spite of fears of blindness, she felt compelled to look at the sun.

There, at the edge of the forecourt, she stopped, waiting

cautiously for the bolts of electricity that had greeted her before.

"Carlton!" she cried, standing in the wind that howled all about her. Her hair was blowing wild and she actually felt insubstantial, as if she might suddenly blow away.

She took a step forward, onto the marble walkway. "Carlton!" she screamed, her voice reverberating within the forecourt.

It astonished her how new everything looked. All the damage done by Paul and the snowplow had been repaired. The theatre looked brand-new.

No wonder the old man won't help me, she thought. He's gone back in time, just like the theatre.

When Karen was halfway up the forecourt, she stopped, waiting for a bolt of electricity to strike her from above. But nothing happened.

Emboldened, she took another step, but this time a perfect white arc blasted from the marquee.

Karen jumped aside, barely missing the tiny fireball that skittered along the tile and up to her leg.

Glancing ahead, she saw that she had but a few feet to go before reaching the doors. A new bravery seized her, and in a flash she thought of Paul, what he had done for Kenny. She remembered the look on his face after the accident—a serenity like none she'd ever seen before, and now she understood: Through facing the theatre, he had dealt with his past, just as Karen would have to do now.

"Carlton!" she screamed.

With all her might Karen leapt up and ran forward, trying to dodge the two white columns of light that zapped down at her. Holding her breath, Karen lunged ahead and ran between them, slamming up against one of the bronze doors.

"Let me in, you bastard!" she screamed, and she pressed her face to the thick glass.

Inside, the theatre looked even newer than it had when Karen was a child. The white light that poured from the crystal chandeliers bathed a lobby that was utterly restored, as if the theatre had been built only yesterday.

Karen worked her way down the row of bronze doors, trying each one, but none would open. Finally, she turned and looked across the terrazzo, where she spotted a large piece of metal that had snapped loose of the snowplow.

Grabbing it up, Karen ducked another bolt of electricity, then charged at the door with the piece of metal gripped like a jousting lance, screaming aloud as she ran.

The glass shattered into a million pieces while Karen covered her eyes. She reached inside, working the handle to the door, which clicked open easily.

Entering, she was aware of an unpleasant odor—a suffocatingly moldy smell, which seemed in variance with the newness of things.

Karen still held the piece of metal like a weapon. "Where are you, Carlton? You made me kill my child, you bastard!"

Sound drifted from the auditorium and Karen recognized it as coming from Odeon's speakers. A movie was playing.

Moving up to the aisle door, still holding her weapon before her, Karen pulled back the curtain and stepped into the auditorium.

Her eyes went to the screen, where images moved within the white flicker of light. Up there on screen, she recognized herself as a young girl, moving through the kitchen in the house on North Post Road. She guessed she was sixteen.

A narrator's voice boomed from Odeon's speakers: "This is the girl. Her name is Karen Webster. Note how she walks. Already she is interested in attracting a man. She uses her body as a lure for base appetites!"

Karen moved down the aisle and faced the screen squarely. This time the images did not frighten her, and she was prepared to fight them, just as she was prepared to fight the theatre and Forbes Carlton. "Stop it!" she demanded.

But suddenly, the image shifted. She was in the foyer now, just before the attack. "Note how she is truly begging for it," the narrator continued, commenting upon an image of Karen walking to the rest room doors. His voice was so deep and loud, it vibrated Odeon's floor beneath her feet.

A man appeared at the edge of the screen, tall and cadaverous, his skin so pasty white that it barely seemed flesh at all. He moved up behind the young Karen, grabbed her by the neck, and tossed her into the rest room.

"It *was* you, you sonofabitch!" Karen cried out. "I'm going to kill you, you bastard!"

A hissing noise shot from the darkened auditorium, just to her right.

Karen spun to it.

There, before her, Forbes Carlton sat in one of the seats. While he looked exactly as he had in the past and as he did upon the screen, his face was still covered with the makeup of Emma Burnside.

"Enjoying the movie?" he asked.

When he threw back his head and laughed, a horrible stench wafted from his mouth. Karen realized it was the same odor she had smelled upon entering the theatre, only magnified now a thousand times.

She stared at him defiantly, holding the piece of metal protectively before her. "You made me kill my child!"

Carlton laughed loudly. "No, Karen. You killed your own child."

"It was all because of you!"

Carlton pointed to the screen, where Karen now lay inside the stall, naked. In the movie Carlton pulled down his pants and straddled her.

From his seat Carlton laughed at what he watched upon the screen. "Isn't this fun, Karen? Look. Our home movies!"

Karen tried to judge how far away he sat. She guessed it must be twenty-five feet. The metal strip in her hand felt heavy enough to do the trick, if only she could aim properly. She considered moving closer, but she feared he might suspect what she was up to and make her stop.

In an instant she made the decision.

With all her might she tossed the metal strip, watching as it hurtled through the dark space of the movie theatre. Forbes Carlton tried to duck, but a corner of the strip struck his head.

After a stunned beat he looked up at her. Blood oozed down his forehead. It blended with the exaggerated smears of lipstick, so that Karen could no longer tell one from the other.

"Bitch!" he cried.

And then he laughed.

"You make it so much easier to do what I have to do!" he cried, then leapt from his seat, approaching her with his hideous, inappropriate laugh.

In the dark, damp space he heard them. The rats were squealing hungrily, waiting to be fed.

"Quiet," Carl Irvine said. "It's almost time!"

There were hundreds now; he could feel them as they crawled all over his body. He didn't fear them now, for they had become his friends.

"Let's go!"

Carl crawled through the dark tunnel, the rats following behind in a straight phalanx, their paws scratching against the cement.

It was time now, he thought. Time to find out if his little plan would work, and the sound of the rats behind him, eager and in his spell, told him that it would.

Carl stopped at a ray of light that shot up from the surface they crossed. He was in one of several tiny tunnels above Odeon's ceiling. The tunnels were designed for maintaining the hundreds of light bulbs in the cove-lit domes, and he knew its dusty labyrinth well.

Pressing his face to the light, Carl looked through the hole and down to the theatre below. He could see the two of them—Forbes Carlton and Karen.

Yes, yes. It's all happening as I planned.

He had wanted to help her before, those few hours ago when the theatre had them trapped, but he knew he could help her more later—at that moment when she herself was in clear and specific danger.

Just like now.

Carl had no idea what Forbes Carlton's master plan was, but he always had a feeling it would end up like this—a final confrontation between Carlton and Karen. He knew that the theatre had tricked her somehow; he knew it from the explosion of newness that had sprung up full from the rot below.

Carl knew Odeon better than anyone; it sickened him to see the wrinkled flesh of the old woman turning young again, becoming desirable.

When Carl left the hotel that last time, he had started to formulate his plan. For all those days and nights since Odeon had closed, the incident with the rats had bugged him. He had always wondered: *Were* the rats controlled by Odeon or were they, in fact, as he had always suspected, Odeon's only *enemy*?

Before he sneaked into the theatre that night, he used his last remaining dollars to buy up some food to live on while he hid in the theatre.

But he also bought nourishment for them, the rats, for he knew that if his plan was to work, he had to gain their trust entirely.

And it was difficult at first, for the rats were skittish and fast. Whenever he approached them, they would dart away squealing, their fat stomachs dragging close to the ground.

He began by streaking peanut butter in a long line in front of him. Eventually, the rats approached, dabbing their tongues into the soft, sweet brown mass. Time after time, they ate their way closer to him, until they had come all the way to his fingertips.

Finally, he reached out and touched them; he ran his fingers along their furry backs, stroking them, as if they were tiny kittens.

And after days of this, they had finally become his.

Now he watched as Forbes Carlton drew closer to Karen.
At last, his time had come.

Karen jumped back, but she knew that it was folly to run from
him. Carlton was fast—eerily fast—so that the speed with which
he now walked up to her seemed impossible: a special effect. She
knew that he was toying with her—he could have killed her all
along. He would want her to suffer first.

"All I ask is that you leave Amy alone!" she cried.

Carlton laughed, loud and long, so that his bony shoulders
shook. He wore a thick black coat that covered his inhuman
skinniness. The makeup and blood still crisscrossed his face,
which seemed neither man's nor woman's.

"Your mother was right, wasn't she?"

"What do you mean?"

"This *is* Satan's Church!"

Screaming with a sudden, convulsive laughter, Carlton pointed
up at the screen. "And for our next feature!" he cried.

Karen watched as the curtains, moving faster than usual, swept
apart across another projected image.

Horrified, she looked upon the pale, expressionless face of
Amy, who seemed ever closer to death.

"Damn you!" Karen screamed. "Why the girl?"

"Why *not* the girl!" he cried.

"She hurt no one!"

Carlton laughed. "What does it matter?"

Karen remembered what Paul had done. "Take *me*!" she cried.
"Take *me* instead of the girl!"

Carlton stared at her for a long time, as if making a decision.
After a moment he walked up to her, touching her gently along the
neck. She reacted to his touch, which was as cold as ice, enough
to make her pull back suddenly in response. Up close, the
woman's makeup, which was slathered so carelessly upon the
male face, seemed all the more grotesque and exaggerated.

"Do you know the hell of things?" he asked suddenly, all at
once seeming to ignore her proposition.

"What?"

Karen watched as his expression changed. Gradually, it became
less malevolent, almost sad; the features fell into what resembled
a pout. He might have been a man who had lost his love.

"I asked if you knew the hell of things!"

"I don't know what you're talking about."

And then he spoke very softly—his voice claimed by a gentleness that seemed eerily inappropriate.

"Do you know the hell of love, Karen?"

She looked into his eyes. They were hard and ugly, surrounded by thick purple moons of misapplied mascara. But now he seemed at once a different person, his poignance almost touching; for a moment he was almost human.

"Yes," Karen answered, whispering. "I do."

Carlton smiled at her gently. "Then we *do* have something in common."

"Will you do it? Will you take *me* instead of the girl?"

Forbes Carlton stared at her. For a moment it looked as though he might spare the child.

"I'll take you both," he finally screamed, and with that he lunged for her.

Karen tried to pull away, but he had taken her arm, which he clenched in a viselike grip.

When he held her, it all came back—the memory of his awful touch.

Yes! Yes! He held me this tightly before. My God, it's all happening again!

"You should have listened to Nell!" Carlton laughed. His tone had changed again, filling with hatred. "You should have stayed away . . . stayed away from the theatre then, stayed away from Wallenberg now!"

Karen felt him press up against her, and she saw his face, like some hideous close-up, his mouth opened in a leering grin, so that the odor was almost unbearable—like something rotten and dead lived way down deep inside of him.

"We had so much fun on our first date, Karen," he said, clutching her. "Let's do it again!"

Karen struggled, but she knew it was no use. His arms were remarkably strong for their flimsy appearance, and she felt that his hug could snap her spine.

But now he pushed her down against the hard, cold cement floor of the auditorium.

"Take two!" he screamed.

As before, she heard his breathing; it grew heavier with his excitement, and she knew that her struggle aroused him. Hoping to discourage him, she tried not to resist, but it did no good. He slapped her, over and over, so that she had no choice but to begin her struggle again.

Karen screamed. "Oh God, please! Not again! Not again! Oh God!"

Then the first one dropped.

It fell so close to Karen that the beady little eyes blinked right into hers.

Struggling with Carlton, who did not yet know that the rat was perched on his shoulder, Karen watched as another rat fell beside the first, followed by yet another.

Carlton reacted now, letting go of Karen. Startled, he looked at both of his shoulders, which were now covered with rats.

Starving rats.

His expression turned at once to horror. "Get them off! For God's sake, get them off!"

He stumbled backward from Karen, so that she was able to get away from him. Stunned, she realized suddenly what was happening, that she was free of him, and she started up the aisle in a run.

"Get out, Karen!"

She stopped in the aisle, surprised by the voice that had seemed to echo throughout the cavernous theatre, as if it were the voice of the theatre itself.

She knew instinctively who it was.

"Carl!"

"Get out!" he screamed to her from on high.

Karen looked up, but she could not see him, only the rats that still dropped from the cove-lit dome above the auditorium. They had covered Forbes Carlton completely now.

"You can't do this to me!" he screamed.

Karen watched as Forbes Carlton pointed in her direction, his arm crawling with the starving rodents that nibbled at his flesh.

"You shall die for this!" he screamed.

Karen stared back up the aisle, but suddenly something huge stepped up out of the darkened aisle. Its eyes caught her attention first—enormous, crude, mounted within a hideously misshapen head.

Karen recognized it at once. It was the same monstrosity she had seen at the banquet, the same thing that had prowled through her apartment—the monster from *Night of the Blood Beast*, only this time it was three times as large.

"Kill her!" Forbes Carlton screamed, his voice slowly disappearing within the muffling swarm of rats that covered him.

Karen turned from the monster in the aisle, directing her gaze at Forbes Carlton. "I'm not afraid of you anymore, you bastard! Nothing you conjure up can hurt me now!"

Karen watched as he fell to the floor, the rats so thick upon him that he soon disappeared beneath them.

She turned back to the monster, which still loomed enormous at the end of the aisle. It stepped forward—its horribly misshapen head wobbling on the uncertain structure that held it.

Karen stared at it, all at once furious, for the thing in the aisle had become everything that was wrong with her life—the stuff of both dream and nightmare.

"Get out of my way, you ugly sonofabitch!" Karen screamed. She ran up the aisle, heading directly for it. "You don't exist, you bastard!" she cried, getting closer and closer.

When she reached it, Karen closed her eyes and she felt her heart pounding in that second before she would collide with it.

But then it happened.

It happened just as she had hoped it would.

She passed right through it, as if the monster that stood in her way were only a mass of colored light, and as she passed through it, she felt the heat of that light surrounding her, covering her for a second in the shimmering stuff of its projection.

When she got to the other side, she looked back. The thing was gone. Like so many of the terrible things she had conjured in her life, it had only been as real as she allowed it to be.

Karen then looked at the rats. Their feast completed, they scurried away.

Satisfied.

In the lobby Karen saw what was happening. The walls had begun to buckle, just as they had before, shucking off hunks of plaster and wood. But now the phenomenon was just the opposite: the newly refurbished flesh was returning to its original decayed state. Freed of the power of Forbes Carlton, the theatre was dying. It trembled all around her as it surrendered its new skin, which fell from the walls in pieces of ruined finery.

"Carl!" she cried.

Karen knew that he had to be somewhere, and she would not leave without him.

Ignoring the danger of falling debris, Karen ran to the stairway that would lead her up to the balcony. Halfway up, she saw him and cried out his name.

When he saw her, he turned away, slapping his hands to his face in shame. "No!" he screamed. "I don't want you to see me."

"It's all right, Carl . . . it doesn't matter!"

But he kept moving down the stairway, keeping his face covered as he ran.

"Get out!" he screamed.

Karen followed him as he ran toward the stairway into the basement. "Carl, I know what happened . . . it's all right. You don't have to hide it from me!"

He disappeared down the stairway, Karen following behind.

"Have to set the dials!" he cried. "Go away! You will get hurt. Go away!"

When she got to the foyer, she lost track of him, and she turned herself around in pointless circles, watching as tapestries rotted before her eyes.

"Where are you?" she cried, her voice echoing back off the hard walls.

She heard a squeaking noise, like an ungreased hinge, and she turned and watched as he disappeared into a space in the wall from which he had just removed a large metal grating.

"Carl!" she cried, running up to the space. She looked inside. A tunnel headed off into a black void as far as she could see. Without hesitating, Karen stepped inside and began to follow.

"Have to turn the dials up," he cried. "Get rid of the theatre forever!"

Karen crawled forward on her hands and knees, right behind him, through the dust and debris that had collected in the old theatre for fifty years. This time, she thought, no matter what, I won't let you get away, not until we've resolved all that's gone between us.

"Carl!" she cried, her voice muted and strangely toneless within the tunnel. "The letter! The letter you got from me!"

"Don't want to talk about it!" he cried.

Up ahead, she watched him crawling farther away into the tunnel, and all at once it was like some mad dream to her—crawling through a dusty, hot tunnel in pursuit of a man she had desperately loved since childhood.

Now she saw that they had come to the end of the tunnel, and she watched as he slid out of the other end, entering a large room. He lit a match, which flickered at the other end, guiding Karen the rest of the way.

Desperate, her lungs filling with dust, she kept crawling, wanting more than anything that Carl should know the truth.

"It wasn't real," she cried to him. "Carl, I didn't write you that letter!"

Even in the flickering dark void, Karen could see the expression of shock as it crossed his face.

"That's right," she said, reaching the end of the tunnel. "Nell wrote the letter. I *never* wanted you to leave, Carl. I wanted to marry you."

When he saw that she was looking at his face, Carl turned away from her. Karen stepped out of the tunnel, lowering herself into the boiler room beneath the stage.

"Look at me, Carl!"

"No!"

"It doesn't matter!" she said. "Look at me!"

Carl turned slowly, illuminated only by the tiny light from the match he held. When his face was revealed, Karen tried not to betray her shock and sadness. That someone she had loved so much could have endured such pain sickened her.

"I'm sorry," he whispered.

Karen trembled. "It's all right, Carl."

Carl dropped the match, which had burned to the edge of his finger, then quickly lit another. He knelt to the floor, where he turned up the dials on the boiler and heater to their maximum. Finished, he touched a button that operated the main valve. It made a hissing noise.

"Come on!" he cried, taking her hand.

He led her back through the tunnel and out to the foyer.

"We got just a few minutes," he said, helping her out of the tunnel at the other side.

They ran up the stairway and into the lobby, where everything looked old again. The theatre's beauty was now but a memory.

Carl led her out the bronze doors and they moved along the forecourt, which was still slippery and difficult to navigate.

But the temperature had increased, and Karen sensed it at once. Ice was melting everywhere they looked, and the early morning air was filled with the sound of a million drops of water falling in concert.

"Run!" Carl cried, his hand in Karen's.

They were halfway to Karen's car when they heard the explosion.

Karen looked back just in time to see the whole front facade as it caved in upon itself, the marquee collapsing in a cloud of dust and glass.

Carl pulled Karen to the ground, where they lay still for several seconds, waiting for the awful noise to stop.

When it was over, they looked up at the ruined shell of Odeon.

Karen could feel the air grow steadily warmer, as if the whole outside were suddenly connected to some enormous source of heat. Ice fell in huge pieces, which shattered noisily along Main Street. Wallenberg was suddenly like a town made of glass.

"Are you all right?" Karen asked Carl. She had heard him groan with pain and now he wasn't moving.

He moaned and wrapped his arms around his stomach.

"Carl!"

Quickly, he grew worse, and Karen watched as he rolled about the ground and cried out in pain.

And then she watched as blood appeared along his arm. It was a jagged line, like some sudden, bloody gash formed by an invisible knife.

She cried out his name, but he acted as if he could not hear her. He continued to writhe in pain, his eyes rolling back in his head as he suffered.

The bloodied lines along his arms suddenly grew wider, splitting open, so that blood and pulp gushed from inside.

Then his legs.

His face.

Karen watched in horror as another body began to struggle outward, liberated by the collapse of Carl's flesh, which was nothing more than a shell.

But the arms that groped at the air were naked, fresher, stronger, and the torso that twisted free of the old was no longer hunched and twisted.

Soon, Karen saw what had emerged—a different version of Carl. She watched as the new and naked body studied itself. He picked up Carl's old shirt, using it to wipe itself clean, and in the warmer air he sat comfortably, unashamed of his nakedness.

"Carl?" Karen said softly, and the new person looked at her blankly. After a moment he smiled at her and nodded, and Karen, overwhelmed, realized who it was that stared at her with such love.

It was Carl Irvine, the way he was supposed to have been, as if the accident had never happened.

Freed at last of Odeon, he took Karen into his arms.

An hour later a squad car arrived from Haleyville. When Karen had turned up missing, it hadn't taken them long to figure out where she had gone.

Karen was relieved when she saw them, for she was far too exhausted to drive.

"We were all kinda worried 'bout you," said one of the troopers.

His partner held open the rear door of the squad car for Karen, who helped Carl get in ahead of her. He had become a little dizzy and had a difficult time walking, but he was smiling now, moving steadily in his new body. Karen had run to Carl's room at the hotel, getting clothes for him to wear. The squad car had picked them up on the hotel porch.

"He gonna be all right?" the trooper asked as Carl settled into the back seat.

"Just fine," Karen said, getting in beside him.

Karen had difficulty finding the courage for her next question. "How about the girl? Do you have any idea how Amy Bradley is?"

The trooper smiled. "They asked me to tell you. The fever broke and she came out of the coma. Just a little while ago. Told me to tell you the fellow's doin' better too. What's his name? Paul?"

Karen closed her eyes in a silent prayer of thanks.

They were about a mile out of Wallenberg when Karen noticed a folded piece of paper in the pocket of the shirt she had given Carl to wear. Careful not to wake him, she pulled it out and unfolded it, reacting when she saw what it was—the letter that Nell had written to Carl.

It broke her heart to read the cruel words that Carl had thought she had authored, and she imagined all the unnecessary pain it must have caused him.

After rolling down the car window, Karen ripped the letter into as many pieces as she could, then tossed them out, turning in her seat to watch them fall.

In the distance the tiny bits of torn letter fluttered through the air. They tumbled and pitched, caught up by a new rise of wind, which was warmer now out of Wallenberg. Karen held on to Carl, but she could not keep her eyes off the pieces of letter—Nell's lie, which had caused so much pain.

Now the pieces of paper scattered away from each other, still adrift in the air, until at last they settled back to earth, falling with the patience of snow.

• Epilogue •

Two months later Jack MacGruder stood before the ruins of Odeon. A work crew had dismantled what was left of it, demolishing those particularly stubborn pieces of the theatre that had somehow managed to survive the explosion.

From behind a fence, Jack had watched the whole process, just as sixty years ago he had watched the theatre's rise from dirt and clay. He felt that his whole life had come full circle.

"Jack?" a voice called from behind him, and he turned and regarded an elderly woman, whose face formed a pleasant smile.

"Hello," he said, returning her smile and tipping his hat, all the time wondering who she was. It was rare for Jack to encounter a face in Wallenberg that he did not recognize. After the tragedy the town had been filled with journalists and other media people, but they had long since left, filling up their tabloids with tales of Odeon.

And besides, he thought, this woman didn't look like a reporter.

She stared off wistfully toward the wreckage. "It must be very sad for you, Jack."

Jack removed his hat. "I'm very sorry, ma'am, but I don't recall your name."

She laughed. "I'm not surprised. It's been a long time."

"Do you live here in Wallenberg?"

"Not now. I live in Los Angeles. I have for thirty-five years. I'm up visiting my sister."

"You grew up here?"

"You really don't remember me, do you?"

"No, I don't."

"It's warm," she said. "I could use a cool drink. Would you join me?"

At the Busy Bee she sipped a gin and tonic while Jack sat across from her with a scotch.

"You and I went to school together," she continued. "You were a couple of grades ahead of me, so that's probably why you don't remember."

"I'm really sorry, but I don't remember. I wish I did, but I don't."

"It's like that sometimes," she said, putting down her drink. She sat quietly for a moment, toying with the swizzle stick in her drink, stirring it so that the ice cubes clattered noisily against the sides of her glass. She looked up at him. "You see, Jack, I was in love with you."

"What?" Jack felt himself blush.

"A kind of infatuation, I guess. I thought you were something special."

"Why didn't you say something?"

"I was afraid. Shy. Besides, you were sort of off in your own little world, Jack. At least, that's the way it appeared."

"I guess I was."

"You loved the movies so much. It's all you ever talked about."

He thought about it a moment. He remembered a little boy in his bedroom, going through his box of movie star photographs. "I was lonely."

"I was there that night," she said, almost like a confession, "the night Odeon opened up for the very first time."

"You were?"

She laughed. "I was one of the cowgirls. I was all done up in one of them corny outfits, carrying one of those pink silk banners. Do you remember?"

"Of course," he said, remembering the bright snap of banners in the wind, the clip-clop of horses' hooves as he crossed the busy street and returned to Odeon, summoned to the balcony by Mr. Peabody.

"I looked at you, Jack. I looked at you in your usher's uniform. My God, I thought you were the handsomest thing that ever drew breath."

Finishing his drink, Jack signaled for another. "It was quite a night," he said. He looked her in the eyes a long time. "I wish you *had* said something."

They stared at each other, so that it became a bit uncomfortable for both of them, the woman finally breaking their silent connection with a nervous laugh. "Things are like that, I guess."

"Too bad."

"It wasn't long after Odeon opened that my father got a new job. We moved away. I went to college, became a teacher. I got married." She held up three fingers to indicate her children. "All three are grown now. Lives of their own. You know how that goes."

Jack nodded, but he had no real idea what she meant. "What about your husband?"

"Cranky as ever, but I love him," she said. "And you, Jack? Did you marry?"

"No," he said quietly, "I didn't."

In the silence that followed, his drink arrived.

"I ended up owning the theatre," he continued. "I ran it for several years. I showed movies, and I was happy . . . for a while. Until they changed."

"Until what changed, Jack?"

"The movies. Life."

"You must have loved that old theatre, Jack."

"I did," he said.

From across the table she smiled at him, her expression friendly and inviting, so that it encouraged him to talk.

He talked about movies—the way they had been in the past. He spoke to her of magic columns of light, of sequins that sparkled in the dark, as curtains parted elegantly across a screen.

He was an old man who had never loved anyone—not a woman, not a brother, not even a friend.

He was an old man who had loved a movie theatre, and now that theatre was gone.

And if he had enough to drink, he would tell her that his heart was broken.

Paul tucked the boy into bed.

"We goin' to the movies tomorrow, Dad?"

"Sure are, pal."

When Kenny was secure beneath the covers, Paul stood up, still a bit unsteady on his left leg, which bothered him when he stood a certain way.

"Dad?"

"Yeah?"

"I'm glad Mom changed her mind. I'm glad we don't have to go to that stupid trial again."

Paul smiled. "Me too."

Indeed, he had finally found a certain peace with Rita. Ironically, the whole business had brought them closer. While they would never hope or want to recapture the feelings that had led them to marriage, they had at least become respectful partners in the business of Kenny's welfare.

"Dad?"

"Yeah?"

"Isn't it neat I don't have those stupid spells anymore!"

Paul smiled. "Sure is."

Quickly, he turned and left the boy alone, for these days he felt like a hero to the boy again, and he didn't want Kenny to see him cry.

Karen bolted awake.

"Amy!" she cried, but she knew the girl wouldn't answer. She knew that Amy was gone, just as she'd been gone all those other nights during the past few weeks.

Karen got out of bed, threw on her robe, then checked the front room, where she found the hide-a-bed empty.

Amy had gone off into the night again.

Alone.

Dressing as quickly as she could, Karen considered the last two months, which had gone by so fast.

After that night in Wallenberg, Carl came back to Los Angeles with her, but the adjustment was difficult for him. He insisted upon being alone, just to think things over.

While his need for privacy initially disappointed Karen, she still saw him frequently, visiting him at the small furnished apartment he'd found in Hollywood. Even though he resisted, Karen lent him money for expenses. Meanwhile, she understood his need for time.

But Amy had never entirely recovered. The trance had ended with the fever, but elements of her odd detachment remained.

Karen had insisted that the girl move in with her, and while it was clear that Amy was making extraordinary progress (just the other day, Amy had laughed uproariously at a TV program) Karen knew that it would take a long time for the girl to recover fully, if at all.

But the nocturnal episodes, such as this one, scared Karen most of all. Without explanation Amy would leave the apartment and catch a bus into Hollywood, traveling in the night with her glazed eyes staring from the window of the bus.

She always ended up at the same place.

Twenty minutes later Karen parked along a quiet street in Hollywood, then walked up to Hollywood Boulevard, which bustled at almost midnight with its gaudy collection of freaks.

Karen moved swiftly past the poster shops, fast-food cafes and brightly lit stores that blasted rock music, finally approaching the movie theatre, where she knew she would find Amy.

As before, the girl stood in front of the box office.

"Amy!"

The girl turned to her, as if she had expected Karen to come. "It's closed," she said.

"I know. It's always closed. They're going to tear it down."

Karen pointed to the same sign she pointed to the other times: CLOSED PERMANENTLY. PLEASE STAY OUT! "You see?"

Amy turned to her. "People live in there, you know. Street people. They sneak in at night and they live there."

"What does it matter?" Karen said, then took her hand. "Let's go home, honey."

In the car Karen reached for her keys while Amy sat beside her in silence.

"It's going to be all right," Karen said, but now that eerie glaze had fallen across the girl's face again, shutting Karen out.

As she turned the key, Karen noticed something in the rearview mirror. She'd only had a fleeting glimpse, but she thought she had seen two men, watching her from the sidewalk.

Turning to look, Karen caught them staring, and the two men turned away, moving quickly up Hollywood Boulevard—a fat man and a thin man.

Troubled, Karen turned back to the steering wheel, where she sat and tried to calm herself. After a moment she looked at Amy, whose unearthly silence terrified her.

"Amy!" she cried, hoping for a reaction, but there was nothing, only that endless, silent staring.

Karen started the car and pulled into traffic, wondering what she should do next.

When she got home, she would first try to decide what was real and what was not.